FRANCIS BRETT YOUNG

THIS
LITTLE
WORLD

WILLIAM HEINEMANN LTD
MELBOURNE :: LONDON :: TORONTO

First Published 1934
Reprinted 1934 (*three times*)
First Published in the Severn Edition 1939
Reprinted 1940, 1946, 1950

PRINTED IN GREAT BRITAIN
AT THE WINDMILL PRESS
KINGSWOOD, SURREY

For
VICE-ADMIRAL W. M. JAMES, C.B.,
and the Staff of
The Battle-Cruiser Squadron.

My dear James,

I want you and Tower and Pertwee and Reid to have the dedication of this book, partly because the first words of it were written in your cabin on board the *Hood*, in those delightful days when we rounded Cape Wrath, lay hidden in the Sound of (so appropriately) Sleat, and played long bowls with the *Warspites* off St. Kilda; and partly, too, because, like most sailors, each of you cherishes in his heart the vision of some particular village ashore; so that I see you at Churt, and Tower in Kent, and Peter at Ellon. Unfortunately you can't carry your villages to sea with you, so here is an imaginary village, complete with imaginary inhabitants, between the covers of a book, which you may take with my blessing (and my envy) on your next Autumn Cruise.

Yours always,

FRANCIS BRETT YOUNG.

Craycombe House,
May 30th, 1934.

"Take any one considerable circle where you know everybody, and the condition of that circle will teach you how to judge pretty correctly."

—*William Cobbett*, 1833.

"The cherfulnesse of the people is so sprightly up, it betokn's us not drooping to a fatal decay."

—*John Milton*, 1655.

CONTENTS

PREFACE

THIS book must always occupy a special place in the author's affections on grounds which may be described as "sentimental"; and for this reason the work itself, together with its appendage, *Portrait of a Village*, runs the risk of acquiring the same description. Yet this I can neither regret nor resent. Both books were written in a mood of which I am not in the least ashamed: in the transport of joy and tenderness that arose from my return, after twenty-five years of distant exile to the county in which I was born and to the scenes of my childhood.

I had come back to these in a spring of unimaginable beauty in which all things seemed familiar yet piercingly strange. The shapes of the landscape—those "blue, remembered hills" of my long-lost youth, the Clents, the Abberleys, the Malverns, the Cotswold escarpment, the great dome of Bredon, the "high reared head of Clee"; the rivers of mine own country, proud Severn and gentle Avon and woodland Teme; the villages of half-timber and mellowed stone; the Worcestershire speech, with its words and phrases which remained so natural to my ears—all these brought me back to the Eden of an untroubled childhood, to the physical delights and the long thoughts of youth. I felt that, after long wanderings, I had come home; and, like that other Worcestershire Lad whose nostalgia has made the hills and brooklands of Shropshire immortal; I found the familiar beauties tinged with a certain wistfulness; my eyes saw the recovered scene in a light which, for all its enchantment, was somehow unreal, in the half-mystical manner of one of the earliest of my literary idols and influences, Thomas Traherne:

The green trees, when I saw them first through one of the gates, transported and ravished me; their sweetness and unusual beauty made my heart to leap and almost mad with ecstasy—they were such strange and wonderful things. The skies were mine, and so were the sun and moon and stars—and all the world was mine—and I the only spectator and enjoyer of it . . .

Out of these ecstatic emotions came *This Little World*: an admittedly inadequate expression of a part of what I felt, a poor thank-offering for the joys of the lost world which I had recovered. I placed my imagined village in the very heart of my own country, amid the devious and narrow lanes of the Lenches in which even a Worcestershire-born man may easily lose himself. I tried—again most inadequately—to express some aspects of the impact of the new world, made swift and restless by the advent of the internal-combustion engine and the mechanized life, upon the old. I tried to emphasize the continuity of life in these remote villages and to fix, as it were, a few of the ancient beauties that are passing away. If the mood in which this book was composed may be called sentimental, the depth of the emotion from which it emerged was genuine beyond doubt, and the work for all its obvious shortcomings, an Act of Faith.

PRELUDE

In this island there are certain localities predestined by Providence for the permanent habitation of birds, beasts and men, since the life of all three is conditioned by the neighbourhood of water. Chaddesbourne D'Abitot, in the county of Worcester, is one of these. Here the Roman, pushing his conquest through primeval Arden to the West, where his wild foe hid, found his progress checked by the marshy confluence of Stour and Severn. Beyond either stream formidable hills looked down on the matted forest through which he had hacked and consolidated his way; between him and these a network of clear rivulets, gushing from the gravel-beds of the Clents, dispersed themselves in impenetrable morasses; and there, on a shelf of higher ground (since the water was sweet and his front immune from surprise) he felled a wide clearing in the wood of scrub oak, established a post, and paused to consider the planning of bridge-head and causeway.

Of the Roman's earthworks, if such were made, no traces remain: those hills catch the south-west rain; and the falling streams (to this day) are subject to sudden floods. Even the causeway which doubtless gave passage dry-shod to the shallows (at the place now called Stourford) lies sunk beneath fathom on fathom of tawny alluvium. Yet one block of hewn stone, foreign in texture, which the legionaries proudly erected to mark one more dogged mile on the road to Wroxeter, survived—who knows how?—the assaults of flood and the slow teeth of time. It lay there still— like those other alien boulders shed from the track of the Arenig glacier—five hundred years later, when another wave of invasion broke and was checked on the same obstinate barrier. Long-haired Saxons, men of the Hwiccans, found it and came to stare in ignorance at its legend. These people were forest-folk; the woods held no fears for them; the red loam from which the woods sprung was not too stiff for their ploughs; and a thane whose name is forgotten (though that of his sovereign Offa has clung to the hill called Uffdown) found the soil and the water to his liking, and set up a long stockade on the brink of the stream in the clearing the Romans had made. Chad, the Mercian bishop, on a journey from Lich- field to Winchcombe, passed that way and blessed the anonymous thane's habitation; so the place, which was now an established settlement, took the name of Chad's Bourne to honour his sanctity. By the spring where this saint had preached, a rude shrine arose, into whose foundations—since rock was scarce in that clayey land—some careful builder imbedded the Roman milestone; and soon afterwards (for time began to move swiftly now) a Norman, kin to that D'Abitot whose greed made his name anathema in monkish ears—*Hight thou Urse? On thee lie Goddes curse!*— replaced the oaken structure by a square tower of stone with lancet windows (convenient, at a pinch, for bow-men) and a round arch heavily indented with dog's-tooth carving—in atonement, perhaps, for Urse's wolfish ways, but with a weather eye on the Welsh always crouched beyond Severn.

Other towers the D'Abitots reared to enforce their dominion; but their stones, less durable than the hated name, have vanished. One remnant persists; a low mound, hardly perceived, in the field still known as Tump Piece, to the north of Chaddesbourne Hall, the seat, for the last four hundred years, of the Ombersley family, the Lords of the Manor and hereditary squires of the village. Of the D'Abitots, indeed, no material trace remains at Chaddesbourne save the broken effigy of one prostrate crusader set up-right with crossed knees in the northern transept of the church. For however sternly the D'Abitots may have established themselves—and in Domesday *"Guy D'Abitot holds Chadsborn for a knight's fee with two mills and a fishery"*—time has given the dispossessed a sure revenge. The Norman's dominion passed like a brief and violent dream. Though his blood (and that of the Roman and Brython, for that matter) persists, it has certainly suffered ample dilutions. On the monuments of the church, on the humbler stones of

the graveyard, on the tablet which commemorates the
fallen of the Boer War, a small group of names,
Saxon all—Bunt, Hackett, Lydgate, Sheppy,
Ombersley—recurs and preponderates: it would
almost seem that no stranger had ever died there.
And since the spirit of a place takes its colour and
shape from the dreams of its dead no less than from
the thoughts of its living, the soul of Chaddesbourne,
sustained by such continuity of habitation and race,
seems peculiarly, richly English.

Its spiritual meridian runs straight as a wood-
pigeon's flight betwixt Piers Plowman's Cleobury and
Shakespeare's Stratford; if the line do not cut the
precise and physical heart of England, it is as near as
makes little matter. Fifty miles from the Dyke which
Offa heaped to keep out the Welsh, and twenty within
that shadowy limit beyond which no nightingale sings,
Chaddesbourne D'Abitot lies lost (or found with difficulty) in a region of moated farmsteads and blossomed
orchards, of straw-thatch and half-timber, of tawny-
sanded brooks feeding one great river, of pastures perpetually green in seasons of drought and red-clodded
arable, of unruly hawthorn hedgerows and minty
ditches, of blowing banks afire with gorse and foxy
coverts smelling of autumnal leaf-mould, of isolated
oaks which have groaned in the wind since Rosalind
roamed Arden and elms that sprang, folk say, from
the Roman's budding vine-poles, yet appear, by adop-
tion, as autochthonous as the oaks themselves.

And all this store of beauties, too humble, too intimate, too unspectacular, too familiar, perhaps, to be
noticed by those to whose condition of life they are as
essential and natural as the atmosphere in which their
scents are suspended, are washed, enveloped and made
magical by the ebb and flow of limpid Atlantic air,
magnificently roofed by the pageant of Atlantic clouds
searching the tidal basin of Severn as though, indeed,
it were still a part of their marine dominion—save
only when the wind sets northerly, blowing over the
lip of the Black Country's smoking cauldron. Then
the landscape suddenly fades, the Atlantic air loses its
limpidness; the sky droops duskily on woods and
fields, its density seems to flatten the very contours
of the land. "It's the blight," people say. "When
the wind shifts it'll clear." And the wind shifts
sure enough, for here the south-west is lord, and
colour shines out anew on wood and field and hedgerow.

Paradoxically, it is the very neighbourhood of those
smoke-breeding cities—with North Bromwich and
Wolverbury as chiefs—which has blessed Chaddesbourne D'Abitot with a happy obscurity, which has
allowed it, as I say, to lie lost. For where once the
main tides of human commerce set steadily westward
to the ford of Severn, during the last hundred years
the iron magnet has swung them eastward. Severn
itself is no longer a waterway, nor the road which the
Romans made and the Saxon followed a channel of

trade. The freight-trains of hardware go clanking and roaring, by day and by night, through a gap in the hills five miles eastward of Chaddesbourne village; the main road South, with its metal core of Shropshire granite and its facing of Trinidad pitch, carries perpetually whirring wheels shod with tropical rubber an equal distance to the West; and neither of these two impetuous streams takes heed of Chaddesbourne, which sleeps in the silence midway between them like a green stagnant pool. Even the solitary signpost which stands where the metal road cuts the track that still links it with Bromsberrow market bears a name scarcely legible, and the grass-grown surface of the lane itself, together with its hesitating contortions, leads the traveller who follows it to fear that he may find himself mired in the cul-de-sac of some farmyard. In short stretches the lane assumes a promising dignity, with wide verges of grass flanked by oaks that resemble an avenue preparing the eyes for the sight of some stately mansion. Overhead the oak-branches meet and are interwoven: a squirrel might cross and recross for a mile without touching the ground. Very possibly a squirrel (and a red one at that) may be seen, his erect tail feathered with light, or be heard, impatiently chattering on a bough that swings with his weight, or, more likely still, a white-waistcoated stoat may halt and peer from the centre of the track with his kittenish face. But when promise of an end seems highest the lane degenerates again into a straight burrow running eternally between thickets of hazel and holly. It is with a gasp of surprise, if not of awe, that one emerges from this green tunnel to see, from a sudden brow, a vista of incredible magnificence: all the heaped hills of Shropshire and Wales from the Holy Mountain to Abdon Burf—so remote as to seem part of the sky rather than of the earth. Severn, slinking between her undercut banks of marl, lies sunk in the green middle-distance, unheard and invisible; but right at the traveller's feet, so startlingly near as to appear larger than natural, spreads the cluster of dwellings, with its mysterious complement of human sorrows and joys, loves and hates, aspirations and despairs, which is called Chaddesbourne D'Abitot.

From this viewpoint, where the village no less than the traveller is caught, so to speak, unawares, its outward shape may be examined with a leisurely detachment. It is seen to consist of less than a score of cottages, for the most part half-timbered and thatched, with tall chimneys of brick to carry their smoke through the eddying air, disposed at unequal intervals on either side of a single street. At one end of the street a short avenue of rook-haunted elms approaches the Hall, a rectangular mass of masonry impressively masked by a pedimented Georgian façade and portico. When winter thins the shrubberies, curious eyes may catch a glimpse of a paved terrace and the gleam of a sheet of formal water. At the opposite end

of the street, where another clump of elms holds a
second rookery, stands the church, with Guy D'Abitot's
Norman tower of tawny sandstone commanding a
more fragile nave and transepts of Late Perpendicu-
lar; and hard by, the Vicarage, mid-Victorian Gothic,
slate-roofed, and mercifully concealed by shrubberies
of laurel and overcrowded conifers of the kind called
"ornamental."

Between these two poles of Church and State, embraced, as it were, by the magnetic field which they
generate, lies the domain of the commonalty. Save
in the midst of the village—where the bakery, the
butcher's and grocer's shops, the post-office (which
also sells sweets), the village hall, the smithy and the
surgery, together with two or three prim, spinsterly
dwellings of a minor gentility, create a nucleus of relatively modern brick about cross-roads dominated by
the "Ombersley Arms," whose dilapidated stables pro-
claim its former state as a "posting-house," the cottages
of Chaddesbourne show a typical individuality.
Though they compose the village street they appear
to retire from it. No single one resembles another—
save in a general air of irregularity and disrepair—
and each is separated from the road and its neighbours
by gardens which have nothing in common but the
pride and ingenuity with which they are tilled and
embellished and the uniform latched gates at which,
when smoke goes up straight and the rooks fly home
on a summer evening, a man, having dug his potatoes,

may stand in his shirt-sleeves and gossip at his ease. With their thatched roofs and mossy pathways, their porches and arbours entwined with sweet honeysuckle and glowing clematis, their old-fashioned roses and casual sweet-williams, each and all make "a picture" of idyllic peace to bring tears to enraptured eyes. That most of the thatched roofs leak when rain pours, that the bedroom windows are sealed hermetically by rot or by ivy, that the living-rooms are unlighted and paved with damp-sweating stone, that the water bucketed from their picturesque well-heads is reasonably suspect, that indoor sanitation is unknown to them, and that the agricultural wage is fixed in those parts at thirty shillings a week, are circumstances that do not enter into the calculations of a casual sentimental observer of rural England. For the Chaddesbourne villagers, as well as their cottages, are "unspoiled." The women, who live to a great age, wear faded sunbonnets and have faces like wrinkled pippins; the little girls curtsy; the older men actually touch their caps when a motor-car passes. They vote . . . but who knows how they vote? That is the only fly of suspicion in the emollient which seems spread with such satisfying smoothness over the surface of this sweetly old-fashioned spot, this fragment of an old-English landscape by Nature after David Cox, compactly caught and preserved within the silver snare of the Chaddesbourne brook. Over this little world, for a period of three-score years, Roger Ombersley ruled, a benevo-

lent autocrat, till, having neglected a winter bronchitis, he took to his bed and died within forty-eight
hours, and Miles Ombersley, his son, reigned in his
stead.

THE HEIR

THE Chaddesbourne brook was in flood on the day when they buried old Mr. Ombersley in March, nineteen hundred and twenty-two. Rain had teemed—as, heaven knows, it can teem in those hills—for three days on end. At some farms they lost lambs. Little sodden bodies were washed down and wedged the foaming sluices at Chaddesbourne Mill, where Eli Lydgate the miller and his man were busy dragging sacks of meal into safety. They could hear the angry water roaring and bubbling outside as they worked, ankle-deep; but below that solitary obstruction the flood grew silent; released, it spread over the drowned fields in a lake with a lapping edge fringed with froth and dead leaves and broken twigs, beneath whose surface the stream itself ran unperceived till, meeting its next obstruction, the stone bridge on the road to Wychbury, it grew noisy again. The stone bridge lay nine inches awash at either end, and farmers' wives who had come from the Wychbury side "to see the vault opened," were forced to turn back for fear of wetting their petticoats and catching their deaths of cold. "One funeral makes many," old people say in those parts. To this day, though neither had fatal consequences, Mr. Ombersley's funeral is remembered by that flood and the flood by his funeral.

His death, as *Berrow's Journal* proclaimed, marked an epoch, the end of an era. The old man—he was eighty-eight when he died—was in himself a museum piece, removed by no more than two lives, and a spiritual gap even smaller, from that other Worcestershire squire, Sir Roger de Coverley. The vault, about which the countryside was so curious, had actually not been opened for forty-five years on the day when Miles Ombersley ("the Colonel," as they called him) succeeded to a home which in formal dank desolation was not unlike it, a thousand odd acres of land, for the most part neglected, and a staggering load of death-duties, for which, characteristically, his father had made no provision.

When Colonel Ombersley heard of the old man's death he had just been transferred from his regiment, in the Army of Occupation at Cologne, to a staff job at Aldershot. The news reached him a few hours after he had signed an agreement for the lease, at an exorbitant rent, of a furnished house on the outskirts of Farnham. As soon as he heard it he got leave and set off for Chaddesbourne, leaving his wife behind to collect the two children and follow him.

As a soldier's wife Helen Ombersley was accustomed to alarms and excursions. Indeed, in her twenty-five years of married life she had rarely known the delights of a permanent home, and this new convulsion seemed a mere jolt to her.

She had married Miles, then a captain in the Thirtieth Hussars, on the eve of his sailing to fight in South Africa, and her two elder boys, Dick and Roger, both born under the shadow of one war, had reached manhood in time to lose their lives in the next: Dick, the heir, a mere child, on the Somme, and Roger, the younger, at Gheluvelt, with the Worcesters. These two blows, falling one on another, still numbed her and deprived her of the capacity of feeling. She had long since reached a state of mind in which it seemed relatively unimportant where she went or what she did, so inured to the idea of death, that to be packed off to another funeral appeared to her the most natural thing in the world.

It did seem a pity, in a way, that the two younger children—Catherine, now a girl of twenty, slender and precocious (and what wonder!), and Jack, who, escaping the holocaust by bare months, was now at Oxford—should be snatched out of their comparatively cheerful lives to assist at such a sombre affair; but the precise mind of Miles had declared their presence necessary, and had arranged for it with an admirable and typical piece of staff-work in black and white. She knew, and respected, the strength of his sense of duty, and never questioned the rightness of his judgment in matters of propriety; in addition to which she herself had been born a D'Abitot and reared in a school as careful of tradition as his.

So, apparently self-possessed and unhurried, though her life still moved in a dream, Helen Ombersley set about packing and sending telegrams, and thanked heaven that, anyway, she wouldn't have to worry about mourning, since Jack had a tail-coat, a relic of his last half at Eton, and Catherine and herself were already provided with black. Then she shut up the Farnham house and sent the two servants she had just engaged on a holiday, and set off with Catherine to Brown's Hotel in London, where Jack had been told to join them. She went up to town third-class, as was her custom unless she was travelling with her husband; but her luggage had printed labels: *The Hon. Mrs. H. Ombersley*, and railwaymen, even when they didn't notice this, always treated her with particular respect: there was something fine and gentle and proud about her calm face, her steady eyes, her body, so erect and remarkably slim for her age.

Catherine, sitting beside her, presented an immature version of the same distinction. She was as tall as her mother, and as erect, but even slimmer, with the angularity of youth. She had the same candid eyes, too young to have known real pain, dark grey, at once gentle and fearless, beneath brows that were so slightly curved as to give the forehead a swift, impetuous air. The skin of her face had the pallor and fine texture of a creamy petal; her mouth was the mouth of a child, generous, passionate, innocent, and the hair which appeared beneath her black felt hat was the colour of beeswax. During the journey they rarely spoke to one another, and then so quietly that nobody heard what they said; but when their eyes met, the hurt eyes and the unhurt, they smiled, and sometimes their gloved hands touched in little instinctive sudden gestures of affection. The people in the compartment took them for a war-widow, recently bereaved and pathetically courageous, with her younger sister. Such sights were common enough in those days; but this one commanded respect.

Miles Ombersley, meanwhile, had reached Chaddesbourne on the previous evening. Mr. Healey, the agent, who combined the management of Chaddes-bourne with that of a number of smaller estates, had sent a high dog-cart to meet him at Wychbury Station. This was the only vehicle in the stables in a passable state of repair; the brougham and the closed wagonette had gone moth-eaten through disuse, and the old squire had always set his face against motor-cars.

Miles Ombersley was chilled to the bone but, as usual, observant. He was pleased by the salute which the station-master, a stranger, gave him, and by the fact that the wooden platform smelt just the same and was lit by the same bleary oil-lamps as in the days, long ago, when he used to come home from school. The lane leading to Chaddesbourne was as rough and narrow as ever, with its cuttings of damp sandstone and clipped holly-hedges, whose wet leaves shone in the beam of the dog-cart's lamps. "Here at least nothing changes, thank God!" he was telling himself, when, approaching the brook and expecting the shade of an avenue, he saw, on either side of the road, like the track of a hurricane, huge elms lying prostrate where they had been laid by the axe.

"What's this?" he asked sharply. Though it wasn't on Ombersley land, the tops of the avenue had been visible from the Hall gates, and anything that happened so near to Chaddesbourne concerned him.

"Beg your pardon, sir?" The groom was asleep.

"What's all this?"

"Them old trees, sir? Why, that's Mr. Hackett, that is."

"And who's Mr. Hackett?"

"The gentleman what's bought Green Hill. A gentleman from North Bromwich."

"A gentleman from North Bromwich!" Miles Ombersley thought. "That's a contradiction in terms." He said: "What's he felled the trees for?"

"Well, that I can't rightly tell, sir. He's pulled down the farm, and they say he's building a mansion."

"A mansion on Green Hill? That's the first I've heard of it."

"Putting in ten bathrooms, they say, sir, and a garridge for six. It's a rare slice of luck for Chaddesbourne, they say, a gentleman like Mr. Hackett coming and settling here. It'll liven things up no end. There's a great dearth of real gentry in these parts compared with what used to be, more's the pity; and this Mr. Hackett—well, they say that money's no object."

Colonel Ombersley grunted. Of course this disaster was only to be expected. He had urged his father again and again to buy Green Hill. Æsthetically that smooth upland, with its fringe of poor woods and the half-derelict black-and-white Tudor farm on the top of it, was an integral element in the Chaddesbourne landscape; as a mere piece of property it should have "rounded off" the Chaddesbourne estate; but, of late years, the old man had rarely troubled to answer his letters, during the war sterner duties had erased the project from his mind; and now some damned profiteer—the type was implicit in every word the groom had spoken—had stepped in with his "money no object" and snapped up the coveted morsel from under his nose. He could see Mr. Hackett with his "mansion," his "ten bathrooms," his "garage for six!" The fact that from ignorance or caprice he could fell that fine avenue spoke for itself. "If I'd been on the spot," Miles Ombersley thought, "I'ld have managed to stop him. I must get to know the fellow and take him in hand. . . ."

The rain came down steadily, in torrents; the flood was already lapping the crown of the bridge when the horse splashed through it. At the Hall Dr. Selby, whom the squire had reluctantly summoned to attend him at the end of his illness, and Dudley Wilburn, the family lawyer from North Bromwich, awaited the heir's arrival. James Langley, the butler, in honour of the event, had lit a heaped fire in the dining-room; but the room itself had not been used since the beginning of the war, and though the flames scorched their calves and made Colonel Ombersley's damp trousers steam as they stood talking uneasily in front of the blaze and waited for dinner, all the space beyond that fierce radius remained icily cold: the chill of prolonged disuse seeping out of the walls from which the eyes of six frozen Ombersley ancestors contemptuously surveyed them.

Mr. Healey was the only sprightly member of the party. An aura of unabsorbed whisky enveloped his ingratiations. Miles Ombersley, catching a whiff of it, made a note. That would never do. Dudley Wilburn, ponderous at the best of times, wore a worried look. ("That man's ill," Dr. Selby thought. "Kidneys, probably. I wonder if he knows?") He drew Ombersley aside and spoke in an undertone:

"I shall try to have everything ready for you by to-morrow evening. The last will was made over forty years ago, at the time of your mother's death. All the witnesses, oddly enough, predeceased the . . . er . . . the testator. Not that that will make any difference; but I do wish he'd made another. There's a codicil which may surprise you. You will also find a number of charitable bequests, quite reasonable then, which may cause you temporary embarrassment. In those days, as you know, life was easier and he was much better off."

"We shall have to meet them, however embarrassing they are," Miles Ombersley replied.

"Oh, of course, of course. It's a pity, all the same. He was obstinate, if I may say so, increasingly obstinate."

The last sentence, spoken as he turned, reached the other couple. Mr. Healey sniggered, as if to say, "Don't I know it!" then cleared his throat loudly to hide the tactless sound. Dr. Selby made no pretence of not having heard. He was a clean-shaven, keen-eyed man on the far side of thirty, with the confidence of four years of war-service behind him.

"It was admirable obstinacy, Wilburn," he said. "The squire fought for it to the last. As an example of sheer will-power I take off my hat to him. I've never seen anything gamer. He had determined to see the war finished and the Germans beaten, and did it, with nearly two years and a half to spare. I'm proud to have known him. If he'd only condescended to take a little more care of himself he'd be alive at this moment. He had a beautiful elastic pulse till the end—the arteries of a man of forty. Well, well, it was a remarkable innings, and he could hit out hard to the end. You realize, Colonel, that he refused to let me send for you?"

"Of course, doctor. You were perfectly right,"

Miles Ombersley replied. "A man I can trust," he thought. "He looks like a soldier and speaks like a gentleman."

The butler proclaimed the self-evident fact that dinner was served. Miles Ombersley took his seat, for the first time, at the head of that table; they proceeded to eat the kind of meal which had always been served at Chaddesbourne, authentically English, from the gravy soup flavoured with sherry to the admirable port. If he had let down everything else, the old man had kept up his cellar. Every spring, till the war began, he had laid down a year's supply of sound wine from Bordeaux and Oporto. Miles Ombersley noticed that the butler spared himself the trouble of offering Healey claret, and that Healey pointedly cut short the quantity of whisky the man mechanically poured out for him. Miles Ombersley's keen eyes were noticing everything that evening; his mind, habitually precise, was quickened by a kind of sombre elation. The moment when he sat down in his father's chair at the head of the table was, in a manner, climactic: not the end of an ambition, but the beginning. All his life, up to this, had been a period of probation. From this instant he was going to take neither men nor things for granted, and poor Mr. Healey's too-pointed abstemiousness decided his fate.

When the port had come home for the second time, the doctor said: "I suppose you would like to see him, Colonel? He's in his old room. Perhaps you'ld rather I came with you?"

Miles Ombersley shook his head. "Thank you, doctor; I know my way. I shan't be long. Won't you pass the wine round again? You had better stay here where it's warm."

Outside, in the hall, it was certainly deathly cold. An oil-lamp with an opaline globe shed a doleful, subaqueous light on the flags, the dim family portraits, the high ceiling darkened by smoke. Miles Ombersley, guided by an instinct that survived from his boyhood, moved mechanically towards an oak table at the foot of the stairs, where an odd assortment of brass candlesticks stood in rows. He lit one. Accompanied by a moving shadow he climbed the uncarpeted stairs. Though he had not considered them for years, every canvas that lined the staircase-wall was familiar to him, and he paused for a moment to gaze at the portrait of a grey Arab stallion by Stubbs, and the superb presentation by Snyders of a thundery sky, in which a heron on its back fell, driven to earth by two falcons. Both seemed better than he had imagined, and both, he reflected, were valuable: from being mere pictures they had suddenly become possessions. "I must get a new valuation made," he thought, "and the catalogue revised. I wonder if we're properly insured against fire."

At the head of the stairs he found himself faced by a Tompion timepiece whose ticking and resonant chime had been in his boyhood the pulse and voice of

B

the landing. The escapement was silent now. So, seeing that the clock had stopped at five minutes to seven,
he re-wound it methodically and, turning the hands
to the time as shown by his watch, was startled by the
sound of the chime, which his setting released—so
startled that, pursuing the habit of years, he found
himself tapping at the dead man's door for leave to
enter.

That really, he told himself, was a stupid thing to
do; yet the absence of the gruff answering "Come in!"
brought home to him, more definitely than anything
that had happened before, the reality of death. Up
till now his seriousness had been no more than the
correct reaction of a grown man of the world. At the
moment when, carrying his candle, he walked on tiptoe into that room, Miles Ombersley was moved,
deeply moved; and since the prime tenet of his code
constrained him to conceal emotion, he felt thankful
that he had rejected the doctor's offer of his company.

What was it that moved him so deeply? Had he
ever loved his father? (He had, indubitably, passionately loved his mother. But that was ages ago; he was
a mere child when she died.) Their relation, indeed,
had never been really intimate: yet no less intimate,
now that he came to think of it, than his own with
Richard, the boy who had been killed on the Somme.
Affection, in the sense of personal tenderness, could
never, where the Ombersleys were concerned, be displayed between men—just as their very relationship

of father and son, of a man and his heir, precluded,
by family custom, any degree of confidence. It was
almost an accepted convention that the relations between the Ombersley in possession and his heir should
be strained. As a matter of fact these two had not
spoken for twenty years. Respect, admiration of a
sort. . . ? That was rather nearer the mark. Yet, even so,
the qualities he had admired in his father were not personal: their two natures were far too like each other
for that. No, the admiration he felt—and his present
emotion showed that this was genuine—was for what
his father represented as the vehicle and instrument
of a tradition, the incarnation of that sense of duty,
that faith—in their Chaddesbourne, in England—
which had devolved on every bearer of the name for
the last four hundred years. That old man, lying
there with his cold features waxen in candlelight,
had kept the light burning for the better part of a
century. He, Miles Ombersley, was prepared to carry
the torch a stage further—into what grim vicissitudes
(for the world changed so rapidly nowadays) he could
not presume to guess—and the prospect of doing so
filled him with the taut enthusiasm he had felt when
first he led his squadron into action during the Boer
War.

Only one moment of disquietude weakened this
iron mood when, slowly lifting his eyes from the contemplation of his father's face and gazing into vacancy,
be became aware of another, his own, which appeared

to regard him sardonically from a Chippendale mirror in which it was reflected and, coming into focus, recalled him violently to himself. Perhaps it was a trick of pale candlelight, perhaps of the mirror's flawed surface; whatever it may have been, Miles Ombersley had the illusion that this face was not his, but a grim simulacrum of the cold features at which his eyes, detached from his brooding mind, had lately been gazing. If that face was indeed his own (as it surely must be, though he had always taken it for granted that he resembled his mother), it was evident that he was more deeply harrowed than he cared to admit. It was white and lined, and shadowed with mortality. The sight of it struck cold on his heart, reminding him that of the short span of human life he had already lived more than two-thirds. Fifteen more years—thirty, perhaps, for the Ombersleys were long-lived. And then . . . this. He pulled himself together deliberately, and became, in spite of mirror and candlelight, his soldierly self. Yet when, moving briskly downstairs, he rejoined his guests at the table, he thought it as well to fortify himself with a third glass of port. The doctor, narrowly watching, saw that the hand that tipped the decanter was steady.

"But the fellow looks as if he had seen a ghost," he thought.

He had; but Miles Ombersley was not the man to be frightened by ghosts, not even the ghost of himself.

II

THE FUNERAL

On the morning of the squire's funeral, the rain ceased at dawn. The water-washed air was so limpid that far hills could be seen; trees and hedgerows showed swelling bud; there was a touch of spring in the air, and each puddle reflected blue sky. This sudden change in the weather was a blessing for everybody, but particularly for Miss Loach, to whom, although she could take no active part in the ceremony, a funeral—and such a funeral—was meat and drink.

Miss Loach had been established in Chaddesbourne for more than thirty years in the midst of that nucleus of Georgian brick, contemporary with the Hall, which marked the cross-roads. Her house was by far the primmest of these prim dwellings, having two tiers of bay-windows projecting into the street on either side of a door surmounted by a fanlight and painted bright green. It was, in effect, a minute town-house that had been dropped complete into the heart of a village, and its air of urban formality was enhanced by the polished brass of the knocker, the letter-box, the door-handle and the two bell-pulls (one marked

"Service") and by the whiteness of the scrubbed steps descending to the pavement.

If the outside belonged to an earlier age, the contents of the house, its mistress included, were definitely Victorian. The drawing-room, which lay on the left of the doorway as one entered and was thawed into life once a week after middle-day dinner on Sundays, was a perfect example of the period of blue china, peacocks' feathers, clasped photograph-albums and milking-stools. On a mantelpiece draped with a tasselled canopy of maroon chenille, stood an oblong mirror with a rounded top, of the kind through which Alice climbed into the looking-glass world. The mirror, in fact, provided the puzzled observer with a key to the nature of its owner; for, when once the resemblance was grasped, one became aware that Miss Loach herself was the spit and image of the Red Queen. Like that lady, Miss Loach was spare, with the most waspish of waists and the boniest of black satin bodices above an ample black cloth skirt; like her she possessed a bony, angular face, a prominent mouth, alternately grim and pugnacious, narrow eyes, and thin hair, preternaturally dark, secured, in a padded bun, by a black silk net of coarse texture; like her Miss Loach was a tyrant and subject to fainting-fits. The only feature in which Miss Loach did not resemble her looking-glass prototype was the queen's remarkable mobility; for Miss Loach was an invalid—the villagers called her a bed-lier—and had rarely, in the last thirty years of her domicile at Chaddesbourne, emerged from her canopied mahogany four-poster in the room above the drawing-room.

This is not to suggest that Miss Loach, at any hour of the day, failed to keep herself informed of what happened in the village, whose minutest activities were the object of her interest and censure. On the contrary, she was as sensitive as a seismograph. No woman stood gossiping, no man entered the tap-room opposite or the doctor's surgery next door, no school-boy shouted and no dog barked in the street without the occurrence being reported to her in detail and its cause and significance discussed by her handmaiden and slave, Jane Trost, a less desiccated spinster with the eager bleached look of a ferret, who kept watch, from behind the lace curtains of the window, for that precise purpose. In the easy pre-war days, when dividends were more generous and taxes lower, Miss Loach's researches had been spread wider afield by means of a one-horse victoria, in which, on fine afternoons, she had taken the air; but since her groom, whom she had heroically sacrificed on the altar of economy and patriotism, had failed to return from Flanders and her income simultaneously declined, her excursions were now limited to the meaner radius of a bath-chair pushed by her maid and steered by herself in a leisurely progress from the Church to the Hall gates and back again.

On the morning of Mr. Ombersley's funeral, for

the first time in thirty years, Miss Loach rose from
her breakfast-tray of tea and dry toast and two kinds
of medicine, and established herself in good time for
the show, well propped-up with pillows and enveloped
in a black Shetland shawl, within the bow of the
drawing-room window. From this point she enjoyed
a wide-angle distant view of the whole village street,
from the entrance of the Hall-drive to the vicarage
and the Church's lych-gate, and a point-blank scrutiny
of the buildings immediately opposite: the post-office,
the school, the policeman's house, the forge and the
inn.

At the moment when Miss Loach took her station,
with Jane Trost at her elbow, the street showed no
signs of rising to the occasion, apart from the lowered
blinds in Mrs. Webb's shop and the policeman's house.
Outside the forge a tired plough-horse stood tethered
with drooping head; in its black interior she could see
the pulsating glow of Joe Atkins's gleed and hear the
irreverent tinkle of hammer on anvil. From the open
windows of the school-house there issued a vaguer
sound, resembling the rustling chatter of starlings in
autumn reed-beds. At the door of the "Ombersley
Arms" (whose blinds were not lowered), the maid-
of-all-work, who came from "away," was down on her
knees scrubbing steps. Mr. Hadley, the landlord,
came and opened the door to gaze at her. He was
smoking a cigarette—in the middle of the morning,
Miss Loach observed disapprovingly—but, in any

case, Miss Loach disapproved of Ted Hadley. Though
she liked a biscuit and a sip of port wine in the middle
of the morning, to keep up one's strength, and half a
glass of Australian Burgundy at dinner to make blood,
she considered the drinking of beer by the poor, on an
empty stomach, a social evil, and the "Ombersley
Arms" a plague-spot. She had often verbally complained to Dr. Selby, and once in a carefully-worded
letter to old Mr. Ombersley, who was chairman of
the licensing magistrates, about the language which
reached her ears in bed from over the road at closing-
time; but the doctor, less sympathetic than usual, had
said something about "banishing poetry from the lives
of the labouring classes," and the squire (of course he
was growing old) had not even answered.

As a practical protest she had rung for Jane Trost
and told her to open the window and bring it down
with a bang; but even that, pointed as it was, had
failed to stop them. If one wanted an example of
what beer-drinking led to—as she remarked to her
maid—one had only to consider Ted Hadley himself,
standing there, with a cigarette on his lip, in the tap-
room doorway: such a fresh-faced, respectable young
fellow before he went to the war and got invalided,
somehow or other, from Egypt—and look at him now,
with his purple complexion (*she* didn't believe it was
heart) and his figure all gone to seed, and that bar-
maid-looking wife (if she *was* his wife) with the
peroxide hair whom he'd picked up in London. It was

B*

typical of the man's unseemly attitude towards life, his lack of decency in everything that mattered, that he probably had no intention of lowering the blinds in his front windows. "I never, *never* interfere in other people's private business," Miss Loach affirmed, "but Respect for the Dead is another matter entirely. Please step over the road, Jane, and ask Mr. Hadley, with my compliments, if he'll do me the favour of kindly pulling them down. Ah, here comes the Vicar. . . ."

Mr. Winter emerged from the laurels of the vicarage drive, a tall figure clad in black cassock and biretta. When she saw the biretta Miss Loach's grim mouth hardened. Her late father, on such an occasion, would have worn the damaged mortar-board which he preserved to the end (Miss Loach had it still), as a relic of his association with Keble College; and she frowned on the biretta, not only because she found it new-fangled, but also because it suggested doctrinal flirtations with the Scarlet Woman, the Whore of Babylon. Her father, in fact, escaping the seductions of the Oxford Movement, had always mounted the pulpit in black, and drawn the line at a surpliced choir. Miss Loach, without being so rigid as that, was a strong Evangelical. Though she knew they existed, she was glad that she had never set eyes on the candles and vestments (the "thin edge of the wedge," she called them) which had crept into Chaddesbourne since Mr. Winter's institution. When he first came to the parish she had sent for Mr. Winter and catechized him and feared the worst; but the worst, in his case, had been tempered later by the fact that, however misguided he might be, he was deeply interested in his cure and a real hard worker. He didn't, like the vicar who preceded him, resent being sent for at inconvenient moments, or regard reading the Office for the Visitation of the Sick and the administration of the Sacrament as a bore; he was patient and kindly and—unlike so many modern clergymen!—a gentleman-born; and if his lean ugly features wore, at times, a quizzical look, if his fine violet eyes (so luminous in that swarthy face) showed occasionally at the corners a crinkling that, in anyone but a cleric, might have denoted amusement, he was always ready to discuss serious questions—such as the Morals of the Village— with gravity. As for the vestments and the candles, which were only lit four times a year: his attitude towards these had an odd, inappropriate resemblance to that of Dr. Selby on the subject of beer-drinking. He had actually made use of the same word—Poetry! —though what poetry had to do with religion, which was surely a serious matter, any more than with the life of the Labouring Classes, Miss Loach couldn't imagine. Still, Earnestness, after all, was the thing that counted; and however much humour (or poetry) got the better of him at times, in matters affecting the root principles of Christianity, such as his dislike of Dissenters and Socialists and the Marriage of

Divorced Persons and Deceased Wives' Sisters, Mr. Winter was earnest to a degree.

Mr. Winter's black figure swerved into the lych-gate and Jane Trost returned, out of breath, to Miss Loach's elbow.

"Well, what did the fellow say?" Miss Loach demanded.

Ted Hadley had actually said: "Tell the old cat to mind her own business," but Jane Trost, being tactful, translated his answer freely.

"He said—'Thank you kindly, ma'am, for reminding him' "—and Miss Loach smiled and preened herself at the thought that, through her timely watchfulness, the proprieties had been preserved.

But by this time the empty street had begun to exhibit a certain liveliness. The horse which had just been shod emerged from the forge and rejoined his tired team-mate. Joe Atkins, the blacksmith, appeared in the doorway in his leather apron. He wiped his hands on his trouser-seat and looked at his watch, then closed the wide door of the forge. From the direction of the Hall a group of old women laboriously approached the cross-roads; they were dressed in black, with old-fashioned jet-spangled bonnets, and picked their way between puddles, lifting their skirts. They all knew Miss Loach, and looked up at her shaded window to see if she was there; they nudged one another and whispered, but were far too shy to salute her. From the opposite end of the street a farmer's dog-cart drove up. Its wheels were spattered with mud and the cob's fetlocks soaked. It was driven by a tall, red-faced man of fifty in a flat-topped felt hat; a woman with a pale, anxious, patient face, sat beside him. As they reached the inn yard a lumbering youth with a florid face jumped down from the hinder-seat and held the cob's head while the driver dismounted. The led horse and trap disappeared into the yard. The tall man entered the inn. Miss Loach shook her head in disapproval and glanced significantly at her maid. "Poor, poor Mrs. Cookson . . . poor woman!" she said. "Such a fine man, too."

"They say he's all right except on market days, ma'am," said Jane Trost in extenuation.

"You have only to look at his face, Jane," Miss Loach replied, "to see that he's not what he was. George Cookson is going downhill and so is the farm, in spite of all the money he made in the war. It's a sad pity to have to say that of a man in the prime of life, a good-natured man, who's a Churchwarden and a staunch Conservative. But there it is,"—Miss Loach folded her mittened hands in resignation—"there it is and, however unpleasant it may be, the truth must be spoken."

"They say that young Jim and he don't hit it off any too well, and I can't say I blame the young man. Mr. Cookson is a regular tyrant by all accounts. The boy don't dare open his mouth when his father has taken a drop."

"That is all very well," said Miss Loach sententiously. "Jim Cookson's place is beside his mother, poor soul. If it were only the drink it would be bad enough; but there are other things too, unfortunately. . . ."

She paused, with pursed lips. Whatever the "other things" were—and Jane Trost's goggled eyes were already gloating—Miss Loach made it quite clear that no further definition should soil her virginal lips. There were limits to the intimacy permissible between mistress and maid, and this subject exceeded them. In any case it must have been closed; for, at that very moment, a new cause for indignation had arisen. It was eleven o'clock, the hour of the morning break, and the subdued starling chatter of the school-house had risen to a clamour as the children, released, stampeded, shouting and scrambling, into the asphalt playground. They screamed round in dizzy circles, crossing and re-crossing, like gulls fighting for offal, the ruder and stronger establishing themselves along the stone parapet which bordered the road.

"Disgraceful, abominable, monstrous!" Miss Loach's vocabulary gave out. "The idea of letting them behave so uproariously on such an occasion! I shall write to Mr. Winter and ask him to complain to the authorities about this exhibition. Not a shadow of discipline, and the girls as bad as the boys! Though, indeed, what can one expect with that dreadful young man? In the old days. . . ."

Miss Loach's mind went back to the time when her father had been Vicar, and the Church School not merely a Church School in name; remembering how he used to "pop in" when he happened to be passing by at the time of the Scripture lesson and pat the children's heads and question them on the order of the Kings of Judah and Israel or parts of the Catechism, explaining how every true Christian was bound to submit himself to his Spiritual Masters and Pastors and believe all the Bible literally, and how the stiff-necked and uncircumcised would assuredly be cast into a lake of fire—besides other vital points of behaviour in daily life (quite forgotten nowadays), such as not throwing stones or shouting, and doffing your hat or curtsying when you saw a lady or a gentleman.

In that golden age, of course, before that iniquitous, blasphemous Education Act (for which she would never, never forgive the Liberals—but what could you expect?) school-teachers were chosen by clergymen, with a proper regard to their characters and religious beliefs. Now, Miss Loach lamented, any young man or woman who had scraped enough book-learning to pass through a training-college was licensed to put wrong ideas into children's heads. If you wanted an example you had only to look at that dreadful young man, Mr. Jones, standing there, caring about nothing but his salary, while the children ran riot and squealed and hung over the wall. Miss Loach hated his black Welsh hair waving in the wind and his savage white face. If he wasn't an atheist and a socialist (and she'd heard rumours of both) he certainly looked the parts. When she had tackled Mr. Winter on the subject, he had merely puckered his eyes in the odd way he had and told her that Morgan Jones was "an interesting fellow"—as if being interesting had anything whatever to do with becoming a school-teacher whose influence could blight the beliefs of innocent children!

"There's a fire in that young man, Miss Loach," Mr. Winter had said, "a smoky fire, which may produce something particularly fine, or particularly unpleasant." Miss Loach could guess which. "If *I* had my way . . ." her soul cried. But the vehemence engendered by imagining just what she would do if she had it was so great that her head went swimmy all of a sudden; she felt faint, and in urgent need of her glass of port and her biscuit, which Jane Trost, in the excitement of the morning's events, had forgotten to bring her. At that moment, indeed—almost as if her mute protests had come to him telepathically —Mr. Jones emerged from his pallid and sinister meditations. He tossed his black head and shouted an order, at which his pupils trotted obediently back into school; and the tenor-bell in the church-tower began to toll.

Arthur Winter heard it, standing alone in the vestry and waiting. He could hear not only the boom of the passing bell, but the rasp of the rope that the sexton pulled and the rhythmical creak of the mounting. The tenor bell had a rich and melancholy tone. It reminded him how, on the day when he first came to Chaddesbourne, only a few months ago, he had climbed alone up the dark spiral steps that pierced the solid stone of the tower like a corkscrew, and gazed through the belfry louvres at the village whose souls had just been entrusted to his keeping. The tenor bell was more modern than the rest of the peal. He had read its inscription, in chaste eighteenth-century lettering:—*Consider man when you hear me, that I ere long may ring for thee. Richard Sanders cast all we. 1719.* The naïve doggerel came back to him now, beating into his brain with its rhythm, like the creak of the mounting, filling his mind with monitory import, yet not perturbing it, for he was a Christian, and the idea of death, if it awed him, evoked no terror. Rather, brooding on that day when he had stood in the belfry gazing down on the village, touched and humble and full of high hopes, he became aware of the spiritual loneliness which, strive how he would, was the lot of a country parson living alone in a gaunt imitation-Gothic vicarage besieged by laurels—of how, the age of passionate faith having waned (and it was worse since the war), a man like himself was condemned to lose his fine edge and accumulate rust. Even in Chaddesbourne, tiny as it was, there was plenty of scope for his energy. He loved his people. Heaven knew he had reason to love them, for no day passed by in which he didn't find himself touched by some shining proof of their goodness and fortitude. They liked him as well, he humbly believed; on the surface they showed respect for him (or his cloth); and yet something—perhaps it was nothing but that respect—seemed always, somehow, to get between him and them; which, since he, by his office, was their means of approach to the throne of grace, seemed disastrous. Men and women alike could never forget that he was a parson; instinctively, when he approached them (they rarely approached him, alas) they assumed a protective colouring not only of speech, but also, he suspected, of thought, which, because it was assumed, made them incapable of religious communion as he understood it. He had blamed the war; one blamed the war for everything; yet in the war, in the trenches and dugouts, he had often, gratefully, beheld—or believed he beheld—the bare souls of men; he had been able to discover their doubts and agonies and exaltations, to share and occasionally, by the grace of God, to help. Those burning, ecstatic moments had passed, it seemed, irrevocably. Only one naked human soul had he glimpsed since he came to Chaddesbourne, on the day when he had quoted Swinburne to Jones, the school-teacher, and the impact of that white-hot soul had made him uncomfortable. It was alien, suspicious, perhaps even hostile. He had invited Jones to drop in some evening and smoke a pipe with him. Jones had thanked him, effusively, he thought, but hadn't come. He was no longer, he felt, a fellow man, a comrade in arms, cold, mud-soaked, spattered with blood, but a gentleman leading a soft, sheltered life in a grey coat and clerical collar, who got up in the pulpit on Sundays and begged people who came there, because it was the right thing to do or because they liked singing hymns, to share in the Holy Sacraments, as, indeed, a few of them did.

In the war he had known the spirit of religion without its forms; now he felt himself throttled by the forms without a vestige of spirit. And what could he do about it? Of course he could pray. He knelt down on the vestry floor and prayed simply, fervently, humbly, for guidance, till, suddenly, the heat of his aspiration having waned, he became aware of a sound detached from the measured creak and clang of the bell, a brittle, fluttering sound like that of a dead leaf come to life; and, looking up to the bleared diamond panes through which sunlight blinked obliquely, he perceived the source of the sound, a small tortoise-shell butterfly which the sudden warmth of March sun had relaxed from its hibernation. It fluttered and clung to the leading with weak-clawed feet, and Mr. Winter saw in this solitary sharer of his loneliness the ancient and appropriate symbol of the soul, winged Psyche warmed into vague immortality—which brought his thoughts back to old Mr. Ombersley (by this time, surely, the cortège must have left the Hall?), and reminded him that this transitory life was, perhaps, after all, a dream, and the life to come the only reality. So he rose from his knees and began to put on his surplice.

The tenor bell tolled on. In that gusty air, to which the shrill blue of March gave a crystalline quality, rooks were busy building their nests in wind-tossed trivets. The quivering vibration of the bell broke in on their cawing and, because it was unusual, aroused the birds' apprehension. They sat perched on the swaying twigs, an alert, black-coated congregation, and solemnly contemplated the odd phenomenon, till, deciding that it boded no good, they began to slip away—first a single bird, then small groups of three or four, till, the impulse having accumulated strength, the whole rookery straggled across the sky like a tattered black pennant, in flight for their second citadel in the elms that shadowed the Hall.

Here too, it appeared, some questionable activities were afoot. In front of the portico a two-horse wagon waited, and the drive was scattered with black human shapes that stood talking in groups and looked suspiciously like a shooting party; so the foremost rooks, which were already swooping to alight, changed their minds and swerved and soared steeply into the cold upper air, where an eddy of sudden wind caught them and blew them this way and that, like fragments of charred straw whirled in the draught of a bonfire. The figures on the drive were disturbed by their cawing; a dozen turned pale faces skyward. Roberts, the keeper, spat on the gravel and said to his neighbour:

"Just you hearken to them damned birds, John; there's a sight too many on 'em. Last year was the first the old squire didn't shoot the young 'uns. That showed he was failing, now that you come to think on it. I don't mind a rook-pie myself." And John Sheppy answered: "Ay, they be squawking up there just as if they knowed all about it, and I reckon they do, Harry. They say them rooks be uncommon knowledgeable birds. . . ."

Helen Ombersley, who was waiting with Catherine and Jack in the cold drawing-room for the procession to start, saw the men on the drive staring upward and heard the rooks' clamour, and the sound spread over her rigid features a soft relaxation, reminding her of the rooks that built in the elms round Stoke Priory when she was a child, and filled all her girlhood with their monotonous cawing.

"I'm glad there's a rookery here," she thought. "No Worcestershire house would feel right without its rookery. I do hope Miles won't shoot them too heavily; they might go away. And there ought to be lambs in the park," she thought, "but perhaps it's too early for them."

Then her eyes, which had been dreamy and remote, became aware of Catherine, who, exploring the unfamiliar room like a strange kitten just let out of a basket, was cautiously lifting the dust-sheet which, like a pall, enveloped the grand piano.

"I expect it's a horrible old thing," Mrs. Ombersley thought, "and all out of tune, but that's where her heart is. When we're properly settled here she must go on with her music. Perhaps it won't cost a terrible lot to have that piano put in order. Or we might exchange it for a good one," she thought, "and pay something extra. It would be nice for her to have a good piano of her own and a big room for practising, after all the horrid little houses we've always been forced to live in. It's a wonderful resource for a girl to be musical, and the child's been starved of it quite long enough. When they see a piano," she thought, "they simply have to touch it." Having no music herself, Mrs. Ombersley regarded that art in a detached way, as if it were Sanscrit roots or Economics; but she hated to think of Catherine being deprived of anything. These two children who had grown up under the pressure of the war were entitled to every kind of compensation (even odd ones, like music) which life could afford them.

Colonel Ombersley suddenly, solemnly appeared in the doorway and said: "They're ready now, Helen. I think we'd better be starting."

"Poor Miles!" Mrs. Ombersley thought. "What a wretched time he's been having! It's making him look quite thin—unless it's the black clothes. Soldiers always look odd out of uniform." She said, brightly: "Yes, darling."

.   .   .   .

Into the private bar of the "Ombersley Arms" the note of the bell came booming and buzzing like some enormous vagrant insect. "It's the set of the wind that does it," Ted Hadley explained as he fastened the window-catch to exclude it. "Sunday morning it's the limit: you can't hardly hear yourself speak. Have another, Mr. Cookson? Just one more. There's time for a short one."

Mr. Cookson smacked his lips. "I don't mind if I do, Ted. There's nothing like a tot of the craythur in the middle of the morning. But, mind you, this has got to be mine."

Ted Hadley laughed as he took the kettle from the hob. "Yours be blowed," he said. "The bar's not open till midday. I'm a law-abiding publican: that's what I am." He sliced lemon, dropped in a lump of sugar, and passed the glass with a reasonably steady hand. "Well, here goes! Cheerio! Here's crime— coupled with the name of sweethearts and wives!"

He winked as he drank. Mr. Cookson drank too, with a gulp; but his shrewd blue eyes, suffused with blood at the corners, showed a hint of uneasiness. "Look here, Ted," he said. "That reminds me. I ought to be moving. My missus and Jim are waiting outside in the yard. I told her I wouldn't stay more than a moment. She'll be wondering what's up."

"Well, we'll soon put that right, Mr. Cookson. Why didn't you say so before?" Ted Hadley limped to the door (it was the gout getting into his woun

that made him lame) and shouted: "Hi, Gladys. Just
come here a moment. Come on . . . get a move on!
Don't take a month over it!"

Mrs. Hadley—if indeed she *was* Mrs. Hadley—
appeared: a much-bangled young woman, perhaps
twenty-seven, who, to judge by the roots of her hair
which showed above her straight bang, had been dark
before reconditioning as a bar-parlour blonde. She
had once, too, probably, been slim and hungrily
vivacious; even now, the greed having been sated at
the expense of her figure, the remains of vivacity
showed itself, in the presence of a strange man, by an
automatic quickening of the big, soft, stupid eyes, and
a smile that displayed teeth too good to be true,
on a face which, in colour and texture, resembled
a large pink fondant. At the sight of the strapping
figure and red face of Cookson her manner became
kittenish.

"Well, well, Mr. Cookson," she cried. "Why,
you're quite a stranger. We'd begun to think you'd
forgotten us. Hadn't we, Ted?"

Mr. Cookson smiled heavily; his eyes approved the
lax full-bosomed body which they were expected to
approve. But Ted Hadley was businesslike.

"Look here, kid," he said. "Just pop out at the back
and ask Mrs. Cookson to step in for a moment. Say
I'd no idea she was there and I hope she's not cold."
He turned to his guest: "And now what about just one
wee drappie more, to settle the others?"

Mrs. Hadley fluttered out into the yard knock-kneed, all girlish innocence. She saw Mrs. Cookson sitting, a monument of patience, bolt-upright in the trap; her thin, drawn, sweet face; the hair dragged back under the old-fashioned hat. "My God, if that's her do you wonder?" she thought. She also saw Jim, long-limbed and powerfully built like his father, with a big, red, shy face, and was so interested in him that she became more girlish and fluttering than ever.

"Good morning, Mrs. Cookson," she said. "It *is* Mrs. Cookson, isn't it? My hubby asked me to say he's so sorry. He didn't know you were out here. And please won't you step inside for a moment?"

Mrs. Cookson smiled wanly. "Oh, thank you very much, Mrs. Hadley. I think we ought really to be going on to the church. I hate being late at a funeral. If you'd just be so kind as to tell my husband I'm ready . . . and thank Mr. Hadley for his kind offer."

Her tone was polite—she had been brought up in an old school of behaviour—but the heart within her went cold with bitterness and scorn. "So this," she thought, *"this* is what he goes out at night to see, this is what he admires! Mrs. Hadley here, Mrs. Hadley there! though it wouldn't matter so much—I'm past caring now, since the day he pushed me in the fire, even though he did cry afterwards and say it was an accident—it wouldn't matter to me if she didn't happen to live on licensed premises, where money

just goes like water. No, you needn't take all that
trouble," she thought, "to show me your wedding-ring.
I can see it all right—the great vulgar thing. It's
your hands I'm looking at; you can always tell what
a woman's worth by her hands." And she thought
of her own sinewy red fingers chapped with cold
and roughened by dairy work, and the wedding-
ring, worn thin by marriage like herself, which she
nervously slipped up and down inside her black-cotton
gloves, till, suddenly, she became aware that this
woman and Jim were looking at each other, and that
Jim was blushing, and terror, combined with protective fury, overwhelmed her politeness.

"Don't stand there gaping like that, Jim," she said.
"Come and help me down, and then tie up the horse
while this lady gives dad my message. Thank your
husband for me, Mrs. Hadley, and tell him I'm much
obliged." She turned her back. "Come along, hurry
up, Jim."

Mrs. Hadley sulkily returned to the bar and jerked
her head backward. "She won't come in," she said,
"and you've got to go out at once. If you don't, I bet
you'll soon hear all about it, Mr. Cookson." And she
laughed derisively. "That's a nice-looking boy. You
can see who his father is."

But Mr. Cookson was far too furious to grasp the
compliment. He banged down his empty glass on the
table and rose. His face had the dark morosity of an
angry bull's.

"I've got to go, have I? There, what did I tell you, Ted?"

But he went, all the same.

"I think I can see the wagon now, ma'am," said Jane Trost excitedly. "It does seem funny, doesn't it, for people in that position to have a walking funeral? You'd have thought they'd have had a motor-hearse."

"Mr. Ombersley never countenanced motor-cars," said Miss Loach severely, "and I think it was very fine of him. A walking funeral, though fatiguing, is reverent and dignified, and it's no great way, after all, from the Hall to the churchyard. If you'll raise that front blind a few inches, Jane, I shall be able to see much better, and none of the mourners, if they're keeping their eyes down as they should, will notice the difference or consider it disrespectful. Ah, there goes Mr. Cookson at last, walking yards in front of his wife, poor creature. It looks as if they've been quarrelling. . . ."

"Oh, and here come the children, ma'am!"

"Well, it's to be hoped that young man will keep them in order this time."

They marched out, the boys grinning sheepishly, the girls primly solemn, and stood by the playground wall in two rows. Morgan Jones, though he controlled these proceedings, resented them inwardly. This parade had been more or less ordered by Mr.

Winter, whom he liked, but, because he was a parson, suspected of some masked designs on his soul. Morgan Jones, as he often assured himself, was the captain of his soul. He wasn't, however, regrettably, the master of his fate, which lay at the mercy of the six school-managers who had appointed him—and Mr. Winter had all the other five in his waistcoat pocket. It was a scandalous thing, he thought, that young children should be paraded like this to witness the pomps of death. Mr. Ombersley was "our Chairman," as Mr. Winter put it; but during his two years at Chaddesbourne Morgan Jones had never set eyes on him. That wasn't the real reason of this exhibition. Not at all. It was just another barefaced attempt to prop up the out-of-date feudal tradition, though among the old people in this benighted backwater, the feudal tradition seemed strong enough to stand of itself—as witness the crooked black figures that now came hobbling out of their garden gates to join the procession down the whole length of the road. There could hardly, he thought, be a soul in the whole blessed village who hadn't turned out that morning. There was none of that nonsense left, thank God, in Wales, where he came from. . . .

"In Wales . . ." he thought; and immediately his romantic face grew tender. Even now, as he lifted his eyes, he could see the humped line of Abberley, beyond Severn. If one climbed to the top of those hills sight could compass the whole cloudy splendour of the Radnor March and the line along which Saxon Offa had dug his dyke. "Land of our Fathers," he thought, as the tune, sung by sweet Welsh voices, came into his head. Here, in Chaddesbourne, he told himself fiercely, the old feud persisted; the fair-haired louts mimicked his rising intonation and scorned him for being a Welshman! Wasn't it a Welshman, a Welsh peasant like himself, who had won their war for them?

But by now the slow horses had dragged the wagon abreast of him. At the sight of the plain oak coffin and the thought of what it contained, his emotional heart, for all its gusty bitterness, grew grave. Death was moving at all times, even the death of a grim old man whom he had disliked, but had never seen. Morgan Jones's mouth stiffened. This solemn thing must be faced. The wheels of the wagon creaked by in a mortal silence. He saw the set faces of the principal mourners, the new squire and his wife; hard faces, he thought, but, most enviably firm. There was something admirable though hateful in their aristocratic composure. Then, suddenly, before that envy had faded, his eyes beheld Catherine Ombersley, and he held his breath, for he was a poet, cruelly susceptible to woman's beauty, and it wounded him to think that any loveliness should look so cold, so remote, so utterly unattainable, as that of this tall, rather angular girl with her proud, pale face and her unconscious distinction of movement. And because his mind was

drenched with poetry he found himself thinking of
"Maud":

> *All that I saw (for her eyes were downcast, not to*
>   *be seen),*
> *Faultily faultless, icily regular, splendidly null,*
> *Dead perfection, no more. . . .*

He hated that tranquil beauty, and all the more because her colouring—dull gold, clouded amber, lustre-
less honey—was of the quality which always had power
to ravish his black heart and send him mad.

"You shall turn and look at me," he thought,
fiercely. "I *will* you to look at me. . . "

But Catherine Ombersley, unscathed by his will,
passed on with her downcast eyes, and Morgan Jones,
nursing his hatred, expelled the unattainable image
from his hot brain, replacing it by another of the same
colour, neither cold nor contemptuous nor yet unattainable: the image of Elsie Cookson of The Moat,
who had blushed when his eyes devoured her in
church, and to whom, though no living soul suspected
it, and she least of all, he had written so many pages of
passionate verse, walking to and fro between the desks
of snivelling schoolboys, or stretching out his hand in
the darkness to find a pencil.

"Come along, you boys," he said hoarsely. "Go
back to your places."

He stalked into the schoolroom importantly, sombre

as Hamlet; the hushed children streamed in before
him.

The rich moment for which Miss Loach had been
waiting all morning arrived. She wished now that,
while there was time, she had dared to raised the front
blind just a trifle higher. In order not to miss anything she was forced to duck her head in an attitude
that made her jutting face resemble the Red Queen's
more closely than ever. The passage of the wagon and
the led horses did not excite her, though she noticed,
with approval, the plainness of the coffin and the
absence of what she called floral tributes, which was
quite in keeping. The spectacle on which her keen
narrow eyes were focused so eagerly was provided by
the principal mourners, Miles Ombersley, his wife, and
the two children, whom, because of the family quarrel
(she had heard vaguely about *that*), she had never seen,
and the excellent view she obtained of it made her
face go red with mild satisfaction.

The Colonel, to begin with, looked everything that
a soldier should be, though it would have been better,
she thought, if he had appeared in uniform, with his
medals and a band of black crape on the arm of his
tunic as a mark of respect.

He was tall, very tall, and admirably erect, with a
typical cavalryman's figure, spare and sinewy. As he
walked he gazed straight in front of him with the
level, unwavering gaze of a man who is facing his

duty; and the profile of his rather small head, which the close-cropped grizzled moustache scarcely modified, had, she saw, the authentic classic Ombersley features: sloping forehead, obstinate jaw, firm lips and predatory nose—the features, in short, of his father (who had disliked her) and of his bachelor uncle, the general, with whom she had played backgammon and mildly flirted in the decade before he was killed in the Boer War. The mere fact of this family resemblance filled Miss Loach with the sensation of vicarious pride which she felt when she heard the first notes of *God Save the Queen* (*the King* it was nowadays) and *Rule, Britannia,* or saw the aspiring stone of Worcester Cathedral or (long, long ago) the Round Tower of Windsor Castle, with the royal standard above it, or hounds pattering down the village street, with a huntsman in pink, or a bishop's gaiters. Like each of these sights, the persistence of the family profile in Colonel Ombersley assured her that in spite of that firebrand Ramsay Macdonald and the recent railway strike (in spite, even, of Mr. Jones, and the State-aided corruption of youth) all was well with the heart of the Empire, and thus with the world. "Even as a subaltern," she confessed, "he gave promise of favouring his papa."

The demeanour of Mrs. Ombersley pleased Miss Loach equally. That lady, she proudly affirmed, was a genuine D'Abitot.

"You notice how tall she is? Nearly as tall as the

Colonel! All the D'Abitots are tall. No doubt it's the Norman blood. And the firm way she puts her feet down—just like a thoroughbred! Though why not?" Miss Loach asked rhetorically. "After all, her father was a viscount and her mother the daughter of a marquess, so what would you expect if not that? You notice the gel takes after her? The same straight nose, the same colouring, though to my mind she looks much too fragile. No doubt the poor child, quite naturally, feels the occasion distressing, though, of course, her deportment cannot compare with her mamma's. She's a graceful creature, but no gels of to-day are fit to carry a tiara. Some say it's the modern dancing and engaging in manly sports; but, if you ask *me*, what their figures miss is a backboard to give shape to the shoulders and a dignified carriage to the spine. I'm told that she plays the pianoforte brilliantly. Possibly that accounts for her stooping. The boy carries himself better, although she's actually taller than he is. That's a pity. Tall men are so much more distinguished . . ."

As she spoke, Jack Ombersley turned his eyes in the direction of the window, and Miss Loach's jutting head was quickly drawn back, but her eyes perceived, with a shock of surprise, that, unlike Catherine, the boy hadn't bred true. His face had neither his father's ruggedness nor his mother's repose. His colouring was sanguine and dark, and the sleek hair, growing to a point, gave the forehead an obstinate air. His mouth was full-lipped, with a certain sensuous beauty

c

which, with the dark eyes—a little lazy and scornful—appeared to demand the background of a cavalier's love-locks, a setting of lace and steel. He had the look, in short, of a cornet in Rupert's cavalry stuffed into a stick-up collar and black tail-coat unworn since Eton, and altogether too small for him. His face, at that moment, was anything but funereal, because he was young and lusty and had lived through the war when, even for children, death was mere commonplace; because, as he turned his eyes, they had caught sight of Miss Loach's face popping back from the window like a rabbit into its hole, and because all this forced solemnity cried out for comic relief; so that he actually smiled, and told himself that he mustn't forget afterwards to tell Catherine what he'd seen. Catherine and he always understood each other, thank Heaven!

Miss Loach saw that smile, and was profoundly shocked by its levity. This young man was handsome enough, she conceded, in a way; but it wasn't the Ombersleys' way, nor yet the D'Abitots'. This discovery, paradoxically, gave her almost as much satisfaction as the fact that the rest of the family had bred true to type, by confirming, simultaneously, her theory that "Blood will tell," and her dark conviction that "Young People are not what they Used to Be."

"You mark my words, Jane," she said: "that boy is going to give trouble. When they told me he wasn't going to Sandhurst after Eton, I knew that something was wrong."

"He's a very good-looking young gentleman, ma'am."

"Good looks are not everything, Jane," Miss Loach answered grimly. "Good looks are of minor importance compared with Distinction. If I wasn't aware who he was, I should never have taken him for an Ombersley, and if I were in his mother's shoes I should feel distinctly anxious. Poor, poor Mrs. Ombersley . . ."

Miss Loach was not greatly interested in the remainder of the cortège. It trudged by, out of step, with an irregular scraping of hobnails on grit. The whole population of Chaddesbourne followed the coffin of this wayward old man, who, though they had not exactly loved him, had always been as much a part of their lives as the brook, or the church, or the hall, or the rooks that cawed in the elms. They were mostly old or middle-aged; for the war had bled Chaddesbourne white, and even before the war came, the power of North Bromwich and the black towns smoking eternally beyond the hills sucked the youth of the village out of the cottages and the fields to court richer adventure amid their sooty activity—as surely as death, and almost as irrevocably. Even the old looked reasonably healthy, thanks to pure air and meagre living, though dank marl and rain-sodden clothes had knotted their limbs and made them hobble. The young married men, lately home from the war, had

a sturdy air, upstanding and frank, with wide Saxon
eyes which accepted life as they found it; and the
young married women, who had stolen shy, proud
glances as they passed at their children standing in
rows behind the schoolyard parapet, had something of
the same stable quality in their looks: the same air of
respect for themselves and the decencies of a life that
was none too easy, so much less easy than when you
were in service—what with children to rear and clothe
and dark cottages to keep clean on a small weekly wage
(thirty shillings, a labourer drew) with so many pence
to put aside for the club and burial insurance, and
always, in the background, the spectre of illness or unemployment or another baby. You never knew. . . .
Yet their eyes were bright (if sometimes a little
anxious); they were not ashamed of their hands, worn
skinny and red with washing; and their plain, honest
faces scrubbed shiny with common soap, looked happy
and eager—a little excited, of course, by this free
entertainment suddenly provided by death and the
hurry of "cleaning-up" so early in the day—but,
somehow, there seems to be no other word for it, good.
Yes, "good" was the only word, Dr. Selby decided,
as he stood behind the gauze screen of his surgery
window and watched them passing. (He had driven
his car axle-deep through the flood to an outlying case
of pneumonia, and returned too late to take up his
proper place in the procession.) There was hardly a
man or a woman among them with whom he hadn't

been brought into contact more or less intimate during the last three years.

"Good, and brave," he thought, remembering that even in the heaviest emergency, mental or physical, he had never known a Chaddesbourne villager "crack" or throw up the sponge. "That is mere insensitiveness," some people might say; but he knew that it wasn't. He had been in the war, and recognized fortitude when he saw it. "Good and brave, but not beautiful," he thought—for, being a natural man, he was not indifferent to beauty in women. By his standards there wasn't a single pretty girl in the parish except that soft minx of George Cookson's at The Moat (poor George Cookson, going to seed pretty fast, by the look of him!) and his tight-lipped, admirable wife. Now that he came to think of it, the Cookson girl, in her colouring, resembled Catherine Ombersley; but "pretty" was not the word one could use for Catherine. Should he say "beautiful"? Perhaps. . . . He wasn't quite sure. If beauty meant fineness of texture, as he supposed it did, then Mrs. Ombersley was actually more beautiful than her daughter. . . .

The wagon had stopped in front of the lych-gate; the six bearers, who had walked on either side of it, were lifting the coffin; and the black cortège, its progress arrested, began to silt up behind. Now, seeing its population gathered together—from the Colonel and his family in front to the last hobbling grandfather in the rear—Dr. Selby conceived an entirely

new vision of Chaddesbourne. It was no longer the
village with which, returning from the war, he had instantly fallen in love and determined to end his days
in, no longer a mere picturesque aggregation of sandstone and thatch and half-timber, no longer merely a
negligible dot on the map, but a spiritual microcosm.

"This is England," he thought: "the thing, the idea,
which we fought for. And that's why, though I don't
actually belong here, I love this place and these people.
If I slip out now nobody will notice me. . . ."

At that moment, indeed, all their eyes were turned
towards the lych-gate where the gaunt, white-surpliced
figure of Mr. Winter stood waiting. The bell ceased
tolling. Its last note, unimpeded by following vibrations, hung quivering and died on the still air above
a silence in which there could be heard the distant
clamour of rooks, the heavy breathing of the bearers
lifting their load, an uneasy bronchitic cough, and a
metallic clink as one of the wagoner's horses tossed
his head. Mr. Winter lifted his hand to claim attention, and spoke in a strained, high voice: "I am the
Resurrection and the Life . . ."

III

INHERITANCE

It was over. The Ombersley vault, having yawned for an hour, was closed. All the lowered blinds in the street had been raised, except Miss Loach's. Miss Loach herself, exhausted by the spectacle, had returned to her bed, where she sat writing a letter to her widowed sister at Bournemouth, in a thin, peaked hand and ink that looked faded before it was dry. *I feel,* she wrote, *that our beloved Chaddesbourne will never again be quite the same.* . . . She had written these identical words (and believed them to be true) after the deaths of Lord Tennyson, Queen Victoria and King Edward the Seventh, though it is doubtful if any one of these had ever heard the village's name.

In the "smoking-room" at the Hall—its name had survived the days when tobacco offended the nostrils of ladies—Miles Ombersley and Dudley Wilburn had unfolded the will. It was a small chamber, opening out of the hall and the long Adam library, of the kind which Victorian ladies playfully nicknamed a "den," though, in this case, the description was not inappropriate. It was dark as a den, even now, in the earlier afternoon; for its ceiling and walls, pickled swarthy with ancient smoke, reflected no light (save, here and there, a cold gleam from the glass that obscured a "sporting print"); and that which might naturally have penetrated it from the sky was obstructed by the shadow of a trio of redwood trees, brought from Oregon in 1860, whose untidy pyramids already overtopped and dominated the house. The room smelt like a den; and that was scarcely remarkable, considering the varied fragments of furry carrion—foxes' masks and brushes, otters' rudders and pads on the walls, pied badger-skins on the floor—which the grizzled wolf who had possessed it had dragged in from the chase.

It was the room of an aged man, too tired to demand or delight in such surface refinements as order or cleanliness. Dust lay like a grey bloom and stank on the shelves of forgotten ledgers and annuals; on the files of pierced bills, on the accumulation of invoices, circulars, charitable appeals and business letters, which had silted up, like the jetsam of a spring tide, on the Chippendale writing-desk, on the floor, on the pipe-littered mantel-shelf and the window-sills—on every available ledge which could possibly support them. There was not in that room a pen that would write or a pointed pencil; the ink in the wells, evaporating, had passed through the geological stage of black slime into the brittle incrustation of a salt-pan; and the stuffing of the one easy-chair—still draped with the moth-eaten plaid which, in time of frost, the old man had wrapped round his shins—protruded from the rubbed maroon leather like straw from a scarecrow's elbows.

Miles Ombersley took this disuse and discomfort for granted; the room had been just the same ever since he had known it. "We shan't be disturbed in here," he said. "There's surely no need to read every word of it?"

"It's quite short and perfectly straightforward," Wilburn replied. "As a matter of fact, it appears to have been drawn up by my father, so that goes without saying."

"I know. A sound lawyer. My father liked and respected him."

"As you know, there is no entail—never has been; but you, naturally, benefit as residuary legatee. There are these two substantial bequests to hospitals—far too big, if I may say so. If he'd consulted us we should certainly have advised him to reduce them in these hard times. But, of course, he didn't."

"No."

"Then bequests to servants: *to all such as shall have been in my employment for eighteen calendar months: one year's wages.* That's pretty generous . . ."

"He always was generous."

"Quite. . . . And a couple of persons mentioned by name. William Frankley . . ."

"The kennel-man. He's been dead twenty years."

"So much the better. For us, I mean. Henry Vowles . . ."

"He's still living, I believe."

C*

"Well, five hundred pounds should cover the lot. Unfortunately it appears he wasn't insured against death duties."

"No. He thought he would live for ever. And he did, very nearly. You mentioned a codicil?"

"Yes. I'm coming to that. I'm afraid it may be a shock to you . . ."

"Carry on, please. I'm used to them."

"Have you ever heard of a woman called Clarke— Mrs. Margaret Clarke?"

"No. Never in my life." ("He lies well," Wilburn thought.)

"She lives in North Bromwich . . ."

Colonel Ombersley flushed slightly. He repeated: "In North Bromwich. . . . I see."

"She was a friend of your father's."

"Is she still alive?"

"Yes. I've never actually seen her; but for more than twenty-five years—ever since I came into the business, in fact—we've been paying her, on your father's behalf, an allowance of seven hundred a year. That allowance is to continue at the same figure in the form of an annuity."

"An annuity. . . . Is this . . . lady young?"

"Well, she can't be very young, can she?"

"Seven hundred a year. That's a tidy sum. Just about as much as my pension's worth if I retire to-morrow. Rather a grim thought, Wilburn!"

"It might easily be worse. You're lucky to have

that in reserve. The rent-roll has shrunk during recent years; your father was easy with the tenants, and I gather from Healey that some of them took advantage of it. He was able to carry on here as he did because—apart from this lady's allowance—he spent practically nothing; he lived on the land, so to speak, and never entertained. Of course, a man of your age with a wife and two young people can't expect to do that. As soon as probate is granted you'll have to deal with Succession Duties. I know nothing of your private resources."

"There's nothing to know: they're practically negligible. As to the scale of Death Duties—I know nothing about them. Can you guess at the figure?"

"That depends on the valuation. They're governed by a sliding scale—from three per cent up to fifty. Of course, if you wish, you can meet them by realising capital—in other words, selling some land."

"Not an acre, if I can help it!"

Dudley Wilburn smiled. "You spoke just like your father then." (He looked just like his father, too, with a faint, dangerous smile on his lips corrected by an equally faint hardening of the blue eyes.) "I was going to suggest . . ."

"Please go on. I'm sorry."

"Not at all. It was merely this. If you *should* think of trimming up the estate on the Wychbury side, there's one outlying property—Uffley Mill, I think it's called . . ."

"I know it quite well. Man named Lydgate. I knew him as a boy."

"Yes, Lydgate. Precisely. Well, in spite of this shocking slump in agricultural land, I believe I could find you a buyer prepared to pay what, in these times, is a fancy price."

"You mean somebody's approached you?"

"Oh, I shouldn't like to say that . . ." ("Of course you wouldn't," Miles Ombersley thought. "You damned lawyers are so secretive!") "I merely hint that a client of mine is interested. I hinted as much to your father some months ago; but he turned it down."

"Naturally."

"Alternatively, of course, we can always arrange a mortgage."

Once more Colonel Ombersley smiled dangerously. "You're encouraging, Wilburn!"

"Well, facts have to be faced." Dudley Wilburn was somewhat aggrieved. "After all, I'm paid to advise you, and I want to help if I can."

"I quite realise that. And please don't think I'm ungrateful. You know more of the facts of the situation than I do. Please go on."

"Then may I suggest—since you jib at my other proposals—that you lie low for a year or two and collect your resources? *Reculer pour mieux sauter*, so to speak."

"Lie low? Forgive me for being stupid. You mean?"

"Go on soldiering, drawing full pay and allowances till you have to retire. There's no hurry. Shut up this house. Leave Healey in charge and make him tighten the strings. By the time when you come to retire ..."

"No, no, Wilburn: that wouldn't suit *me!*" Colonel Ombersley spoke almost passionately. "Healey's getting his notice to-morrow. You may think that precipitate"—(Wilburn *did*)—"but even if I didn't dislike the fellow ... that's in confidence, of course ... I should certainly get rid of him. I'm going to retire from the army at once, and I'm going to live here, in this house, because—I'm aware that this may sound odd and romantic—because I belong here and this happens to be my job. I've thought of it as my next job for the last fifty years. I'm not as young as I was, but I'm going to tackle it. It's an all-time job. If there's one type of man I despise it's the absentee landlord. My wife's with me in that."

"Oh, I quite agree, my dear Ombersley." ("What a boy he is!" Dudley Wilburn thought. "Do these soldiers never grow up?") "Don't misunderstand me," he went on. "I merely suggested that you should temporize, go easy for a year or two—give things time to adjust themselves."

Miles Ombersley laughed. "A year or two! In a year or two we may both of us be dead—there may be another war or a revolution. No, Wilburn, I'm taking no risks and I'm wasting no time. I don't think you quite realize how much Chaddesbourne means to

me—how anxious I am to get going. How long will
it take to get probate?"

"Oh, not very long. Say a couple of months. It's
a watertight will."

"So in two months' time I shall know where I
stand?"

"Yes, you'll know where you stand," Dudley
Wilburn answered grimly. "By the way, Mrs. Clarke
will be expecting a hundred and seventy-five pounds
on the first of April. You'ld like to pay it as usual?"

"If my credit's good enough."

Wilburn laughed. "My dear Ombersley!"

"Well, you never know."

"What I meant to suggest"—Wilburn paused—
"was that, if you felt so inclined, we might contest the
codicil."

"On what grounds?"

"Undue influence. He was eighty-two, and
obviously failing."

"That's why he made it; and you know, my dear
Wilburn, he was as sane as you or I. No, no. Let
it rest. This explains a number of things. It gets
rather dark in here, doesn't it?"

"You ought to have those trees down. They shadow
the whole house."

"He remembered seeing them planted seventy
years ago. Odd, isn't it?"

"They were planted too close together. I suppose
they had no idea that they'ld grow like that."

Miles Ombersley stared out of the window gloomily. "I hate cutting down trees. However . . ."

There were many matters waiting to be dealt with more urgent than the felling of trees. More urgent, and far more complicated: the command of a regiment of cavalry in war-time seemed child's-play compared with them. To begin with, Miles Ombersley had never before, since his days as a subaltern, been embarrassed by lack of money. In the earlier years of his service, his pay and his father's allowance, together with the modest income his wife inherited, had sufficed to free his mind from financial anxiety. Now, the pay, which fell, unperceived, like manna, had been replaced by a pension that didn't amount to half of it; his wife's income, small though it was, showed signs of shrinkage, and, instead of an allowance, he found himself faced with a mass of everyday liabilities, quite apart from the Treasury's immediate and staggering demands in respect of death-duties.

If he had been willing or able to accept his father's standard of life which, for the last fifteen lonely years, had been hardly higher than that of his labourers, Miles Ombersley might possibly have been able to deal with the situation. But, of course, he was neither willing nor able to accept it. He had been accustomed to live the precise kind of life imposed by his social station, without meanness, yet equally without extravagance, demanding, quite reasonably, the same

comfortable, modest existence for his wife and
children. He was accustomed to "do himself well";
to travel first-class (at the nation's expense); to hunt
when he pleased (there were always chargers available); to shoot two or three days a week in the autumn,
and rent a rod in summer on a South Country chalk-
stream; to go up to Town in the season and put up
at Brown's with his family; to frequent his club and
attend a few social functions, with visits to Epsom and
Ascot and Goodwood thrown in. All this part of his
life had been conducted without ostentation; it consisted of things which he had always enjoyed as a
matter of course and expected to go on enjoying until
he was too old to find zest in them.

Yet no sooner had he retired than many of these
modest habits, which seemed as natural and necessary
a part of his life as his morning bath and shave, became questionable, and some impossible. He found
himself suddenly enrolled in the order which had
begun to be called "the new poor." It was a proud
distinction, no doubt, but the pride was tempered by
grave disadvantages. Up till now he had always regarded the Chaddesbourne estate and the Hall as
assets. He soon learnt they were nothing of the sort;
they were liabilities, though the State, whose faithful
servant he had been, declined to agree with him, exact-
ing a toll of death-duties out of all proportion to the
actual value of his inheritance: a levy, in the form of
hard cash, on capital that was not, at the moment,

negotiable. In addition to this it demanded land-tax
on land that, without a further infusion of capital,
could produce no income, and heavy rates on a house
that, by modern standards, was uninhabitable—rates
which, if he made it inhabitable, would become heavier
still. By the end of the year his fluid resources must
be exhausted. And always, like a prisoner dragging
an iron chain, he was aware of the galling weight of
Mrs. Clarke's annuity. Without that accursed handicap he might have made fairish running. As things
were, this crowning injustice was more than he could
be expected to carry. Again and again he felt bitterly
towards his father: not so much because the burden
was unjust to himself, as because it was unjust to
Chaddesbourne.

The old man had been unjust to the property in
other ways, more forgivable because of his age, but
hardly less embarrassing. The confusion of the
"smoking-room" in which the business of the estate
had been conducted was symbolical of an equal confusion in its affairs. On the night of his arrival at
Chaddesbourne, Miles Ombersley had decided, with a
soldier's characteristic ruthlessness, to get rid of
Healey, the agent. He was a mean type, Ombersley
thought, disliking his spindly, gaitered shanks, un-
successfully apeing the style of a country gentleman,
his pale eyes, his thin foxy hair and moustache, his too-
ingratiating manner, the suspicion of alcohol never
absent from his breath—above all, the air of a

specialist handling a mere amateur in which, with a knowing wink, he waved searching questions aside: "Don't you worry about that, Colonel. I haven't the details on me, but I'll soon put that straight. Just you leave the matter to me."

The devil of it was that Miles Ombersley was forced to do so. The fellow was as slippery as an eel—you never knew when you'd got him—but equally, in the present condition of things, he was indispensable: the only guide, trustworthy or false, who could point a way, tortuous or otherwise, through this morass of neglected business. He had given himself fifteen years of life in which to enjoy the possession of Chaddesbourne: it seemed doubtful if that would be enough for him to put the place straight.

Alone in the evening, snowed under by monstrous drifts of disordered documents—bills, leases, contracts, cheque counterfoils, passbooks, receipts, assessments, demand-notes—Miles Ombersley lamented the fact that soldiering was no fit preparation for the rôle of a modern landlord. The army was a good business-show and adequately run; as commanding-officer he had been ultimately responsible for the regiment's complicated finances; he had signed the returns, congratulating himself that the accounts were balanced to a halfpenny; but the work for which he took credit so easily had actually been done by the senior staff-sergeant (what wouldn't he give for him now!), whose documents (being a judge of men, if nothing else) he could sign without a moment's disquietude.

What *had* soldiering taught him, he sometimes asked himself, that was of any conceivable use in his present life? A man couldn't adopt a new and complicated profession at the age of sixty, and there wouldn't be any more wars, in his time at any rate. Jack had shown more sense than he'd given him credit for in declining to try for Sandhurst. When Jack came down from Oxford—let the boy have all the fun he could get for another year!—he would suggest his going to one of those schools that taught "business methods," or, perhaps, putting in a short spell at an agricultural college. He regretted, occasionally, that Helen had persuaded him to send Jack to Eton. All the D'Abitots went to Eton as a matter of course; but he himself was a Wykehamist.

Meanwhile . . . deeply as he disliked him . . . Mr. Healey at least "knew the ropes."

Mr. Healey, in point of fact, knew far too much for his liking of the whole cat's cradle. He knew, Colonel Ombersley guessed, though the subject was naturally avoided, about Mrs. Clarke; he must know —or, at least, suspect, the tight corner into which his new employer had been thrust. These were two further excellent reasons for his early dismissal; but, as long as he was useful, Miles Ombersley determined to use him. Accustomed to command, he gave Healey, who was actually devious rather than dishonest, an extremely thin time. Not only amid the muddle of

papers in the smoking-room, which already began to
look orderly, but also in the open fields, where he
walked the poor agent's spindly legs off his feet,
Colonel Ombersley's curiosity riddled him with questions, rapped out like the staccato of a machine-gun,
till Mr. Healey's too-narrow forehead grew so
wrinkled with perplexity that it almost disappeared.
At the end of these tramps and sessions, observed by
Miss Loach, he retired to the consolations of the
"Ombersley Arms," where the welcome due to so
valuable a customer awaited him.

"Why, Mr. Healey, you look like a corpse," Mrs.
Hadley would say.

"Then I look what I B well feel like," Mr. Healey
grunted.

"Well, I call it a shame: there's no other word for
it!"

After two double whiskies Mr. Healey, revived,
claimed her sympathy.

"It's not what he asks you," he said, "it's the way
he keeps on and nails you to every single word that
you say. 'Taken down and used in evidence'—just
like a police-court! And if you made the least slip he'ld
come down like a ton of bricks. I'm a truthful man,
Mrs. Hadley, but I don't mind saying that beggar
just puts the wind up me. This, that and the other!
You never know where the next question's coming
from. Things you'ld never dream of! And the deuce
of it is, half the time I'll be damned if I've the fog-

giest idea what he's driving at or feeling or thinking. If I hadn't my living to earn, I'ld tell him to go to hell double-quick, and stay there! It's a hard life, Mrs. Hadley."

That, in fact, was precisely what Ombersley intended it should be. Healey's answers to the questions he fired from such various angles resembled those directional waves of wireless by which in fog a navigator contrives to plot his position. By this means, though his course was still too densely beclouded for him to dare to drop this doubtful pilot, to take over the wheel and signal *Full Speed Ahead*, he was beginning, at last, to guess where he was and to grasp the lie of the soundings and reefs which surrounded him; till, finally, from those voyages of exploration in which his splendid physical fitness and clarity of mind extracted the last ounce of virtue from poor Healey's tired limbs and fuddled brain, there emerged a meticulous survey, thickly peppered with soundings, psychological and physical, of his new sphere of activity.

By the end of a month of driving energy and concentration, there was not an acre of pasture or arable over which his feet had not plodded; not a spinney or covert or wood that they had not penetrated; not a farm or cottage or barn that he had not examined; not a single tenant or sub-tenant with whom he had not conversed and whose worth and character he had not assayed. He began, in fact, to see the estate as a whole, assembling, out of multiple details, a unity corresponding to the shape outlined on the finger-smudged sheet of the six-inch ordnance-survey that hung on the smoking-room wall; a lop-sided triangle, roughly based on a line that ran from the woodland belt which encircled the Hall to the bridge on the road to Wychbury, its blunt apex bisected by the brook flowing out of the tangles of Foxhall Wood past Uffley Mill.

IV

UFFLEY MILL

OF all his possessions Uffley Mill held the most cherished place in Miles Ombersley's mind. In his boyhood, when all distance was magnified, it had seemed to him romantically remote and inaccessible. The Mill enshrined memories of heaped farm-house teas and mugs of pale cider and of the one unforgettable moment of triumph in which, instructed by Eli Lydgate, he had caught his first trout.

The Lydgates had rented Uffley for three generations, and the mill was the sole survivor of the two ascribed to Urse D'Abitot, his wife's ancestor, in Domesday. That was why Miles Ombersley had so stiffly resented his lawyer's suggestion of selling it. It was hard to guess how much of the original mill-house remained; for when once a certain degree of antiquity is passed, the works of men (no less than themselves) have an aspect of agelessness. In Miles's memory the building had always been shapeless and old and creaky, with low lintelled doorways beneath which a tall head —such as that of his friend Eli Lydgate—must be ducked; its sagging timbers complained of their centuries of tension; its flagged floor had sunk three feet below the level of the garden—unless, perhaps, it was the surface of the ground which had risen by gradual, infinitesimal accretions of dust and mould. On one side the leat and the stagnant depths of the mill-pond, where pike basked and floundered amid the flat leaves of water-lilies—on two others the trouty swirls of the Chaddesbourne Brook: Uffley Mill, with its dripping, moss-grown wooden water-wheel, stood wellnigh islanded by silent or singing water. And beyond the brook, overhanging its marly banks, lay Foxhall Wood, the impenetrable fastness from which it sprang. Set apart by a space so narrow that at sunset the shadow of trees thrown over the stream seemed to fall like a stealthy paw within a pace of the threshold, the wood and the house, Miles remembered, had both seemed to be watchful and drowsily alive, with a wariness resembling that of wild animals facing each other, crouched and motionless and rather frightening, so that he had not been unwilling to take Eli Lydgate's strong hand when they went in to tea.

Now that he came to think of it, Eli Lydgate must surely be the only friend of his boyhood on the Chaddesbourne estate. Skirting Foxhall Wood on the day of his first visit to Uffley after his return he couldn't help wondering what Eli would look like now. The mill, he supposed, would seem just as it had been, though probably smaller; but "young Lydgate," who was fifteen years older than himself, might be startling; for, apart from his age, the man had had a strange history. In his youth and in early manhood Miles Ombersley remembered him well, as a gaunt, tall figure of a man with bold, rough-hewn features and the remarkable combination of red hair and crisping beard with dark eyes that appeared to smoulder beneath craggy brows. Even with the son of his landlord, Eli's speech had been harsh and habitually curt, his manner ruthless. He lived, it appeared, in a world of his own: a lonely, forbidding world which few neighbours were minded to enter. All the Lydgates habitually "kept themselves to themselves," and it was typical of the family's nature when Eli, in early middle life, chose to marry a "foreigner"—Chaddesbourne left it at that—who had come into the district as lady's maid to the elder Miss Abberley, and to whom he had given a lift one day driving home from Wychbury.

Mrs. Lydgate, who, in fact, came from Belgium, was a small shy creature with jet-black hair parted in the middle and a pale, placid face which, whenever she spoke (which was rarely and with an odd accent), seemed to glow with a swift incandescent vivacity. She was a Papist, so Miles had been told; every Sunday her husband drove her to the Roman Catholic chapel at Stourton to hear Mass. She harboured exotic graces, such as playing the piano (he had bought one for her) and singing quick, pattering songs, supposed to be French, and serving up spiced "kickshaws" fit to rot a man's stomach. It was difficult, indeed, for Chaddesbourne to believe that such a strange woman could be moral. That was why, people said, Eli kept her cooped up at Uffley, so that nobody in the village ever knew more of her than the glimpse of her small, bird-like figure, perched high upon Eli's dog-cart, and of her quick, illuminating smile—until, having borne him three children—two boys and a girl—she died, as quietly and as mysteriously as she had arrived.

After this Eli Lydgate grew more taciturn and Uffley more isolated than ever. His small family grew up and was scattered. He had never "got on" with his sons, and there was no work for young men at Uffley. In the days of his prime—those days that Miles Ombersley remembered—the Chaddesbourne farmers grew wheat and baked their own bread in a cooling-oven. Day by day loaded wagons were drawn to the mill with sacks to be hoisted. Miles remembered the sound of grain as it slid down the shute with a seething hiss like that of a smooth sea slowly cream-ing on shingle, while, below, the great grit-stones rumbled and made the floor shudder. He could see the wheel turning over so slowly that it always seemed to be stopping, yet never stopped; he could see the drops of silver splashed from its buckets and the boil-ing race below churned to rainbow spray. But no grist had come to Uffley Mill for many a day. . . .

Indeed, when Miles Ombersley approached it that afternoon (it was May, and Foxhall Wood was floored with a mist of bluebells), it seemed to him as though the place had not merely shrunk (as he half expected), but gone grey—so silvery were its timbers—and then died in its sleep. It was one of those bad days for Uffley when the north wind blows, carrying over the hills fine dust from the Black Country's smoke-screen and blearing the sky with a yellowish film which absorbs light and flattens every colour in the landscape. As he rode up to the door over the wide bridge that spanned the mill-race, his horse's tread gave a wooden sound, unreal and hollow, and the face of the house looked as blank and disused as if it had been abandoned because of some curse.

Dismounting, he knocked at the door, but nobody answered. Then he heard steps behind him and, turning, perceived a shape, human—or rather sub-human—hurrying towards him with the gait of a land-crab. It was the kind of form that might have been expected to emerge from that mass of worm-eaten timber. Its spine, distorted in youth by the dead-weight of flour-sacks, had been twisted; one shoulder was tilted higher than the other, so that even as he walked (or shambled) he still seemed to carry an invisible burden and his head was bowed. The eyes that peered upward from beneath his furrowed forehead and tangled hair—they were gentle as those of some patient animal, and quite incredibly blue—appeared to regard Miles Ombersley with mingled surprise and pleasure.

"Why, bless us, bistna thee Master Miles!" he said.

"Don't yo' tell tell me yo' dai' remember me?" (Could this be Lydgate? Miles Ombersley thought. Was that possible? He smiled uneasily.) "Yo' remember Joe Warley, Master Miles, what used to dig worms for yo' when yo' came fishing. Us 'as been looking to see yo', me and the gaffer, this long time. Thee 'asna changed that much neither, not considering. Come inside, Master Miles."

"A boy . . . a man . . . a hobgoblin who used to dig worms for me!" Miles Ombersley thought. "Joe Warley . . ." The name raised an echo somewhere, but that was all. Yet this welcome was genuine; the creature seemed pleased to see him. "Of course I remember you," he said.

At that moment the door moved inwards. A young girl had timidly opened it. She had a pink and white face, and cheeks to which colour ran quickly when she saw a stranger standing so close; her eyes were coal-black, her brows straight, like a pencil-stroke in a Japanese drawing; she had a small, tender mouth, lips brilliantly red, which she opened now with a little gasp of surprise. Her hair, drawn smoothly down from the middle line, displayed a white parting.

"A pretty child," Ombersley thought. "She doesn't look English: a Spanish Madonna." He remembered hearing that Lydgate had married a foreigner—but could it be possible that he had a daughter as young as this? "No older than my Catherine," he thought. Joe Warley was speaking:

"Now, Mary, my dear, you run along quick and tell your grandpa it be Master Miles—Captain Ombersley, rather. Hark at me forgettin' my manners!" he chuckled; "but old times is old times. Step in, Master Miles, step in!"

Miles Ombersley ducked his head and stepped down; he remembered the drop of the threshold.

And the house, though no grain had been ground in the mill for long enough, was still permeated (unless that were the hunchback's clothes) by the nutty odour of flour. Joe Warley, still chuckling, followed him as he groped his way over the sunken flagstones.

"So that girl is Eli's grandchild?" he asked.

"Ah, that's our Harry's girl, that is. 'E were lost in the war, our Harry; but his wife took up with another chap before Harry was killed. The wench, she takes after the mistress, her grandma, like. Two steps up, this time. Look out, Master Miles!"

Miles Ombersley stumbled up. Yes, this room was exactly the same as he had always remembered it: black oak furniture, knotted and uneven as if its shape were the product of growth rather than carpentry; bright brass and pale pewter gleaming in the light of a wood fire flickering in vast recesses of chimney; geraniums in bloom on the window-sill (how their hot scent came back to him!), and there, heavily rising from his seat in the chimney corner, less gigantic by far than he had imagined, but somehow the same, the figure of his youth's adoration, Eli Lydgate. Miles

Ombersley held out his hand; Lydgate grasped it.

"So it's you, Master Miles!" the familiar voice said. "I've been laid by the heels, or else I'ld have come to the Hall. And I couldn't get down to the funeral: the floods were out. Joe and I had our hands full, I can tell you!"

"I know you'ld have come if you could. Let's have a look at you, Eli."

"I'm not much to look at. Not too bad for seventy-five, though—apart from the rheumatism."

He moved slowly towards the light. "Yes," Miles thought, "his face is the same, but less harsh than it used to be. With his red hair turned white and his beard cut like that to a point, he's remarkably like Helen's father. It's a face of enormous distinction," he thought; "you could almost imagine the man had D'Abitot blood in him. And why not? The Lydgates have probably been in the district as long as they have —perhaps even longer." He said: "Sit down, Eli, and tell me how things have been going in Chaddes-bourne."

Lydgate laughed defensively. "In Chaddesbourne? We know naught of Chaddesbourne here nor Chaddes-bourne much more of us. Best ask Mr. Healey. He'll tell you."

"He has told me. He's not encouraging."

"*I* pay my rent, don't I?"

"Indeed you do, Lydgate. I wish some of the others were like you."

"Meaning Cookson? That isn't a hard one to guess. I don't like the man, never did; but he's called a good farmer. He's put as much into The Moat as he's taken out. You try farming yourself, Mr. Miles, and you'll learn all about it. Mary's getting us a cup of tea. That won't be the first cup of tea you've drunk in this house."

"No, indeed! . . . Nor the last, I hope."

Miles thought: "He talks to me as if I were still a boy, and makes me feel like one." In the gloom—on these days of "blight" it was always dusk at Uffley—he was aware of the girl, Mary Lydgate, passing to and fro as she set the table. She moved softly, like a shadow; and her deft movements, now that he came to think of it, were what one would expect from the delicately shaped hands and feet he had noticed. "She shows breeding, too," he thought, "but of a different kind;" and, with this, his thoughts went back to Eli Lydgate's odd marriage, of which he knew nothing but hearsay: the vivid, fragile foreign woman and this rough-hewn, taciturn man who, even now, as the two sat together, after forty-odd years without meeting, had not spoken a word for five minutes by the slow-ticking clock. "What a strange life," he thought, "for a friendless foreigner, alone, in this creaky house—so old, so remote—with a husband whose words—to say nothing of his thoughts—she probably never quite understood till the day she died. Yet that's hardly more strange," he told himself, "than the life of this child, coming back, like a little ghost of the other, to flutter through the same shadows, with no company but this frosty old man and that hobgoblin Warley: they might just as well put her in prison!" Then he thought of his own girl, Catherine (who was, he imagined, about the same age as Lydgate's grand-daughter), and how richly coloured her life must be in comparison. Well, that wasn't any business of his, he supposed. If she'd come here from a bad home she probably thought Uffley a paradise. Meanwhile, he desired to pursue the subject of Cookson, from which Eli had deftly retreated.

"This man at The Moat . . ." he began. "You and I are old friends. You can help me by being candid."

Eli Lydgate grunted. "I've told you. Cookson's a good farmer, by all accounts, but not a good manager. He's well liked; and when too many people like a chap it's apt to turn his head: makes him think he's a bigger man than he is and forget his station until he comes down with a bump—and then, maybe, it's too late. George Cookson has too many friends, and they're not all good ones."

"Healey speaks very well of him."

Eli Lydgate was silent. "Ah, that's where the wind blows," Miles thought. "What has Healey been up to? You get on well with Healey?" he said.

Once more Lydgate grunted. "An agent is paid to keep tenants quiet. Isn't that so? I don't bother him much. I know better than that. You ask him."

"You mean there are things that want doing here, and that Healey refuses to do them?"

Eli Lydgate laughed bitterly. "Not one penny's been spent on this place for the last ten years except what I've paid myself. Take a look for yourself at the roof of the barn and the rotten gates and fences and the pumps that won't work. It's your property, not mine, Mr. Miles, and I'm not complaining."

"You know money's been tight, Lydgate."

"I've had cause to know that better than most. And now it's too late, I take it."

"Too late? What d'you mean?"

"If you're going to sell Uffley Mill, you may as well sell me up with it."

"To sell Uffley Mill . . . ?"

"Well, it is for sale, isn't it?"

Looking backward Miles Ombersley saw himself in the smoking-room at The Hall; he saw Dudley Wilburn's solemn face and heard his dull voice speaking: "A client of mine is interested . . . I hinted as much to your father . . . a fancy price . . ." Sudden fury flared up in him. Something happening behind his back! Was Wilburn in it? He said sharply:

"Where did you get that idea from, Lydgate?"

"It's what everyone tells us."

"Then everyone tells you a lie. As long as you're living or I am, Uffley Mill won't be sold. You may take that from me. Not a stone, not an acre of it! Now

D

you know where you stand. Let's shake hands on it."

They did so in silence. That hand-clasp was an odd gesture for a man so habitually contained as Miles Ombersley. Yet this return to Uffley Mill, with its poignant reminders of youth and of inexorable time, together with the wistful atmosphere of that solitary house, the black wood that watched it, the mournful water, had induced in him a mood that was perilously susceptible to those emotional sentiments which he dreaded and usually suppressed. The tension was broken, fortunately for his self-respect, by a laugh from Lydgate, who said brusquely:

"In that case, Mr. Miles, you'd better have a look at the roof of that barn: I reckon it's not quite past saving, if you can spare the cost of repairs."

"I'll do what I can for you, Lydgate. Never fear that. When you want a thing done, come to me."

And Miles Ombersley meant what he said. This strange visit, oddly enough, though he had found it disturbing, had done more than anything else during the reaction which set in after his first triumphant enthusiasm on succeeding to Chaddesbourne, to strengthen his sense of rightful possession, his re-solve—in spite of the odds against him—to do his duty and win through. That corner of the estate, dilapi-dated though it might be, was a unique survival of the Chaddesbourne he had dreamed of. The Lydgates had lived at Uffley a hundred years before he was born: a Lydgate still lived there in precisely the same manner as his forbears. "Continuity," he thought. "A symbol of continuity. And that's what I'm here for, too."

Such reflections and aspirations continued to warm and to comfort his soul as, crossing the bridge, he walked his horse down the length of the village. Here the blight which had muffled Uffley all afternoon had been dissipated or transformed by the westering sun into an aureate haze that appeared not merely to lave, but to permeate and infuse the familiar shapes it enveloped. In this light he saw all Chaddesbourne, transfigured, grow golden—from the tawny surface of the road to the quickening hawthorn hedges; from these to the slopes of thatch and their rising smoke; from these, again, to the bursting leaf-buds which, beyond their bare boughs, fledged the ultimate airy twigs of the elms with soft plumage. It was that grateful, that elegiac moment when all creatures that have laboured turn homeward. He passed a hesitant trail of cows, with swaying udders and heavy, sweet breath, and a boy who whistled as he drove them; beyond these, two belated labourers, who halted and stared and touched their caps before they trudged on. From behind a hedge he could hear the impacts of a plunging spade; he could see the stooped shoulders of an old man planting potatoes, the flicker of a robin darting to seize the grubs he upturned; and the smell of the broken soil came over the hedge to meet him.

There was no sweeter odour on earth, Miles Ombersley thought.

By the gates of the Hall he heard rooks overhead coming home from their foraging with a babel of harsh cries, a rustle and creak of wings. Leaning down from the saddle, he pushed the gate open; it swung to, the latch clinked. And there, down the length of the terraced walk, between the still water, where Irish yews were mirrored like cypress-spires, and the tulip-splashed border, he perceived a small, lonely shape: the figure of his wife, who, startled by the clink of the gate, looked up, turned towards him, and slowly waved her hand.

That small gesture, made, somehow, pathetic by distance, precipitated Miles Ombersley's tender mood. He felt almost inclined to tie up his horse to the block and join her; to share with her the last ecstasy of that golden hour. He would slip his arm round the frail slenderness that was so dear to him (she had suffered so much and so bravely!); they would walk to and fro together between the still water and the tulips; she would tell him, like the eager child she still was, of her gardening plans. She herself, indeed, had that pale golden grace which, in autumn, tricks the fancy into sensations of spring.

For one moment he hesitated between inclination and the duty which had forced itself on him during his ride home from Uffley; and, as usually with him, duty won. He rang for the groom, and entering the house made straight for the smoking-room—they called it the office now—where he sat at his desk and composed a careful letter, in which he gave notice to Healey. By the time that it was signed, sealed and stamped the gold outside had faded.

V

PORTRAIT OF A LADY IN BLACK

HELEN ÖMBERSLEY noticed particularly the confident mood in which Miles returned from Uffley that day. Though he habitually kept his anxieties and encouragements to himself, she always became aware of them through those intuitive perceptions which sheer physical proximity has the power of developing between married people—even between those, she thought, who were married unhappily. "Not that *our* married life has been anything but ideal," she told herself, stooping down to pick handfuls of groundsel from the long border at right angles to the house, in which now, as the Darwen tulip-buds coloured and opened, she was daily finding surprises of disappointment or delight.

Their marriage had begun, indeed, as a passionate romance in the days when her father, Lord D'Abitot, still lived at Stoke Priory, and Miles—he was a subaltern then—had ridden over from Chaddesbourne to court her.

Thinking back on that period now (her thoughts had a deliciously vagrant habit when she was gardening) she could remember, she could almost hear the

clop-clop of his horse's hoofs on the red gravel drive
—and there she stood waiting for him, a child even
younger than Catherine, under the benignant eyes of
the two great Van Dycks in the Adam Hall! She could
hear her heart beating fast as the rhythm of trotting
hoofs became leisurely and stopped; the thud on the
gravel as he dismounted, the bridle's clink as he tied
his horse to the ring in the portico. Slowly, slowly—
for even in love Miles had been methodical—he
mounted the steps one by one, until, being able to
bear the sweet agonising suspense no longer, she
opened the door and smiled at him, and Miles, advancing, swept off his hard hat and bowed to her with
a gesture Van Dyck's cavaliers could hardly have
bettered, displaying his chestnut curls (officers wore
their hair longer in those days) and releasing that waft
of pomade which, together with faint memories of
Cuba, was the characteristic aura of a late Victorian
soldier.

She could smell that masculine aroma now as, in
memory, he bowed over her hand and whispered:
"Have we time to take a short turn in the garden
before tea?"

Then he offered her his arm in the courtliest
manner: such a robust young man; so clean, so neat,
so confident (and why not?) in his soldierly, hard
integrity of body and mind; proud too (and why not,
again?) of being a Chaddesbourne Ombersley; proud,
enormously, of his regiment, yet without an atom of

pretentiousness, because all these things, in spite of his pride in them, were a matter of course.

"Have we time to take a short turn in the garden before tea?"

It was in the topiary garden at Stoke Priory, she remembered, amid the smooth yew hedges, the chalky statuary, that Miles had asked her to marry him (a cuckoo was calling then; a cuckoo called now) and she had accepted him. Their spring courtship had all the atmosphere of Lord Tennyson's *Maud*—a poem which nobody dreamed of reading in these days. But what poetry! Helen Ombersley thought, and glowed, recalling it. *"There has fallen a splendid tear from the passion flower at the gate. . . .* Love was really splendid and passionate in those days," she thought. Men reverenced women, like Arthur and his knights (with the exception of poor Lancelot), and no nice girl ever went to a Hunt Ball without a chaperon. Whereas now. . . .

"These tulips are all old varieties," she thought. "And I'm sure that wretched man Follows has never lifted them for years. That's why they've deteriorated. And Follows has deteriorated too, because he's not been lifted either. I want new kinds of tulips, but Miles can't possibly afford them; and I want a new kind of gardener too, but he's been here so long that if he were lifted now it would probably kill him. I shall have to arrange this herbaceous border myself," she thought, "and for once, I shan't have to leave it." Her mind went back to the numerous gardens she had made and been forced to leave. Wherever her husband's life took her she attempted to make a garden. Hot cannas in Egypt, gigantic zinnias in Poona. Sometimes she had been torn away from them before they came into flower.

"And our early married life," she thought, "was just as ideal." (*Cuckoo . . . cuckoo. . . .* Would that wretched bird never stop?) All its intimacies had been governed by—what should she call it?—decorum, respect. It was a relationship which had never lost its fineness in the haphazard familiarities that were current now even among people of their own type of breeding. Miles never forgot—as quite nice people, or people who ought to be nice, forgot now—that he was a gentleman and she a well-born lady, so that their union had kept the flavour of formidable alliance between "high contracting parties."

To a certain extent, of course, they had lived their own lives. That, no doubt, was one of the reasons why romance had survived. In those days ladies had not presumed to share all their husbands' activities. The regimental life of a serving soldier was, quite properly, a separate existence, held, tacitly, as inviolable as the doors of his club. One accepted these minor separations along with the major ones, such as the regiment's tours of foreign service in Egypt and India and the three years' frightening hiatus of the Boer War. They passed swiftly, too—that

D*

was natural enough in the life of a woman who
had borne four children and considered it her duty
to devote herself to their upbringing and education.
And although one's husband seemed almost a stranger
when he came home from South Africa or from peace-
time service abroad, it was surprising how quickly, how
gladly, one picked up the threads of one's married life,
almost as if they had never been broken—"because
marriage of our kind," she thought, "the old-fashioned
civilized marriage, isn't a thing of loosely-knit sentiments and easy emotions, but a firm-woven texture of
mutual faith and respect, quite superior to degrad-
ing suspicions and little, mean jealousies and petty
selfishness—a life as stable and dignified as a house
like this. . . ."

For now, rising from her knees at the end of the
border, she saw the warm, red-brick flank of Chaddesbourne Hall. It did not appear, from that angle
of view, a beautiful house. It was too deep for its
height, and the slates of the high-pitched roof which
showed through the stone balustrade had a purplish
tinge. Yet its strongest effect was one of four-square
solidity; the man who planted it there had intended
it to stay. It was eminently a reticent house. There
were no fussy gables (as in that horror of Mr.
Hackett's which made Miles so savage); no wilful or
whimsical decoration distracted the eye from its sober
horizontality; it expressed, through the medium of
the local material—that masonry against which the

cascading panicles and pale leaves of wistaria appeared so luminous—the poise, the self-respect, the staid common sense of a Worcestershire squire of the late eighteenth century; it was an architectural expression of wisdom rather than culture, of security rather than riches, of comfort rather than aspiration, of confidence rather than pride, of moderation in all things: a complete expression (now that she came to think of it) of its present possessor, her husband.

"A house to be lived in, not looked at," Helen Ombersley thought, slowly removing the earth-stained gloves which she wore for gardening. The fact that a word like "lived" came into her mind was an encouraging sign. Since the slaughter of Dick and Roger she had merely existed, like the tail of a worm which still wriggles when a spade has cut it in two. She had accepted life—if this paralysis of all feeling deserved that name—not because she found any vestige of savour or joy in it, but because she believed God wished it, because, she supposed, it was her duty to live for Miles and dear Jack and Catherine. She had sometimes wondered if Miles had suffered half as deeply (the children, of course, were too young, too buoyant for true desolation); but in moments of real emotion his lips were closed automatically; apart from occasional "short leave," he had never left his brigade, and when they met, in those brief and poignant moments, she had contrived—at what cost none could guess—to exhibit a fair imitation of the

Roman mother, and known, by the way he played up to her rather than by any weakening gestures of tenderness, how much he admired this hollow show of fortitude. When first Miles came home she had made up her mind to force herself to speak of their sons just as if they were still alive; but when the time came she knew that she dared not face this risk to her false composure and his, so that their names remained unspoken; and this knowledge of her own limited courage had taught her a new canon of discipline which forbade her not merely to speak those names, but even to shape them in her mind, obeyed so successfully that from that day to this they had never yet crossed her lips.

That was why she was shocked when, on this bland evening, dreamily aware of the mass of the Hall's flank enkindled by sun, of the wistaria's falling plumes, of bees searching the limes, of a gust of white lilac, she surprised herself saying to herself: "How Dick would have loved this!" She was shocked because the escape of those words, slipped free, in an abstracted moment, from her steeled inhibition, produced none of the retribution she was schooled to dread: neither anguish nor tears, but rather the incredible relief of rain after drought—more than that: of birth after travail. "How Dick would have loved this!" She murmured the words aloud; and it seemed to her now as if they rejoiced in their release, floating happily away like white puffs of cloud or blown cherry-blossom, and that a softness like that of the lilac-perfumed air stole into her cold, empty heart, by the way they had passed and warmed it, salved it, filled it with vague incredible content.

"Something strange has happened to me," she thought. "I believe I am coming alive. And they want me to come alive. I'm sure they are glad of it. I'm going to be happy here. It's as though they were smiling. . . ." And she found she was smiling herself, no longer bravely—as often she smiled—but serenely, unconsciously—she almost dared to think happily. "Can it really be over?" she asked herself. "Is this going to last?"

She distrusted this miracle, above all for its suddenness. Perhaps she had reached the term set to her mourning by Time, the slow healer of all things. Perhaps this strange lightening of the spirit resembled one of those jewelled landscapes, disclosed instantly and then gone for ever, that flash through sudden thinnings of mountain mist. Yet even when that transfiguring light had faded from the rosy walls—as it did at that moment—and left them cold, she still felt, for the first time in many years, most oddly at home. If her Dick would have loved Chaddesbourne Hall, she loved it too, for some quality transcending mere beauty. Why? she wondered. . . . Perhaps because it resembled Stoke Priory, the house she had always thought of when she used the word "home"—not so much in itself (though the date and style of the build-

ing were the same) as in its familiar surroundings: the
great elms, the cawing of rooks, the still water in
which it was mirrored, the orchard-lands falling
towards Severn, in that sense of an immanent invisible
girdle of peaceful hills. Was there some healing
quality, particular to herself, in this sweet native air?
Did her spiritual roots run as deep as Miles's, though
she did not know it, into this tawny soil? A stray
stanza of poetry sang through her mind and seemed
to answer her:

> "In my own shire if I was sad
>   Homely comforters I had:
>   The earth, because my heart was sore
>   Sorrowed for the son she bore;
>   And standing hills, long to remain,
>   Shared their short-lived comrade's pain."

Thus the Worcestershire poet spoke for her. Perhaps
that was it. She had come home for healing to the
waters of Abana and Pharphar, to Severn and Avon,
the rivers of her own country; to its smell, to its
speech. Hadn't she smiled when old Follows—who
was such an incompetent gardener, had called elder
trees "ellerns," and wood pigeons "quices," and green
woodpeckers "stockeagles," and complained when the
rooks grew busy in the walnut trees, that "them there
great crows was gullocking the bannuts;" yet she
knew what he meant, and those fine Saxon words were

the music of all her childhood, like the cracked village chimes and the singing notes of the handbell-ringers at Christmas. She had returned to a world in which nothing had to be learned anew, to a kind of life of which she was mistress by birthright, a world in which, without effort or adjustment, she could regain her long-lost self and be true to it, as Shakespeare said.

"I believe," she thought, "I am going to be happy again." Yet happiness, in her case—unlike unhappiness—could never be the mere product of a personal mood. It depended too much on the state of mind of her husband and Jack and Catherine. Were they going to be happy at Chaddesbourne? Miles certainly was. His single-mindedness, his capacity for living in the present and taking things as they came, made him happy (though never excited) wherever he might be; and the rehabilitation of Chaddesbourne, for all its difficulties, was the task to which he had looked forward ever since he was a boy. But Jack and Catherine . . . would Chaddesbourne mean anything, or at least the same things, to them?

It seemed unreasonable to expect that it should. Until the day of their grandfather's funeral they had never set eyes on it. To them it must seem at first sight a gloomy and not even comfortable house tucked away in the wilds of the country miles from anywhere: just another—and not a particularly pleasant—halting-place amid the many peregrinations of their war-ridden childhood. She had noticed with some concern (for she always watched him) Jack's restlessness and obvious boredom on that first visit. It was a pity, she felt, that he wasn't going to Sandhurst. All the Ombersleys were born to be soldiers (or ought to be) and soldiering would have settled him. But he wouldn't. The war had knocked all the romance and glitter out of military life; and Jack, though in most things he didn't resemble his father, had all Miles's obstinacy, with none of his respect for tradition. Modern Oxford, he told her, was stiff with "temporary" captains and majors and colonels, who stalked down the High as if they thought they owned it and blithered about the old war from morning till night, and regarded him and his Eton friends, who had more right to be there than they had, as childish intruders. When Miles talked to him about Sandhurst Jack had gone positively mulish. None of his friends were going into the army, he said, and why should they? There wouldn't be another war in his lifetime, anyway!

Then what *did* he propose to do? Miles sternly enquired. (It wasn't the least bit of good being stern with these war-time children: she knew that to her cost.)

"Oh, I don't know, Father," Jack said. "There's no need to worry about that yet. Most of my school friends are going into business."

"Into business?" Miles laughed. The idea of an Ombersley going into business tickled him.

But oddly enough (providentially too, Helen Ombersley thought, for she knew her son better than he), Miles hadn't insisted on Jack's going into the army. He had something else, as she knew, in the back of his mind. He was determined that the mistakes of the last generation should not be repeated in this; he was going to catch his son young and train him thoroughly for his proper destiny as the next owner of Chaddesbourne; he was going to teach him to know the place through and through and love every acre, to make it the central pride and devotion of his life. The sooner Jack began to think of it in that way the better. They would work things out and talk things over together, father and son: the ideal combination which he had missed. As Jack said, there was no hurry. In the end he would come to it naturally. He was an Ombersley. . . .

Perhaps. She wondered. Jack wasn't the same kind of Ombersley as her husband. The difference was not merely physical, though there, too, it was striking. It was a difference of texture. Though he had plenty of physical courage, Jack's fibre was so pliable (she wouldn't admit it was weak) compared with her husband's. He didn't, she guessed, take Miles's infrangible standards of conduct for granted; even when he submitted to them, as he generally did, he couldn't always respect them. Institutions that Miles reverenced blindly because they were English, games like cricket, for instance (one of the first things he had done at Chaddesbourne had been to put ropes round the pitch in the park), appeared to Jack slightly childish and dreadfully slow. Slow. . . . That word, she believed, was the key to the difference between them; explaining why he had jibbed at the army, why, she feared, he might jib at Chaddesbourne. He was impetuous, nervously, callously impatient of all things smooth and leisurely, of old books, of old songs, of (she sometimes feared, though he tried not to show it) old people. His mind was on wires, like his body, incapable of repose.. Neither one nor the other could stay fixed for five minutes on end, and when either moved it went off like a screaming rocket. For speed—this insensate, bewildering modern speed— was his god.

That was why he had made such a friend, first at school and then at Oxford, of Trevor Tregaron, the son of the man who made motor-cars, whose eccentric grandfather had died, more or less bankrupt, at her old home, Stoke Priory. The Tregaron boy was quite nice, he had charming manners; but she couldn't help feeling that his influence on Jack was pernicious: they were always risking their lives together at Brooklands on racing-cars, and Jack's last letter from Christ Church had told her they were learning to fly (she hadn't dared to tell Miles)—as if enough unfortunate boys hadn't lost their lives flying in the war! Besides which, young Tregaron's father was a millionaire; he had far too much money to play with, and set the pace there as well. Of course Jack was only a child, she reminded herself. But such a ruthless, passionate child! Could a nature like his, as Miles fondly believed, consent to "settle down" so soon in the sober routine of Chaddesbourne?

Once or twice she had ventured to speak of these doubts to Catherine. Jack and Catherine had grown up together and still shared their secrets. But Catherine was almost as much a puzzle to her as Jack, which seemed wrong: a mother should certainly understand her own daughter—*"your daughter's your daughter the whole of your life,"* the old saw insisted. The strained atmosphere of the "home front" had been more wearing for girls than for boys; boys, at school, were kept busy with games and lessons and drilling, and isolated from the contagious anxieties and sufferings of their elders; while Catherine, who was older than Jack and, being a girl, developed more quickly, had been much more aware, in those sensitive years, of the distress that surrounded her. A young girl, condemned to live alone with a broken-hearted mother, had so little chance of losing herself in normal activities; she just wondered and brooded. That was why—even though Helen Ombersley didn't wholly approve of it—she had consented to Catherine's joining the V.A.D. and working for a time in Lady Bemerton's hospital at Wyshford. Bea Bemerton was a woman of the world with an unquestionable sense of propriety; and Wyshford Abbey, of course, was an officers' hospital—though in those days, as Miles bitterly complained, the word "officer" didn't necessarily signify "gentleman."

However, there were quite a number of "nice" girls nursing at Wyshford, and when first she went down there to stay a week-end she was encouraged to see how quickly Catherine had improved. In the space of a few short weeks that languid, coltish child had become a woman. The severe nurse's uniform, with its great red cross, became her; her cheeks glowed with colour; she had acquired an astonishing air of poise and self-possession. "Your girl is a beauty," Lady Bemerton told her. "I can foresee many hearts being broken." Then she saw Mrs. Ombersley's face grow anxious, and declared she was only joking. "My dear Helen," she said, "you needn't worry your head about *that*. . . . Our patients, poor lambs, are too proper for words, and I keep my eye on them. I can assure you that things of *that* kind don't happen at Wyshford."

Yet something *had* happened at Wyshford in spite of Lady Bemerton's eye. What, exactly, it was, Helen Ombersley never knew, for Catherine never told her, and for that very reason she suspected it must have been of *that* kind. When the Armistice came and the Bemertons' hospital was closed, the Catherine who rejoined her in London was not the Catherine she knew. She was older—but so many years older! The colour had faded from her cheeks. And though she was as sweet and thoughtful as ever—with a kind of chastened sweetness (and, Heaven knew, Helen Ombersley needed it), her soft eyes looked hurt. It was a strange thing, Helen thought, for the two of them to be living together, each trying to help the other with little forced gaieties and unreal bright smiles, each hiding, and with such virtuosity, her awful emptiness.

"If she'ld only confide in me," Helen Ombersley thought, "it might make her feel easier. It's this awful suppression of feeling that desolates her." Sometimes when Catherine came to kiss her good night and she took the child in her arms, so that the hurt eyes were hidden, she had a sensation that Catherine was on the verge of telling her, or crying, perhaps, and held her breath. Then, quietly, determinedly, Catherine would raise her head, her eyes tearless, her sweet lips set in a deliberate smile. She would put her hand to her forehead and smooth back her beeswax-coloured hair.

"Shall I put out the light, darling?" she would say. "Are you sure the window's not open too wide? I'm afraid it may rattle. The wind's rising."

And Mrs. Ombersley would say: "No, I'm sure it won't rattle. I love to feel the air on my face. Good night, darling child." She saw Catherine stepping to the door—she was a beautiful mover in spite of her tallness—and her pale, lovely face, so ineffably simple, so child-like, illumined for one ghostly moment till the switch clicked under her long fingers and the light went out and the door softly closed behind her, and each returned to her soul's own proud solitude.

It was a great blessing, Helen Ombersley thought, in those days, that Catherine could "lose herself," as people were supposed to do, in her music. That was another world of sensation which she couldn't share with her daughter—none of the D'Abitots or Ombersleys were musical or ever had been—but when she heard Catherine playing her piano for hours on end (until she sometimes feared she would wear herself out), she imagined and hoped that the child was finding some form of emotional expression denied to herself. She had an extraordinary delicacy of touch, people said, combined with a power that was almost masculine. At times, when she played, the house seemed to rock with wild music like a ship in a storm. It was as though then—and then only—in these birth-pangs of sound her passionate nature found speech. Sometimes, when the communicable stress of her playing became well-nigh unbearable, Mrs. Ombersley would stand listening at the door till she could stand it no longer, and enter to see Catherine turn round with a startled look and as pale as a ghost.

"My darling," she would say. "Are you never going to stop? You'll tire yourself out!"

And Catherine would blink and smile: "Oh, Mother, you frightened me. What time is it? The clock's stopped. I haven't the least idea. Let's go out and get some fresh air."

They went walking together—they were living in Chelsea then—along the Embankment. Barges breasted the sallow ebb and gulls screamed noisily above them. They walked briskly, side by side, the two tall, slender black figures, each immersed in her separate dream, until suddenly one or the other, made conscious of a neighbouring loneliness, would smile or put out a gloved hand. In those days London still bristled with reminders of the war: well-fed officers home on leave swaggering in their be-ribboned uniforms, soldiers in hospital blue, here and there the pinched face of a man who had lost an arm or a leg or hobbled with a stick. For them the war was well over; the gulls in the bleak sky screamed gaily; securely—for what mattered now?—the strung barges stripped the tide.

But gradually the uniforms, khaki or blue, grew rarer and rarer; you could walk for an hour on the Embankment without meeting one. People were bored with the memory of the war, and many contrived to forget it. So soon, Helen Ombersley thought, so soon forgotten! But neither she nor Catherine could forget.

That was why it had come as something of a relief when Miles, with his regiment, was brought home from the Rhine and ordered to Aldershot. It had meant leaving London, which didn't really suit Catherine; the hurried uprooting, the physical jolt of setting up house in Farnham. And then came a second jolt; her father-in-law's death, and the even more radical transference to Chaddesbourne. If what Catherine needed was shaking out of herself, these two should help her, quite apart from the healing effects of Worcestershire air which, Mrs. Ombersley firmly believed, had sovereign virtues. How otherwise could she account for the gradual change in herself which had culminated this afternoon in that very odd moment of exaltation and hope? It seemed likely that Catherine, with the natural resilience of youth, would recover even more quickly. "Though she still looks so pale," Mrs. Ombersley thought, "and moves so languidly. Perhaps she needs iron. If she doesn't improve, I must get that nice Dr. Selby, whom Miles speaks so well of, to come and prescribe for her."

VI

THE SURGERY

IT is doubtful if anyone in Chaddesbourne was happier during the spring than "that nice Dr. Selby"; it is certain that nobody was busier. That year the fourth wave of the direst pestilence since the Black Death, the influenza of nineteen-eighteen, swept Europe. This wave, though less devastating than its predecessors, had still enough foaming spite left in it to upset and suck back in its deadly recoil a few victims made feeble by age or undermined by the stresses of war. The old man called Sheppy, for instance, who had hobbled so painfully in the funeral procession, was swept off his tottering legs; he made a second, a far easier journey in the same direction (this time they carried him), and did not return to the cottage in which he had been born; but John Sheppy was so gnarled and mossed and shaky in any case, that his passing created no more surprise or concern than the fall of a dry elm bough that crashes in the night.

For the most part Dr. Selby's practice was not clinically exciting. It consisted of the maladies of a typical village community, picturesquely and badly housed, somewhat meagrely (and often injudiciously) fed, incredibly ignorant of the first elements of hygiene, but, on the whole, healthy. Older folk of both sexes, of course, showed signs of wear—"bad legs," the legacy of haphazard child-bearing, that refused to heal without rest which could not be given them; old ruptures, the penalty of forgotten strain, crippling rheumatisms and chronic bronchitis, the result of patient exposure to wind and weather. In addition to these he was met by the common casualties of a labourer's existence: falls from ricks or from ladders; feet crushed by a horse's stamping or pierced by a fork; fingers "poisoned" because some neglected puncture or tear had gone septic.

Every morning, at nine to the tick, his housekeeper, Mrs. Hussingtree—an ex-cook (in "good service"), who, together with her husband, an ex-under-gardener, looked after the doctor, his house, his car and his garden, for two pounds a week—unlocked the door of his surgery, a converted stable, providentially placed (for Jane Trost guessed quite enough as it was) on the side of the house remote from Miss Loach's observation. And there, by the time that the doctor stepped briskly across the yard and took his seat at his desk in the shabby consulting-room, whose air was drenched with an odour of sharp antiseptics and vinous tinctures, the debris of Chaddesbourne's leisurely activities drifted up: hobbling pensioners, stalwart young men with their arms in splints or bandages, housewives dragging children with swollen

faces tied up in handkerchiefs, muffled convalescents
taking their first outing after a fortnight in bed. As
each entered the surgery, which, in winter, a quick
fire made comfortable, the bell on the door of the
waiting-room rang. They sat down on the varnished
deal benches, patient as cattle, exchanging not only
the tales of their private ailments, but the gossip of
their neighbours—so that this bare room, scrubbed
clean and smelling of lysol, became a kind of club
where news and opinions were exchanged far more
freely and comfortably than in the public-bar of the
"Ombersley Arms" (since sickness frees tongues as
quickly as liquor), and "going to the doctor's" became a social occasion, for which one put on one's best
clothes and manners, like "going to church." They
sat there and talked, discussing themselves and their
neighbours, till another bell on the doctor's desk
pinged; till one patient came out to tell them the re-
sults of his consultation, and another entered the con-
fessional. For that, in a sense, Dr. Selby's consulting-
room was. Though he had only arrived in Chaddesbourne after the war, he was less of a "foreigner" in
the village's eye than the admirable Hussingtrees
(who came from the next village, Wychbury), or Mr.
Winter, or (more reasonably) Morgan Jones.

For Dr. Selby's regrettable alienism was excused
and discounted by his function, more intimate, if
possibly less sacred, than that of the vicar. Like a
man who, succeeding to the headship of a mystical

cult, assumes the hieratic name of his predecessors, he was known to all as "the doctor," and rarely as anything else. Even his house—though a faded inscription on the garden gate declared its correct designation to be "Ivy Cottage"—had been known, for longer than even Miss Loach could remember, as "the Surgery." He possessed, in fact, in the shabby black bag which he carried and which contained, in addition to dressings and hypodermics, the awful instruments of minor surgery and obstetrics, the social equivalent of a red diplomatic passport, admitting him, without let or question, within the most jealously-guarded domestic frontiers. Wherever he entered people said: "Oh, it's only the doctor." Harassed minds grew calmer; tense faces softened with relief. Even women in labour momentarily forgot their pangs and smiled at him with pale, anguished eyes, anticipating release.

This last department of his practice was one which, except in desperate emergencies (which were rare), he would gladly have forgone. Quite apart from the fact that it frequently dragged him from bed in the middle of the night and condemned him to fruitless vigils in unpleasant surroundings, he considered it was not a man's job. Furthermore, from the standpoint of present economic conditions, he considered that there were already quite enough children in Chaddesbourne—rather more, in fact, than the village wage-list could support. But now, since a score of demobilized married men had come home from abroad, the birth-rate was rising rapidly.

This phenomenon, which Dr. Selby, who knew that more mouths must be fed, found disquieting, was a source of high satisfaction to Mr. Winter, who boasted to him that the number of christenings in the parish church was the highest recorded since the beginning of the war.

"So there'll be plenty to fight in the next one," Selby told him. "That's fortunate, isn't it?"

Mr. Winter went red in the neck, but refrained from explaining what he meant, which, of course, wasn't that. This was one of those little sardonic jokes which made his friendship with Selby (and friendship it was) exasperating. They felt much the same about many important things, such as the superiority of Rugby football to Soccer, of pipes to cigarettes, of claret to Burgundy and of either of these to champagne; they shared, to a larger degree, the same views on politics—were in theory free-traders, but leaned towards tariff reform, thought the House of Lords individually superb and collectively a danger, and agreed that the Unemployment Donation, lately christened "the dole," was a humiliating catastrophe and entirely necessary; yet in matters of religious dogma and even religious principle, of which, patently, the abominable thing called birth-control was one, Mr. Winter knew that he and the doctor would never see eye to eye.

He regretted this: he not only liked Selby person-

ally, but also admired him for his candour, his kindness, his humour (within limits) and his courage.
There wasn't a man in Chaddesbourne with whom he
would rather find himself in a tight hole, nor one
whose life, in practice, more nearly reflected the spirit
of his Master. He was encouraged, when he first
came to Chaddesbourne, to see Selby in church—for
doctors, he knew, were not uncommonly infidels—
and hurt more than shocked when he found that Selby
was not a communicant. One day, choosing his
moment tactfully, he had broached the sore subject.

"Well, you see, I'm afraid those things mean
nothing to me; they're left out of my composition,"
Selby had said.

"Yet you come to church sometimes?"

"Ah, that's quite a different matter. I come to
church, first of all, because the building is beautiful—
by far the most beautiful work of man in Chaddesbourne—and because I find your noble Anglican
liturgy sublime. I come there again because I believe
in tradition and—what shall I call it?—continuity of
experience, religious or otherwise; because the people
of this place have been worshipping on that spot for
more than a thousand years and have left something
behind them—an atmosphere that's worth sharing.
Then, I come to church because it's a good example—
no, I'm not being priggish—and think the beauty
and quietude and all the other things I find there are
good for their souls. Incidentally I like to feel I am

sharing good things with the people around me. And lastly I come, quite frankly, because I enjoy it. I like to hear people singing hymns and forgetting themselves. And you happen to be one of the very few padres I know who don't talk nonsense. But as for your sacraments—the mystical part of your religion. . . ."

"The most profoundly important part of it. . . ."

"Ah, there you have me. I suppose, if you want the truth, I'm not really religious. We'll leave it at that."

Mr. Winter supposed they must, although he hated doing so. What puzzled him most of all, and indeed made him envious, was the clear fact that Selby was actually more closely in touch with his parish than himself. It seemed odd, it seemed almost unjust that in spite of his prayers, his fasting, his consuming desire for their welfare, his brotherly love for them (and this was no empty phrase), the people to whom he was ready and willing to devote his life denied him that entrance to theirs which they accorded to this mere layman, whose mission was not reinforced by the divine sanctions that he possessed.

Dr. Selby, in fact, was that rare type of human creature (even among doctors), a man with an enquiring mind, absorbed and fascinated by every aspect of his calling—concerned not only with the bodies that, for reasons grave or trivial, ran the gauntlet of Jane Trost's scrutiny and entered his surgery, but also with the far more mysterious minds which compelled those

bodies to enter; with the factors of heredity and
environment which made those minds, no less than the
bodies they controlled (or failed to control), what they
were (or imagined they were); concerned with the
very dreams, immediate or atavistic, which haunted
those minds and, unconsciously, influenced them; with
the souls—he was sufficiently modern to believe in
souls—which, apart from bodies and minds, yet not
immune from their association, revealed, in defiance
of matter, such astonishing energies and apathies, such
odd manifestations of essential goodness or evil.

Because of the mystical conception of life which
a study of its material aspects had forced on him—a
mysticism more profound than that which Mr. Winter
professed as a matter of faith—Dr. Selby regarded the
little pathetic world of which, when he adopted it, he
had made himself part, with a benevolence which was
more tender than the vicar's because of its detachment,
more effective because it was less vague and also less
critical. For this reason, though he had no intimates,
all the village was his friend; his life was a solitary
life, yet never lonely; his vision of Chaddesbourne,
though realistic, was unclouded by pessimism.

Indeed he was aware that he had much to be thankful for. First of all, he was young—and apart from a
fragment of shrapnel in the lung, quite reasonably
healthy; he was alive—and, but for a freak of chance,
or Providence, or the law of averages, might have been
dead; he was independent, in a modest degree, financi-

ally; he had interests, only a shade less absorbing, out-side his work—in the natural world (here seen at its loveliest), in books, in music.

This last passion, indeed, would have afforded him a rare escape—had escape been needed—from the more grim obsessions of his medical life. In the sunny room at the back of Ivy Cottage, which he consecrated to his leisure, stood a small Blüthner grand piano, which he had bought, years ago, with his first pro-fessional earnings. During the war the poor thing had languished in a North Bromwich repository, so sadly neglected that when first he installed it at Chaddesbourne the very keys seemed to have for-gotten the touch of his fingers and become insensitive. Now, coaxed back to life, the piano had recovered its soul. It stood there, a stark shape of lustrous ebony, against the cream wall from the midst of which, like some blank-eyed oracle, brooded the death-mask of Beethoven which, in days of younger enthusiasm, its owner had brought back with him in triumph from Leipzig.

Mrs. Hussingtree regarded the instrument with pride and awe; its unusual shape gave the house dis-tinction, though its lid, unlike that of any other piano she had met, was dedicated to an austere and un-natural nakedness. "Not so much as a vase or a mat of embroidery or a photograph!" she complained. After a number of earnest but unsuccessful attempts to supply appropriate decorations, which no sooner

E

appeared than they were ruthlessly swept away, Mrs.
Hussingtree gave in. "I'm bothered if I know what
he *does* want," she said—though she might have
guessed.

Dr. Selby was not a good pianist; his fingers were
clumsy, for this passion had come to him at a time
of life when they had lost youth's flexibility. Yet, to
balance this lack of skill, he was fortunate in possess-
ing a faculty (more æsthetic than mathematical) for
extracting, almost at a glance, the essence of the music
he tried to play. His tastes were not easily classified.
In the days of his early enthusiasm they had been
frankly romantic; he had been sweetly ravished by
the songs of Schumann, ensnared in the silken threads,
like dew-drenched gossamer, out of which Debussy
delicately wove his tissue of crepuscular sound, carried
clean off his feet, exhilarated (though half protesting), by the full flood of Wagner—impetuous, irresist-
ible as the surge of the Rhine-music sweeping through
Siegfried's Journey in *Götterdämmerung*. Since the
war his liking for sentimental heroics had waned. He
suspected that sentiment and cruelty might be the
poles of the same emotion; he had seen the bright
Nordic panoply of Siegfried, the pomps of Valhalla,
uncomfortably translated into terms of cold steel or
high explosives; and his mind, which now craved for
an expression less chaotic, less volatile, had discovered
it in the pellucid profundities of Bach, the ripe wisdom
of Brahms, in the vast serenity of his first love,

Beethoven, in Hugo Wolf's poignancy, in the peculiarly intimate quality—as native to his soul as Piers Plowman or Wordsworth's Prelude—which he found in the later work of the English Elgar.

It was a solitary passion. So far as the doctor knew, there was not, in the whole of Chaddesbourne, a single soul who could share it. Mr. Winter's eyes, it is true, had shown a faint glimmer of interest when they discovered on Selby's piano copies of Bach's Mass in B Minor and *The Dream of Gerontius*. But that interest, as the doctor divined, was not artistic but ethical: the result of a hope that the presence of these works denoted a secret change of heart in the direction of orthodox religion, which, of course, they didn't. That the vicar was devoid of any vestige of a musical "ear" was evident from his uncanny skill in avoiding, when he intoned, the note which Miss Burton, at the organ, gave him. For him—and indeed for the rest of the village—Miss Burton was the arch-priestess of musical mysteries: she had actually contrived to teach the school-children four-part glees (which were anything but gleeful) and carols; to produce in church (on appropriate occasions) recognisable versions of Lohengrin's Wedding-March and the *Dead March* in "Saul," and to perform, with more confidence (and therefore with much less noise) Handel's *Largo* and a selection of Mendelssohn's *Songs Without Words*. On occasions, intoxicated by these successes, she had been known to improvise. . . .

Those lamentable modulations and progressions were the cause of Dr. Selby's delight when he discovered in the unmusical wilderness the hint of an oasis. One spring afternoon, finding himself close to the Hall, he had taken the chance of catching Miles Ombersley at home and reporting on the condition of Roberts, the keeper, who had wrenched his ankle in a rabbit-hole. He approached the front door with diffidence—not because the Ombersleys were unfriendly—the colonel and he, on the contrary, understood one another perfectly—but because workmen still haunted the house and the family were not yet "settled in."

Remembering his visits during old Mr. Ombersley's last illness, he had always regarded the Hall as a gloomy, inhospitable house. It surprised him to find how the atmosphere of it had changed. The drive had been strewn with new gravel and rolled, the encroaching shrubberies cleared, the festoons of ivy stripped from pilasters and pediment; and the flagged entrance hall, in which his old friend the butler welcomed him, was no longer the dim, dank crypt which had made him shiver. The dull purplish tinge, which formerly absorbed and suppressed every glimmer of light that entered, had been banished from the walls and replaced by the colour of time-mellowed parchment, which not only reflected light but also seemed to retain it, revealing an unsuspected wealth of plaster-work in low relief, that, freed from successive incrustations

of paint daubed on without stippling, now displayed
the formal delicacy of a Georgian craftsman's hand in
swags and medallions, and defined, in the flicker of
fire-light, fluent traceries whose shapes might well
have been carved in old ivory.

"I'll see if the Colonel is in, sir," the butler said,
"if you'll wait here a moment."

Dr. Selby, alone, continued to contemplate the
astonishing changes in his surroundings. In the
times he remembered, the place had not merely
seemed gloomy and depressing; it had actually
been boorish; it had seemed not only resentful of
physical light, but also of the spiritual illuminations
of grace or culture. It had seemed savage, unhomely,
reflecting the material slovenliness of its owner, the
typical blindness to beauty of a mid-Victorian squire.
Even the painted eighteenth-century Ombersleys on
the walls had appeared to withdraw themselves in
frigid disdain of this decadence in manners which they
loathed but could not resist. Now, revived and encouraged, they seemed to have taken heart, looking
down with pride and complacence from canvases in
which the rich hues of brocades and velvets and the
whiteness of wig-powder resumed the glowing trans-
parence of their original pigment. It was not so much,
Dr. Selby thought, that the place had been brought
to new life as that its old submerged life had been
restored. It demanded, he thought, a habitation not
stately, not even formal, but gracious and dignified:

the kind of existence which was symbolized for him—
he found it natural in matters of "atmosphere" to take
his symbols from music—by Mozart, by Scarlatti, by
Vivaldi, or by the "little" Bach.

"Yes, that," Dr. Selby mused, "is what this house
needs to lay the last ghost of its ugliness; the old
music it remembers—or ought to remember—returning to the familiarly-proportioned spaces through
which its faint echoes once wandered. If only these
charming Ombersleys realised that! But I know what
will happen. That nice-looking boy from Oxford will
bring down a gramophone, and that gentleman in
brocade on the wall over there, whose toe is already
pointed to tread a minuet, will have his fine sensi-
bilities affronted by jazz. And then. . . ."

The amused, half-bitter flow of his thoughts was
checked suddenly; he strained his ears. For, somewhere in the house, so distantly that the sound could
not be traced, he heard a faint strain of music that
might have been evoked by his meditation. It was
his "little" Bach: the slow movement of the Italian
Concerto. If he had racked his brains to find one, he
could not have chosen a strain more appropriate to
his mood than that sweet meandering melody with
its slow falls and hesitations. These tenuous sounds—
for he knew and loved every note of them—filled him
with an odd excitement; not only because the invisible
(and almost inaudible) player understood, as he
understood, the value of the movement's pale gaiety,

its melting sadness, but also because (to make the effect more ghostlike, and therefore more real) it seemed, at this distance, to be played on some old sweet thin-toned instrument.

"A well-tempered clavier," he thought; "but, of course, that's impossible. People don't play clavichords nowadays, nor even harpsichords. It's just possibly a spinet. Upon my soul, I believe it's a piano: an ancient piano of the kind that one might expect to find marooned in a house of this kind—unless the whole thing's an illusion, which isn't like *me*. But the player. . . . Who can that be. . . ?"

The butler returned. The rhythm of his steps on the stone pavement broke in on the music and drowned it.

"I'm sorry, sir," he said. "I can't find the colonel anywhere. I thought he was in the garden, but I'm afraid he's ridden over to Uffley. If you could leave a message. . . ."

A message! No, no, that could wait. He said: "Who is that playing, Langley?"

"Playing what, sir?" The man looked puzzled. "I beg your pardon?"

"Can't you hear? Someone's playing the piano."

"Oh, that, sir! Why, that'll be Miss Catherine practising. Yes, that's what it'll be. At first I didn't catch your meaning. She goes on by the hour like that, sir." He spoke as though her persistence required an apology. "But we don't hear it much, sir. These old walls are very thick."

So this wasn't an illusion after all. It was Catherine Ombersley. Catherine Ombersley. . . . A beautiful-sounding name; a pale, luminous name (like reliefs in old ivory); a gentle, sweet-smelling name, with something in it of the Worcestershire fields and orchards in this green-growing season of young grass and plum blossom. As he turned away from the steps—for now that the clue had been broken he was no longer tempted to explore her labyrinth of faint sound—Dr. Selby's mind went back to the day of old Ombersley's funeral and to the thoughts which had passed through his mind as he watched the procession. He had decided then, he remembered, that this Ombersley child might, perhaps, be called beautiful. Only perhaps. . . . Only if beauty denoted in chief a certain fineness of texture. With a girl of her breeding one might almost take that for granted, together with composure, quietness, restraint, good taste: all quite admirable qualities no doubt, yet all of them (if not actually negative) rather neutral, rather cold—rather discouraging, in fact, to a man like himself whose upbringing and daily life were concerned with different social strata; to a bachelor whose contacts with women, thanks to the war, had been mainly professional, and therefore unsentimental; to a shy man, in short, who generally preferred, out of habit perhaps, the society of men.

Till that moment he had not felt an inclination nor taken the trouble to speculate on what qualities or deficiencies lay hidden beneath that placid (but wasn't there beauty in placidity?), that fine-textured exterior; yet now, at a single glimpse of its mysterious content, his imagination, his curiosity were fired. In that moment Catherine Ombersley slipped into her place as a half-human figure, delicate and tender as the little Bach tune she had played (and what was more, understood, as he himself understood it) in a setting formal and gracious, designed by Adam, and irradiated by ivorine light—rather distant still, but indubitably, mysteriously alive.

That mystery provoked him. He was curious about Catherine Ombersley. She suggested a virginal realm which challenged his exploration, but lay just out of reach. Perhaps the one sample which had come to him of the treasures it held—that little Bach tune—was fortuitous and misleading; perhaps disappointment (and that wouldn't be the first of its kind!) awaited him. None the less, he felt eager now to review his first impression; to see what effect this newly-discovered tinge of colour would give to the static, inanimate figure. Mr. Winter was encouraged by seeing Dr. Selby more frequently in church. He was flattered to notice that the doctor had changed his seat for one nearer the pulpit, which happened also (though this did not strike him) to be on a level with the chapel in which, amid their dead ancestors' monuments, the living Ombersleys, still feudally distinguished from their neighbours, performed their weekly devotions.

E*

Mr. Winter hoped, though without much confidence, that the bread he had cast on the waters in those lamp-lit winter colloquies was returning to him. Perhaps Dr. Selby had suffered a change of heart?

Well, perhaps he had. It was possible (to use an appropriate clinical metaphor) that Dr. Selby's mind had already become unconsciously infected with the vagrant virus of love which no filter of reason can exclude—or that, at this moment (May's mildness favouring) his resistance happened to be lowered and that the germs of infection—against which previous attacks unfortunately confer no immunity—were ready to fulminate in their favourite culture-medium of a lonely heart. There was a lot of measles—and love—"about" in Chaddesbourne that spring.

VII

ENTER MR. HACKETT

THE second of these endemic afflictions (or miracles) began to exert its full power about the time when the rooks, more hardy in these matters, had finished building and hatched their brood—when the apple boughs' coralline buds of blossom opened to pink and the call of the cuckoo became monotonous. Then the village street which, up till this, had shown after dark no more sign of life than a wintry gleam of lamplight in cottage-windows, became murmurous with soft voices and hushed laughter. On Sunday evenings after church, the field-paths and lanes around Chaddesbourne were scattered with slow-moving couples who made love (as love should be made) in a bloom-scented dusk.

Employment, too, remained reasonably brisk, in spite of the steady drift of demobilized men coming home from the war. There was work going on at the Hall (as much as Miles Ombersley could afford) that absorbed unskilled labour: the uprooting and clearing of the mournful shrubberies of laurel which throttled it, the widening of the drive to give motor-cars room to turn, the conversion of part of the stables into a garage, the felling of the great sequoia. That, indeed, was a job! Before the axes would bite, a six-inch felting of fibre must be stripped from the trunk. When it leaned and crashed, like a falling church spire, the whole building shook; the men who were working in the house—painters, plumbers, carpenters —all rushed to the windows to see what had happened, and light flooded the house like a sudden burst of sunshine. It made everything look shabbier than ever, Helen Ombersley thought; yet what did that matter compared with the ponderable spiritual relief that the influx of light brought with it, and which seemed more like the lifting of a weight than the mere removal of a shadow?

At Green Hill more ambitious works were afoot; the red bricks of Mr. Hackett's garages rose course by course. Every evening, when the day's business was finished, Mr. Hackett himself drove over from North Bromwich in his huge Pearce-Tregaron car, painted pillar-box red, to watch the growth of his pet monstrosity. Its erection, Miles Ombersley thought, was an offence to the landscape's amenities even more brutal than the felling of the elms by the bridge. On the first night of his return to Chaddesbourne he had vaguely conceived the idea of calling on this new, unwelcome neighbour and "taking him in hand"; but the obvious, unmitigated vulgarity of a fellow who could drive such a car and build such a house deterred him. That eyesore, endowed with powers of malignant growth like a cancer, shot up till its peaked confusion of blue-slated gables possessed and dominated the whole countryside. Even in the privacy of the Hall garden the eyes could not escape it; for its unavoidable bulk, overtopping the trees, stared out like a fiery ulcer on the flank of that green declivity, and the drive that led up to it, faced with gravel, cut Green Hill diagonally with a raw, red slash. The unspeakable outrage was there and must be endured. Miles Ombersley washed his hands of it and its owner.

The village, on the contrary, accorded Mr. Hackett complete approval. The building of the mansion on Green Hill was equivalent to the discovery of a mine, from whose output (to say nothing of leakages) a steady stream of gold would find its way into empty pockets. The tale of Mr. Hackett's wealth was exaggerated, like the number of his bathrooms. The house couldn't be run, anxious mothers decided, with less than ten maids; by the time it was finished their daughters would be ripe for service. If the garden were made to match the house—men were busy levelling and terracing the ground at the back of it—it couldn't possibly be "kept up" without six or seven gardeners. Mr. Wood, the butcher, could count on supplying the servants' hall, where the consumption of meat ran in geometrical proportion to the number of mouths. The only shopkeeper in the village who did not welcome Mr. Hackett's establishment with unmixed delight was Mrs. Webb, the postmistress, who foresaw an increase of work in sorting letters and attending to the telephone exchange, unlikely to be balanced by the staff's consumption of peppermints or gelatine lozenges, which were the staples of her trade.

And, whatever the future promised, the benefits of the present were not to be sniffed at. Already more than a score of workmen were paying top prices for lodgings in Chaddesbourne, consuming Mr. Wood's meat, Mrs. Webb's cigarettes, and (Miss Loach was pained to observe and to hear) Mr. Hadley's liquor. With their jokes and their songs and their free-handed ways—to say nothing of the stuttering exhausts of their motor-bicycles—they "brightened up Chaddesbourne no end."

This process of "brightening up" was, naturally, not without casualties. The builder's foreman, for example, fell from a scaffold and broke his leg in two places. He lodged, disregarding expense, at the "Ombersley Arms", and he was not a teetotaller. Miss Loach, for one, was not in the least surprised at the accident; those two facts explained everything, even though Dr. Selby, minutely cross-questioned, assured her that his fall was due to a lack of caution and not to an excess of alcohol. "An abstainer would have kept his balance," Miss Loach affirmed.

Then Nellie, the younger of those two dreadful Bunt girls, produced a baby—an "osbud," they called it in Chaddesbourne. Nobody told Miss Loach of this second accident until after the child had been born, and nobody but Miss Loach (and, according to herself, Nellie Bunt) was surprised. "It's all them workmen chaps knockin' about," said the village. The monstrous thing was that Miss Bunt had already presented the too-tolerant world with a war-baby. "It's all them soldiers knockin' about," the village had said then. But the Armistice, as Miss Loach severely remarked, had been signed three years ago. The world was at peace, and offences which she had once been constrained to overlook (though *never* to condone) in the interests of patriotism, could no longer be countenanced.

She told Mr. Winter so, flatly.

"When this sort of thing happens," she said, "I always consider the vicar of the parish directly responsible."

"Oh, hardly *directly*, Miss Loach," Mr. Winter mildly protested.

"Then who *is*, I should like to know?"

"That's a difficult question. I am doing my best to get the child taken to a home, but the mother is adamant . . . adamant."

Next she tackled Dr. Selby, when he came on his weekly visit, and asked him what he proposed to do about it: "This is the second, remember," she said. "That girl is becoming a scandal."

Dr. Selby looked wise and shook his head slowly. "Don't you realize," he said, "that the Bunt girls are born for trouble as the sparks fly upward? If you'd seen the cottage they live in you wouldn't be surprised—or, perhaps, you would. I'm proposing to make myself unpopular at the Hall by asking the Sanitary Authority to have it condemned. Four adults and three children in two rooms, each the size of your china-pantry, and the man out of work. He lives 'on the panel,' as they call it. I put 'rheumatism' on his certificate, but the disease from which he's actually suffering is malnutrition. Now that Ombersley's rabbits have begun to breed he'll get to work with his snares, which means he'll be better fed and so will his family. The only astonishing feature in the case is that the child appears to be healthy. Sound stock on the father's side, whoever he may be. . . ."

"It's the Bunt girl's duty to say who he is."

"Very possibly she doesn't know, and it's no good bullying her. She seems to be fond of this child. The other one died."

"By the mercy of God," said Miss Loach. "As to the cottage they live in, I can only say I entirely disagree with you. It's one of the prettiest in the village; I know the outside quite well. I always remark on the clematis over the porch. And understand this, Dr. Selby: in my dear father's time things like this never happened in Chaddesbourne."

"What, never, Miss Loach?"

"Well. . . ." Miss Loach perceived the allusion and stopped just in time. "If that cottage is condemned," she said with some satisfaction, "it will mean, of course, that the Bunts will have to leave Chaddesbourne. There isn't another cottage available, is there?"

"Unfortunately, no. Mr. Hackett's proposing to build some."

"Mr. Hackett? You don't mean to say that that wretched man's going to be allowed to spoil our village with his horrible modern building?"

"You never can tell. Mr. Hackett's the kind of vandal who may possibly prefer sanitation indoors to a privy at the bottom of the garden. He may even insist on bathrooms."

"On bathrooms, indeed!" Miss Loach tossed her head. "They'll only keep coal in them."

"Perhaps . . . if they're lucky enough to have any coal," Dr. Selby replied.

He left Miss Loach puzzled but unshaken in her convictions. She often wished that her old friend Dr. Weir, of Wychbury, was still alive. This young man, though undoubtedly clever and even considerate, had the knack of making polite conversation disturbing; his words left an after-taste which she couldn't immediately get rid of. As for his hint that environment had something to do with Nellie Bunt's morals (which, as every churchwoman knew, were entirely a matter of conscience and religious teaching), this, now that she came to think of it, had a smack of socialism. If only people would leave her dear Chaddesbourne alone!

Her one consolation was the fact that the village's rightful proprietor, Miles Ombersley, had returned, and would soon put its politics (as well as its morals) to rights.

If Miss Loach's winter-cough had not defied the healing influence of spring, she would certainly have been pushed or pulled to the Hall, and have satisfied her sense of duty by instructing Miles Ombersley in his. But Miss Loach, despite that malignant vitality of spirit which, through four months of seclusion in her stuffy bedroom, had worn Jane Trost to a bleached rag and had even made Dr. Selby (whom she now distrusted) dread the sound of her voice and the sight of her, was, physically, a poor little old woman—far older than she confessed—with the frailest of bodies. The cough kept her awake at night—it kept Jane Trost awake too—and in the morning, when she put on her Red Queen's wig, the least waft of air set her houzing and tissacking again. So, propped up in bed amid a thicket of medicine bottles, in a black knitted dressing-jacket, she set out her complaints in that thin, pointed, underlined hand of hers and in the third person. *Miss Loach presents her compliments to Colonel Ombersley*, she always began. But, apart from this, her remarks were not complimentary.

These letters, delivered by hand, like the notes of diplomats (for Miss Loach knew that if they passed through the post, Mrs. Webb, the postmistress, would speculate on their contents), accumulated like a drift

of beech leaves on Miles Ombersley's desk. They had
amused him at first; but now he was no longer amused
and had no time to read them. He had no time for anything outside the routine of his estate. The spiritual
relief he had gained by getting rid of Healey had disadvantages: though it saved him a calculable sum of
money, it involved him in matters at once distasteful
and inconsonant with his personal dignity. People
employed an agent, it was said, to do their dirty work
for them; and the work that now fell to him, if not
dirty, was at least unpleasant, for it made him appear
to be mean, hard, unsympathetic, when, in fact, he
was merely trying to pull things together and do his
duty by everybody—himself and his heirs included.

How complicated that duty was, nobody in
Chaddesbourne could, and, he felt rather bitterly, nobody attempted to guess. People thought of him as
a man with a substantial income from land, whereas,
in fact, mere taxation forced him to draw on his
capital.

There was, for instance, this matter of Aaron Bunt's
cottage, about which Selby was bothering him. Aaron
Bunt was a congenital waster, a ne'er-do-well, and an
inveterate poacher, who had even (this always stuck
in Miles Ombersley's gullet) contrived, somehow, to
slink out of serving during the war. Dr. Selby, who
was reasonable in most things, had reported, in his
brisk, businesslike manner, that the cottage which
Bunt inhabited and Miles owned was uninhabitable.

It was his duty, he said, to convey his opinion to the local authority, unless, to avoid that unpleasantness. . . . The suggestion, with its flavour of blackmail, put Miles Ombersley's back up.

"Bunt's cottage," he replied, "is structurally neither worse nor better than a dozen others in Chaddesbourne." (That was only too true, Dr. Selby eagerly agreed; but in *this* case. . . .) "In this case—and you know it as well as I do," Miles went on, "you've a fellow who's never made the slightest attempt to keep the place decent or help himself in any way. I take it you'll agree that all the responsibility is not always on the landlord's side? Incidentally," he added, "Bunt hasn't paid a farthing of rent for the last four years."

Dr. Selby was not in the least surprised. Bunt hadn't a farthing to pay.

"Then why doesn't he look for a job of work and earn something?"

"I suppose one must say: because he's not made that way."

"My dear doctor, that's all very well! I've kept a roof over this fellow's head for more than four years, mind!"

"Yes . . . a roof of sorts. It leaks pretty badly, you know."

"So does mine. But that, of course, is far less important in these days. If I did my duty to myself— or to the village, for that matter—I should clear Bunt out, lock, stock and barrel. But I can't. The law won't let me. So what *can* I do?"

"Either make the place fit to live in or else demolish it."

"Demolishing will hardly mend matters, will it?"

"Well, I'm not so sure about that."

"Demolition costs money. And as for repairing the place. . . . Have you any idea how much that would run me into?"

"Pretty nearly as much as building a new cottage, I suppose."

"More or less. And, of course, that would ruin the whole village street."

Dr. Selby laughed. Miles Ombersley stared at him. He wasn't aware that he had made a joke; and humour, at that moment, was not in the best of taste. He went on:

"Quite apart from that, the proposal's uneconomic. Supposing I had the capital to spare (which I haven't) and supposing that Bunt paid a proportionate rent (which he won't)—even then, at the present cost of materials and labour, the outlay would scarcely pay me two per cent. I've gone into these figures, and there it is. That's not my fault, is it?"

"Indeed, no. Let's call it your misfortune . . . and Bunt's, too. His cottage, as you say yourself, is not the only one; it's merely the worst. And don't think, for heaven's sake, Colonel, that I don't see your position. I'm not 'taking sides.' In this matter I'm a public servant. I'm paid—not very well, by the way—as

Medical Officer of Health for this Rural District; and, as far as I can see, there's no alternative to my making an unfavourable report. Or only one . . ."

Miles Ombersley stared into space.

"You are perfectly right," he said at last. "I'll do what I can, doctor."

He was always doing "what he could," or a little more—though nobody (except, perhaps, Mrs. Ombersley) guessed how difficult he found it. The new roof he had rashly promised Lydgate for his barn had cost two hundred pounds; he would rather have left it to fall in than make a bad job of it. That was only the first of a score of claims on his cheque-book which Healey, more expert at wriggling out of them, had managed to postpone. New fencing, new gates, new pumps, new drainage. . . . Every week the tale mounted up and appalled him; while the things which (in the first flush of succession) he had counted on doing, the things he would have enjoyed putting straight, receded farther and farther beyond the verge of possibility.

Week by week money ebbed away, like water from a leaky can. That, indeed, was an appropriate figure for his proud inheritance: a battered tin-can full of holes and corroded with rust: an affront, whenever he looked at it, to the military ideals of "spit-and-polish" in which he had been nurtured.

And always, as though the devil himself had invented him for the sake of an odious, mischievous

comparison, Miles Ombersley found himself faced
with that damned interloper, John Hackett, whose
vulgar affluence was corrupting the village's old
monetary standards just as surely as (witness Nellie
Bunt) his town workmen had corrupted its morals.

Mr. Hackett, he heard, must have "the best of
everything," and didn't care what he gave for it. Mr.
Hackett's two principal gardeners, who came from
North Bromwich, were paid urban wages, and the
men engaged locally would share the same privilege.
Mr. Hackett's head chauffeur boasted that not a man
on the Greenhill Estate (as they called it now) drew
the local standard agricultural wage; the workmen's
children were to be supplied with free milk from a
pedigree herd of Friesians, their tables with free
vegetables; even their lamps (until electricity came,
and that wouldn't be long) were to be filled with oil
bought in bulk and supplied at wholesale prices; while
their families, who didn't "come under" the National
Insurance Act, would be covered by an extension of
the scheme already in force at Mr. Hackett's factories.
The chauffeur, who drove (in addition to two other
cars) the pillar-box-red Pearce-Tregaron, was the
principal agent of this propaganda. He sat like a
satrap, every evening (for his hours were short), reflecting his patron's glory in the most comfortable
corner of the private bar at the "Ombersley Arms,"
where he shared with George Cookson the admiring
attentions of Mrs. Hadley. It was from him that the

village learned what it was prepared to believe, and what was probably true: that Mr. Hackett could "buy up" Colonel Ombersley ten times over without turning a hair.   Mr. Healey, who was already managing a couple of farms which Mr. Hackett had bought on the Wychbury side, was in a position to know the truth of this and would vouch for it. Mr. Healey did, willingly. Let the tenants of the two estates compare notes, he said, and judge for themselves.

Not all of these details, so impressive to the village's ears, reached Miles Ombersley's.   His personal servants were loyal, and, in any case, knew better than to repeat them. He was aware, none the less, of the new invasive influence and of its symbols, constructive and destructive, which still leered at him—even now, when the trees were in leaf—from the flank of Green Hill.

The deuce of it was that "this damned fellow Hackett" or "this damned outsider" as the colonel habitually thought of him, had actually as much right to inhabit Chaddesbourne as the Ombersleys themselves. He wasn't, historically speaking, an "outsider" at all.   A good fifth of the graveyard, to judge by tombstone inscriptions, was cluttered with Hackett bones; and although no bearer of his vulgar name had yet presumed to invade the preserves of chancel or transept, Hacketts, variously spelt, showed an obstinate preponderance in the earlier manorial rolls as occupants—and, at one time, as possessors—of that typical piece of Ombersley property, Uffley Mill.

In the days of Napoleon, when the contemporary Ombersleys had been freezing with Moore at Corunna or bleeding with Picton at Waterloo, the last Hackett of Uffley had migrated to North Bromwich and established himself as a working gunsmith in Steelhouse Lane. During the following century, every war which had bled the Ombersley stock had nourished the Hacketts; and the last and bloodiest of all, in which Miles himself had fought and lost his two sons, had furnished "this fellow Hackett" with a fortune of fantastic proportions, and leisure for which the devil (Miles felt) had found sinister employment. Miles preferred—as was his habit with other unpleasant people and things—to pretend to himself that John Hackett and his works simply didn't exist; and succeeded in doing so until, one Sunday afternoon when he had surrendered himself to the persuasions of the *Observer's* "leader," Langley, the butler, brought in a card.

The quality of this card, which was printed, not copperplate, and announced "John Hackett" without the conventional "Mr.," had persuaded Langley who was more of a snob than his master, to leave the visitor standing on the steps outside. That would never do, Miles Ombersley thought—for he prided himself on a politeness which, exaggerated in the case of people who were "betwixt and between," amounted, at times, to a positive refinement of insolence. So, having discarded his reading-spectacles, he went to the door in person and invited John Hackett into the next degree of hospitality—the hall, decorated by Adam, in which Dr. Selby had suffered such strange adventures of the spirit.

Miles Ombersley was wearing the shiny blue serge suit in which he had read the lessons in church that morning; the dark cloth accentuated the neatness of his tall, spare figure, the classic regularity of his features, the whiteness of his bony hands, and lent his wiry limbs a deceptive air of refinement, almost of fragility. Beside him, John Hackett, who was clad in rough tweeds, gave the impression of being a creature of a different species on whose creation less time and less skill had been expended. He was thick-set, with short legs, disproportionate to his longish body, and the legs were not shapely. His cropped hair, black streaked with grey, had a coarse, unruly texture. He wore a bristling, ill-trimmed moustache, much greyer than his hair, above thick lips, firm to stubborn-ness, but not unkindly; and the skin of his face had the pallor, not necessarily unhealthy, of those who live under gritty skies where sunshine is rare, with, here and there, a blue speck of carbon imbedded in it.

It was, perhaps, in the hand which, without any lack of confidence, he extended towards Ombersley that the physical difference between the two men was most marked. Of an equal strength, it lacked form and flexibility: it was like stationer's print compared with copperplate. And John Hackett's speech, when he spoke, had the same comparative defect. It was tolerably educated; the words he used were the current coinage of polite conversation; yet, somehow, their vowel sounds seemed less purely shaped, their consonants less elegantly clipped. A different mint. Print and copperplate over again. . . . He said:

"Colonel Ombersley, I hope you'll forgive an intrusion at this unconventional hour. I've been bold enough to hope that my name may be familiar to you."

Miles Ombersley fixed his monocle and appeared, quite unnecessarily, to examine the card with distaste. Then he let the glass fall and smiled—dangerously, if Hackett had known it. "Of course," he said. "Then I've not been too bold after all," Mr. Hackett said heartily. "Sunday afternoons are the only time I get free. I'm a business man, Colonel Ombersley. As you probably know, I've lived in North Bromwich all my life; but my ancestors came from your village." (Miles acknowledged the compliment.) "I'd always known this," John Hackett went on, "but until a couple of years ago I was kept far too busy to worry my head about them. To tell you the truth, when I *did* come to Chaddesbourne it was a case of pure accident, trying to find my way in a car cross-country from Bromsberrow to Lord Wolverbury's place at Stourford. I'm afraid this long story bores you?"

"Not at all. Not at all." Colonel Ombersley was not impressed, as he should have been, by Lord

Wolverbury's name. New people . . .

"Well, I'll try to come to the point," John Hackett
went on. "When I dropped down the hill over there
that day I hadn't the very foggiest idea where I was.
I never carry a map in the car when I push off on
my own for a breath of fresh air. Of course, I could
see at once that I'd stumbled on one of the most charming villages in England. But that wasn't all. Outside
business matters—where that sort of thing is essential
—I'm not an imaginative man. But as soon as I set
foot on the ground—something made me pull up the
car and get out and look round, you know—I was
ready to swear—and still *am*—that I'd been here before!" He laughed: "Sounds ridiculous, doesn't it?
But there you are! Every stick and stone of it
familiar! I assure you it made me feel queer. Then
I met an old man—he's dead now, a chap called John
Sheppy: jolly name, by the way—and asked him the
name of the place. 'Chaddesbourne D'Abitot,' he said.
Then the whole thing came back, clear as daylight. I
remembered the stories my old grandfather told me
when I was a kid. It still gives me a shiver to think
of it!"

Miles Ombersley shivered, too. On this spring
afternoon, with no fire, that stone-paved hall was as
icy as the gaze with which his Georgian ancestors on
the walls appeared to regard Mr. Hackett. He was
thinly clad, and this long-winded visitor's enthusiasms
showed no signs of coming to the point. He waved

Mr. Hackett courteously towards a door on the left—
"Won't you come this way? Rather warmer inside!"
—and ushered him into the library.

Mr. Hackett beheld what was, perhaps, the only
completely beautiful room in the house. All, even that
cold hall, were finely proportioned, having been
plotted in a classic age when the nice disposition of
space was almost an instinct; but this, in its grace of
conception and restrained wealth of ornament, was a
sheer work of art, to which more than a century of
serene habitation (if not of culture) had given a *patina*.
Whether Robert Adam himself (as tradition affirmed)
had planned it—"Adam after the Fall," a witty purist
suggested—was a matter of doubt; but, beyond any
doubt, a master's taste had begotten those mouldings
of plaster; that frieze, that tasselled cornice; those
delicate ceiling traceries from whose midst descended,
like an icy stalactite, the brittle cascade of a cut-glass
chandelier.

Two pairs of pilasters and pillars of *giallo antico*
divided it; and three walls, including that which was
broken by the fireplace and that through which they
had entered, were clothed (that seemed the just word)
with shelves of books, whose bindings of tawny calf-
skin and gilt appeared—no less than the furniture of
satinwood and pale mahogany—to reflect the soft
light, resembling the radiance that kindles autumn
beechwoods, with which, at this moment, the atmosphere was suffused. Autumnal . . . that was the word

for this room's serenity. The autumn of the classical style; the autumn of a civilization. Though he knew he had left spring outside—calling cuckoos and blue-bells—this sense of autumn haunted and perplexed him. The worn needlework carpet, with its faded Aubusson garlands, felted their tread as they entered like fallen leaves or beech-mast; autumnal scents proceeded from the Worcester bowls heaped with withered rose-petals; only one tall vase of coppery tulips spoke of spring, and even the colour of these foreshadowed autumn.

To John Hackett, his ears attuned to the crash of stamping-machines, the whirring of bands and lathes, the perpetual bustle of the strepitous North Bromwich streets, it seemed as though he had suddenly been dipped in a quiet pool composed of some foreign element amid which he floundered uneasily, against which he instinctively rebelled. His new house at Green Hill was not like this house, he told himself. Not with all the money he had spent on it could he have made it like this, supposing he'd wanted to—which, of course, he hadn't. These old-fashioned mansions, all empty grandeur and no comfort, could be picked up anywhere nowadays for a mere song. Their unfortunate owners were almost ready to pay you to live in them if you'ld only keep them from fall-ing completely to pieces and pay rates and taxes.

Awed, ill at ease, but firmly refusing to be intimi-dated, Mr. Hackett became suddenly aware of the figure of a woman motionless against the light. She sat writing at a satinwood table, so dreamily absorbed in pondering her next word as to be unaware of the two men's silent approach; and John Hackett, seeing her thus for the first time in profile, was immediately struck by the fragile grace of the unconscious pose, the slim straightness of the erect figure, the delicate suspension of the fingers which held the pen, by an emanation of tender innocence which, somehow, in that autumnal room suggested Spring. Politeness compelled him to speak:

"I'm afraid we're intruding. Your daughter . . ."

"My wife," Colonel Ombersley said shortly. "Helen. . . . If you'll excuse us . . ."

The frail dreamer rose; she turned and smiled, collecting her papers. "Of course. I didn't hear you come in, Miles," she said in a voice which John Hackett found singularly deep and composed. "I was trying to work out a plan for a herbaceous border. It's difficult, isn't it? There are so many lovely things nowadays."

John Hackett agreed that there were. That smile, that brief hesitation, those unnecessary words, were, he guessed, a gesture of friendliness, a tactful palliative to any awkwardness he might possibly have felt at not being "introduced." Mrs. Ombersley, standing, appeared to be taller than he had imagined, and the erectness of her carriage made her seem taller still. He had not been deceived when he gave her a young girl's figure; but now that she faced the light he was surprised to see that she was certainly over fifty, and probably older than himself. Her fine-spun hair had a sheen and a pallor not of silver, but of platinum; her features, which still showed concern for the stranger's comfort, and her dark eyes, which regarded him frankly but without disapproval, were still beautiful, if a trifle sad. "How lovely she must have been!" John Hackett was thinking. "How is it," he asked himself grudgingly, "that the women of this sheltered class can manage to preserve the shadow of their beauty when ours have lost it? It isn't just a matter of money . . ." And he saw (he, himself, was a widower) the wives of his business friends, the girls he might possibly have married, now middle-aged.

Mrs. Ombersley, hesitating, glanced swiftly from John Hackett to her husband; then, seeing that his intentions were precise and included no introduction, smiled a soft "Good-bye" and discreetly vanished. Miles Ombersley sat down behind a massive Chippendale writing-table, with the air of a regimental commander in his own orderly-room.

"That is better," he said. "Please go on, Mr. Hackett—and do sit down."

Mr. Hackett, standing, went on: "As I've told you, I happened to discover Chaddesbourne by chance. My life, Colonel Ombersley, has been a pretty full one. We North Bromwich folk are not sentimental. We don't bother about our ancestors or anyone else's; we take people as we find them, you know: that's a good rule in business. But I don't mind confessing it gave me a bit of a shock when I first felt—well, what shall I call it?—the 'pull' of this place and realized, for the first time in my life, that I actually belonged somewhere. When a man gets to my time of life and has made all the money he's ever likely to want, I believe that kind of feeling isn't uncommon. Well, to cut this long story short. . . . Do you mind if I smoke?"

"I'm sorry. Won't you have a cigarette?"

"Thanks." He had pulled out a cherry-wood pipe; but thought better of it, and lit the cigarette Miles Ombersley offered him. "I got hold of a bit of land, as you probably know. There was more than sentiment in that, for I don't mind telling you I bought it dirt cheap; land's a drug in the market nowadays, as I'm sure you realize." (Colonel Ombersley smiled.) "Then I thought: 'Why not run up a house?' Not a grand place like this, you know, but a snug little house for a quiet week-end. So I pulled down the farm—it was falling to pieces—and built one; and the more I came here, the more I fancied it. Then the next thing I did was to look up the vicar—nice fellow, Winter—and dig into the parish records, births, deaths, and so on. They go pretty continuously back into the seventeenth century. Before that there's a gap . . ."

"There was a fire in the vestry in sixteen-forty. Ralph Ombersley's time. That fellow over the

F

mantelpiece. Killed at Powick Bridge. The portrait's by Janssens. Not a bad one."

"That's awfully interesting. I see I should have come to you first."

John Hackett turned eagerly to examine the picture of a cavalier in a steel cuirass against a dark background, and it suddenly struck him (perhaps it was merely a trick of the light) that the eyes and the hands were the eyes and hands of his host.

"That gap holds me up," he went on. "Up till then, going backward, it seems that my Hacketts were pretty continuously established at a place which belongs to you: Uffley Mill—Chaddesbourne Manor, they called it in those days—and when once you get hot on a scent like that you don't feel like 'calling off,' do you? Well, that's why I'm wasting your time to-day. Mr. Winter's suggested that I might find a lot more material in the manorial rolls, which I believe you possess."

Miles Ombersley nodded. "The vicar's quite right. I do. What is more, they're almost complete, going back to the time of my wife's people—the D'Abitots, you know. If you'ld like to have copies made of the records which concern your forbears, you can have them with pleasure. Of course, you may draw a blank."

John Hackett laughed. "I'll risk that. This is exceedingly kind of you, Colonel Ombersley. Now, supposing I come . . ."

"*You?* I wonder if you realize the technical difficulty? You'ld be dealing with monkish Latin and Norman French in every conceivable kind of lettering. I can more or less gather the sense of the rolls myself, because I happen to have made a hobby of family history. It's a disease, as you say, of middle age; but I got it early—when I was a subaltern, in fact. For any systematic research I'm afraid you'll have to employ an expert. If you like, I can give you the name of a reliable man whom we can both of us trust. The work needs skilful handling as well as knowledge."

"That's most kind of you again," Mr. Hackett said. "I'll be guided by you, if I may. Of course, the whole matter's entirely outside my province. As long as I get what I want, or what *is* to be got, I shan't grumble about what it costs me. I should like it to be understood that money's no object. I want the best, and I'm quite prepared to pay for it. Now, if you have this expert's address . . ."

"I'll find it and send it to you." Miles Ombersley spoke as politely as ever. Only, at the moment when the visitor began to talk about money, his mouth had winced and a harder glint had come into his eye. John Hackett, too pleased with the result of his visit, or, perhaps, too innocent, failed to observe these phenomena foretelling the onset of frost. With a frankness that on any other subject than this would have been engaging, he went on gaily: "And, Colonel, if there's anything

else you want doing in the village, any public convenience—that sounds odd, but you know what I mean—in
which a man who doesn't mind putting his hand into
his pocket will come in useful, all you need do is to
drop me a line and tip me the wink. That reminds
me—if you happen to send those particulars about the
expert to me at Chaddesbourne, you might address
them to Chaddesbourne Manor . . ."

"Chaddesbourne *Manor?*"

"Yes, that's what I'm calling it. Just a matter of
sentiment again. That was the name they called Uffley
Mill by when my forbears lived there, so I thought
I'ld revive it. Green Hill's not much of a name when
you come to think of it, is it?"

It was certainly less distinctive, Miles Ombersley
agreed. "All the same," he explained, "a manor is a
definite thing. For what it is worth—and, of course,
it means nothing nowadays—I happen to be Lord of
the Manor of Chaddesbourne D'Abitot myself . . .
not that I can prevent you from calling Green Hill
any name you fancy."

Mr. Hackett was obviously surprised and distressed.
"Look here, Colonel," he said. "If you want me to
change it again, it's not too late. I've no wish to tread
on anybody's toes, I assure you!"

"Of course, you will do exactly what you think
right," Miles Ombersley frigidly replied.

Once more Mr. Hackett floundered. "Looks rather
as if I've put my foot in it! You know, sir," he said,

"there's one way out of this muddle, if you don't mind my mentioning it. . . ."

"Not at all."

". . . and that is: if you'ld care to sell Uffley Mill. You can name your own price."

Miles Ombersley flushed slightly. "Am I right," he said, "when I guess that you've made this proposal before?"

"As a matter of fact, I did once mention it to Healey, who put it up to your father."

"Who turned it down."

"So I gathered. But there's no harm, is there, in mentioning it again? I'm a business man, and I know what death-duties mean. Quite apart from that, I don't think you get a big rent from your present tenant."

"You seem remarkably well informed on my private affairs, Mr. Hackett."

"In any case, I can see you don't like the idea," Mr. Hackett replied imperturbably

"No. It doesn't appeal to me."

"No offence, I hope, Colonel?"

"You've a perfect right to ask me if I want to sell."

"But you don't. So that's that. I'm sorry. I'd always had hopes . . ."

"You had better abandon them, Mr. Hackett. You shall have that address to-morrow."

Miles Ombersley rang the bell for the butler to show his visitor out. Mr. Hackett left, smiling, continuing to make protestations of thanks, yet feeling, all the time, that in some inconceivable way he had, as he said, "put his foot in it." Funny people, he thought, these poor country gentry! You never knew quite where you were with them, and so damned polite with it all! He climbed into the red Pearce-Tregaron and roared back to Green Hill.

"This is more my style," he thought as, entering the hall-lounge (or lounge-hall—he was never quite sure which it was) over the new parquet floor that still smelt of bees-wax, he encountered a puff of warm air, impregnated with paint, from the latest type of radiator. "This is more my style. . . ." Yet the second time the words shaped themselves they had lost a little of their relief and most of their boastfulness. The house was "just his style"—and, somehow, he wished that it wasn't. He couldn't see a woman like Mrs. Ombersley living in it. And he knew that he couldn't call it Chaddesbourne Manor. Miles Ombersley had left the decision to him. That was deuced clever of him. "These fellows, they have a way with them, you know," Mr. Hackett thought. "But he's dead wrong about Uffley Mill. If he'd any sense he'ld be glad to let me have it. It's the chance of a lifetime for him, and he's a fool not to see it."

VIII

THE MOAT

THAT was rather what Miles Ombersley himself would have been forced to admit if he had been able to consider the question of Uffley Mill with a level mind. But he couldn't. First of all the rumour that the place was for sale had put his back up. And now the infernal cheek of this fellow Hackett who, out of sheer clumsy ignorance, was proposing to call his new red-brick abortion by the name that had once belonged to it, case-hardened his obstinacy. If he ever had to sell Uffley Mill—and he wouldn't sell anything if it could be avoided—it certainly wouldn't be sold to John Hackett, Esquire! In the meantime he couldn't afford to keep tenants who didn't pay their rent punctually. Something would have to be done about Cookson, for instance, sooner or later. Something extremely unpleasant. . . .

Mrs. Cookson knew this. Since the end of the war things had been going from bad to worse; and this, after twenty-five years of pride and respectability, seemed hard to bear—particularly at a time of life when everything looked difficult and Dr. Selby, whom she consulted in secret, advised her to "take things easily." Perhaps, up till now, they had been too evenly prosperous: human life had a way of tempering rough with smooth. Yet when she worried—and now worries never left her—she couldn't help thinking wistfully of her early married life, when she had come, a young bride, to The Moat, and all her friends had envied her.

Now, when she was dusting the drawing-room—for however hard they were pressed it was still her pride to keep the house bright and speckless—she paused in front of the photograph which had been taken on the day of her wedding, and her mind turned back with wonder to think that she had ever been capable of such gay hopes, such unclouded happiness as showed itself there on her smiling, tremulous face.

The guests had been grouped in front of the green-house (one could see, through the panes, the stalks of ghostly geraniums) on the strip of lawn behind her father's draper's-shop in Stourton; they had been dragged out, laughing and talking loudly, from the luncheon-table, where the health of the bride and bridegroom had just been drunk in real champagne, and Mr. Moyle, the photographer, had been so facetious that none of the bridesmaids could keep their faces straight. There was her father, James Timmins, in the frock-coat he wore when he took the collection in church; her mother wearing a bonnet trimmed with forget-me-nots and a blue velvet mantle—dolmans they called them. And there, towering above herself, with his head thrown back proudly, stood her husband,

George Cookson. Such a handsome young man he had been in those days, so gallant, so impetuous! He was handsome still, Mrs. Cookson thought, still gallant (alas!), still impetuous. But the fine curling moustache, on which everyone remarked in those days, was gone—he had shaved it as soon as it went grey because it made him look older—and the lack of it now showed his mouth to be child-like and petulant, good-humoured generally (although he *had* pushed her in the fire), but weak—yes, that was the trouble—good-humoured but weak.

That weakness showed itself in the way that his figure as well as his face had gone soft; in his plethoric complexion which one saw, at close quarters, to be due to a plexus of fine blood-vessels permanently congested; in the tremulous hand with which when he came in from market, already a trifle "peart," he would slop out a tot of whisky; in the quick gusts of temper, like flame spurting from a hissing log, with which he would shout the house down (the servant could hear him, too!) when he found she had locked the cupboard in the massive mahogany sideboard and hidden the key. Yet even now, when George chose to "look after himself," she couldn't help being proud of him. He was generous—generous to a fault. That nobody denied. And respected: wasn't he still the people's churchwarden, vice-chairman of the Parish Council, president of the Farmers' Union? Didn't he speak for the whole of the district at the Poultry Fund

dinner? A good farmer, too. There wasn't to-day in
the whole of Bromsberrow market a better judge of a
beast or a sample of corn; and there, on the sideboard,
stood the trophies he had won at cattle-shows and the
pieces of plate presented by firms selling dips and
fertilizers for the best crop of swedes, the cleanest
fields, the tidiest farm. That, of course, was years ago;
but even now as they drove into Bromsberrow shop-
ping on Thursdays, there wasn't a soul who didn't
smile and salute him when he called out a cheery good-
day in his rich tenor voice. Even the tradesmen to
whom they owed money seemed glad to see him.
"George Cookson's all right," they said.

But she knew that he wasn't all right. She knew
that better than he did, for the bills came to her.
George had "no head for business"—indeed, he had
always been proud of it—and she, with her trades-
man's daughter's upbringing, had always looked after
that side as well as the dairy which, of course, was a
farmer's wife's privilege and perquisite. In the old
days, when everything seemed easier, in spite of the
anxieties of bearing children and bringing them up,
she had taken a pride in balancing accounts month by
month. If she was out by a halfpenny her conscience
would keep her awake at night, and George, seeing her
worried look, would play little jokes on her, producing
sixpence and telling her he'd found it under the table!

It would take several thousand sixpences now to put
matters straight. Every post brought in masses of bills

—and all "account rendered"—some with coloured tickets stuck on them bearing requests polite or peremptory. She paid them as best she could; she made him sign cheques for them, one here and one there, to keep as many different people quiet as possible; but now, when she made him sit down to his cheque-book, he appeared to resent it.

"Why d'you bother about *them?*" he would say. "They know I'm all right. We've dealt with that firm, me and my dad before me, for the last fifty years. What you women don't understand about farming is that it's all ups and downs. It's always the same. We had a good time in the war, and now it's the time of the seven lean kine, as it says in the Bible. If you'ld only stop worrying. It doesn't improve your appearance. Every time I come into the house you look like you've come from a funeral!"

That was all very well; but what about the Michaelmas rent?

"Oh, we'll find that all right," he would say. "If we can't you won't go to the work'us just yet: I can square Joe Healey. He'll put in a word for me with the squire. He's a good friend of mine, is Joe."

"A bad friend, you should say," Mrs. Cookson thought, "like the whisky you drink with him." She remembered—she could never forget—a thing that had happened when she was a girl at Stourton. A neighbour of theirs, a draper, her father's chief trading rival, had "got into difficulties"; he had come to her father one evening, with a face like death, trying to borrow money. When he had gone away empty her father had said: "They've got the bum-bailiffs in at Rogers's"; and the sinister horror of those words had stuck in her mind ever afterwards; for, though she had never seen a bum-bailiff, she had always imagined them as creatures of an almost inconceivable brutality and ugliness, trampling and spitting all over the house and turning out drawers and poking their noses into everything. Supposing these monsters ever came to The Moat!

She loved The Moat and was proud of it, too. It wasn't like an ordinary farmhouse. There were pictures of it in all the county histories; learned societies came from miles away to examine it. Mr. Winter brought people, too.

"A wonderful example of late fifteenth-century half-timber," he said. "Now I want you to come round to the other side and look at the chimney-stack. Stone ashlar at the bottom, you see; they were taking no risks of fire. Then, at the level of the gutter, two brick octagonal bases with trefoiled panels on every face of the octagon, and above the bases those two quite lovely circular brick shafts with corkscrew mouldings. The loveliest chimneys in England, I sometimes think! And now, Mrs. Cookson, *may* my friends just glance at the frieze?"

Of course they might. She wasn't ashamed of anyone seeing her dining-room: the mahogany table shining like ice and the massive sideboard loaded with George's plated trophies. They could examine the whole house from cellar to attic without finding a speck of dust or an unscrubbed floor. She stood by while, peering through the dusk (it was always dusk in the dining-room); some visitors spelt out the motto of the frieze word by word, and others secretly preened themselves in the mantelpiece mirror.

PLENTI : AND : GRASE : BI : IN : THIS : PLACE :
WHYLE : EVERI : MAN : IS : PLESED : IN : HIS :
DEGRE : THERE : IS : BOTH : PEASE : AND : UNETI.

"How true that is! Just fancy them saying that all those years ago!" the visitors exclaimed. "But Mrs. . . . er . . . Cookson, don't you find it too terribly damp, with the moat all round? And are there any ghosts? There *must* be! Or bricked-up skeletons?"

No, the house wasn't damp, she said, with her sweet, tired smile, and there wasn't a single ghost or skeleton that she knew of.

"Not even a skeleton in the family cupboard?" they joked.

Then her pale cheeks flushed, and her heart went cold; for she thought of the stacks of bills locked up in the kitchen bureau and the laughing ghost of the handsome George Cookson that had been; and then that horrid memory of the bailiffs in Rogers's shop returned to her. Calamities like that, she remembered her father saying, never came by chance; people brought them on their heads. But that wasn't quite true: things happened, in spite of one. She didn't blame George, for instance, for the change that had lately come over him—even though he *had* pushed her in the fire. It was just middle-age: the spiritual equivalent of his face going red and lax and his figure falling to seed; of the physical change in herself which woke her up suffocated with hot fumes, made her feel like death—and almost long for it—in the morning. Only George, of course, refused to admit he was any different. He had been furious with her when, taking no risks, she had sent that Bunt girl packing. He had been angry when she caught him rifling her dairy-money box—the odd pounds and humble shillings, scraped together by butter-making before he was out of bed, on which she relied, more and more, for meeting current expenses.

She wouldn't even have minded that so much if he had only kept her company, as he used to do, through the long evenings. But now, as soon as the tea things were cleared, he began to look sly and restless and hummed and clear his throat.

"Well, I think I'll just take a turn," he would say; and a moment later she would hear the cranking and sputter of the muddy Ford in the yard, and a grinding of gears as the car rattled off down the drive, to return, by good luck more than judgment, after the "Ombersley Arms" was closed.

"Perhaps," she reflected, "he'll stay home at night when Elsie comes back. He's always been mad on the child. I suppose it's because she takes after him, and not after me, like our Jim."

She was thankful, for other reasons, that Elsie had passed her examinations and was coming home. George had spoilt the child—that was the truth of it —by trying to make a young lady of her; sending her first to that boarding-school in Leamington and then to the Training College. Quite apart from the cost, it put grand ideas in her head and made her forget that she was a farmer's daughter who ought, rightly, at her age, to be making herself useful about the place and helping her mother with the housework (so many dark corners to keep clean!) and the hens and the butter-making.

Of course, Elsie was as pretty as a picture, with her dad's blond colouring, her skin, like a petal, her soft violet eyes, the wavy bobbed hair that she tossed back so petulantly, and her elegant, mincing speech. If she wasn't his daughter you'ld have said that George was in love with her, the way he kept gazing at her and handling her and pinching her cheek or her neck. (He never does that to me, Mrs. Cookson thought; but then, why should he?) But beauty of that enticing kind was in some ways a danger. It meant shoals of young men buzzing to and fro on their motor-bikes like wasps round a jam-pot; and young men from the towns, by the tales one heard, had no vestige of principles. Not that she didn't trust Elsie to look after herself. Elsie's head, on the contrary, was more tightly screwed on than you'ld credit in a girl of her age. Her assurance, the contemptuous way in which she ordered her admirers about, was almost comical; those soft, violet eyes, those delicious lips could become imperious. She could be as hard as nails, and ruthless, and selfish, and obstinate, and capricious beyond words, when anyone crossed her. Her father laughed at her tantrums; but it wasn't a laughing matter.

"How strange, how unnatural it is," Mrs. Cookson thought, "that I should be thinking of my own daughter, the flesh of my flesh, like this, just as if she were someone else's!" But it wasn't really unsympathetic, she told herself. It was only another aspect of the general feeling of apprehension and uncertainty which beset her. It was for Elsie's sake as much as her own that she dreaded as well as welcomed the child's return. Such a change from the highly-coloured life she had led in North Bromwich! No *palais de danse* (or whatever they called them), no shops, no "movies," no cocktails (whatever they were), no smart young men with money to spend on her! For, after a time, all these would forget her—out of sight, out of mind! And there wasn't a boy within miles of Chaddesbourne at whom Elsie wouldn't turn up her nose, as witness the way she had ridiculed her partners —and particularly that poor Mr. Jones—after the dance in the schoolroom last Christmas. "And now,"

Mrs. Cookson thought, "she will just have to settle down the same as the rest of us; she'll hate it like poison, but she'll have to put up with it. After all, she's a farmer's daughter—no use pretending otherwise—and this is where she belongs. WHYLE : EVERI : MAN : IS : PLESED : IN : HIS : DEGRE : THERE : IS : BOTH : PEASE : AND : UNETI," Mrs. Cookson thought, her glance suddenly straying to the lettered frieze and observing, with concern, that one of the fat-bodied spiders which haunted the crevices in the beams had spun his web between the words BOTH and PEASE. "That's the worst of an old house like this," she thought; "there's always some finicking job to be done —you can never keep pace with them, and I can't reach the ceiling properly without steps. I shall have to ask Jim to carry them in for me when he comes for his tea."

When she thought of her son, Mrs. Cookson's eyes, which were pale with anxiety, grew warm and tender. "If it wasn't for Jim," she thought, "I don't know what I should do. Always cheerful, and nothing in the world too much trouble for him. What a thing it is to be young! And he's mine," she thought. "He never thinks of a woman, thank God!"

Jim Cookson, indeed, had no time to spare for this sort of diversion. Like Elsie, he had spent the best part of his adolescence away from Chaddesbourne. Their father had definite ideas as to his own social position (to say nothing of his wife's), and objected to his

children's sharing the education that the rates provided
for those of his labourers. Jim had acquired his, such
as it was, as a day-boarder in the Grammar School at
Stourton, where he lived with the uncle who had
succeeded to his grandfather's business. It wasn't a
bad education of its kind, but Jim Cookson never made
much of it. In the matter of book-learning his brain
was slow to act and full of insensitive spots, as
cumbrous in action as his unwieldy body. His mind
lacked the quick apprehensions of town-bred children:
even in games they outstripped him; and though
everyone liked him, because he didn't, apparently,
mind being laughed at, most people, including his
masters, put him down as a good-natured fool. George
Cookson took this rather hardly. He had always
looked forward to boasting about his children as other
men did; and though Elsie was smart as paint (so far
as that went, pretty girls had no need of brains and
were better without 'em) he felt it a grave reflection
on himself that he should have a lout for a son. "I'm
damned if I know where he gets it from," he complained continually. "It doesn't come from my side
of the family." Mrs. Cookson sighed—she had begun
to sigh even in those days. "You don't understand
the boy," she said; "you never give him a chance.
If you'ld leave Jim alone instead of nagging
him . . ."

George Cookson laughed bitterly. "Nagging?
That's good! I like that from you, Annie!"

"Give him time. Don't hurry him. I know Jim better than you do."

"Well, one thing's quite certain. I've no intention of throwing good money after bad. I've paid through the nose for his education, and I've had enough of it. See?"

Mrs. Cookson saw. At the age of sixteen Jim came home from Stourton. For this reason alone his mother was thankful that he hadn't shown signs of brilliance. She was lonely already, and hungry for the kind of affection and understanding which neither Elsie— sweet as she could be when it suited her—nor her husband provided. And Jim understood everything, instinctively. She didn't have to waste breath explaining her feelings to him. When they sat alone facing each other beside the log fire at the end of a hard day's work on a winter evening, too tired for talk, there was no need for words between them; and when Jim kissed her good night, as he always did (George hadn't kissed her for years) Mrs. Cookson's frail body became conscious of a mysterious infusion of vitality from her son's strong arms. And how strong they were! He resembled his father in that, if in nothing else. By the time he was eighteen he had grown fully as tall as George; his unwieldy limbs had lost much of their awkwardness. Sometimes when George came home early from the "Ombersley Arms" or the "Crown" at Bromsberrow and started baiting him, she shuddered to think what might happen if these two great men came to grips; for though Jim was the harder, George Cookson had made a fine name as a fighter in his youth. If Jim ever lost his temper. . . . But Jim never did lose his temper, and since there is small fun in baiting a bull that won't turn, his father soon contemptuously abandoned the sport.

"That boy of yours hasn't even the guts to stand up for himself," he complained. "If he had any brains there might be some excuse for it. But he hasn't. It's sheer, slow stupidity. Not the brains of a rabbit!"

Mrs. Cookson kept silence. That, she knew, was the liquor speaking. Her boy was no fool. He had plenty of brains of a sort, and sufficient wisdom, as well, to appreciate his father's—to realize that, in spite of an advancing decadence, George Cookson was still a shrewd and skilful farmer, whose judgment, in technical matters, was an invaluable prop to his own inexperience. So George Cookson, though he continued to grumble and refused (because it made his wife angry) to admit the least virtue in Jim, began, gradually, to drift into the way of least resistance, leaving more and more of the direction of the farm to his son, and indulging his own taste for appearing as a popular figure (which, indeed, he was) at all the local markets and Midland cattle-shows, presiding at meetings of the Farmers' Union and the Board of Guardians, and returning, unsteadied by triumph, to the well-earned appreciation and flattery of Mrs. Hadley, "the only woman in the world who under-

stood him"; and Jim, growing ripe with responsibility
before his time, spent his huge strength ungrudgingly
in the vocation for which it had been given him.

For, despite his father's contempt for his brains and
his incapacity for book-learning, the boy was a born
farmer, and gifted, in that one direction, with instincts
and intuitions transcending reason. In relation to the
earth and its creatures, his keen sight, his enormous
hands, appeared to acquire a special, an elemental
sensitiveness—just as his limbs, hugely thewed like
those of a shire plough-horse, seemed adapted by
nature to labour in a particular element: the tawny
Keuper marls and stiff clays of the Severn basin,
through which, following plough or harrow, he moved
erect with a splendid unhurried ease. At such times
Jim seemed no longer awkward or clumsy; the rhythm
of his stride was serene as that of the seasons; his great
limbs were proper to the sweeping curves of the land.
He loved that land for itself, its colour, its shape, its
texture. He knew its varying nature by heart; how
here pasture was sweet and there sour; how here
hidden clay struck cold and there friable loam was
generous; how water flowed here unseen and there
land lay arid; and, almost as though the land itself
acquiesced in a partial assimilation, not merely his
clothes—stained ruddy with use and smelling of byre
and stable—but his very physical fibre seemed dyed
and permeated by the hues and odours of earth, so
that when he stalked into the yard, his caked hobnails

ringing on the cobbles, he appeared less a human being than an embodiment of the forces with which he was dealing.

When folks asked him a question, he had an odd habit of delaying his reply; he gazed at them for a moment with those wide and rather childlike blue eyes of his, as though he were anxious to fathom, before he answered, not merely the immediate significance of the question itself, but the mysterious sequence of thought from which it had sprung, and other thoughts, still unspoken, in the enquirer's mind. This pause gave an impression of slowness, though Jim was not slow, and when, at length, he spoke, his eyes smiled and the deep, soft voice (the smile, too) had a quality one might almost call beautiful, and an element of surprise: for though his voice had the tones one associates with culture, the speech he used was the land's ancient dialect, and contained not only words, but also inflexions and rhythms foreign to town-bred ears. When Elsie came home she mimicked her brother's broad accent, and George Cookson complained of it:

"You'ld think there'd been nothing spent on his schooling," he said. "The boy talks like a ploughman and stares at you like an animal."

Perhaps that was why the labourers who worked on the farm and its animals were so devoted to him. He could do what he liked with the men; they took orders without a murmur from Jim, which George Cookson, for all his imperious bluster, would never have dared to give them. They confided to him their small family troubles, trusting his silence; they borrowed money from him, and generally repaid it. Even Aaron Bunt, that notorious poacher, told him his secrets. There was no hour of the day or night when the hands weren't ready to help him cheerfully. If the farm failed to show a profit, it was not through bad service. He had "a way" with animals, too. Dogs, particularly, adored him. They obeyed his least word or whistle. One of the sheep-dogs, caught overnight in a poacher's snare and half mad with pain and terror, lay sullenly growling with bared fangs at the men who dared not approach. At the sight of Jim Cookson the beast's terror vanished. When Jim knelt down beside it, it rolled over on its back and licked the big hands that fumbled with the wire. If a vicious horse must be drenched or a savage bull gelded, the neighbours sent for Jim Cookson to "lend them a hand." Wherever fierceness spelt fear he could do what he liked with them: he feared no animal just because no animal feared him. It was almost as though he possessed some strange power of communication, denied to others. Even the bloodthirsty, pink-eyed ferrets he fondled never nipped him.

It was the same with wild creatures. He had a nose like a hound for their scent, eyes cunning to see where a vixen had curled round her cubs, or a badger rolled, or a fox's brush swept the dew. He knew the tracks of the little otters (unhunted in those parts), which crept up from Severn in summer, when the salmon had passed, to bloat themselves on frog-jelly spawned in the ditches; the holes in the roots where squirrels hoarded their nuts; the kingfishers' noisome larders. Love, no less than instinct, gave him a sympathy with all these wild kinds of life which, by some mysterious vibrations, must have revealed its benevolence; for quick eyes, bright with terror at the tremor of a footfall or the shadow of most human shapes, accepted his presence as part of the natural landscape (which indeed it was), so that, seeing him, they went on with their play or their hunting, with no more concern than if some stray bullock had thrust its head through the brambles to gaze at them with mild eyes.

For all this, Jim Cookson was in no way less human than his fellows nor less capable of natural passions. It was only that his emotions, strong though they were, had a brooding quality. At their strongest, he found it hard—and almost distasteful—to express them in action or, above all, in words. Beneath that contained exterior they flowed invisibly like the undercurrent of Severn rolling to the sea, and those who saw only the surface knew nothing of them—not even his mother. Perhaps not even himself.

IX

MR. WINTER PROPOSES

IT was by chance—or rather by one of those combina-
tions of chances which are the perpetual wonder of
lovers (who can never believe their meeting to have
been the result of anything less than a miracle)—that
Jim Cookson met and fell headlong in love with Mary
Lydgate. Though Uffley Mill marched with The
Moat, Eli Lydgate, who kept himself to himself and
rarely left the immediate neighbourhood of the mill,
had little in common with George Cookson, except
their boundary, the maintenance of which was a cause
of contention rather than of friendship; and each, for
a different reason, disliked the other.

In this case Mr. Winter, quite properly, acted as
the envoy of Providence. From the day of his arrival
in Chaddesbourne—that day when, with tears in his
eyes and warm aspirations in his heart, he had surveyed his cure from the elevation of the belfry-
windows—the vicar had been distressed by the
village's lack of organized social life. As soon as his
congregation had streamed out of church on a Sunday
evening he felt they were lost to him; and like any
good huntsman (or shepherd) he believed it his duty

to keep his hounds (or his flock) under an imaginary tablecloth. It was this lamentable scattering, he thought, that accounted for such unfortunate vagaries as Nellie Bunt's baby. He explained this to Dr. Selby, who, as time went on—and in spite of his unsettling opinions—had become his principal confidant.

Dr. Selby listened patiently to the vicar's complaints, because he liked him and because he was rather sorry for him. Dr. Selby habitually liked and felt sorry for most people.

"Of course I know just what you mean," he said, "and I quite agree with you. But we English people—particularly those of us who live in the country—are such individualists. Our homes are our castles; we're always on the defensive. Five hundred years ago (and that's not long for Chaddesbourne) we jolly well had to be. Then our lives, though you'd hardly believe it, are tremendously full, and as different from another as—what shall I say?—as our cottage gardens. We hate being what you call 'organized'—unless we're convinced that it's absolutely necessary for some specific reason. A war, for instance. . . ."

Mr. Winter sighed and shook his head sadly.

"And even then," Selby went on, "though we take it like lambs, we like to pretend that our organization is voluntary. This war, with its conscription and ration-cards and restrictions and drills and all the rest of it, has made us less fond of being organized than ever. We want to go back to living our own lives in

our own lazy way. We've been herded together un-
naturally in regiments and factories for four precious
years. That's why we've come to hate crowds and
leagues and societies of all sorts. That's why the
benevolent schemes of the Church Militant don't
appeal to us."

"Yes. . . . I know. I quite realize that," the vicar
said plaintively. "That's the tragedy of the whole
thing. During the war one couldn't help feeling the
country was spiritually alive. People's minds were on
fire—not merely with war-like enthusiasm—you
didn't get much of that in the trenches anyway—but
with all kinds of fine and lovely emotions flickering
up where you'ld least expect them. All our senses were
quickened, even our sense of beauty—that sounds odd,
but it's true. Selfish men became generous and cowards
heroes: you must have seen that yourself a hundred
times, Selby. And, however grand or humble we were,
we forgot all about it. We were brothers one of
another; we all worked together on a plane of devotion and ardour so infinitely higher than anything
before or since. That's what sticks in my throat: the
fact that a monstrous and devilish thing like the war
should have been able to bring out these lovely qualities of high passion and patience and absolute human
goodness, and that now that the ghastly business is
over, the flame sinks to ashes, and here we are—just
where we were!"

"Not just where we were, my dear Winter. Not

just where we were. . . ."

"Rather worse than we were, I sometimes think, God forgive me!"

"It may look like that sometimes. A pendulum must swing if it moves at all. There's the law of stimulus and reaction. Hot air (you'll observe the metaphor) rises, and cold air falls. Exaltation of the spirit is followed by spiritual lethargy. Night follows day. I could go on irritating you by saying things of this kind for a week. They sound like a copybook. But they're true. Human spirits, like human bodies, are subject to a kind of thermostatic control."

Mr. Winter sighed hopelessly. "Is there any reason on earth why we shouldn't be able to revive all the noble emotions of which we've shown ourselves capable in the cause of destruction, and use them constructively?"

"Yes, the best of reasons. We're tired. Give us a chance to recover ourselves. And then wake us up if you like with a religion . . . a religion, mind, not thirty-nine articles. But for God's sake don't hurry us."

From the mass of these abstract discussions, in which, though he teased him, Dr. Selby agreed with the vicar, a number of communal activities, unknown before the war, came to birth in Chaddesbourne. These included Boy Scouts led by Morgan Jones, who, with his thin white knees and rebellious hair, looked sufficiently unmilitary to satisfy any pacifist; Girl Guides, whom Miss Burton's neatness made look much more war-like; a branch of the County Library, housed in the schoolroom; a club for young men, encouraged by the doctor and intimidated (though he didn't know it) by Mr. Winter, and a Women's Institute, a branch of the one in Wychbury. The Hall, though it patronized these activities, did not yet share in them, and Miss Loach disapproved of them all, because none of them had existed in the Golden Age of her father's vicariate.

Even so, Mr. Winter remained unsatisfied. There was still, he maintained, no such thing as a corporate village life. You shook people together, but they still remained units. "It isn't," he said, "that I want to improve them. I want them to enjoy themselves without being self-conscious. I want to give them more fun."

"With a pinch of your own private medicine in the jam. That's what they'ld suspect," the doctor warned him.

"Of course. That's the trouble. To tell you the truth, I've been thinking of folk-dancing."

"Merrie England and all that? No, Vicar, that hobby won't gallop. You see—here I go again!— England *isn't* merry by nature, and I doubt if it ever was. We have no abandon. We're stiff Northerners, self-conscious and reserved. You can't *make* us unbutton."

"I was thinking of a party at Whitsuntide. Quite

undenominational. Say a dance and a whist drive in
the schoolroom."

"Well, try it by all means. Make the tickets as
cheap as you can. We like value for money. And, for
heaven's sake, Vicar, no speeches. By the way, don't
forget to rope in the Ombersleys."

Mr. Winter determined to risk the experiment and
to make it a success. He flew hither and thither on
his bicycle, his sallow cheeks flushed, his eyes glowing
like violets. First, naturally, to The Hall, where Mrs.
Ombersley, delicate as a wisp of old lace, received
him in the library. She came there from the garden,
where she had been working, she said, with a pretty
flush on her cheeks. When she slipped off her muddy
gloves he could see her slim white fingers; her voice
was so quiet and the syllables of her greeting were so
deliciously, limpidly precise—like rock-crystals on a
string—that Mr. Winter, whose ears had grown used
to the homely accents of Chaddesbourne and Dr.
Selby's plain speech or Miss Loach's prunes and
prisms, thought: "Really, what extraordinarily nice
people these Ombersleys are, and what a pity we don't
see more of them!"

Helen Ombersley smiled as she listened to him,
but her eyes were distrait, for the thoughts which she
had taken out with her into the garden, where one
can think more calmly, had accompanied her indoors.
That morning she had received a letter from her
cousin, old Lady Clun: a disturbing letter, which

hinted that Jack, whom she had been picturing en-
sconced in the monastic seclusion of Christ Church,
was "interested" in a young woman of a most undesir-
able class—a "dance-hostess" (the word was vaguely
familiar and unpleasant) in a London night club
whose name she had never heard: *The Blue Fox. I
think*, Lady Clun had written, *it is my duty to tell
you* (Duty and pleasure combined, Helen Ombersley
bitterly reflected) *that Ledwyche has seen Jack three
times at this place, which is most disreputable, in this
woman's company. As you know, my dear Helen,
these creatures stop at nothing. She's probably found
out that Jack is an only son. Ledwyche asked me to
drop you the hint—so here it is!*

Mrs. Ombersley's first emotion on reading this
letter had been a wave of white-hot fury against
Evelyn Clun, who was always a cat, and her son, Lord
Ledwyche. What was Harry Ledwyche, a middle-
aged man who ought to know better, doing in this
most disreputable place? And what right had Ledwyche, with *his* reputation, to question the honourable
nature of her Jack's relations with this young woman,
whoever she might be? Yet this, when she came to
think more calmly, was the paradoxical crux of the
business. If Ledwyche had surmised that Jack's attitude towards the young woman was merely dishonour-
able (supposing such an old-fashioned word to exist
in his vocabulary) he would probably hardly have
troubled to mention the matter. It was, ironically, the

innocent and honourable nature of Jack's intentions that made the case serious. He might be (or imagine himself to be) in love; he might even—and this was what Ledwyche's warning meant—be thinking of marriage, which would be simply too dreadful—because if Jack did anything rash of that kind, Miles would never forgive him.

That was why—with a sense of guilt, for the idea of hiding anything from her husband hurt her—she had taken such pains to conceal Lady Clun's warning letter. Life had been (or seemed) far less difficult before and during the war. Dick and Roger, the sons she had lost, had obligingly conformed to the pattern of which Miles himself was such a perfect example. But Jack was different from his brothers. Of course, he had only been twelve, a mere baby, when the war broke out; and the people who actually fought in the war, like Miles, could never quite understand what those who didn't went through—young children, particularly, growing up in the midst of all that suppressed emotion and anguish, growing up without any proper allowance of vitamins (nobody had ever heard of them then), growing up in a world which, in spite of what everybody said, was, in fact, just a little bit mad, which had lost its bearings.

They came back from the war, these grim heroes, Mrs. Ombersley thought, and expected the new generation, which knew nothing of their old, wrecked world, to conform to standards it had never known or cared about; and when they laid down the law, the new generation stared and gaped in surprise, for the very language of heroism was now archaic, and words which before the war had meant one thing now meant something totally different. That, in essence, was why Jack and his father couldn't understand one another. Even when she knew they meant the same thing, they put it differently. It was her task, by virtue of the breadth of love which embraced them both, to act as an interpreter, to reconcile, to defend (though that sounded ridiculous) each from the other. And that task wasn't easy!

Mrs. Ombersley, still smiling and listening to Mr. Winter's enthusiasm, sighed. The sigh made him start, and, seeing this, she recovered herself, for Mr. Winter was not only entitled to respect as the vicar of Miles's parish, but as a good and earnest man. She said brightly:

"I think your idea's quite excellent, Mr. Winter. Of course, I can't make any promises for my husband —he has so many things on his hands—or for Jack, who is working so hard at Oxford: I do think the examinations are terribly stiff nowadays, don't you? But Catherine and I shall be only too delighted to look in and see you all enjoying yourselves. We feel rather guilty, to tell you the truth, about having seen so little of you; but if you only knew what a business it is getting into an old house, without any conveniences, that has been neglected like this one, I'm

G

sure you'ld forgive us. And the garden! You've no idea what a wilderness! The roses are just coming into bloom—I expect you have masses of new kinds of roses up at the vicarage—and when I see how they've been neglected I can't help thinking how wonderfully courageous the lovely things are. Only look at these delicious La Frances. Such a silvery pink, and so much more scent than most of the new ones!" She bent over her roses and slowly inhaled their faint fragrance. "Don't you think so?" she said.

The rhetorical question came to him so pleadingly that, even if he hadn't agreed with her, he would probably have assured her that he did. The gentleness of this lady stirred him strangely. It suggested a cloistered innocence—which seemed odd in a woman of the world who had borne four children; a graciousness untouched by the dusty business of everyday life; her presence left him with a remembered fragrance like that of a flower—"like silvery La France roses," he thought, and yet that wasn't right. "Rather, a fragrance of withered petals," he told himself sentimentally, "of faded pot-pourri in a silver bowl. And lavender. Decidedly, lavender."

How different Helen Ombersley was from any ordinary woman Mr. Winter realized when, having left her, he called on Miss Burton. Miss Burton, whom he had always described as "refined" and "superior"! There was something unsatisfactory, he noticed, about Miss Burton's shape. It was a stubborn little shape with extremely practical limbs precisely adapted to the functions which they would be called upon to perform—among which allurement did not take a prominent place. It wasn't that Miss Burton appeared to him less modest than Mrs. Ombersley, but that, in spite of her youth and health, and her passable looks, she appeared so much less attractive. When Mr. Winter proposed to her that she should provide the music for his dance, her face, which was given to this affliction, flushed quite prettily —not because the vicar's searching scrutiny embarrassed her, but because, during the spring, she had contracted a liking (which, since schoolmistresses may not marry without their managers' permission, was not merely disturbing, but improper) for her colleague, Morgan Jones, who would certainly be of the party and might ask her to dance with him. That was why Mr. Winter's complimentary invitation had two sides and cut both ways; for she knew that, chained by duty to the piano-stool, she must suffer the agony of seeing Morgan Jones dance (if he so condescended) with women less worthy of him than herself.

"But at least," Miss Burton thought, "I shall be with him—perhaps alone with him—when we decorate the schoolroom."

And she saw herself daintily poised on a pair of steps, with her feet in the first position, while Mr. Jones, gazing upward, fascinated, handed her wreaths of evergreens and ivy or coloured paper; and she was glad that her married sister in Dulston had sent her a pair of silk stockings for Christmas, because, without being vain, she knew from what friends had told her that her ankles were her best feature, and a step-ladder was so revealing. There was always the chance, of course, that Mr. Jones, with the savage Welsh Puritanism which she dreaded and admired, might flatly declare that he disapproved of dancing, and this chance of romantic intimacy be lost. But Mr. Jones, in the event, condescended to approve of the occasion, because he hoped (though Miss Burton little suspected it) that Elsie Cookson might come to the dance and that the vicar might introduce him.

The only person of importance in Chaddesbourne whom Mr. Winter failed to consult was Miss Loach, who, as soon as she heard what was moving, peremptorily summoned him.

"What is this I hear, Vicar?" she asked. "A dance in the schoolroom?"

Mr. Winter expounded his motives. He felt sure Miss Loach would agree. But Miss Loach, reserving her judgment, remained hurt and silent.

"I never remember a dance in my father's time," she said at last. "Not a dance in *that* class, I should say. The Hunt Ball, of course, is quite different. In any case, I hope you will strictly forbid the performance of modern dances. From what I have heard and read in the newspaper, they appear to be of a revoltingly animal nature. Their names speak for themselves." She shuddered. "The fox-trot, the rabbit-hug. If you insist on old-fashioned, dignified dances such as mazurkas and quadrilles, and permit no rowdiness—although there *are* dangers, of course—I shall offer no objection. But I trust you won't keep it up after ten o'clock. The early hours of sleep are the most beneficial."

As Mr. Winter moved to escape from the looking-glass world, like a schoolboy who was expecting to be caned and got off with a lecture, Miss Loach stopped him.

"There is only one thing that I have to add, Mr. Winter," she said, "though I feel I need hardly mention it. That dreadful Bunt girl must not be admitted to the dancing-floor under any circumstances."

"I don't think you need worry about that," the vicar replied. "Nellie Bunt has just gone to a situation in Wolverbury."

"A situation? And with what kind of reference, may I ask? Do the unfortunate people who have engaged her realize the girl's character?"

"I expect Dr. Selby, who got her the place, has informed them. They are friends of his, I believe. I shouldn't have told you that. Will you please forget it?"

"In any case, I should have known this sooner or later. I respect your confidence, needless to say, Mr. Winter. But there are certain things one cannot and should not forget. This is one. It confirms my suspicions."

Miss Loach did not say—and the vicar was too tactful to ask—what, exactly, her suspicions were. He wanted, above all, to make his dance representative not merely of the people who came to church, but of the whole community. He was delighted to find how many new people the scheme put him in touch with, and how unjust this contact proved many of his prejudices. Ted Hadley, for instance, against whom Miss Loach and others of the righteous had particularly warned him, turned out, on nearer acquaintance, to be—not exactly a sheep in wolf's clothing, but an average decent fellow of the kind he had met by the dozen in the war. On the steps of the "Ombersley Arms," observed with horror by Jane Trost, Mr. Winter and Hadley discovered that they had actually served in the same brigade.

"Of course I'll take tickets, Vicar," Ted Hadley said heartily, "*and* sell them, and do any mortal thing that I can for you. Glass and crockery: that's in my line. You leave that to me. And my missus—you don't know her, I'm afraid: she's not much of a churchgoer any more than myself—but I can tell you this, she's a dab-hand at catering. She'll take your refreshments in hand if you'll say the word." He limped into the passage and shouted: "Hi, Gladys! Where is the damned woman? Excuse me, sir. Won't you kindly step in a moment?"

Mr. Winter, still observed with increasing horror by
Jane Trost—(Indeed, Mum, she said, I could hardly
credit my eyesight!)—stepped in. He found Mr.
Hadley's bar-parlour extremely cosy. All its contents
were neat and shiny, from the waxed linoleum floor to
the gleaming parade of bottles and glasses and pewter-
pots, the mirrors, advertising whisky and stout, the
glazed prints of hunting and cock-fighting. Even its
faint odour of spirits and casks was not unpleasing; he
could imagine a man feeling strongly inclined to settle
down here for an hour or so with his pint of beer and
his pipe on a winter evening. Even now . . .

"Not a bad little hole," Mr. Hadley agreed. "And,
mind you, I keep it decent. I wasn't a regimental
quartermaster sergeant-major for nothing! It suits me
and Gladys first-rate. You can hear what they're
saying in the tap-room and give 'em what-for if they
start creating." Mr. Hadley tentatively picked up a
glass and a bottle. "A tot of hot whisky with sugar
and a slice of lemon. That's mine! I suppose, sir, you
can't be tempted?"

Mr. Winter, acutely tempted, was protesting that
he couldn't be, when Mrs. Hadley appeared. She gave
a start and her hands went up to her head, for, at that
hour of the day, her blond waves were still gripped
by curlers. Then she switched on a girlish smile and
carefully pulled up a scrap of grubby lace in the "V"
of her bosom.

"Now, Gladys, lovey," Mr. Hadley said. "We're

talking about this dance. I've promised the vicar here to sell all the tickets we can, and I've told him you'll run the buffet. That's O.K., isn't it? But what you want most of all, sir," he went on, "is a first-rate M.C. These Chaddesbourne people, you know, sir, they're not half-awake. They need loosening up, you might say. And if you'll forgive my mentioning it, it's a deuce of a job to loosen them up on minerals. You want someone, in a manner of speaking, to throw them together and put some pep in them. Otherwise, I give you my word from what I know of Chaddesbourne, this show will be like a funeral—and you don't want *that*, do you now?"

"He ought to get Mr. Cookson, Ted," Mrs. Hadley said eagerly.

"Mr. Cookson! When you know just as well as I do, George Cookson's laid up with sciatica! Come off it, Gladys! I'ld offer to take on the job myself, but I know, frankly speaking, sir, you'ld much rather have a churchman—though, mind you, I was C. of E. myself for the duration. Let's think now . . ."

"There is rather a dearth of gentlemen in the district, isn't there?" Mrs. Hadley put in sympathetically, still fidgeting, to the vicar's embarrassment, with her bit of lace. "Of course, there's that Mr. Jones."

"Mr. Jones? Mr. Jones? That black-haired, white-faced. . . ." Ted Hadley pulled up just in time. "Don't try to be funny, Glad! No . . . I've got it! I've got it! The man for that job's Dr. Selby."

Mr. Winter nodded. "An excellent idea. I'll ask him."

"Now wait just one moment," Ted Hadley went on, with enthusiasm. "You'll pardon my putting this plainly as one man to another; but these Chaddesbourne people are touchy—you've no idea. If you ask one and don't ask another they'll think they've been slighted and take offence. So you must have a list of outside people who don't see the notices and let them know somehow. Dr. Selby'll help you there, too. There's nowhere he doesn't go. They're all on his books. And there's one thing more. If you want to get hold of a thumping big subscription—and, mind you, these shows always cost a lot more than you'ld think—the only thing you need do is to send a notice to Mr. Hackett, who's just come to Green Hill. You don't know the gentleman, sir? Well, that makes no odds. His chauffeur, Mr. Martin, drops in here pretty well every evening, and I need only drop him the hint. Yes, I'll do that with pleasure. Now, if there is anything else . . ."

There wasn't, as far as he knew, Mr. Winter assured him. Mrs. Hadley saw him to the door ("No trouble at all. It's a pleasure," she coyly informed him) and shook hands on the doorstep. Jane Trost witnessed this parting. By the ormolu clock on the looking-glass mantelpiece Mr. Winter had spent exactly seventeen minutes in the "Ombersley Arms." His gait she reported, did not seem noticeably un-

G*

steady; but his face was as red as a beetroot—as well it might be after the intimate way in which Mrs. Hadley had pressed his hand.

At this point, Dr. Selby, in his turn, became Fate's lieutenant.

Uffley Mill was, to him, the most romantic building in Chaddesbourne. Its age, its remoteness, its watery isolation, and the neighbourhood of the great wood, more ancient still, all fascinated him. Chance had made Eli Lydgate one of his earliest patients, and when the bout of bronchitis was over Eli had asked for his bill and insisted on paying it—a proceeding so unusual in Chaddesbourne as to be startling. Dr. Selby liked Eli Lydgate not only for his physical distinction—those magnificent craggy features, that white Van Dyck beard—but also for his mind, which was not the mass-produced product of a penny newspaper, but that of an individual, full of blind-spots and prejudices, but acute and signally just. He liked Joe Warley, too. That antic figure partook more intimately of the unchanging soil than any other in his practice. His grotesque head resembled a shard long-buried in the earth, with a hoard of obsolete coinage, being mysteriously crammed with vestigial fragments of lore which living folk had forgotten—odd superstitions and saws, expressed in words which Piers Plowman would have found familiar. Almost as much—though for different reasons—Dr. Selby was interested in Mary Lydgate; that dark, shy, delicate girl, with her placid, virginal face, who, almost too tenuous to be real, too young to be true, passed in and out through the shades of Uffley, herself a shadow. He often wondered, being given to speculation, what the inner life of this evanescent creature—who, since she was a child, had known no other—could be: what unimaginable dreams, discontents, aspirations, joys, might lie hidden beneath a surface as quiet as that of the mill-pond by which she lived, if that suspended existence deserved the name of living.

That was why, when the vicar planned his party at Whitsun, Dr. Selby's thoughts turned towards her in pity—and also, perhaps, a little in mischievous curiosity—wondering what would happen if the charmed circle were broken and the sleeping beauty released.

On the eve of the dance he drove over on purpose to Uffley and asked Eli Lydgate's permission to take Mary with him. The adventure was risky, for he knew the old man's obstinacy. It gave him the sensation of abducting a nun from a convent; yet he believed that Lydgate trusted him, and had confidence in his own persuasive tact to carry the matter off.

"The child never sees a single creature of her own age," he said, "and I don't think that's good for her. Young people should not be shut off from their own kind of life altogether."

"I've no fancy for Chaddesbourne folk, young or old," Eli Lydgate told him. "As for company of her own age, she'll have all that she wants of that, come next week. There's a letter from Steve this morning —my eldest boy Harry's son, who went for a sailor. His ship's to be laid up at Barry or some such place; so he's out of a job and wants to come here for a bit till he gets another, and I reckon I can't turn him out, though I would if I could."

"A grandson? I never knew you had one, Lydgate."

"Why should you? Harry and I never saw eye to eye. He left Uffley forty years ago. He was killed in the war, the same as Mary's father. As for Steve, as they call him, I know nothing about him, except that he's got on pretty fair at sea up till now. But blood's thicker than water, they say, and he's the only one of the name that's left, barring Mary. I don't want him here—don't you think it!—but there it is. As for Mary. . . . I reckon the child's happy enough without putting new ideas in her head. She never complains."

"Of course she doesn't complain. But I think she's a right to. You needn't be frightened, Lydgate. I'll look after her. I'll drive up and fetch her to-morrow evening and bring her safe home again."

"Aye, but that's only the start of it. You know what I mean. I don't fancy a lot of young bulls coming hanging round Uffley. She's too young for that nonsense."

Selby laughed. "You know, Lydgate, she's not so young as all that. She's a woman. If you'd any

eyes you'ld see she's an attractive woman. Sooner or
later some young man will find her out, and you won't
be able to stop it. The great thing is to see that she
doesn't get caught with the first one that comes along,
and I'll take good care to keep her clear of the wrong
'uns. I know pretty well who they are."

Eli Lydgate grunted. "I bet you do, Doctor. Well,
since it's yourself, you can do what you like about it.
That is if she'll let you. That's her business, I reckon,
and the child's got a will of her own like her grandfather. Go in and ask her yourself. You'll find her
down in the dairy. Do you know your way?"

Indeed Selby knew his way through the dark
labyrinthine flagged passages with their pitfalls of
steps that here rose and there fell until, at last, the
grilled window, illuminating the cool moons of milk-
pans set on slabs for their cream to rise, admitted a
glimmer so dim, so green, so like that of some dripping grotto, that one wondered if the place were not
sunk below the level of the brook whose watery music
enveloped it. So the fancy took him; and indeed,
when he came to think of it—for his eyes were still
dazzled with May sunshine—wasn't there something
of a water-nymph in the sweet, cool, delicate presence
of this girl, Mary Lydgate: her arms and throat moon-
white as the pans of milk, her eyes pools of blackness
beneath the dark brows and smooth hair? His steps
startled her.

"Oh, Doctor!" she cried. "You frightened me."

Then she laughed—which meant, of course, that she wasn't frightened.

"Now listen, Mary," he said, and told her his errand.

"But I shouldn't know anyone there," she said, quickly alarmed. "And I've never danced since I was at school, and I've nothing to go in. They'll all be so grand . . . girls like Elsie Cookson. And then—then you've no idea, Doctor, how busy I am just now. Steve's coming. Has Grandpa told you?"—Her voice quickened with excitement. "He may be here any day now, and I must have things ready. So you see . . ."

"Now don't fly into a panic like that," he begged her. "It won't be a bit grand. It's only a village affair. And I'm sure you can find some frock that'll do for the party. In any case, you'll look . . ." He was going to say "delicious"; which was true, but hardly professional, so he put it differently. "In any case, you'll look quite as nice as any girl there. So that's settled, isn't it? I shall come in the car and fetch you and drive you home again. And you'll enjoy it immensely. I'm ready to promise you that."

"Have you spoken to Grandpa?" she asked, rather timidly.

"Yes. He'ld like you to go. You're entrusted to me for the evening, and I've promised that nobody shall run away with you. Now say 'Yes' quickly!"

"I should like to go very much."

"Then I'll call for you. Remember: Thursday evening at eight."

That was how it began.

X

INVITATION TO THE WALTZ

As soon as afternoon school was over and the children had burst out into the street with their jackdaw babble, volunteers, directed by Mr. Winter, began to strip the schoolroom. Police-constable Page, regarding this as a semi-official occasion, and having discarded his tunic and rolled up his shirt-sleeves, was only recognizable by his uniform trousers and boots, above which and a mufti waistcoat his big, honest face, well-nourished on plain country fare, had the look of a healthy schoolboy's. Joe Atkins, the blacksmith, also brought his huge strength to the job, moving ponderously, like one of the plough-horses he spent his days in shoeing. When he saw Morgan Jones, his pale brow beaded with sweat and his thin chest pumping, pushing this way and that at the desk which was his seat of authority, Joe Atkins's horny hands descended on it like steel grapples; they hove it aloft and swung the whole massive weight over his shoulder.

"You leave him to me, Mr. Jones," he said. "It be knack as does it."

Morgan Jones, still panting, smiled grimly and thanked him, but envied that brutal strength and was glad that Miss Burton, in whose eyes he knew he was god-like, had not witnessed his physical discomfiture by this uncouth Titan, even though (he told himself) Joe Atkins was only exhibiting the qualities of a beast of burden, and had never read Swinburne's *Ode to Proserpine*. But Miss Burton, who was busy at the other end of the room collecting and stacking school-books, had seen everything—because her eyes never left Morgan Jones. She had been longing to beg him to leave the big desk alone in case he should strain himself, and was not (if he had only known it) in the least impressed by Joe Atkins's physical prowess, be-cause, for her, brute strength counted for nothing com-pared with culture and intellect, and Mr. Jones's chief charm in her eyes was the combination of brains, which must be revered, and fragility, which might possibly be mothered. What she really wished she could do was to remove Mr. Jones from this hurly-burly of dust and clatter, entreat him to reserve his strength, and give him a cup of tea; but nothing, it seemed, was going to work out as she had imagined it, and though she had put on her silk stockings in anticipation of that intimate scene in which, working quietly together, they were going to decorate the schoolroom, Mr. Winter had decreed that no decorations were necessary, and in any case, it appeared, there wasn't time for them. So, as she stacked the school-books and carried them into the cloak-room, she tenderly watched Mr. Jones out of the corner of her eye through her owlish spectacles, disappointed and still wondering what she had done to make him snap at her like that when she asked him a reasonable question; not knowing that Mr. Jones, who had just heard Dr. Selby say that George Cookson was in bed with sciatica, was himself in a state of irritation and dread lest this meant that Elsie wouldn't come to the dance . . . in which case all this dusty, detestable turmoil would go for nothing! "After all," he thought, "why should *I* go straining at things and making my heart beat like this, when any lout or loafer in the village can do it better than I can?"

"Loafer" meant Aaron Bunt, whom Ted Hadley had bribed in from the gutter to help by the promise of a pint of beer later on in the evening. He was a half-starved wisp of a man with a tiny insect-like head and sloping shoulders, the skin of his wrinkled, ill-shaven face made as swarthy by weather as if it were stained with walnut-juice; he had lank, greasy hair, and black eyes, set too close together, which gave an impression of cunning mingled with furtiveness in keeping with his slinking gait which resembled that of a gipsy's lurcher, and he wore a tweed coat which had once belonged to old Squire Ombersley and was far too big for him, in the skirts of which enormous pockets were concealed. Though he worked well enough with the rest, those black eyes of his were always alert and defensive, for the two natural enemies of his kind, Harry Roberts the keeper and Police-constable Page, were there; so that his wariness was like that of a sharp-nosed jackal slaking its thirst at an African water-hole in the uncertain company of lions and leopards. This encounter, which resembled an armistice, provoked the keeper and the constable to exchanges of ponderous humour.

"'Ave you got an 'ole in them pockets, Aaron?" Roberts enquired, with a wink.

"I've a pair of handcuffs in mine," said the constable. "Like to see them, Aaron?"

"I thought I seed Aaron last Monday anent Foxhall Wood, but behappen I only fancied it, for when I run up there warn't naught there but a rabbit-net and a stink of gill-ferret. Yo' dain't 'appen to 've dropped a net, Aaron, do you?"

"Nets? Get along, Harry! Aaron Bunt 'asna' got no nets to lose, nor gill-ferrets neither! If Aaron was up by Foxhall Wood 'e was after the bluebells and primmyroses. A great lover of flowers is our Aaron."

Aaron Bunt only laughed. He knew by experience how dangerous it was to bandy words with these tyrants. Before you knew what you were saying, out popped a notebook and a stub of pencil, and anything you said might be set down and come up in court. But though he said nothing, the mind of the hunted—and hunter—was quickly at work, for he knew that to-night, when the moon was up, both these bullies who played with him now like two cats with a mouse would be safely engaged in this silly party of theirs, and that the coast would be clear; that he could take his time and work his ferrets on a string, with the warmship of Ted Hadley's promised pint in his belly, and not be scared into leaving his nets behind. More than that, if the dogs would keep quiet—and on moonlight nights they often kept barking for nothing—he might even treat himself to the taste of one of Roberts' fowls, and none be any the wiser; for when once a fowl was plucked and the feathers gone up the chimney, not even Roberts himself could swear to it, and with all them cars of Hackett's tearing along he might say he'd found it in the roadway if questions were asked. And foxes were desperate plentiful round Chaddesbourne. "More than one sort of fox," he told himself, chuckling.

"What are you laughing at now?" Harry Roberts barked at him.

Aaron Bunt put his head on one side and solemnly winked.

Miss Loach, of course, had seen him enter the schoolroom. For the first time since the squire's funeral she had left her bed for an arm-chair placed in the window. But the sight of Bunt working there— or pretending to work—was not nearly so distressing to her sense of propriety as the vision of Mrs. Hadley, her peroxide hair frizzed up like a Jezebel's and her pink blouse so low in the neck that, at a distance, one could only guess where silk ended and flesh began. If Mrs. Hadley, however immodestly she was dressed, had behaved with modesty, Miss Loach might have felt less indignant; but, true to her type, she didn't. She was joking with all the men, who laughed and appeared to enjoy it, and once went so far as to touch Mr. Winter's arm, which not only betrayed her lack of respect for his cloth, but also reflected, beyond any doubt, on the nature of their relationship. Remembering Jane Trost's account of the vicar's protracted visit to the "Ombersley Arms", and suspecting—if not the worst—unforgivable laxity, Miss Loach braved the risk of pneumonia by opening six inches of window to the lascivious May air in the hope of hearing what Mrs. Hadley was saying; but all she heard was a peal of outrageous laughter in which Dr. Selby, who ought to know better, joined.

"It looks like they're enjoying themselves, ma'am," Jane Trost said, rather enviously.

"Decent people can enjoy themselves without behaving like laughing hyenas," Miss Loach affirmed. "Kindly shut down the window, Jane, and draw the blinds. The air has a nip in it. I've always heard that May is a dangerous month."

The air was delicious that afternoon, Catherine Ombersley thought; it was almost like summer. Sitting there at the old Broadwood piano, whose tones were so feeble and sweet, with gust after gust of indefinite perfume entering the open window and swaying the glazed chintz curtains whose coloured tendrils and blooms, as the sun shone through them, glowed like ancient stained glass, she saw her mood reflected

in the Mozart *rondo* she had just been playing, which
was tender and gay, yet somehow ineffably pathetic,
like a landscape seen through glancing rain or tears—
because the beauty of summer, whenever she felt it
now (and summer at Chaddesbourne was utterly
drenched with beauty) reminded her of the brief enchantment she had known in the hospital at Wyshford
when she had fallen in love.

It had been such an obvious thing for a girl who
was nursing to fall in love with a wounded airman
who, when he was cured, had gone back to the front
and been killed. When she read his name in the
casualty list it was as though she herself had died; her
heart went on beating, miraculously, in a body that continued to live without any reason or purpose; but now
that she came to look back on that period of wonder
(so short, for his wound had been trivial and it had only
lasted three weeks) it was, oddly enough, the atmosphere of Wyshford Abbey that she remembered—the
wide lawns, cedar-shadowed in sunlight, the Palladian
façade—rather than the face and the voice and the
touch of the boy she had loved. For he was only a
boy, after all: a mere child like herself, with a quick,
charming smile and nice, clumsy hands and beautiful
teeth. Of his mind she knew nothing, except that he
said he loved her; and that, together with his pitiful
wound and the pathos of his predestinate youth and
eager gallantry, was enough in those strangely unreal
days when so much youth, so much gallantry danced

momently, like brittle ephemerids, in the deadly air, and fell and perished, when every emotion—perhaps pity and love more than any—partook of the same pervasive and perilous exaltation. For a long time after his physical image had first become blurred and then faded—time wasn't the unit for measuring feelings of that kind!—there had remained in her mind a vague memory of sensation rather than of sight; but now that summer came round again for the third time, there were moments in which even that memory seemed to be submerged and lost in a secret (and almost shameful) physical contentment—as though the welling of warm air and of light had succeeded in thawing at length the frozen wastes of her mind in which now, as in Alpine meadows, starry flowers incredibly appeared.

When she first came to Chaddesbourne such a new birth of life and of hope had seemed unimaginable; to her languid senses one place was as lonely as another; she couldn't pretend to share her father's enthusiasm. Yet insidiously, out of its loneliness, healing had come to her, and her heart, in which love had died, had begun to love it. She was beginning to take interest in the present and think of the future, to look forward to the fun she and Jack would have together when he came down from Oxford; rich summer delights, the long rides and walks and discussions which one could only share with a girl or a boy of one's own age. There would be village cricket, too, in the hot August days.

Her father, she knew, looked forward to that. All Ombersleys and D'Abitots were cricketers, he himself had once made forty-seven against Harrow. Already they were preparing the pitch in the park. All yesterday afternoon she had heard the mowing-machine and smelt the green smell of mown grass in the air; and to-day a dear horse in big leather boots was pulling the roller. It was a pity that Jack couldn't share her music, but with him that didn't matter; they had such a wealth of childish experiences in common: little family jokes and catchwords that meant nothing to anyone else. And music, after all, was at its best a solitary passion: people liked the same things as you did, but you could never tell if they liked them for the same reasons, because, really, there weren't any reasons. Still, it would be nice, Catherine thought, if there were two persons in Chaddesbourne, or even one —her own family were hopeless!—who knew the difference between Bach and Offenbach, or had ever heard of either. It would have made a difference simply to know that such people existed; to feel that the notes she played might just possibly be heard by somebody passing the drive gate who would stop suddenly and listen and say, straining their ears: "Ah, that's the slow movement of the *Waldstein*!" instead of being convinced that the sounds just drifted away into utterly empty air and went on vibrating until they reached Vega or Sirius, which, naturally, didn't care whether Catherine Ombersley could play the *Wald-*

stein sonata or not. As things were, there was nobody but Miss Burton; and this reminded her that Miss Burton would certainly be let loose on the piano at this dreadful dance which her mother, humouring Mr. Winter, had let her in for. It might have been rather less boring, she thought, if Jack had been with her; for then, at least, they would have seen the same comical things and laughed over them afterwards; though one oughtn't really to laugh, because Chaddesbourne was their own village, and it was their duty, her father implied, to take part in the village life—as she certainly would, turning horrid little girls into guides and so on, as soon as she ceased to be the stranger she was at present. "But now," she thought, "I shan't know a soul in the room, except Mr. Winter, who'll think it his duty to dance with me while everyone stares at us—Mr. Winter and 'that nice Dr. Selby,' as Mother calls him."

She smiled, thinking how Mrs. Ombersley had fixed epithets like that for everybody; yet, when she considered it, Dr. Selby *was* rather nice. He had not pretended to be solemn and wise, like most family doctors, on the day when her mother had insisted on his examining her. He hadn't, in fact, examined her at all. He had just looked at her quizzically with the ghost of a twinkle in his shrewd eyes (they were grey, she remembered) and said: "My dear Mrs. Ombersley, you needn't worry about her. People always feel lazy at first when they come to Chaddesbourne. The village people will tell you it's just the 'strong' air—which is rubbish, of course; what they mean is: one needs acclimatizing—and that's true in most places."

Catherine had been grateful for that, though she had a feeling that Dr. Selby saw—or guessed—far more than he said. "Very searching grey eyes," she thought, "that notice everything. It wouldn't be easy to deceive them." And, anticipating further scrutiny, she began to ask herself what dress she should wear. For an occasion like this, the plainer the better, she thought.

This was precisely the problem which Mary Lydgate was debating at that very moment, though in her case, alas, there was no embarrassment of choice. It was fortunate, she thought, that she had hardly grown an inch taller since she came to Uffley. There was a white silk dress she had worn before she put up her hair at her last school-party, and skirts, providentially, had "gone up" a little since then. She stood solemnly contemplating it now in her ill-lighted bedroom—all the upstairs windows at Uffley were so small and so heavily leaded that no more than a glimmer of daylight could penetrate the old glass—and saw that the silk, although she had folded it carefully, had grown crinkled by its own weight, like a field-poppy's petals, and would have to be ironed. So she carried it downstairs, spread a blanket and sheet on the table, and set a smoothing-iron to heat on the gleed. It was strange, she thought, that the two greatest excitements she had known for years—the news of her unknown cousin's arrival and Dr. Selby's invitation to the dance—should have coincided in this bewildering fashion. All day she had been hard at work preparing the best bedroom for Steve; going down on her knees to scrub the floor, and sweeping and dusting, and airing the sheets, thin with age, that she took from the black oak press with its odour of lavender. She had been working so hard to make everything sweet and speckless for Steve that, now it was finished, her back and her legs were aching, and she felt sure that she must look a sight with those great black eyes in a paperwhite face. "But," she thought, "if it's nicely ironed, white silk will suit me. I shall be all black and white."

Too black in one place: that was the tragedy. For, search as she might, she couldn't find anywhere the white cotton stockings that "went" with the white silk dress—which meant that she would be forced to wear her best black cashmere stockings (since tan wouldn't do), and these, beneath a short skirt, would make her legs look enormous . . . "though of course they *are* naturally rather thin," she thought, "that's one consolation, and this silk 'comes up' beautifully, though it has gone a little yellow."

At The Moat sunlight lingered later than at Uffley. There was no black shadow of Foxhall Wood creeping up to the threshold, and in most of the rooms upstairs the casements had been replaced by sashes, so that at this time of the year a girl could dress for a dance quite easily without lighting candles or a lamp, as Elsie was doing. On the same floor, George Cookson lay sunk in a feather mattress on the great mahogany four-post bed—complete symbol of every Victorian domestic virtue—which he had shared for the last quarter of a century with his wife. He didn't particularly like these sleeping arrangements. It was not much fun sharing your bed with an elderly woman who lay wide-eyed and worrying half the night, waiting to pounce on you the moment you woke, and talk about money. But Mrs. Cookson insisted on his sleeping with her, and though he had grown clever at evading her, he dared not cross her. Over and again he had pointed out, feebly protesting, that most of the gentry slept separate at their time of life. But Mrs. Cookson had a maggot in her head. "We're not gentry," she said, "we're plain farming people. If you went and slept in another room the girl would notice it, and it'ld be all over the village in a week. A man ought to show respect for his wife, I consider."

"Well, don't I show you respect? I damned well have to!"

"Respect . . . when he pushed me in the fire!" Mrs. Cookson thought bitterly. But she didn't say what she thought, because, though it was justified, she knew George would call that "nagging." She was grateful to Dr. Selby for having kept her husband in bed— though Heaven knew when the poor man's bill would be paid—and maliciously pleased that he had been

"done out of" going to the dance and making a fool
of himself (and her) with Gladys Hadley. The least
movement gave him such pain that he lay there at her
mercy—if it had been anything but sciatica she knew
he would have kept slipping downstairs for a drink—
and that afternoon she had taken advantage of his
helplessness and immobility to confront him with
the desperate state of the family finances, carrying up
to the bedroom the accumulation of bills and requests
for payment and threatening letters which she had
never succeeded in making him face before. He lay
there, like a sulky child, and had to listen to her—"a
sulky, lovable child," Mrs. Cookson thought; for a
week's rest in bed and isolation from whisky had made
George look younger and quite undeniably handsome.
There wasn't a grey hair in his head, and his naturally
good-natured face, no longer suffused with liquor, reminded her of the stalwart, upstanding, successful
young man she had married. But that, though it made
her wistful, didn't soften her sense of duty. "What
we ought to do, George," she said, "and you know
that as well as I do, is to sell up the farm and most
of the stock and settle down quietly in a nice little
place about a quarter the size of this. Pay our debts,
George, and start over again: that's what we ought
to do."

George Cookson wallowed impatiently in the
feather bed.

"Oh, stow it, Annie! Don't go on like an idiot! A

small place, indeed—and me President of the Farmers'
Union!"

"Well, that's nothing. We needn't stay here. We
can leave the district."

"So that's what you're after, is it? Look here: I
was born in Chaddesbourne. And it'll take someone
better than you to drive me out of it," he added hotly.

"Away from that woman at the 'Ombersley Arms,' "
Mrs. Cookson thought. "Well, you'll have to do something about it," she said.

"I'll do something all right if you'll only keep your
mouth shut. And there's one thing I tell you straight,
Annie . . ."

What that one thing was Mrs. Cookson never
heard, though she could easily guess, for, at that
moment, Elsie came dancing into the room.

"Will I do, Dad?" she said, and swept him a
curtsy.

"Come here, then," he said, "and let's have a proper
look at you. What do they call this stuff?"

"Taffeta. I'm tired of this rotten old frock, but
anyway, it's good enough for Chaddesbourne."

"Want a new one, do you, chicken? Well, ask your
mum. I like my little girl to look smart."

"How dare you—how *dare* you!" Mrs. Cookson
thought. The blood flew angrily to her neck. Then
came fear. Was he going mad, perhaps? There was an
uncle of his who went queer!

"Here, what's this on your cheek?" George was

saying. "It comes off red on my fingers!"

"Oh, Dad, don't! You're spoiling my make-up."

"What do you want with make-up, I should like to know?" Mrs. Cookson asked.

Elsie smiled. "Mum's old-fashioned, isn't she, Dad? You and I know better. You don't want me to be different from everybody else, now, do you?"

"I know one thing. I wouldn't be seen dead painted up like that," Mrs. Cookson said.

"And I know another, darling," Elsie laughed. "You never will be. Oh, Dad, I *do* wish you were coming. It's such a bore!"

In the farmyard below, the old Ford began to sputter.

"There's Jim with the car," Mrs. Cookson said. "Hurry up, now. Don't keep the boy waiting."

"I keep every man waiting. That's one of my habits. Dad, you've never once said I look nice, and now I shan't kiss you."

"Just as well, I should think, with that nasty red stuff on your lips," Mrs. Cookson said.

Jim sat stolidly in the car, his big figure shaken by the decrepit engine's vibrations. Elsie made no attempt to get in. "I think you might open the door, Jim, and wipe the seat for a lady," she said, rather grandly.

Jim stared at her. "This here seat's as clean as it ever will be. Come on, jump in, or we shall be late."

"The best people are always a little late, darling,"

Elsie informed him. "I don't mind betting Miss Ombersley won't come before nine." She stepped daintily, distastefully into the car, which gave a leap forward that nearly unseated her. "Oh, Jim, do go slowly," she cried, "my hair will be blown away."

"All right, keep it on. But we *are* late, you know," he said grimly.

As they rushed through the air (for the car had no curtains) Elsie examined her brother critically. Jim's neck, which looked red at all times, was redder than ever by reason of the high collar that constricted it, and the edge of the collar itself was smeared with blood, because, taking unusual pains in shaving, he had scraped the skin under his ear. He looked, indeed, as pathetic and awkward as yokels must look in their Sunday best; and in order to correct this impression with a touch of elegance, he had smartened his bird's-eye necktie with a gold pin which had belonged to his grandfather, representing a race-horse and jockey in full career. The sight of this ornament filled his sister with horror.

"Oh, do take that dreadful thing out of your necktie!" she cried.

Jim felt rather hurt. "It belonged to Dad's father," he said, "and it's real gold."

"Why, I never saw anything so vulgar in all my life!"

"It's a race-horse. Bend Or. Belonged to the Duke of Westminster."

"Well, I'm certain no duke ever wore a great ugly thing like that. Please give it to me. I'll put it in my bag and take care of it, I promise you."

Jim surrendered the tie-pin reluctantly, and drove on with fury. As they reached the main road, Mr. Hackett's red Pearce-Tregaron droned past like a shell in flight. Elsie sighed. "Now that is the kind of car I should like to ride in!"

"I daresay you would. But you never will," Jim said grimly.

"Well . . . you never know." Elsie smiled.

It was very lovely, that mild May evening, in Chaddesbourne. As they ground past the church the clock was chiming the hour (they were in time after all) and the notes of the sweet, cracked bells, released from the louvres of the belfry, round which swifts whirled and soared with shrill, trilling cries, seemed to hang on the limpid air like the smoke suspended in wisps above cottage chimneys. The schoolroom lamps had already been lit; a light shone from Miss Loach's bedroom, a third light flickered in the front upper room of the smithy, where Miss Burton, who had been busy till the last moment, was washing her face and bathing her tired eyes in cold water to make them sparkle; and these scattered lights, too feeble to compete with the fading sky's luminous turquoise (in the lakes of the western horizon it was almost green) or to turn the windows behind which they burned into lanterns, were seen as crystal pin-

H

points, like fallen stars, save when Miss Burton carried
hers to the mirror and it became a firefly. Then, before the harmonics of the chime had died on the air,
the tenor bell, which sounded the hours, struck eight.

"We've just done it!" Jim Cookson said, pulling
up with a squeak behind the red Pearce-Tregaron.

"Yes, and look at my hair," Elsie grumbled.

Dr. Selby came up to the pavement kerb in a
hurry. "Is that you, Jim? (Good evening, Miss
Cookson.) Will you do me a favour? I've just had a
call to the other end of the village. Bunt's baby. And
I promised to fetch Eli Lydgate's granddaughter
from Uffley Mill at eight o'clock sharp. Will you turn
round as quick as you can and run out to Uffley to
fetch her? Just explain why I couldn't, and tell her
you've come instead. Go quickly, Jim, there's a good
fellow. You won't mind being deserted, Miss Cookson? That poor child will be wondering what's happened to me." He smiled, waved his hand, and was
gone.

"Well, I like that!" said Elsie Cookson. "What
about *me?*"

"Oh, just go in and wait, Else. I won't be long.
There's Miss Burton. You know her, don't you?"

It was Miss Burton indeed. When she saw Elsie
Cookson in her rose-coloured taffeta she almost
gasped; it was so grand. How could mere sterling
worth such as hers compete with this dazzling
elegance? "But her face is made-up," she thought.

"It looks positively garish in daylight; and I'm sure that a man of education and taste wouldn't look at her."

Wouldn't Morgan Jones look at her! He had spent the whole of that day in a nervous fever of anticipation, aggravated beyond words by Miss Burton's respectful but clinging confidences. Had this woman the right—just because they happened to be members of the same profession and to teach in the same school —to exhibit, before all the world, this possessive intimacy, to treat him as though he belonged to her? As the day wore on and each grew as tired as the other, his irritation increased. Once or twice he had snapped at her—as who wouldn't?—and seen two patches of crude colour come into her shiny cheeks (like the dabs of paint on a Dutch doll's); seen her eyes look liquid and hurt behind the round lenses of her spectacles. "Must you ask me *everything*, Miss Burton?" he had said. "Have you no ideas of your own?" And now that he had been home to his lodgings at the post-office and bolted his food and scalded his mouth with hot tea in his hurry to get dressed in time, he felt even more agitated; for just at the moment when he saw the Cooksons' Ford rattling up with Elsie in it, when his heart beat wildly and cried: *"She is coming, my own, my sweet!"* and she stepped to the pavement, who should converge on him from the opposite side, her face wreathed in silly smiles, and impulsively place her hand on his arm, but Miss Burton herself!

Morgan Jones's eyes blazed. With a violent movement he shook himself free, and in doing so lurched
into Elsie. He said "Pardon!" at once. For one instant her eyes met his. They were as lovely as he had
imagined, but full of a withering contempt for his
clumsiness. Without a word of acknowledgment for
his apology, she picked up her taffeta skirt and swept
past him into the schoolroom. Morgan Jones stood
watching her, helplessly, with a face like Hamlet's.

In the kitchen at Uffley Mill the grandfather clock
struck eight. Mary Lydgate had been waiting there,
ready dressed, for a quarter of an hour. The white
silk frock, in spite of its yellowness, had "come up"
beautifully; there was a fichu of white tulle round the
neck, which she had fastened in front with a brooch
that had belonged to her grandmother, a Belgian gold
coin. Eli Lydgate was busy with Joe Warley in the
field they called Tyning Leasowes, where one of the
ewes was in trouble with a late lambing, and so neither
of them had seen her and told her how she looked
in her party dress; but, apart from those dreadful
stockings, she thought she might have looked worse.

She stood, in spite of her aching feet, because she
didn't want to crease the newly-ironed dress; but the
minute-hand moved on slowly from the hour to five
minutes past and then to ten, and still there was no
sound of the car that was coming to fetch her, so that
she began to wonder if the doctor had forgotten his

promise, and to see herself being left there in the kitchen like Cinderella, which was dreadful to contemplate after all the trouble she had taken to make herself nice. There was no sound, indeed, but the perpetual murmur of water (which was Uffley's silence), the slow tick of the clock and the bleating of a lonely lamb, for the foxes in the wood didn't begin to bark until it was dusk. If she had known that there would be so much time to spare, she thought, she would have slipped out into the garden and picked a few cottage-tulips to put in a jar on the dressing-table of the room she had prepared for Steve; because by now he must surely have left his ship and might turn up at any moment, and she was anxious that he, their first visitor, should find everything perfect.

Then, suddenly—unless it were a gust of wind that had made the mill-race sound louder—she heard the noise of a motor-car's engine, and hurriedly slipped on her coat and ran to the door. It was a motor-car after all, but not Dr. Selby's. She knew Jim Cookson by sight, for she had seen him in church with his father and mother, though she had never spoken to him. Jim sprawled out of the car and advanced with his cap in his hand and his face like a beetroot. It seemed odd to her that such a big young man should look so distressingly shy. He said: "You are Miss Lydgate, aren't you?" (A foolish question. Who else could she be?) "Well, Dr. Selby's sent me to fetch you. He's been called to a patient. I'm sorry I've kept you waiting. Will you get in, please?"

She got in, and Jim took his place beside her; but he didn't look at her, nor did he speak a word until, rattling down past Moat Farm, he suddenly turned and pointed to some cattle grazing in a field by the road.

"Those there bullocks are mine," he said eagerly. "I mean they're my own, not Dad's. I bought them with my own money and he gives me the feed. They're a well-sorted lot, grade Herefords. Beautiful beef they make. Don't you think they look champion, Miss Lydgate?"

Mary Lydgate had thought nothing at all; but Jim's eagerness was so appealing that she had to say something. "They look lovely," she said.

"I knew you'ld like them," he answered proudly. "You couldn't help."

It suddenly struck her that she hadn't yet thanked him for the lift. "It was awfully kind of you to come and fetch me," she said. "You'll be late for the dance, I'm afraid."

Jim sighed. "Oh, that's nothing. I shouldn't have gone at all if Dad hadn't been laid up. You see, I had to take Elsie in, anyway. This sort of thing's not in my line. I'm not much for dancing." He paused, struggling with words. "But I'ld give anything to dance with *you*. You don't mind my saying that, do you?" he added timidly.

"Of course not. But I'm afraid I'm not much of

a dancer myself. If you dance as badly as I do we should make a rare mess of it with everyone looking. I'm frightened of dancing, anyway."

"Well, if we're both of us frightened, that makes it better, doesn't it?"

Mary laughed. "I'm not sure about that."

"But you will dance with me, won't you, Miss Lydgate?"

"Yes, I suppose so," she said.

"You see, now I've seen you. . . ." He hesitated. "I've no wish to dance with anyone else. That's not just a compliment, Miss Lydgate. I mean what I say."

From the obvious effort the saying cost him, it seemed that this must be true. Yet what could one say in answer to such bald directness? Though she found it as strange as the rest of this odd encounter, and had no wish to encourage him, this lumbering boy's simplicity touched her. It was almost childish; one couldn't be rough with a child; and whatever she said, in truth or in coquetry, would be taken literally. So, flattered yet slightly embarrassed, she kept silence until they reached the schoolroom, where she thanked him again and, again, he found speech.

"But you mustn't thank me, Miss Lydgate," he said. "I think this is the best bit of luck that's ever happened to me. I shall have to take the car round to the yard, I'm afraid. Don't forget what you promised!"

Mary smiled. "No, I won't forget."

Inside the schoolroom Miss Burton was playing a polka.

It was Nellie Bunt herself, Mrs. Hussingtree said, who had come flying to the surgery with that message.

"But we sent her to Wolverbury a month ago; I gave her the money for her fare," Dr. Selby replied.

"Nellie Bunt's not the first bad penny that's turned up before it was expected," Mrs. Hussingtree sniffed. "She says her sister sent her a postcard to say the baby was ill, so she's left her place—run right out of the house, the flighty bizzom!—and walked most of the way, though she did get a lift from a man in a lorry between Wednesford and Stourton. She says that the baby's dying, and the language she used . . . well, she didn't learn *that* in Chaddesbourne, I'm certain sure!"

It was a shame to disappoint his little friend Mary Lydgate, but a call was a call, and this one seemed urgent. Dr. Selby turned round the car and drove to Aaron Bunt's cottage. He approached it with distaste, for the wretched place was still on his conscience. Miles Ombersley had promised to do what he could about it, but nothing had been done, and the house was unfit even for the habitation of people grown used to its damp and squalor, let alone for a new-born child.

Nellie Bunt stood waiting for him at the gate in a fever of agitation: a slip of a girl with lank gipsy hair like her father's, who, had she been properly fed, might almost have passed for a beauty; for her long-lashed eyes had a sort of smouldering fire in them (like a sullen animal's, Selby thought), and the skin of her throat and bosom, liberally displayed and be-decked with a glass-bead necklace, had the firm, fine texture and pallor of a magnolia petal. The excite-ment of running the length of the village had coloured her cheeks. It wasn't surprising, he thought, that un-savoury young men (or their elders) ran after a creature so clearly born for pursuit and easy posses-sion. Nellie's mouth—that sure index of virtue—was a harlot's mouth; he had seen its like, and shrunk from it, a hundred times in the streets of London. Even now, in that moment of desperate agitation, the mere sight of a man—of an unlikely man, such as him-self—made her body assume, instinctively, automatic-ally, a pose of invitation and acquiescence that froze him and made him speak sharply.

"What's all this about?" he said. "I thought you were at Wolverbury."

The girl's face worked; she burst into tears; Selby felt like a brute.

"It's the whooping-cough, Doctor. Mam says she's been badly three weeks. And it's turned to the croup now, Mam says. I know us be goin' to lose her. I ought never to a' left her."

"Don't meet trouble half-way now, Nellie." Selby patted her arm. It was cold to the touch, and she

H*

shivered. He entered the cottage and was aware of its composite smell of damp walls and floor, rotten thatch, decaying vegetables, the tang of choking wood-smoke, the acrid odour of dirt. In front of the fire, where the smoke hung heaviest, stood a wooden box padded with rags, over which two women were bending: Nellie Bunt's elder sister, a more slatternly version of herself, and the swarthy, witch-like figure of her mother. In the foul receptacle itself lay a pitiful bundle, indistinguishable from the rags in which it was huddled, inert as a sick lamb. When Selby entered, the two women rose and made way for him. He knelt and took out his stethoscope, and unfolded a poultice of sodden green leaves from the baby's chest. As he did so, there came unbidden into his mind the memory of a Victorian picture which he had often seen on the walls of middle-class homes. It was called "The Doctor," and, as he remembered it, he was aware of the contrast between himself, the doctor of reality, firm, sceptical, ruthlessly materialist in all matters of clinical fact, and the bearded, sentimental figure which the painter idealized; for the feeling uppermost in his mind at that moment was not patience or benevolence, but anger and extreme irritation at the ignorance and stupidity which (as the stethoscope told him) had condemned this small, pitiful wisp of humanity, unwanted and uncared for, to die. As he listened to the rasping sounds which came from the baby's choked chest he heard also, distantly, the unceasing flow of Mrs. Bunt's ghoulish commentary:

"I told our Nellie, I told her straight, she'd no call to send for you. *I* know what the chin-cough is, and I know what to do with the croup. Leastways, if I don't, doctor, I ought to, seeing as I've carried four to the churchyard with it myself. This here baby's been houzing and houssacking for three weeks on end, day and night, I told her. Some gets over it and some don't, I says. So long as the poor mites can yox up the fleem. . . ."

Dr. Selby looked up, interrupting her. "What's this thing?" he said. He held up a fragment of something that looked like a stick on a loop of string.

"That's the foot of an oont—a mole as you'ld call it—what Dad catched for her. There bain't no better cure for the chin-cough than that."

Selby threw the fragment of carrion on the fire.

"Why didn't you send for me before?" he asked sharply.

Mrs. Bunt seemed shocked by the question. "Why didn't I send? Well, who's going to pay for the doctoring? I should like to know that. I'm an honest woman. As I says to Aaron last night. . . ."

"You know perfectly well you could have got an order from the parish. The truth of the matter is, Mrs. Bunt, that you didn't care. And you don't care now. Get the child away from this smoky fire and give it some air. Send your husband up to the surgery for some medicine at once . . . and mind you give it her! I'll look in later on to-night."

"Aaron's gone out for a walk, and I don't know when he'll be back," Mrs. Bunt said weakly.

"Well, come yourself then. Let Nellie look after her baby. If anything happens I shall have rather more to say to you."

As he moved to the door, Nellie clung to his sleeve:

"Oh, doctor. . . . Her little legs is gone all fady, doctor. She bain't going to die? Do promise she bain't going to die!"

"It's a case of pneumonia, and that's always serious. But we'll do all we can for it, Nellie. I'll promise you that."

"You mean her be going to die." She stared at him with wild, dark eyes—like those of an animal made fierce by fear they were now, with flecks of flame in them. She spoke in a rapid monotone—"If my baby dies, doctor, I'll do somebody in—either myself or another. If my baby dies, I won't go back to service. I'll go to the bad, I will. I'll go on the streets just to spite them. What's the use of being good and keeping straight, like they say, if they take my baby off me? What harm has her done?"

No harm in the world, Selby thought, driving home, except being born into a world that, through our mismanagement, is too full to hold her; no more harm than that apple tree, so lovely, now, in the fading light, on whose blowing boughs no more than a hundredth part of the set bloom would come to fruit-

ing when cold winds or late frosts had rusted and
thinned it. Her little legs were all fady. . . . Yes,
that was the word. The trees in the Chaddesbourne
orchards, those gnarled, cankered apple-trees, suffered
losses for much the same reason. When fruit clustered
too thick on the bough it went "fady" and fell and
rotted in the springing grass, giving back its juice to
the earth from which it had risen in sun-warmed,
moon-drawn sap. But Nellie Bunt, though near
enough to the earth (and perhaps too near for her
comfort), was less submissive. The desperate anguish
and fear he had seen in her wild eyes haunted him.
They were the hurt eyes of all the stricken mothers
of this world—of Rachel, mourning for her children,
stony Niobe, Hecuba—for she knew, as well as he,
that her baby would die, and though nobody else
wanted it, she did; and so he was sorry for her. This
lapse into personal pity, an emotion proved useless, of
which, though no doctor is immune from it, every
doctor who strives to perform his duty unshaken must
beware, became transmuted by the subconscious habit
of discipline into another less treacherous and more
valuable: indignation against the immediate cause of
this tiny catastrophe which had come to shatter the
star-powdered universe for poor Nellie Bunt.

That cause, beyond any doubt, was the appalling
condition of Aaron Bunt's cottage (not even the sweet
evening air could purge its reek from his nostrils) and
the person responsible for this condition was that

amiable and, indeed, conscientious landowner, Miles Ombersley, whom he respected as much as he liked. Because he liked Ombersley, because he respected his character and had been anxious to make allowances for his undeserved embarrassments, Dr. Selby had compromised with his conscience and held his hand. But he couldn't do that any longer now. The Bunts' cottage was only one of seven, each a potential source of disease and death. To-morrow, without fail, he must frame a damning report on the lot and make himself highly unpopular at the Hall—which was the one house in Chaddesbourne where he particularly wanted to be popular. "If only," he thought, "Colonel Ombersley had a little of John Hackett's money: if only John Hackett had a little of Miles Ombersley's taste."

XI

DANCE RHAPSODY

MR. HACKETT, fortunately for himself, was quite unaware of his deficiencies. When he drove down to
the schoolroom that evening in the red Pearce-
Tregaron, he felt, perhaps, more pleased with himself than ever before. During the previous week he
had finally sold his interest in the family business in
North Bromwich and secured, as the culmination of a
year's hard bargaining, a capital sum sufficient to
found half a dozen "county" families. He was still,
he told himself, a man in the prime of life, unhampered by any connections apart from a few pensioned
relatives. For the first time in fifty years he possessed
the time, as well as the money, to amuse himself; to
build what he liked, to grow what he liked, to change
the whole face and economy of the soil he had bought,
as the fancy took him; and this inclination was the
stronger because, somewhere deep down in the limbo
of heredity, there survived a remnant of that feeling
for the land itself which, three generations ago, his
humble ancestors had carried with them from
Chaddesbourne to North Bromwich.

This mystical inheritance impressed Mr. Hackett

deeply because, apart from his business (and even in this he had profited by imagination), his mind was incurably and innocently romantic. It filled him, now, with feelings of overwhelming benevolence towards Chaddesbourne, and some sense of his own importance, as of a rich uncle returned from abroad, or a fairy godfather, on this evening, which marked his first public appearance among the community which had secured his favour.

"This is real country life, an expression of the true village spirit," he told himself as he entered the schoolroom and saw fifteen couples dancing to Miss Burton's uncertain rhythm on the floor which Ted Hadley had sprinkled with a top-dressing of boracic powder. "This is homely and light-hearted," he thought, "without any of the artificial excitement with which people whip themselves up in a dance-hall in town. This is simple enjoyment of a kind that has gone out of fashion. It's clean and healthy and natural; and I don't feel a stranger, I'm part of it. If I hadn't been blind and dumb I should have settled down here fifteen years ago. Though I don't know a soul, I feel this is where I belong."

Mr. Winter, who saw him standing in the doorway with a contented smile on his face, moved over to give him welcome. He looked slim and refined that evening in his black silk vest.

"I'm so glad you've come, Mr. Hackett," he said, "This is a great success. I can't thank you enough for the five pounds you sent me so generously. It's re-lieved us of all anxiety about the catering, and I assure you it's much appreciated."

"Oh, that's nothing," Mr. Hackett told him. "What's five pounds, after all? Look here, Vicar, forget there *is* such a thing as money. If you find that you're down at the end of it, just you let me know, and I'll foot the bill, see? I reckon I've got good value for my fiver already. Now don't waste your time talking to *me*. I can look after myself. Colonel Ombersley isn't here, is he?"

"No, I'm not expecting him; but Mrs. Ombersley and her daughter will be looking in later."

Mr. Hackett sniffed. "Rather like royalty, eh? Who's that pretty girl over there . . . the dark one in white?"

"Eli Lydgate's granddaughter Mary, from Uffley Mill." Mr. Winter smiled. "That's a place you're interested in."

"Even more than I was when I saw you last. Yes, I've had copies made of all the Manorial Rolls. I must tell you about that later. Fancy that, now. The heiress of Uffley! But I mustn't keep you."

Mary Lydgate had embarked on the physical perils of dancing with Jim Cookson, which were real enough, because her feet were always in danger; for Jim's brain was so overwhelmed and exalted by this in-credible privilege of touching her (her hand lay in his, warm, soft, submissive!) that it became incapable of

exercising its normal function of directing the movement of limbs, even less of transmuting into words
the bold thoughts which formed themselves in his
mind, yet fell into fragments as soon as his tongue
tried to shape them. Every moment his feet grew
more wayward and the unusual constriction of his
starched linen collar less bearable; so that Mary
Lydgate, looking up shyly to smile her encouragement (for the poor boy *was* doing his best) after a
particularly unfortunate error in navigation that
hurled her, like a dinghy dashed by a wave on to the
side of a portly brigantine, against the liberally-
cushioned beam of Mrs. Hadley, whom Healey the
agent, a breezy tug-boat, was pushing before him,
became seriously concerned lest the poor boy's face
should burst like an over-ripe tomato.

"How different he is from his sister," she thought,
as the next stumbling gyration of the waltz brought
her face to face with Elsie, the full-blown skirts of
her rosy taffeta swinging outward like the hoops of
a Dresden shepherdess, an incarnation of neatness and
fashion, in Ted Hadley's arms. Not that Mary entirely approved of Miss Cookson's style of dancing,
which was the latest, combining more intimacy than
seemed necessary with an expression of blank boredom
on her smiling face which suggested that the movements of her feet (how neat they looked in their high-
heeled silver slippers!) had a life of their own detached from thought or volition. They were the kind

of feet, Mary thought, which might go on dancing, with the same exquisite precision, if their owner were not merely bored but had fallen asleep, like those fantastic creatures who competed in tests of endurance. "But she isn't happy," Mary thought. "She's discontented; though if I were as pretty as she is and had a rose taffeta dress and flesh-coloured silk stockings instead of these dreadful black ones, *I* shouldn't complain. Oh dear, oh dear, I do hope this dance won't last much longer," she thought, just as Miss Burton decided to bring it to a close with a final bang, and Jim Cookson, whose feet she had spent all her skill in avoiding, stepped backward, with all his determined weight, on Morgan Jones's.

Morgan Jones gave a gasp and a snarling cry, and Jim Cookson slewed round.

"Oh, Mr. Jones, I *am* sorry. I'm afraid I didn't see you."

Morgan Jones's face went whiter than ever with pain and anger. All his feelings were near the surface that night. His lips twisted back in a dog-like grimace of rage at this big lout's clumsiness; but before he had quite lost his temper and snapped, his quick wits realized that the author of his pain was the brother of Elsie Cookson, and he turned the grimace into a smile.

"It's no consequence, Mr. Cookson," he gasped. "It was my fault as much as yours. I ought to have kept my eyes open."

Which was true, more or less. His eyes, in fact, had been so fiercely fastened on Elsie (just as Miss Burton's, whenever she knew what came next in the music, had been fastened on him) that he was completely unaware of anything or anyone else. She was dancing, he saw, with that gross, hulking Saxon, Ted Hadley. "With a drink-sodden publican," he thought bitterly; for, in spite of his inconsistent admiration for Omar Khayyám, Morgan Jones had been brought up in a strictly teetotal home where all strong drink was anathema, and had assumed the blue badge of abstinence at the age of seven. But what hurt him far more than the sight of Elsie Cookson dancing with Hadley was her submissive attitude, which Mary Lydgate had recognized as a symptom of boredom, but which Mr. Jones, being jealous and extremely unworldly, interpreted as rapturous abandonment. Such a sight was enough to drive any man—and particularly a poet— to desperation, to provoke in him an access of chivalrous gallantry such as King Arthur's knights— who were all of them Welshmen, like himself— habitually displayed in the freeing of damsels in durance. A naïve Galahad (with a suspicion of Quixote), he had almost determined to defy convention, to dash splendidly into the mêlée, as soon as the dance was over, and rescue the lady from Hadley's arms without any introduction, when no less than twelve stone seven of Jim Cookson came down on his foot like a pile-driver and sent him limping, dizzy with pain, towards the buffet where Mrs. Hadley, all pink and white and gold, stood dispensing free lemonade.

"Why, goodness gracious, Mr. Jones," she said, "whatever's the matter? If you feel faint you'd better sit down and I'll give you a spot of something." She winked. "I've a bottle of Johnny Walker under the table that Ted's brought for his friends," she whispered. "No doubt it's the heat of the room. Being stout like I am I feel it myself. Now you've only to say the word. . . ."

Morgan Jones declined the offer stiffly and turned away. This was the first time that Mrs. Hadley had ever spoken to him, though she evidently knew who he was, and the smiling familiarity of her address was as improper as he had imagined it would be. Mr. Hackett, on the other hand, wandering to and fro with a look of vague benevolence, had heard the whispered colloquy. His chauffeur, Martin, had often mentioned the Hadleys, and the appearance of this plump good-natured woman confirmed Martin's favourable report. Mr. Hackett had ideas which were not Miss Loach's (or even Mr. Winter's) on the function of a village inn which, he felt, in the absence of a club, should be an important centre of communal life, and this jolly, business-like creature, with her bustling efficiency, was the very woman to make it one. He could guess that, in spite of her easy manner, she would stand no non-sense, she would know how to deal with a man who had taken a drop too much; and her husband too, with his waxed moustache and air of an old sergeant-major, performing, in Selby's absence, the functions of a Master of Ceremonies with such tact, such good humour, such spirit, such likeable humanity, was an equally valuable man to have in a village community —not only because he knew its individual weaknesses but also because he was sufficiently generous to allow for them.

"I ought to make friends with these people," Mr. Hackett said to himself. So, approaching the buffet, he leaned over towards Mrs. Hadley—so close that he caught a strong whiff of frangipani—and said:

"Did I hear you mention the words Johnny Walker?"

"Why, of course, Mr. Hackett! It *is* Mr. Hackett, isn't it? Pleased to meet you, I'm sure. Well, this really is an honour! But for goodness' sake don't tell the vicar I gave it you, will you?"

Mr. Hackett laughed. "Tell the vicar? You bet I won't!"

"Well, there's no harm in it, is there? A little of what you fancy, like poor Marie Lloyd used to sing. Ah, *there's* Dr. Selby. So now my poor Ted will be able to join us. Goodness gracious, doesn't the doctor look solemn! There's a party-face for you!"

Selby was feeling a little solemn. That baby (and the whole problem of the Bunts) was still on his mind. It was an odd change to step straight out of that scene of squalor and anguish into this light-hearted company. His preoccupied eyes were searching the room intently. They saw Mary Lydgate, who was sitting by Jim Cookson (that was a fortunate accident!) and smiled at him; they saw Mrs. Hadley and John Hackett laughing together; Elsie Cookson, alone, delicious, and a little sulky; Mr. Winter, his swarthy face radiant with satisfaction, courteously bending above the plump black satin figure of Mrs. Webb, the postmistress, as though she were a duchess; Miss Burton, at the piano, the chaste bun at the back of her head jerking to and fro in time to the music; Morgan Jones, pale as death, greedily gazing at Elsie Cookson, yet too shy to approach her: he saw all these faces and figures, but not the ones he was looking for. It appeared he was still in time. Catherine Ombersley and her mother had not yet arrived.

Ted Hadley limped up and slapped him playfully on the back. "So here you are, doctor! Where the devil have you been hiding?" He looked flushed and well pleased with himself; his red cheeks, above the skewer of moustache, were shiny with sweat. "Everything's going off champion," he wheezed. "Talk about throwing 'em together! My word, but it's hot! What couldn't I do to a pint? I'll get them to open a window."

His wandering eye caught sight of the solitary figure of Elsie Cookson. "That won't do," he said seriously. "That poor kid's not enjoying herself.

She's the prettiest piece in the room by long chalks, too. Well now, what can we do about it? Let's see. . . ." He snapped his fingers in triumph. "*I've* got it," he said, and walked over to Morgan Jones. "Look here, Jones, my boy, do you happen to know Miss Cookson? That pretty kid over there in the pink frock with what-d'ye-call-ems. Festoons . . . no— what is the word?—flounces. Yes, flounces. That's right. You don't? Well, you're damn well going to, my son; so move along quick!"

It had come . . . the moment of moments for which Morgan Jones had lived—he could say that with truth—for the last six months. Yet it came so suddenly now, and presented him in such questionable company, that he felt almost inclined to plead some excuse and escape—for what would this refined creature think of a man thrust on her by such a vulgarian as Ted Hadley? But Mr. Hadley was taking no chances. It was his office that evening, in his picturesque phrase, to "throw the young people together and put some pep into them," and he almost literally threw the astonished Jones into Elsie's lap, with an introduction that made him shrivel into his shell like a hermit-crab.

"Here you are, Else," he said. "You look a bit down in the mouth. Here's someone who'll liven you up! Allow me to present Mr. Morgan Jones, the celebrated humorist. Mr. Jones: Miss Cookson. Or is it the other way round? I always forget. Now, my children, sit down and get on with it!"

Morgan Jones, his face miserable with angry embarrassment, his hands damp with nervousness, sat down and was dumb. In the black of night he had imagined this meeting over and again, choosing the setting with care and investing the dialogue on both sides with the sense of poetic drama in which (when alone, or on paper) he knew he excelled. In those scenes the hero, a somewhat Byronic figure, dark, Celtic, mysterious, had spoken fluently in a rapid monotone, and the words he uttered, though plain to simplicity, had vibrated with a dark undercurrent of passion which the heroine, and nobody else, must understand. And indeed, in token of this, deeply moved, she had always lowered her eyes to escape the dazzle of this blinding eloquence, contenting herself with sweet, hushed monosyllables, which, of course, kept the dialogue going, leading on, by calculated degrees, to the moment chosen for avowal. Thus the artist had planned it; but—Life being, in the contrivance of *scènes-à-faire*, less competent than Art— it was Elsie, so much more self-possessed than himself, who spoke first and upset the cues. And the words she spoke were pathetic.

"Mr. Hadley's too priceless, isn't he?" was what she said. And Mr. Jones, unable to speak to this unfamiliar cue, mumbled: "Yes," and was silent.

"You're not really a humorist, are you?" she said. "I don't think you look like one. Though, of course, you may be killingly funny when people get to know you. . . ."

Mr. Jones said, first "Yes" and then "No," and left it at that.

"This is awful," he thought. "If she could see the poem I wrote on the day when I saw her first! If I could only put down my present feelings in writing! If I didn't look like a dumb idiot and could be what I am! If that damned Burton woman would stop staring at us like that through her beastly spectacles!"

This embarrassment, at least, was quickly removed. At that very moment Ted Hadley, emerging from the cloak-room, where he had secreted a bottle of beer, conducted Miss Burton, who was too dazed by the spectacle of Mr. Jones in Elsie's company to resist him, to the piano and ordered a waltz. Miss Burton, still haunted by that bitter vision, began to play. Morgan Jones rose stiffly and offered Elsie his arm. "May I have the pleasure?"

"Well, if his feet are no better than his tongue," Elsie thought, "God help the pair of us!" She said, with the insolence of conscious youth and beauty: "There's no harm in trying."

Mr. Jones smiled grimly. His feet, in fact, were much nimbler than his tongue. He had a Welshman's innate sense of rhythm, and considerable skill, with which, in spite of his crushed toes, which were just "coming round" (or perhaps, since pain is a nervous stimulant, because of them), he proceeded, literally, to take Miss Cookson's breath away. He danced like a black tornado, spinning and whirling—though less destructively—through the crowded floor. In his grip Elsie Cookson was as helpless as a straw caught up in a whirlwind, and the sensation, though terrifying and slightly indecorous, was also exciting—more exciting than anything she ever hoped to encounter in Chaddesbourne. This small dark man with the pallid, agonized face at whom she had turned up her nose was by no means contemptible. He was strong, and, apart from physical strength, he had power of another sort—the kind of suppressed and dangerous power of which one was aware when one stood and gazed at the drum of a dynamo, spinning silkily, silently, yet charged with crackles of lightning. As they danced she was never unconscious of this high potential. She was not at all sure she liked it—at moments she hated it—and yet, if he had asked her if she wanted to stop, she would have said "No" without hesitation. This young man was so utterly different in every way from the nice-mannered boys whom she had allowed to pilot her round the dancing-floors of North Bromwich and take her for drives in their fathers' motor-cars and buy her boxes of chocolates. His manners, by those suburban standards, were as uncouth as his dress and his unruly hair; his social station was that of a mere elementary schoolmaster, without a past or a future, whom, under ordinary circumstances, she would never have met; there was, not only in his appearance but also in that part of him which did not appear yet was felt, something foreign to her and even antagonistic. He wasn't in the least to her taste, though odd tastes were sometimes acquired. In the meantime he danced . . . divinely, the conventional word, didn't fit—say, rather, thrillingly; and even Miss Burton was playing better than usual.

Miss Burton was conscious of this herself. When Ted Hadley took her and set her down at the piano her heart was so full of anguish that she scarcely knew what she was doing; but when once they had touched the keys her fingers became possessed; all the emotion which had been pent within her since Morgan Jones despised and rejected her on the doorstep seemed to pour through them into her playing and was released in tumultuous waves of rhythm and sound which she heard, and into which she flung herself like a suicide desperately plunging into the sea. "This is strange," she thought. "Either I'm inspired or else I'm going mad; but whichever it is, it's really of no consequence, for now that I've seen them together I know the worst." So she played and played in a dream, quite forgetting to stop, until Ted Hadley came and tapped her on the shoulder and woke her.

Morgan Jones let his arm fall from Elsie's waist; they were both flushed and panting.

"Well?" . . . he said. That was all. But his eyes shone with triumph; he was clothed in wild glory.

Elsie laughed. "Oh dear. . . . I didn't know you

could dance like that, Mr. Jones."

"I can do lots of things besides dancing," Morgan Jones said quickly. He wanted to add: "I can write poetry . . . burning words. And I can make love!" But now that the music had stopped and people were buzzing about them he was beset once more by the self-consciousness he had managed to forget, and, instead, he said in the stiffest of tones: "Thank you very much, Miss Cookson; that was most enjoyable. May I have the pleasure of the next one?"

Elsie smiled. "Yes, of course you may. But I hope they won't start just yet. I'm quite giddy and out of breath, and so are you. It *was* a long one, wasn't it? I thought that wretched woman would never stop playing."

"And I wish she hadn't!" Morgan Jones's soul fiercely protested. "Heaven is timeless, and that was heaven. Don't you realize that yourself, you lovely thing?" But his soul was dumb, and in its silence he fell to earth, becoming aware of the corn which that clumsy lout Jim had crushed, and of a shoe-lace untied; so that, though Elsie made room for him on the bench beside her, he bowed and left her abruptly.

As he crossed the floor on his way to the cloak-room he saw that all eyes (except those of Miss Burton, which were reproachfully fixed on himself) had been turned towards the entrance. Mr. Winter, abandoning Mrs. Webb, nearly collided with him in his eagerness to reach the door in time to receive Mrs.

Ombersley and her daughter.

"These English parsons are all the same," Mr. Jones thought bitterly. "Snobs and tuft-hunters every one of them: there he runs like a hare to go twittering round that old woman and that stuck-up girl who have condescended to come here and stare at us as if we were animals. Why? Because she's an 'honourable,' the daughter of some duke or other! When the world revolution comes there'll be none of that toadying nonsense; and parsons will have to pull their weight and put in an honest day's work like the rest of us if *I*'ve anything to do with it!"

He stood glaring at the back of poor Mr. Winter, whose only anxiety, at the moment, was to find Mrs. Ombersley and Catherine comfortable seats and put them at their ease, though, as far as Helen Ombersley was concerned, the second of these aims was superfluous. Throughout all her girlhood at Stoke Priory, when her parents were alive, she had been accustomed to "looking in," as they called it, at village functions; and though twenty years had gone by since she last attended one, she had no sooner set foot in the schoolroom than she felt completely at home. If she had been brought there blindfold she could have guessed where she was; for this room had the identical odour of the schoolroom at Stoke; of ink and floor-boards newly scrubbed with soft soap; of paraffin lamps, badly trimmed; of dress-lengths, newly "made up," still redolent of the draper's bales; of rock-cakes and buns and ham-sandwiches; of steaming tea-urns and overheated humanity. And, opening her eyes, she would have seen again on the walls the same yellowish varnished maps, the same texts in Gothic type, the same oleographs of wild animals, through an air that echoed the same hubbub of rustic speech, the same subdued laughter, the same clatter of crockery. So familiar to her senses was every element in that scene, that she welcomed them all (and even the least pleasant) with the thrill of recognition that an exile feels returning to the streets of London, and her face, though she did not know it, became tender, and her eyes shone.

"It was awfully good of you to come . . . and Miss Ombersley, too," Mr. Winter was saying.

"But I love it," she told him. "I adore seeing people enjoy themselves. I've told Catherine this is our first public appearance, so we must be careful how we behave. And we don't want to monopolize you either, Mr. Winter. Please remember that."

"I've been keeping two seats for you here," Mr. Winter said, leading them up to the dais on which, in school-hours, Morgan Jones's desk stood.

"Oh, but this is too dreadfully grand," Mrs. Ombersley protested. "Mayn't we put our chairs on the floor? Would you mind?"

"Well, of course not, if you prefer it." Mr. Winter lifted one chair from the dais and Dr. Selby, hurrying up, removed the other.

"Ah, here's one old friend, at any rate," Helen Ombersley said. "Dr. Selby, you promised faithfully to inspect my garden, and you've never come. And now it's too late. All the tulips are over. Catherine, darling, a tragedy! I've come without a handkerchief. Dr. Selby, my memory's incurable. Could you do anything for it, do you think?"

"You should keep a Remembrancer, like the Lord Mayor of London . . . or is it the King?"

"Well, I have one. You see? Thank you, Catherine darling. She knows all my weaknesses. Isn't she wonderful?"

Selby surveyed Catherine Ombersley gravely, as was his medical habit; he smiled, but made no answer. Was she wonderful? The question seemed worth examining with scientific detachment. She was certainly different from what his mind, running on and elaborating the memory of their first encounters, had imagined. She was neither a child nor the frail incarnation of a wistful tune by Bach performed on the clavichord, but a tall, strong, eminently self-possessed young woman—a trifle too pale for his liking, but otherwise patently healthy in body and mind. And how like her mother she was! The resemblance pleased him; for he had observed that mothers provide a valuable (and often a disheartening) glimpse into their daughters' futures, and felt ready to wager that Catherine's figure, in thirty years' time, would be very little different from what it was now. As to what was inside that proudly-poised head or behind those grey eyes, he didn't presume to guess. But there was nothing like trying; and before the evening was over (he never was in a hurry) he meant to find out, in a spirit of cold, impersonal psychological research. At the moment there seemed no chance of beginning investigations, for Mr. Winter, who had darted away like an anxious blackbird foraging for her brood, returned, dragging with him a substantial morsel in the shape of Mr. Hackett.

"Our new neighbour tells me," he said, "that he hasn't the pleasure of knowing you and Miss Ombersley. But I'm sure you know who he *is*, Mrs. Ombersley, and you've seen his house at Green Hill."

"Oh yes, indeed I know that quite well," Helen Ombersley answered sweetly. "And I think, as a matter of fact, Mr. Hackett and I have met. You came to see my husband, didn't you, Mr. Hackett?"

"Colonel Ombersley didn't introduce me, you know."

"How naughty of him! He's extremely forgetful. But won't you sit down? Oh, this is my daughter Catherine."

Mr. Hackett bowed. "That isn't a hard one to guess. Do you know, that day I came to the Hall I mistook you for her? I did, honestly."

Helen Ombersley smiled. "How very charming of you! Tell me about your new house, Mr. Hackett.

I

I suppose it's quite finished now, with all kinds of wonderful modern conveniences which would fill me with envy?"

Mr. Hackett rose like a trout to a mayfly. "Well, of course, you know, it's a very ordinary house; its outside doesn't flatter it. As I said to the architect: 'I'm not out for show. A plain man like myself doesn't want any fancy Elizabethan manor or Tudor castle or gloomy Georgian stuff. You can cut out the battlements, I told him, and go strong on the plumbing. I want it warm and I want it snug and I want it convenient. And if you'll give me that, I don't care what it costs."

"That was nice for the architect, but wasn't it rather rash?"

"Well, I'm like that, you know, Mrs. Ombersley. When I get what I want I don't mind paying for it. After all, what's the use of money if you don't keep it moving?"

"Oh, of course, and I'm so glad you didn't go in for battlements. Large houses with battlements are terribly expensive to run," Mrs. Ombersley sighed. "Though to *you* that would make no difference, would it? And you're going to be happy there?"

"Happy? Happy isn't the word. Mrs. Ombersley, I feel as if I were just beginning to live all over again. This place has taken a grip on me. I was always reckoned to be pretty keen on my business, but I'm keener on Chaddesbourne than ever I was on that!

Of course, it's quite natural, in a way . . ."

"In what way?"

"Didn't the Colonel tell you? Well, it seems even more natural now than it did when I saw him. I've been routing up all sorts of things in the Manorial Rolls, and it appears . . . I'm afraid this won't interest you."

"But it does. Immensely. Please go on."

"Well, it appears that my family, the Hacketts, you know, were once just about the biggest noise in the district. They spelt the name with one 't', but they were my folk all right. At one time—twelfth century, that was—they owned the Manor of Chaddesbourne."

"But didn't that belong to my people, the D'Abitots?"

"That was just after the Conquest, and they took care to get hold of it again later on. But you see . . . I hope this won't offend you . . . one of the Hacketts, Maud was her name, married into the D'Abitots."

"How amusing! In that case, we're cousins."

"Well, I wouldn't presume to say *that*. Not exactly cousins. Connections. But all this stuff I've been able to rake up, through your husband's kindness, does explain, in a way, the feeling I have for Chaddesbourne. If it doesn't belong to us now, I do feel we belong to *it*; and I feel . . . well, I feel I want to *do* something for it. That's what I feel, Mrs. Ombersley."

Helen Ombersley gazed at him steadily. Mr.

Hackett was moved, deeply moved. When he had spoken of his money his words had jarred on her; but since then it had struck her that the man hadn't really been boasting—he was merely, honestly, ingenuously, clumsily, revealing a mind that, in spite of this tiresome feature, was simple and kind. When she looked at him now, observing his broad Saxon face with the specks of carbon in it, the wide-set blue eyes with their odd mixture of defiance and shyness, and the ill-trimmed moustache; when she listened to his speech, which was nearly—but not quite—that to which she was accustomed, and perceived the enthusiasm which gave his dull words a glow of poetry, Helen Ombersley began to feel kindly towards John Hackett, and rather sorry for him (quite needlessly, since Mr. Hackett was not in the least sorry for himself) as a man whose instincts, in spite of his ignorance and uncouthness, were, probably, radically decent. It was a pity, she felt, that Miles had taken such a dislike to him—Miles, of course, was as full of ridiculous prejudices as a public schoolboy, and if she questioned them he need only point to that dreadful house on Green Hill—but, because she was a soft-hearted woman, and more than three parts mother, she suddenly wished she could take Mr. Hackett in hand and tell him quietly, as one speaks to a boisterous child, that however rich he might be, it was "bad form" to mention it, and that he ought to trim that moustache, and go for his clothes to Miles's tailor in

Sackville Street. . . . Would he mind? she wondered.

Mr. Hackett, apparently unconscious of her scrutiny, went on:

"Yes, I want to *do* something for Chaddesbourne, Mrs. Ombersley, and I don't know where to begin. For instance, it's struck me to-night that this schoolroom's a poor sort of place for a show of this kind. What they want is a village hall. And why shouldn't they have one? Now supposing I came to your husband and said: 'Look here, Colonel Ombersley; if you'll give us a bit of land in the middle of the village—say, just opposite the church—I'm ready to build one to-morrow. I've a smart young architect fellow on my hands at this moment—the chap who's designed my new house—you can see for yourself he's cram-full of the latest ideas—and if you'll give us that field we can cut down those old trees in a jiffy and start work at once'—what do you think he would say?"

Mrs. Ombersley had not much doubt what her husband would say; but Mr. Hackett was so warmed by his subject that he spared her the necessity of shirking the question.

"Then there's other things," he went on, "that are crying to be done. We're behind the times, Mrs. Ombersley: there's no getting away from it. Do you realize that there's not such a thing as a petrol-pump between here and Wychbury? How can you expect to attract motorists to a place—I ask you—that hasn't a filling-station? And the roads. . . . Why, the main street of Chaddesbourne isn't fit to drive over. I've broken two springs in three months on my Pearce-Tregaron. What we want—and I've been on to the County Council about it already—is a thorough widening and a proper surface of tarmac with a nice, regular concrete kerb to finish it off. *And* proper street lighting. The electric main isn't more than a mile away from us. I'm proposing to bring current over the hill to my house, in any case—as a matter of fact, I've just written to your husband about the way-leave, and you'll be able to tap it in the park—so why shouldn't the village have the benefit as well? When you go down this street at night, as I sometimes do for the sake of a walk, I often ask myself how people in these days can read the newspaper with nothing but a smelly oil-lamp. Do you wonder they know nothing of the world? Why, bless my soul, Mrs. Ombersley, there isn't even a motor-bus service! This place, I maintain, ought to be linked up with North Bromwich by a regular time-table. Just think of it: over there, not fifteen miles off, there's three-quarters of a million people who've never set eyes on a place like Chaddesbourne! Not set eyes? Why, they don't even realize that such places exist. When I brought the men from my works here last August Bank Holiday on their annual outing, I can tell you it opened their eyes. I assure you, it was touching to see them—just as if they'd never tasted fresh air in their lives. And it's wrong, Mrs. Ombersley, it's wrong. We can't say it isn't. But what can you do about it?"

This time Helen Ombersley answered him:

"I think it's a pity to do anything—don't you?—in too great a hurry. Village people, you know, Mr. Hackett, are terribly conservative. They hate being pushed into anything." She was thinking: "Oh dear, my poor Miles! Thank goodness he can't hear all these dreadful heresies. Does he guess what he's in for?"

"Now there, I'm afraid you've hit the nail on the head, Mrs. Ombersley. They're not half alive. They want a good gingering up, and before I'm much older they'll get it! Well, I must say I'm glad to have had this opportunity of a chat with you. It's nice to find somebody who understands what one's driving at and sees eye to eye with one. You might just drop the Colonel a hint about what I said *re* the village hall— smoothe the way, so to speak . . ."

"Oh, I think," Mrs. Ombersley said anxiously, "you'd much better write to him."

"Well, just as you please. No doubt you know best."

"And please don't try to do all your gingering-up at once," she entreated.

"Ah, that's all very well; but life's short, you know," Mr. Hackett told her gaily.

He was pleased with himself. Now there was a sensible woman! None of your jabbering kind, but one who knew how to listen intelligently and could grasp what a business man meant. Not a bit stuck-up either. "That's real aristocracy," he thought. Some women—the new Lady Wolverbury, for instance—would probably have taken offence when he mentioned that ancestress of his who had married a D'Abitot. But she'd merely said: "Then we're cousins." Could anything have been more friendly than that? "And she's no fool!" Mr. Hackett thought. "Though she didn't say so, she knew just as well as I do that if I set to work opening up Chaddesbourne in the way it should be—decent roads and electric-light and a bus service, and all the rest of it—it'll send up the value of their property fifty per cent. A remark-able woman," he thought. "I'm damned glad I've made friends with her. She's the sort that could twist me round her little finger, and I don't mind betting she could do the same with her husband. Why didn't I mention the matter of Uffley Mill?" Mr. Hackett thought; "she would have seen at once what my feel-ings were, and might have put in a word for me. 'Don't be in too much of a hurry,' she said, and, by gad, I believe she's right. It's slowly as does it. I'm sorry I didn't get a chance of speaking to that girl of hers. She must have slipped away from us while we were talking."

She had been smuggled away, in fact, by Dr. Selby, who had been hovering near them, wonder-ing, impatiently, when Hackett would stop, and seeing no prospect of this, had bent over and asked her to dance. "If you won't be too critical," he said, "for I'm no good at this sort of exercise."

Catherine smiled. "And the young lady's rhythms are rather baffling. However, let's try. I've not danced since the war."

"That sounds wrong. You were made for dancing. In spite of the problems Miss Burton sets us. Why haven't you danced since the war? Surely not for lack of opportunity? People dance too much nowadays. I call it Tarantism."

"No. Lack of inclination. What is tarantism? It sounds horrid."

"It is. It's a pathological state of uncontrolled movement, resembling modern dancing, produced by the bite of a spider called a tarantula."

Catherine shuddered. "Oh, don't! I hate spiders . . . the ones with fat bodies. It sends a shiver down my spine just to mention them. Have you a long name for *that?*"

"An atavistic phobia. It's common—I have it myself—and quite incurable. Cats are another. But I love cats. Short-haired ones."

"I adore them, too. Particularly Siamese, with chicory-blue eyes. But they're cruel, aren't they?"

"All wild animals are. So are we. You look better, Miss Ombersley."

"Thank you, Dr. Selby. Is this a consultation?"

"No . . . a compliment. My bedside manner. Polite social small-talk. When I prescribed for you I made

I*

a mistake. If I'd known you then as well as I do now . . ."

"But you don't know me any better!"

"Ah, there you're quite wrong. I do. I was going to say I should have changed my prescription. I should have cut out certain imprudences and excesses in your spiritual diet . . ."

Catherine laughed: "What *are* you talking about?"

"Psychotherapy. The cure of malaise of the soul. I should have cut out Chopin and Schumann and Tschaikovski and Scriabin and, yes, I think, Wagner and Debussy—much as I love them—and insisted on heroic doses of Bach and Beethoven at least three times a day, and very occasionally Brahms. One prelude and fugue of the forty-eight after every meal, and a Beethoven *rondo* at bedtime. It's a pity you don't sing."

"It would be a tragedy if you heard me! But what is the meaning of all this? Of course, there is nothing the matter with me; but if there were, what has music to do with my . . . I suppose you'ld call it my 'case'?"

"Far more than you think. I should call it nothing of the sort. I treat people, not cases. But please let me finish my prescription."

"Very well."

"Then . . . a new piano."

"Oh, Dr. Selby, that's cruel. If you only knew!"

"I do know. Shall we say Blüthner?"

"That makes it worse. You see, we're so frightfully hard up that there's no earthly chance of my ever getting one."

"And I have one. . . . A pre-war *Flügel*, in perfect condition, because I tune it myself."

"A Blüthner grand in Chaddesbourne? That's quite incredible. You see, I had no idea you were interested in music."

"Nor had I that you were, until the other day when I heard you playing Bach."

"What was I playing?" she asked quickly, shrewdly.

"The Italian Concerto. Slow movement."

"So you really *do* know? That sounds dreadfully rude of me; but such heaps of people talk 'music' and know nothing about it, just as people talk 'books' when they've only read reviews. I expect you play marvellously."

"Appallingly. I've a surgeon's hand, not a pianist's." (Catherine looked at his hand. "A nice hand, a good hand," she thought.) "But let me go on. Ten minutes from the Hall—and three if you bicycle—there's a Blüthner piano standing alone and longing to be played on in an empty room—the owner goes out to work for his living—with nothing else in it but books and music. There's a Mrs. Hussingtree, too, who will be at your service. And I want you to use it—if you'd like to—whenever you feel inclined. That's the end of the prescription. What d'you think of it?"

"I think you're a very good doctor. But . . . but

don't you feel a piano—one's own piano—is a frightfully personal thing? Don't you think it might resent a stranger's intruding?"

"My Blüthner won't. It will love it. It knows about you already."

"I might leave something of myself behind. You never know."

"That's just what I'm hoping. . . . Will you?"

"Will I use the piano? Of course I will, Dr. Selby. How did you come to think of me?"

Selby thought: "My sweet child, how shall I ever think of anything else?"

Then the music stopped.

"I must tell Mother."

Catherine glowed as she spoke. It was a lovely illumination, Selby thought: like spring sunlight whitening the sprays of a wild cherry-tree in blow, yet warmer than that—say, rather, the radiance of still beech-woods in May when all their fans are fledged with translucent green. Catherine Ombersley bent over her mother and whispered ("And now," he thought, "she is a silver birch swayed by the wind"), and Helen Ombersley's face brightened, too, with a milder, later glow ("It's the same face," he thought, "but this is an autumn light and almost as lovely") as she raised her soft eyes and smiled at him gratefully, yet with a shadow of reserve—for, though she liked Selby personally and Catherine's happiness was nearer to her heart than most things, she couldn't help asking herself what dear Miles would think (being what he couldn't help being) of the proposal of this sudden young man who wasn't really so young—he must be twelve years older than Catherine—and about whom, apart from his skill and good nature, they knew nothing whatever.

"But this sounds too exciting, Dr. Selby," she said. "Won't you come and sit down? Catherine, darling" —she took Catherine's hand and stroked it—"you have quite a colour this evening. Tell me, please, Dr. Selby, who is that delicious, demure little creature in white on the other side? She's so pretty and shy, and that great big boy by her side is making such heavy weather."

"In white? Oh, that is my own little girl, Mary Lydgate. She's lovely, isn't she? This is her first appearance in Chaddesbourne, and I'm responsible for it."

"I congratulate you. She's the belle of the ball. Don't you think so?" (Catherine thought: "His own little girl. So that is the type he admires. She's little and dark. Of course, she *is* very pretty.") "It's such fun, sitting here and watching people's faces," Mrs. Ombersley went on. "The plain young woman who's playing, for instance, I'm beginning to feel sorry for her. She goes on pounding that poor piano and has none of the fun, and all the time she looks more and more tired and unhappy. She doesn't enjoy it a bit."

"Mother . . ." Catherine said suddenly. "Do you

think she'ld resent it if I went over and offered to play for her?"

"Of course not, darling. Do."

Dr. Selby's face fell. He had looked forward to at least one more dance with Catherine, and feared that, if once he lost her, that hope would vanish. Yet, as though she knew that some compensation was due to him, Catherine turned and smiled as she left them to join Miss Burton at the piano. She touched Miss Burton's shoulder, and Miss Burton jumped; for a moment she thought that it might be Morgan Jones.

"I think they've been working you much too hard," Catherine said. "Won't you let me take your place for a little while, and go and enjoy yourself?"

Miss Burton smiled wanly. "Oh, I'm not a bit tired, really, Miss Ombersley, though it *is* rather hot, and I'm always subject to nervous headaches." ("Enjoy myself!" she was thinking. "*Enjoy myself!* If only she knew!") "And the next one I promised Mr. Hadley to play is the 'Lancers.'"

"Well, let me play that."

"I'm afraid it's not very easy to read at sight, with the repeats and all that."

"I might have a try, anyway, mightn't I?" Catherine said. "Let me look at the music." (Miss Burton sighed and surrendered it.) "Oh, I think I could manage this all right, and if I can't, it won't be your fault."

She sat down at the piano. Miss Burton stood by nervously. "Now that he sees I'm free," she thought, "will he ask me to dance?"

"Take your partners for the 'Lancers,' ladies and gentlemen," Ted Hadley was calling. Miss Burton saw Morgan Jones. He was looking beyond her. She knew where, instinctively. He was looking at Elsie Cookson. He walked past her without turning his eyes. She noticed he was limping. She felt rather faint. "If I went to the buffet for a glass of lemonade," she thought, "I could turn my back on them without anyone noticing."

"Take your partners for the 'Lancers.' Now hurry up, ladies and gentlemen!" Ted Hadley bawled. "Come along, you young people, come along! Don't be shy!"

"I'm afraid I can't manage this one, Miss Lydgate," Jim Cookson said.

"Oh, let's try it. I've forgotten the figures, too. All you have to do is to follow someone who does know it."

"Well, if I get mixed up . . ."

"I think it's the limit, don't you, Mr. Jones, putting on an old-fashioned dance of this kind when they might have a fox-trot."

"Oh, it's still very popular in Wales, Miss Cookson. I'll promise to pull you through."

(Miss Burton thought: "Ah, she doesn't want to dance with him! Perhaps!")

"Now, come along, Glad, we'll show these kids how to do it!"

"O.K., Ted. Miss Burton, d'you mind looking after my buffet?"

"Not at all, Mrs. Hadley. Don't give it another thought."

"Oh, thank you so much, Miss Burton. It's a shame you're not dancing yourself."

"Well, I've rather a headache, to tell you the truth. It's the heat."

"You wait till you're as stout as I am, my dear. Then you'll know what heat is!"

"Thirteen . . . fourteen . . . fifteen . . . Mr. Winter, we're only one couple short! Won't you make up the number? Last dance of the programme!"

"Ought clergymen to dance?" Mr. Winter thought. "That sounds like a newspaper headline." He looked appealingly at Helen Ombersley, who smiled and shook her head. The "Lancers," he thought, is not an intimate dance. Surely no breath of scandal could attach itself to the vicar and the postmistress. "Mrs. Webb, may I have the pleasure?" Mrs. Webb beamed.

"I can't have it said I refused the vicar, can I?" she said.

They stepped forward. "Bravo, Vicar!" Mr. Hadley cried loudly. He clapped his hands. The whole schoolroom was laughing and clapping.

"Goodness gracious, I feel just as if I were being married all over again," Mrs. Webb declared.

"All serene! I thank you, Miss Ombersley. Music, please!"

They were off in a ragged start, while Ted Hadley's drill-sergeant's voice thundered out directions: "Make your bow . . . Set to corners . . . Now then: ladies to the centre! . . . Next the visiting figure . . . No, that's wrong, Jim: the other way round . . . Go and visit your sister first . . . It's like driving sheep . . . That's better: I believe the vicar knows more about it than anybody!"

"How I wish I could read music at sight like that!" Miss Burton thought. "Why, she makes the piano sound quite different from when I play it. The Cookson girl doesn't look as if she's enjoying herself, and I don't believe *he* is. I wish I could hear what he's saying!"

He was saying: "May I look in at The Moat some evening next week after school?"—and then, because Elsie didn't answer him at once and he feared a rebuff: "I should like to see the house. I've heard such a lot about it."

Elsie laughed her brittle little laugh. "I'm sure Mother 'ld be charmed to show it you. People come there in shoals. She's almost as good as a guide-book."

"And you?"

"Oh, I'm no good at that musty old stuff. I hate everything old."

"I meant: shall I see you?"

"See *me*? What d'you want to see me for? I'm out

most of the time. You see, my friends run over from North Bromwich and take me for rides. I love motor-biking, don't you?"

Should he say that he hated and despised it? There was no time to say anything.

"Last figure of all!" Mr. Hadley cried. "Now this one's great fun!"

Jim whispered: "I do wish your grandad could have a look at those bullocks of mine, Miss Lydgate. You might mention you've seen them. I've always been told he's a wonderful eye for a beast. And I wish you could meet **my** mother some day. I feel sure you'ld like her."

"I shan't have one **moment** to spare when my cousin arrives."

"When is he coming?"

"Oh, any day now. To-morrow perhaps."

"That's just like my darned luck!"

"Grand chain!" Mr. Hadley shouted.

Grand chain . . . A swift, rhythmical weft of hurrying figures; alternate clasping and unclasping of hot hands that met, some casually and others eagerly, and then swept on. Mr. Winter, Mary Lydgate, Jim Cookson, Morgan Jones, Gladys Hadley, Elsie Cookson, Ted Hadley, Mrs. Webb, weaving round and round, the files twisting in opposite movement, till the music momentarily released them—and then, once more, *Grand Chain*. . . .

Miss Loach, sitting up in bed with her night-light

burning in a glass cup, heard the stamping, the laughter, the jolly surge of the music. She looked at her father's gold watch. It was nearly midnight, and still they kept her awake. They were clapping their hands and cheering now in the most unseemly fashion. Such an orgy had never been heard in the street of Chaddesbourne before. "Mr. Winter," she thought, "shall be made to suffer for this. To-morrow without fail I shall write to the bishop about it. Making the school—the Church School!—almost as great a nuisance as the 'Ombersley Arms.'" And now, it seemed, they were singing *God Save the Queen* at the top of their voices without any restraint or reverence. In her dear father's time every meeting of that kind had closed with a prayer. "No good will come out of this," Miss Loach thought.

They were pouring into the street. Mr. Winter politely attached himself to Mrs. Ombersley, while Selby, scheming, had possessed himself of Catherine's coat—a long, silk-lined coat of black faced-cloth with a silver-fox collar. "Such a wisp of a thing!" he thought as it hung on his arm.

"You must put this on," he said. "I don't want you laid up with a cold."

"But the air is like milk," she said, "and I'm burning."

"All the more reason."

She submitted gently. It seemed beautiful of her to submit.

"It was good of you to play for her," he said.

"I loved playing. They seemed to be having such fun. But Miss Burton didn't dance after all. I'm afraid nobody asked her. What a shame! There's your little protégée looking at you quite wistfully. I believe you've neglected her."

"Yes, I mustn't. Excuse me a moment." He took Jim Cookson by the arm. "Look here, Jim," he said. "I shall have to go back to my patient. When you've dropped your sister at The Moat, will you mind taking Mary Lydgate home to Uffley?"

Would Jim mind! He was so excited that he could hardly speak.

Helen Ombersley held out her pale hand to Selby, saying good-bye as though the party had been hers. "I'm so glad you were able to come."

"If you're walking," he said, "and if I may, I'll come with you. I've a patient I promised to see at your end of the village."

"But that will be lovely, won't it, Catherine, darling?"

They walked down the street, the lights and the hubbub fading behind them. They walked slowly; Catherine had slipped her arm through her mother's; and the sight of those two girlish figures, so near to each other in grace and refinement, so frail, so tranquil, struck Selby as an experience of unusual beauty, a new aspect of life in which he wished he could share, but knew he couldn't. They walked quietly; their light

steps scarcely seemed to impress the dust—almost as
quietly as the moon shadows (it rose late) which
moved before them. A tingling silence seemed to
possess the mild sky lapped in milk of moonlight; the
trusses of apple-blow hung rigid and pale as ivory;
and he thought—he couldn't tell why—of a little
song of Max Reger called *Maiennacht*, with a languid,
drooping melody and almost childish words:

> *Helle strahlt der Mond hernieder in bezaubernd*
> *stiller Pracht, und die Knospe ward zur Rose in der*
> *lauen Maiennacht.*

Helen Ombersley spoke: "In such a night," she said,
"I feel as if all my rose-buds must long to break."
She sighed. "You only find nights like this in England
and in May. I think summer must have been born to-
night, don't you?"

Selby was silent. It seemed to him that her words
should die on the quietude they had scarcely disturbed.
Through the ragged hedge on their right he saw a
candle's glimmer in the window of Aaron Bunt's
cottage.

"This is my patient's cottage," he said. "I must
leave you here."

But he stood at the gate and watched till he could
see them no longer before he clicked the latch.

Inside they had been listening. At the sound of the
latch a shadow crossed the window; the door was

scraped open and a figure advanced towards him.

"Well, Mrs. Bunt?"

"It's all over, Doctor. 'Er be gone. Thanks be, us 'ad 'er christened before 'er took ill!"

"And how's Nellie?"

"Our Nellie? Her's like a dog with a bone. Her's that spiteful you can't get near her. Best let her be, I say."

"Very well. Send Bunt up to the surgery in the morning for a certificate. Good night."

He walked homeward. It was a very different journey. As he went he was oddly haunted by Mrs. Bunt's words: "Thanks be, us 'ad 'er christened before 'er took ill." What strange remnant of ancient magic clung to this Christian sacrament in that Pagan mind? Did Mrs. Bunt believe in its virtue? Was this child she had killed (for it came to that) made immortal for her by baptism, as it was, doubtless, for Arthur Winter? And he thought—his mind was full of music that evening—of Elgar's *Gerontius* and the priest's solemn words of committal:

Proficiscere anima Christiana de hoc mundo!
Go, in the name of God the Omnipotent Father
    who created thee!
Go, in the name of Jesus Christ our Lord, Son of
    the living God, who bled for thee!
Go, in the name of the Holy Spirit Who hath been
    poured out on thee!

Go, in the name of Angels and Archangels; in the
name of Thrones and Dominations; in the
name of Princedoms and Powers!

"Princedoms and Powers," he thought. "But this
is Nellie Bunt's baby. And nobody cares for its going
but God Almighty and Nellie Bunt . . ." He sighed.
"I wonder," he thought, "if that child enjoyed herself and is safe home at Uffley yet."

The centre of the village, about the cross-roads, lay
deserted and silent before him, for everyone but himself had gone home to bed. Only two lights were
visible, the faint glimmer of Miss Loach's swimming
night-light and the pallid flicker of a candle-flame in
the bedroom over the post-office where Morgan
Jones, prowling to and fro in his shirt-sleeves, was
engaged in writing a poem to Elsie Cookson. He had
made one false start already, which began:

> *Child, by what chance did you and spring together*
> *Ravish my heart so utterly to-night?*
> *Your April beauty and this wild, sweet weather*
> *That woos the nightingale . . .*

But there it had stuck, and, since he must write or die,
he had plunged, as rashly, into a more sombre mood:

> *When, in grey time, you shall count over*
> *Names of this, that, and the other lover;*

Names of dead men whose eyes shone
For lust of a loveliness that's gone;
Amid your triumphs and your shames
One name, above all other names,
You shall remember. . . .

The name which she would remember was, of
course, Morgan Jones, which, in spite of the incandescent spirit it represented and its rich capacity for
rhyme, lacked poetical quality. Against his will all the
words that rhymed with Jones began to haunt him, to
jeer at him; so he crumpled the second piece of paper
and threw it after the first in the empty grate.

"I wonder what she is thinking of me now?" he
asked himself.

Elsie Cookson, in fact, was not thinking of him at
all. She was yawning in the back of the Ford which
jolted her over the ruts on its way to The Moat, and
reflecting that it had hardly been worth while putting
on her rose-coloured taffeta for such a dull affair,
particularly when she remembered how plainly
Catherine Ombersley and her mother had been
dressed. How comically rustic these Chaddesbourne
people were with their 'Lancers!' 'Lancers!' They'ld
be reviving quadrilles and mazurkas next!

Mary Lydgate sitting beside her, was still wide
awake and excited; the mere fact of riding in a car was
sufficiently unusual to be thrilling. When they halted
at The Moat and Elsie got out, Jim asked her to join

him in front. "You'll find it much less shaky here than behind, Miss Lydgate," he said. They drove on, through the moonlight, but Jim was too timid to speak another word till they came to the field where his bullocks were grazing.

"There they are!" he said proudly.

"They look as if they were feeding on moonlight," she said. "Is it mist?"

"No, that isn't mist nor moonlight," he told her; "that's cuckoo-flowers, or ladies'-smocks, as some call them. They grow thick in this piece because there's water underneath. It never goes dry, this field. If it was daylight you'ld see the king-cups, too, though they're nearly over. It's a regular garden here. Do you mind if I stop just a moment?"

He switched off the rattling engine without waiting for an answer, and she felt a little anxious, wondering what he was going to do next. But he didn't do anything. He merely told her to listen.

"I can't hear anything," she said, "except that fox barking."

"Oh, I don't mean that. I heard what I want you to hear just before we stopped. He'll start again in a moment. In that blackthorn-bush over there. Ssh . . . There he is!"

Sweet, piercingly sweet, intolerably sweet, the song of the nightingale held them meshed in its music.

"Isn't he fine? There's nothing to touch him," Jim whispered. "I often come here on a moony night to hear him. They nest here every year."

"I don't think I ever heard one before," Mary told him. "He sings better than a blackbird, doesn't he?" But she thought: "Are we going to spend the whole night here just listening to a bird? What a queer boy he is!"

"Well, I suppose we had better go on," Jim sighed.

He got out to re-start the engine as the nightingale stopped, but before he cranked it the ears of both caught another sound, a crunch of boots on the road's rough gravel.

"Who is it? Who's coming?" Mary asked quickly.

"I can't see; but I don't mind betting it's that scoundrel Bunt. He'll have taken the chance of Joe Roberts being at the dance to put in a few hours' poaching, though if it is him he'll do a bolt as soon as he sees us."

Yet the rhythmical tread grew nearer, and suddenly, from behind the blackthorn-bush where the nightingale had been singing, a man's figure stepped into the moonlight. He was tall, with a handsome, moon-pale face, and he carried a suit-case. When he saw the car he stopped dead.

"Hello," he said. "I was right. I thought I heard voices. I've lost my way. Can you tell me where this road leads to?"

"We've come from Chaddesbourne, and we're going to Uffley Mill," Jim told him.

"Uffley Mill? Then I'm walking away from it.

This is a bit of good luck! I was trying to get there myself, and now you can give me a lift. Lord, I'm tired! I'm not used to walking. Can I get in behind?"

"What do you want at Uffley at this hour of night?" Jim asked.

"Only a bed, my son, nothing else. You needn't stare at me. It's all right. My name's Steve Lydgate."

He hove his suit-case into the car with a bump, then jumped in after it and slammed-to the door.

"Righto, son!" he said. "Carry on!"

Jim obeyed, and the car leapt forward. He felt thwarted and angry. This stranger, who had spoilt the last part of his drive with Mary and prevented him from saying or attempting to say the bold words which he was keeping till the last, appeared to treat him with as little respect as if he were a taxi-driver. He resented, too, the easy familiarity with which, now, Steve Lydgate leaned forward, laying his hand on Mary's shoulder—he himself would never have dared to touch her like that—and said: "Who the dickens are you, I should like to know?"

"I'm Mary," she told him. "Your cousin." Her voice sounded brighter, her tone more eager, Jim thought, than when she had spoken to him.

"But what are you doing out at this time of night?"

"We've been to a dance in the village. This is Mr. Cookson."

Steve laughed. "A particular friend of yours, eh? It's a case of 'Two's company and three's none?' Looks as if I've not half put my foot in it. I don't want to spoil sport. Look here, Mr. Cookson, if you like I'll get out."

Jim mumbled. "You stay where you are. It's all right. Glad to give you the lift."

"It was lucky we met you, Steve," Mary said. "If you'd let us know when to expect you . . ."

"Well, I couldn't, and that's the truth. The crew only got paid off in the middle of the afternoon. I thought: 'What the devil's the use of hanging about in Cardiff?' If you knew Bute Street as well as I do you'ld know what I mean. So I made a dash for the station; changed four times—Newport, Hereford, Worcester and Stourton Junction—and here I am! Dead to the world! Is it very much further? I've only been once to Uffley, and that's donkey's years ago when I was a kid."

"No, we're nearly there," Mary told him. "That's the house, just in front of us."

"I should never have known it. Looks pretty in moonlight, doesn't it?"

The mill rose before them, pallid against the dark wood, more like a house in a dream than ponderable brick and timber. Jim put on the brakes and stalled his engine, and immediately the silence was full of the sound of water. He got out miserably to give Mary a hand, but her cousin reached her before him. Mary thanked him in a pretty flutter. "She's more excited now," Jim thought, "than she's been all the evening!"

And Steve Lydgate didn't take her hand, as he would have done: he caught her in his arms and lifted her bodily down. "Why, you're light as a little feather, Mary!" he said.

Jim stood staring at them. It looked, for a moment, as if she wasn't even going to thank him. He was also aware, for the first time, of Steve Lydgate's face, and saw he was a handsome, big-featured man, with much of Eli Lydgate's distinction, but little of his grimness; it was a frank, bold, masterful face, accustomed to command, yet now, when he smiled, gay, happy-go-lucky, charming, perhaps even generous; and his figure, though rather less tall than Jim's, had something of the face's quality, being supple, though sturdy and easy in all its movements, despite its strength. It was he, in fact, who first turned and held out his hand.

"Thank you, Cookson," he said. "I expect we shall meet again."

"I expect so," Jim said. "Are you staying here long, Mr. Lydgate?"

Steve Lydgate laughed. "That's an awkward question! Am I staying here long, Mary?"

"I hope so, Steve. Thank you so much for bringing me home, Mr. Cookson."

"Oh, that's nothing. I suppose I'd better be going now," Jim said. He re-started the car and reversed it; but when he looked back and lifted his cap the two cousins had turned their backs on him.

"This is great sport, isn't it, Mary?" Steve said. "Far better fun than arriving in the middle of the day. Who's the dumb young man?"

"A neighbour. Mr. Cookson's son, from The Moat. He's a farmer."

"He looks like one. Pretty heavy on the hand, I should say."

"He's quite nice, though he's awfully quiet. Do mind your head, please, Steve. There are steps up and down everywhere."

"Don't worry about that. I can see your white frock going up and down, too, in front. Here, don't run away from me!" Once more he laid his hand on her shoulder; he liked the silk's softness and the shoulder's fragility; he was an amateur of shoulders. "*Now* where are you off to?"

"I'm going to find some matches to light a candle."

"Matches? Why not ask me? Here you are!"

He struck one. A quick spurt of flame illumined the kitchen. From his childhood he just remembered the great oak beams and the yawning hearth. Mary took the match from him hurriedly, it burned so quickly, and their fingers touched. "A small, soft hand," he thought; "Japanese women have small, soft hands."

"Oh! I thought it would burn my fingers!" she cried. But she had managed to light one candle and from that lit another. She stood there with a candle in either hand, her face evenly illuminated.

"You're a pretty, bright-eyed thing," he thought

"I've seen girls like you before. Where? Malaga. . . .
Yes, that's it: Malaga in Andalusia, where we took on
the bitter oranges. But Spanish girls are damned difficult. What good luck I brought the mantilla and the
tortoise-shell comb. They'll suit her fine." He smiled;
and Mary Lydgate smiled, too. It was all, as he said,
such sport—this romantic arrival, and they two alone
like this in the sleeping house!

"You look like a picture standing there," he said,
"with a candlestick in each hand. If you move your
hands you'll spill tallow on your pretty white frock.
So be careful: I might want to kiss you. It's quite right
for cousins to kiss, don't you think so, Mary?"

"I don't know . . . I suppose so," she said.

"Suppose!" He laughed. "Well, I'm going to,
anyway."

He bent forward with deliberation and kissed her
on the lips. It was not the formal kiss she expected.
Indeed, it was quite unlike any kiss she had previously
known, though it was what she had imagined the kisses
of a lover might be. It was the kiss of a man experienced in the refinements of the game (as he counted
it), astonishingly gentle, and yet so determined that,
withdrawing from it in astonishment (and even in
alarm), she felt breathless and weak and light-
headed.

"What's the matter with you, Mary?" he said.
"You're not shy or frightened of me?"

She was a little of both, but denied it.

"You made me giddy," she said, "and I couldn't breathe."

He laughed softly. "One would think you'd never been kissed before."

"I never have . . . not that way."

"You've a lot to learn, child."

"And I did spill candle-grease on the floor. Look, two great blobs of it!"

"No use crying over spilt tallow! What happens next?"

"I'll show you your room. I put everything ready. It's very late. Unless you want something to eat . . ."

"I'm more tired than hungry. I've been up since five this morning—or, rather, yesterday." He yawned luxuriously, opening his mouth wide like some great animal; he had excellent teeth.

"Then here's your candle."

He took it and followed her. She stepped lightly up the old stairs which complained of his following weight; the oak door, too, creaked on its hinges as she opened it and showed him into the room she had prepared for him—a low-ceiled chamber, with an open casement and white lace curtains, smelling faintly of lavendered sheets, of apples stored in the room next door, and of the lilac Mary had set in a jug to welcome him. There was a massive mahogany bed with a tester and looped curtains of rep. The sheets were turned down, and the coverlet bulged in the middle where she had put a baked brick wrapped in flannel to warm the bed. It was a virginal room which breathed an air of sweet-smelling innocence; through the window a shaft of moonshine outshone their faint candlelight and blanched the stiff lilac-plumes. Cool, limpid as moonlight, too, was the watery sound of the brook.

"I shall sleep well to-night, with that sound of water," Steve Lydgate said. "It's almost like being at sea."

"We're so used to it here, we don't notice it."

"That's what I mean. Good night, Cousin Mary!"

"Will he kiss me again?" she wondered. Half hoping he would and half dreading it, she stood waiting for a moment; but his "good night," it appeared, was final; he had already turned to undo the clasps of his suitcase and was whistling softly to himself; so she closed the door softly and left him, stealing quietly along the passage to her own room, where she sat on the bed too excited to undress, her mind still possessed and confused by the events and emotions of this astonishing day.

They swept her mind like a gusty wind, haphazard, churning up sensations one after another like scurrying leaves: her distress, that morning, when she found her white stockings were missing; the shock when, instead of the doctor's car, she saw Jim Cookson's; Elsie's rose-coloured taffeta, the vicar's silk waistcoat; Jim's flushed face, his clumsy feet and his equally clumsy compliments; Morgan Jones's damp hand clasping hers in the passing contact of the Grand

K

Chain; Catherine Ombersley smiling at Selby; the
moon-drenched meadows of cuckoo-flowers; the
nightingale's song. . . . Yet, amid these vagaries
of memory, standing out again and again with the stark
actuality of an oak that looms through thinnings of
mist, the figure of her cousin dominated her thoughts,
his reality reducing the rest to the consistency of mere
shadow. That figure had not the shape she had antici-
pated. Its form was as unexpected as his dramatic
coming. He was neither gentle nor kindly, in the way
that Jim Cookson was kindly: he had not even noticed
the pains she had spent in preparing his room nor the
flowers she had picked to greet him. He was sudden
and ruthless; she could believe he would be cruel. Yet
even here, separated from him by closed doors and
walls, she was excited and aware of his presence to a
degree in which she had never been conscious of anyone
before, not merely as a memory, but as of an overwhelming imminence of flesh and blood. Long after
she had undressed and slipped into bed, lying there
wide-eyed and listening to the owls' wild, quivering
halloos, that consciousness kept her awake.

"I wish he hadn't kissed me like that," she thought.
"It was wrong."

But her heart was glad Steve had kissed her.

When the church clock struck midnight, Aaron
Bunt was skirting Foxhall Wood. Like some creature
that dreads light—even moonshine—he hugged the

shadow of the hedgerow, stooping low, from sheer habit of caution, and sniffing the air like a dog as he went. From time to time he paused to examine those spots in the tunnelled banks where Jim Roberts set his snares. There were not many rabbits caught in the snares that night; the moon shone so clear that it threw a shadow of each noose, and of those that were snared some few had been savaged by foxes. These he left, contenting himself with two that were still alive till he killed them by breaking their necks and slipped them into the skirt-pockets of his coat, where, although they were dead, their hind limbs continued to twitch.

As the clock chimed the quarter he found himself close to Jim Roberts's cottage. There was no light in the windows, so he guessed that the keeper had not yet returned from the dance. He crept close to the back of the house, so softly that no dog heard him. He saw pheasant-coops in rows and a rickety fowl-house with a run of wire-netting round it, and, perceiving this, a mischievous imp in his brain reminded him how, not long ago, Jim Roberts and the policeman had made fun of him, and told him that this was the chance to get his own back. So now, since the dog had not smelt or heard him, he slipped into the pen and crept to the fowl-house. The door had no padlock; a stick held the hasp to the staple. Aaron opened the door and inserted his hand round the corner where the plump, drowsy birds roosted on their perches in rows. His fingers moved cunningly, following a shape,

scarcely touching; then fastened like claws of steel
on a feathered neck and withdrew the fluttering bird
silently. Another sharp twist, and it was dead. . . .

But now a dog barked. He had no time to waste.
When a man leaves his fowl-house door unhasped a
fox, sniffing round, finds some way of scratching it
open. And hungry foxes leave blood on the ground.
Aaron plucked out a handful of feathers and scattered them; then he let blood run from the neck of
the bird and trailed it over the grass. He would have
liked to kill that dog, too—the beast wouldn't stop
barking—and other dogs in the distance (the night
was so still) took up the alarm. If he didn't make
tracks pretty soon, Jim Roberts, coming home from
the dance, would hurry up and surprise him. He slunk
off—not towards the village, but back, by the way he
had come, round Foxhall Wood. The dead fowl, in
the opposite pocket, balanced the two rabbits. He
broke into a loping stride and chuckled as he went.
He was pleased with himself, for he had wiped Jim
Roberts's eye, and the fowl would make a strong broth
for Nellie's sick baby.

XII

MORNING POST

THE birth of these various frail hopes, exaltations, enchantments, each of which appeared to its victim more momentous than the unquiet destinies of Europe, had no more effect on the steady current of life in Chaddesbourne than had those hatches of gauzy insects, duns and spinners, upon the slides of the Brook over which, gilded by slanting sun, they shimmered and whirled and dipped in their iridescent death-dance. Chaddesbourne works for its living six days of the week and some part of the seventh; and mere accidents, such as somebody's falling in love or out of it, are no more than an embroidery to the weft of its workaday tissue, amusing—or even startling— but unessential.

Thus, the morrow of the dance, a mizzling day (as they call it) with veils of grey moisture drooping from the hills, saw the stream of leisurely activity flowing in its usual channels. At his desk it found Morgan Jones, no longer a Byronic hero ablaze with verses, but a pallid, stunted young man in need of a hair-cut, expounding the rule of three to rows of inky schoolboys: at hers it discovered Miss Burton, her features flattened and subdued, as if something heavy had rolled over them (as, indeed, something had), yet full of that morning briskness, that air of having been thoroughly and recently scrubbed with a soapy flannel on which she prided herself, imparting "expression" to her girls' recitation of Wordsworth's *Daffodils*.

From the smithy, where Jim Cookson had led in two heavy horses to be shod, there issued, between pauses filled by commands to "Come over" and stampings, the gay, syncopated tinkle of hammer on anvil and the pungent reek of seared hoofs; from the wheelwright's next door could be heard the screech of a plane: Mr. Bagley was "knocking up" a parish "box" for the burial of Nellie Bunt's baby; from the scullery of the "Ombersley Arms" came a clatter of female tongues and crockery: Mrs. Hadley, blithe as a morning lark, with her hair in curling-pins, was helping to wash up the glass and china that had been used to furnish her buffet. Upstairs Mr. Hadley still slept.

On the opposite side of the road, an unusual number of "panel patients" straggled towards Selby's surgery; for each Friday morning the papers on which their sick-pay for the week depended had to be signed. Among these Mrs. Bunt hurried up, with a black gipsy hat on her head. She felt extremely important, as she always did when she came for a death-certificate; yet, as she passed Miss Loach's door, she looked nervously upward—for Miss Loach was the one person in the parish (beside the policeman) of whom she was afraid—only to see that Miss Loach's bedroom blinds were still lowered behind the sealed windows, as a mute protest against the dance which had spoilt her first sleep. Miss Loach hoped that Mr. Winter would be up early enough to observe this acid commentary on his lack of consideration, and that his conscience, if he had any conscience left, would trouble him; but Mr. Winter, retiring so much later than usual, had overslept, and at that moment, having breakfasted heartily, was lighting a pipe and wondering what had happened to his morning paper.

Fifty yards away from him, at the back of the post-office, his partner of last night, Mrs. Webb, and Sam Homer, the postman, were sorting the mail which had only just come in, having been delayed by smoke-laden fog on the Black-Country side of Stourton. Mrs. Webb was flustered that morning—not only because she wasn't used to late hours and still felt sleepy, but also because she had just emerged from a sharp passage of arms with Mr. Hackett's butler, West, who had rung up twice wanting to know what had happened to the morning letters. Mr. Hackett, he said, was going to write to the Postmaster-General and complain.

"Well, let 'em all complain and stop talking about it!" said Mrs. Webb, confiding her grievance to the postman. Was that the way, she asked, for a gentleman in good service to speak—even over the telephone —to a respectable woman who had kept a post-office since before he was born, she and her poor Henry be-

fore her, without a single complaint that she'd ever
heard on? It was time, she said, for Mr. Hackett's
butler to learn that Chaddesbourne was Chaddesbourne, not London—or wnerever he came from—
and that the people in Chaddesbourne post-office were
expected to take their turn, like they'd always done,
without looking snortified and clearing their throats
and rapping on the counter with their money if a
woman happened to be serving a penn'orth of bull's-
eyes or enquiring after a neighbour's health or gone
to the back to make herself a nice cup of tea! Who
was Mr. Hackett's butler, anyway? Mrs. Webb demanded. Butler, indeed! When he'd been a butler
as long as Mr. Langley at the Hall, thirty years with
one family, it would be time enough for him to start
badgering a woman by telephone.

"But he won't last that long, Sam, nor yet a quarter
of it," said Mrs. Webb grimly. "A young man who
sends off postal orders four or five times a week and
asks a woman to be sure she puts the right time on the
office-stamp, is a betting and horse-racing young man,
you take my word for it, and no good ever came of
betting and horse-racing. Now where are we, Sam?"

"I think them's the lot, Mrs. Webb."

"Well, seeing as it's a bit late, Sam, and the colonel
will be waiting for his paper, I reckon you'd better slip
down to the Hall before you start on your round, like.
Oh . . . but wait a minute. You mind that there
letter for the doctor what I noticed was posted in

Wychbury? Behappen it's a message; so you might just pop it into the surgery as you go out. Then there's that other one for Miss Loach, from her sister in Bournemouth. She gets one from her, regular, every Friday morning, and I know the poor soul looks forward to it, so you might pop that one in, too. And just ask Jane Trost how the old lady's feeling this morning: say I've noticed her blinds are still down. Then, when you've finished at the Hall, Sam, (and you might drop Mr. Langley a word about this butler at Hackett's: not the horse-racing, mind—that's official —only the telephoning), when you've finished there, as I was saying, I should cut across over the hill with that bundle for The Moat, even though they are mostly bills. And don't forget to ask after Mr. Cookson's lumbago. You can leave Hackett's lot till the last. That'll learn 'em to complain! And if that naggy young fellow gives you a misword, Sam, you keep your mouth shut: just you tell him to come and see *me!*"

Sam Homer winked and shouldered his post-bag. "All right, Mrs. Webb." The bell on the shop door pinged feebly behind him as he stepped out into the street. What a kindly air! The soft, summer drizzle enveloped everything: it was so dense that he could not see the time by the church clock, and the tufted tops of the elms were lost in it, too. Yet, if sight was baulked, all immediate sound seemed to gain from this damping of its vibrations a curious intensity; so that, when he walked, he heard the scrape of his own hob-

K*

nailed boots on the road, the babble aloft of talkative rooks; the anvil's tinkle; the soft screech of the wheel-wright's plane; he was even aware of the bleat of Miss Burton's lambs, reciting their poem about the Ulls-water daffodils. All scents, too, lay low and com-pressed—not merely such obvious smells as that of hartshorn from the forge or of new bread from the bakehouse, but earth's subtler essences. The very dust, felted by moisture, smelt of early summer, releasing its proper odour which rose and met in mid-air the mingled sweetnesses of invisible meadows and woods and hedgerows, exhaled slowly, luxuriously, like a sigh of content, beneath the caress of fine rain which, though warmer than dew, settled almost as softly on uncurling fronds and leaves or spent blossom.

"Growing weather," Sam Homer thought as he trudged along. His mind was on the sweet-peas he had sown before Christmas and nursed in a box in the brew-house to bring them forward. A postman didn't pick up much pay, but he did get time for his garden, and everyone who came near Sam Homer's stopped and passed a remark on the show of blooms in the borders and the whiff of his hedge of sweet-peas blow-ing over the road. "This mizzling weather," he re-flected, "'ll bring them on champion." And his heart was glad, for his prime ambition in life was to win a first prize for sweet-peas at Wychbury flower-show and have the card framed and put on the mantel-piece. . . .

"Growing weather," Helen Ombersley thought as she sat at her housekeeping desk in the Adam library and stared out of the window. "Lovely weather! It's only the unfortunate people who live in towns who can't enjoy this soft rain. As soon as the letters come in, I shall go out into the garden without a hat. I want to feel this soft rain on my face, so cool and so kind. Later on, when the sun comes through, one can almost feel things growing. Even from here you can see the slender stalks of the pinks, so slim and alert, and the iris spears and the crimson buds of the pæonies, all straining upward on tiptoe to catch every spot of it! But I won't go out," she thought, "until the letters have come; because this morning there'll almost certainly be one from Jack. It's naughty of him not to write more regularly, though I suppose all children are thoughtless, especially boys. Dear Catherine is much more considerate by nature, of course. And how well the dear child looked this morning, in spite of being out late! That tiresome dance must actually have done her good; which only shows that she ought to go out a lot more than she does, because it's bad for young people, particularly girls, to be thrown in on themselves. What a blessing it is that she has the outlet of her music! When they talked about music last night, she and that nice young man, Dr. Selby, it made her look quite different, and quite lovely, although I say it."

Mrs. Ombersley's brows contracted ever so slightly;

for, thinking of Selby, whom she liked, she remembered his invitation. Was it quite proper, she wondered, for a young girl to visit the house of a bachelor and play his piano—even when he wasn't at home? "When I was Catherine's age," she thought, "it would certainly have been regarded as rather odd. I'm sure, if I'd suggested such a thing, Mamma would never have allowed it; though, of course, in these days people are much nicer-minded and more sensible than they used to be. In London, nobody would notice a thing like that now; but in Chaddesbourne. . . . I wonder. Small villages like this are so gossipy, and people like us *have* to set an example. I don't think she ought to go there, poor darling," Helen Ombersley thought, "unless Miles approves. . . ."

And, of course, she knew perfectly well Miles wouldn't approve. Quite apart from his rigid insistence on canons of behaviour, that necessity for "setting an example" which played so large a part in his life, Miles was much more class-conscious—to put it brutally, more snobbish—than she or any of her family. The D'Abitots, in spite of their more exalted station—or, perhaps, because of it—had always been much more ready than the Ombersleys to accept people outside their own class for what they were. Even on the village cricket-field where, in theory, all men were temporarily equal, Miles was apt, while insisting on the community of sport, to show himself conscious of fine shades of social distinction, all as strictly arranged in his mind as grades of military rank. In these tables, for instance, Mr. Pomfret, the Rector of Wychbury, took precedence over Mr. Winter—not because he was an older man or a Rural Dean, but simply because he happened to be born a Pomfret and belonged to the county (it was the difference between a commission in a line regiment and one in the Guards); while Dr. Selby, as a member of a learned profession definitely lower than the church (if narrowly superior to the law) could never, however striking his attainments or acceptable his manners, take higher rank than that of a warrant-officer, or, at the best, that of an officer risen from the ranks or holding a "temporary" commission.

More than this: Helen Ombersley had lately been conscious of a veiled irritability in her husband's allusions to Selby—as though, under the stress of his general embarrassments (of which she was increasingly aware, though he hid them from her), these die-hard prejudices of his were getting slightly the better of his reason and his existent, though oddly limited, sense of humour. She had regretted it, and hoped that this attitude towards Selby would be transient, for Miles had never found it easy to make friends outside the small group, shrunken by the war, he had acquired in his youth at Sandhurst; and since not one of these lived within easy reach of Chaddesbourne, Dr. Selby, who had served in the war and understood soldiers, offered the most likely substitute. She regretted it even more that morning for Catherine's sake. It was months and months since she had seen the child glow as she glowed last night. "But if I have to choose between her feelings and Miles's," she thought; "of course Miles must come first; and if I didn't confide in him about it, he might feel hurt. . . . I suppose I ought really to tell him about Mr. Hackett as well. And then the fat *will* be in the fire!"

Helen Ombersley sighed; for the intrusion of the idea of Miles (whom she loved) into the stream of her consciousness had flawed its serene flow with an undercurrent of vague disquietude.

"Where is he?" she thought, "and what is he doing? I had better see if he wants me."

Colonel Ombersley, discovered in his "office" lighting his pipe, declared brusquely that he wanted nothing but his *Morning Post*. The reading of this paper, like most other processes in his precisely-ordered life, had become part of a daily (and perhaps a symbolical) ritual. Births, marriages and deaths, which he read as he stood, constituted an *hors-d'œuvre;* with his porridge, he absorbed first cricket, then polo, then racing; passing thence, by way of the *London Gazette*, through promotions, appointments and retirements, he arrived at matters more weightily appropriate to his immutable bacon and eggs, such as politics, foreign and domestic; until finally, under the stimulus of his second cup of coffee, he surrendered himself to the expert guidance of the leading article as to the rigid opinions which a plain soldier of his class and political party should form and hold (for the next twenty-four hours) on the recorded facts. This morning, the absence of his paper, by breaking one link in the chain of the conditioned reflex which began with his icy bath and deep-breathing exercises and ended with toast and marmalade, had deprived Miles Ombersley's breakfast of its proper flavour, had made him feel that the world was out of joint, and that the future of this new day was extremely doubtful. It was ridiculous, he said, that the postal authorities should be incapable of delivering letters at the same hour every morning: the field-post-offices, run by soldiers during the war, had been much more reliable than this flabby civilian machine. Even in Mesopotamia, he said. . . .

But at this point Langley arrived, out of breath with the haste which he knew to be expected of him, and reverently laid the worn leather bag, with its brass plate engraved: Chaddesbourne Hall, on the study table. "Oh, well, here they are at last," Miles Ombersley said. "Do you know why they're late, Langley?"

"It was fog on the line, sir," Langley panted. "Mr. Homer asked me to inform you."

Miles opened the bag. While he dealt out the letters Helen Ombersley stood by meekly, like a little girl waiting to be given a cup of tea in a queue. There were several invitations to garden-parties: *The Misses Abberley at Home . . . Lady Wolverbury requests the pleasure*; a dress show: *Callot Sœurs exhibiting*

their New Season's Models; a piano recital: surely
that must be meant for Catherine? But no letter from
Oxford. And that was all she wanted. "It's too bad
of him," she thought.

Miles had opened his paper and announced earth-
shaking events: "Surrey, seventy-seven, all out; Tich
Freeman took six for forty: nasty bowler on a drying
wicket! Hobbs out first ball. Well, well . . . I suppose I had better get on with these letters, and read the
paper after luncheon. Good-bye, my darling."

He appeared to consent to be kissed, though she
knew he adored it, before she left him. This was no
moment, it was clear, in which to speak about Selby's
offer to Catherine. As she closed the door softly Miles
re-lit his pipe, which had gone out. Now for it. . . .

First a letter from the contractor in Wychbury about
the repair of the barn at Uffley Mill. Mr. Hollis presented his compliments to Colonel Ombersley, and was
sorry to say that the joists were found so far gone with
the death-watch beetle as to make the top floor unsafe.
There was dry-rot in the timbers of the roof as well;
and as neither of these was covered by the original
estimate, the contract had worked out at rather more
than the previous figure. He was confident, however,
that the extra work had been necessary, and would be
found a good job, according to instructions received,
in every respect. He remained Colonel Ombersley's
obedient servant, and enclosed account, as requested.

Reading these words, Miles felt momentarily

annoyed that Hollis had presumed to undertake any work that had not been authorised. In the army the figures of all estimates for constructive work were checked by the technical experts of the Royal Engineers and rigidly fixed. In the looser procedure of civil life it appeared that estimates were regarded as approximate and elastic. This one, which he had always regarded as "on the high side," had actually stretched by no less than sixty per cent. Of course, he couldn't complain. Hollis had promised to do his best to "keep it down," and Miles had trusted him to "make a good job of it." This bill must be paid. Amid so many pressing expenses an odd hundred pounds here and there did not seem, of itself, important. It was rather the accumulation of these various odd hundreds, insensibly mounting to thousands, that began to embarrass him, eating into the narrow margin (if any margin were left) which he had counted on for meeting such immediate emergencies as the repairs to Aaron Bunt's cottage. He had promised Selby to see to this matter. He was a man of his word. Yet the sum he had earmarked for that purpose had vanished, it seemed, in the fulfilment of another promise: the repair of the barn at Uffley.

"If Healey were still with me," he thought, "he would probably have found some way out of the difficulty, some convenient compromise. I suppose that is what he was paid for; but I can't do that sort of thing. I can't compromise, or even temporize. It's my nature to ride straight at my fences, and I'm too old to change it. So here goes. . . ."

He wrote a cheque, in his firm, formal hand, for the contractor's account, and entered the sum on the debit side of the ledger.

Another letter. It was written on a sheet of blue paper torn from a writing-pad and signed, with a flourish, George Cookson. Mr. Cookson had received Colonel Ombersley's note about the half-yearly rent for The Moat, due on Lady Day last. He was sorry to say that one thing and another, including a run of bad luck, had prevented his settling that and the other arrears; and now, just when he had been hoping to make arrangements to meet it, he had been laid on his back with an attack of lumbago and sciatica to which he was subject—due, in part, he felt bound to say, to the dampness of the house, about which he had frequently complained to Mr. Healey, who admitted that the walls needed a new damp-course and had promised to see to it, but probably forgotten—and being laid up like this made it impossible, as the colonel would understand, for him to get into Bromsberrow and arrange the matter with the bank. He didn't want the colonel to think that he had any intention of evading his just obligations. He was not that sort of man, as Mr. Healey and, he ventured to say, everyone else in the district would agree. But that wasn't enough in farming nowadays; you had to have luck; and his own luck during the last year, what with losses of stock and low prices, had been something awful. However, with good harvests in sight and things generally looking up a bit, he was not down-hearted; and if Colonel Ombersley would be patient, he had every hope of arranging matters with the bank and letting him have a cheque within the next few months. He, also, remained Colonel Ombersley's obedient servant.

Miles Ombersley was less patient than Mr. Cookson wished. Mr. Cookson protested a deal too much for his liking. The Moat was by far the largest single property on the Chaddesbourne estate; its six hundred acres represented, or should represent, a rent of twelve hundred and fifty a year, on which Miles had already paid a substantial part in land- and income-tax, though George Cookson, at this moment, was more than twelve hundred pounds in arrears: and those twelve hundred pounds—to say nothing of the rent which would be due, and probably unpaid, in four months' time—were essential to the solvency of the Chaddesbourne estate. It was all very well for George Cookson to boast—and demand confirmation from Healey, if you please!—of the fact that he wasn't the "sort of man" to evade his just obligations. This loquacious letter was nothing if not evasive; and, oddly enough, the thing that stuck in Miles Ombersley's throat and irritated him most of all was the querulous suggestion that he, the landlord, had contributed to Cookson's default by neglecting to provide a damp-course and giving him sciatica! Why couldn't the fellow say simply, in so many words, that he couldn't pay and had a thin chance of doing so?

That, at least, would be honest. But honesty wouldn't mend matters. What would? "Supposing," Miles thought, "I insist on payment and, failing payment, evict him. . . . What will happen? He'll probably go bankrupt—and off flies my twelve hundred pounds, together with what I shall lose while choosing another tenant. Or perhaps, when I've set the proceedings going and been bled by the lawyers, he may manage to raise money somewhere and pay up—in which case no court would allow the termination of the lease, and the same vicious circle of default and unpleasantness will begin all over again. And supposing I do nothing. . . . The man who could write that letter will certainly take advantage of it. He'll think—and quite rightly—that he's on an easy wicket, and go on making excuses till he owes me double! This is a matter for legal advice," Miles thought. "I must go and see Wilburn. And I mustn't waste time. I'll drive into North Bromwich and see him this afternoon. . . ."

But the thought of seeing his lawyers was disturbing in itself. He had an instinctive dread of the law and its sinister processes. One "got into the hands" of lawyers, as people said. It reminded him of the incomplete income-tax return, which, on a third peremptory demand, he had abandoned and fired off to North Bromwich for Wilburn to deal with. It reminded him, too, that in three weeks' time Midsummer Day

would come round, when another instalment of his
father's iniquitous annuity to Margaret Clarke—*Mrs.*
Margaret Clarke—and another payment of interest to
keep the mortgagees quiet, would be due. As for re-
payment of capital. . . .

"Shall I have to go on being bled like this for ever?"
he thought. "Is the game worth the candle? Supposing I did what so many of my friends have done: put
the place up for sale—there's no entail—and got what
I could for it; let the mortgagees take their pickings,
and retired with the rest to some place where living is
cheap and the climate tolerable—Dinard, St. Raphael
—or even Guernsey, where the income-tax-dodgers
go? I could end my days in peace on my pension and
the interest on what was left; I shouldn't be forced
to spend the rest of my life scheming and fretting and
fighting with my back to the wall in a losing battle. I
could sell it to that fellow Hackett to-morrow," he reflected, "if it were mine to sell. . . ."

He stared out of the smoking-room window. The
fine rain had ceased falling, but the air was still
drenched with moisture, its substance made whitely
candescent by the invisible sun, whose light, thus
diffused, afforded a flat and shadowless illumination in
which the colours of lush grass and tender leaves had
the quality of tempera or (where films of water still
gleamed) of enamel. On the wet gravel outside, a
thrush stood cracking a snail, glancing sideways at
Miles between the blows, as though asking for his

approval. In the park's middle distance, young rabbits had hopped out of their holes one by one to nibble the dew-tender grass, unafraid of the men who were rattling the roller over the pitch for Saturday's cricket; in the elms young rooks were garrulous with low confidential colloquies breaking out at times into cackles that sounded like laughter; in the laurestinus thickets a blackbird gave forth her sudden stutter of alarm; at the corner of the window itself, water dripped from a broken rain-gutter.

What he saw and heard was no striking combination of scene and sounds. It had neither far vistas nor shapely forms nor startling colours; it lacked even the heartening compensation of sunlight, being no more, in fact, than an isolated sample of rural England at its least distinguished in the light of a wet summer morning. Yet no sooner had Miles Ombersley's inward eye envisaged the alternatives—the Riviera, Brittany, or Guernsey—than his feelings experienced a passionate revulsion in its favour. He had spent enough time in service abroad to know his own mind. He knew that the only country he cared to live in was England; the only place, Chaddesbourne. . . . "However badly things go," he told himself, "this is my home. I would rather die poor in Chaddesbourne than live in comparative affluence anywhere else. And when Jack is as old as I am, he'll feel just the same. For his sake, as much as my own, it's my duty to carry on. . . . And I must get that rain-gutter seen to."

He scribbled a note on his pad. More letters. The next bore the Wychbury postmark and the address was typewritten; but before he could open it the butler tapped at the door.

"Police-constable Page is here, sir, and wishes to speak to you."

"Very well, Langley. Show him in."

There is a social grade in which the figure of a policeman is frankly regarded as that of a natural enemy of the human race; to another, more firmly grounded in respectability, he still represents the law in its repressive quality; to Miles Ombersley, on the other hand, the constable appeared as no more than a humble agent of that established social order which it was his own lot, by nature no less than as a Justice of the Peace, to embellish and sustain. Constable Page, as the only other local representative of that order, appeared to him worthy of particular patronage and encouragement. Though the Capuan luxury of Chaddesbourne had softened his military fibre, the constable had not entirely forgotten his service ways; at the sight of Miles Ombersley seated behind a desk that resembled an orderly-room table, he instinctively stood to attention and saluted and threw out his chest, on which a row of three medal-ribbons was proudly displayed.

"Well, constable?"

"I won't keep you a moment, sir. Just a warrant for your signature."

"Nothing serious, I hope?"

"It's the worst case I've had since I've been here, I'm sorry to say, sir." (Constable Page's face was lit with professional enthusiasm; he looked anything but sorry.) "It's a man that I've had my eyes on for the best part of a year. Bunt's the name: Aaron Bunt, sir."

Aaron Bunt. . . . The tenant of the cottage which Selby had condemned. Miles remembered that foxy figure with the lank gipsy hair, and its contrast with the well-filled tunic and bulging red cheeks of the constable struck him.

"What has the wretched fellow been doing?"

"That remains to be seen, sir. I have every reason to suspect him of feloniously entering on private premises, Mr. Roberts's, the keeper's, and stealing one of Mr. Roberts's fowls—a Rhode Island Red, sir. Being of a poaching disposition, Bunt is known, from what he's said before witnesses, to have had the intention of wiping Mr. Roberts's eye. On the night of the thirty-first ult.—that is to say, last night, sir— Mr. Roberts being known by Bunt, as I can prove myself, to be otherwise engaged at a soirry or dance in the schoolroom, and returning to his house past midnight, Mr. Roberts observed that the dogs was unduly excited and that some person unknown had entered the fowl-house and stolen one hen. Outside the fence, sir, we discovered signs of a struggle. . . ."

"A struggle?"

"Feathers and blood, sir . . . indicating that the unknown person had intended to give the impression that he was a fox." (Constable Page shook his head from side to side and smiled knowingly.) "But foxes—leastways four-footed foxes—don't carry knives, sir: not knives with blood and rabbit-fur on the handle."

He produced, from his tunic pocket, a packet of official foolscap, which he unfolded clumsily with his spatulate fingers, displaying a horn-handled knife.

"That belongs to Bunt?"

"I'm not in a position to say, sir. That remains to be proved. But I don't mind betting it does."

"What are you proposing to do?"

"I shall visit Bunt's house, sir, and put a few questions to him. Of course, I shall caution him. If he denies all knowledge, as he will, I shall proceed to search the premises. That's why I must have the warrant. An old hand like Bunt knows just where he stands, sir. If I turned my back for five minutes he'ld destroy all the evidence."

"Roberts wants to prosecute?"

"It's nothing to do with him, sir, one way or the other. The matter's in the hands of the police, and I'm glad it is, sir. This man Bunt has been asking for trouble this long time, and I don't mind telling you straight I've had enough of his cheek."

"Very well. Where's the warrant?"

"Here, sir."

Miles Ombersley signed it. He hesitated. "The man's out of work?"

"And always will be, sir. Permanent. A bad family, sir. The girls are a problem as well, and the wife's no better. It would be a good thing for Chaddesbourne if we could get rid of the lot, that's my honest opinion."

"Well, they must live somewhere, you know."

"Yes, more's the pity, sir."

"All right, constable."

Page saluted and turned about. Miles Ombersley automatically returned his salute. The vision of Aaron Bunt's slouching figure came back to him. No doubt the fellow was a wastrel, a nuisance, a thoroughly bad citizen, a creature, too, of defective intelligence—for how, otherwise, could he have been such a fool as to leave his knife behind? Yet somehow, in spite of the conscience which made him aware that a civilized community could not tolerate theft—query: should a civilized community tolerate starvation?—he couldn't help wishing that Constable Page, decent fellow though he was, had been a little less pleased with his own astuteness, a thought less well-fed. . . .

Letters . . . letters! He glanced at his watch. The morning had slipped by insensibly; it was nearly mid-day. And the sun had burned through at last: beyond the roped cricket-pitch a blue-green distance was clearing. The thrush had cracked his snail-shell and flown away. From the drawing-room he heard the tinkle of Catherine's piano. Although he knew next to nothing about music and cared less, he was proud of her dexterity; it was the one thing, since the credit was not his, that he was inclined to boast of. That letter with the Wychbury postmark. . . .

The paper had a printed heading: Chaddesbourne Manor; but Mr. Hackett, in an access of clumsy tact, had crossed the words out and substituted *Green Hill*. It was a friendly letter, and far too familiar for a stranger—at least that sort of stranger—and there was hardly a line where poor Mr. Hackett did not put his foot in it. He began, in his innocent enthusiasm, by taking it for granted that Miles Ombersley would be delighted by the news that he intended to bring the benefits of modern civilization to darkest Chaddesbourne. He was proposing, he said, to tap the line of Bromsberrow Electrical Supply Company at the point where the lane from Chaddesbourne cut the main road running south. The company had already arranged for various wayleaves on the Bromsberrow side of the bank up to the point where the line would enter Ombersley property. They had not written to Miles because, some years ago, there had been some sort of difficulty in dealing with his father, the late Mr. Ombersley, who had, it appeared, an odd, old-fashioned prejudice against electricity—just as *his* father before him, had resisted the passage of the Stourton-Worcester railway. Mr. Hackett had assured the company that in Miles's case there would be nothing of that kind to fear. What he proposed, in short, was to carry the high-tension cable from the edge of Chaddesbourne bank obliquely across the park on masts of steel lattice, which the company called "pylons," in the direction of the end of the village adjacent to the Hall. The masts proposed were anything but unsightly, and had, in fact, been approved by the architect who had planned the new house at Green Hill. At some point, the nearer the Hall the better (but that was a detail) he proposed to erect a transformer for the supply of current of inferior voltage for light and power to the Hall itself and the village. Beyond this point the high-tension cable should be extended in a line as direct as possible to the bridge, on the farther side of which another transformer would deal with the supply of current to the Green Hill Estate.

As I hinted to you the other day (Mr. Hackett went on), *it is a great satisfaction to me to do anything in my power for the improvement of a village with which my family has been associated for so many centuries. That is why I decided, at somewhat increased expense, not to carry the power-line to Green Hill direct, but to take in the village; and, looking upon this, as I do, as a labour of love, I shall be flattered if you will allow me to defray the whole of the cost of bringing the current to your back-door. The company will also undertake to allow supplies to be afforded from any pole, mast or pylon that may in future be erected on your property: a convenience*

the value of which you will realize if, at any time, you
should contemplate erecting any buildings, com-
mercial or otherwise, in the vicinity of the park. I
have been fortunate in persuading them to commence
work on the supply immediately; and if you will drop
me a line conceding the necessary wayleave, I can at
once complete the preliminary formalities.

Yours faithfully,

Jno. Hackett.

P.S.—I am informed that each pair of masts or
pylons will carry a sixty-foot span of H.T. cable.

Miles Ombersley, though a man of quick temper,
was slow of thought and not ordinarily given to precipitate action. In his first reading of Mr. Hackett's
letter the thing that impressed him most was the
fellow's calm "cheek" in taking his acquiescence for
granted. It was only when he read it a second time
that his mind grasped its full enormity. From the
smoking-room window he could see the whole field
of Mr. Hackett's proposed operations. An overhead
cable, crossing the park with its latticed masts placed
at sixty-foot intervals, would be visible in the whole
of its hideous length from the front of the house.
More than this; if it followed the line which Mr.
Hackett so confidently suggested, the slung cable
would actually cross the cricket-pitch, with one mast
at long-on and another at second-slip. If the first

offence was a piece of gratuitous insolence, the second was sheer sacrilege: one might as well propose setting up a roundabout in the middle of the Piazza di San Pietro or a coconut-shy in the Square of the Ka'aba at Mecca! At this point Miles's dislike of Hackett, which had been simmering ever since their first encounter, boiled over; Mr. Hackett became, in his eyes, not merely responsible for this monstrous presumption, but a scapegoat for all other irritations with which he was beset that morning. Miles Ombersley saw red; and, such was his nature, the mere fact of his seeing red imposed on his actions an iron control and on his words a formal politeness more telling than violence. He took a sheet of notepaper and wrote with deliberation:

Dear Mr. Hackett,

I thank you for your letter of yesterday's date, and for your kind offer to allow me to draw a supply of electrical current from the power-line which you are proposing to carry to Green Hill. I am afraid you will think me as prejudiced and old-fashioned as my father when I tell you that I have made it a rule not to grant any wayleaves for the passage of electric cables over the Chaddesbourne estate.

Believe me to be,
Yours sincerely,
Miles Ombersley.

He addressed the envelope: *J. Hackett, Esq.,*

Green Hill, Chaddesbourne, and, having sealed it, brought down his fist on the back of it with a satisfying thud. So much for Jno. Hackett!

After that he felt better. The fact of his having disposed of this odious matter so firmly, re-established his self-confidence in regard to his other embarrassments. If he could deal with Mr. Hackett in such a satisfactory manner, he was in fettle to face the rest. At the luncheon table, in fact, Mrs. Ombersley was pleased by his hearty appetite and his buoyant air in contrast to the grim demeanour he had shown of late. At the end of luncheon he informed her that he was driving into North Bromwich. She did not enquire why. She never asked questions.

Miles Ombersley detested—he had always detested—North Bromwich. From his childhood he had conformed to the family's attitude of treating this growing city, which lay at a distance of thirteen miles as the crow flies and half-an-hour's motor-run from the gates of Chaddesbourne, as though it did not exist. They preferred to ignore it, partly because it happened to be in another and an inferior county, and partly because every one of its million inhabitants was believed to be, more or less, a John Hackett, in various stages of financial development; indeed, none of the older families in the district—Abberleys, Pomfrets, D'Abitots—had ever accepted the possibility of "knowing" North Bromwich people. Such members of this alien race as had contrived by their wealth to establish themselves in the county—industrial magnates such as the recently-created Lord Wolverbury and Sir Walter Willis—were severely left to live in a social *enclave* of their own. Even though the North Bromwich shops were admittedly luxurious and convenient, no Abberley or Pomfret or D'Abitot would dream of dealing with them; they sent orders by post to the Army and Navy Stores, or jogged in, once a week, to Worcester, where the shopkeepers realized who they were and knew how to spell their names, and didn't subject them to the indignity of being asked for references or addresses.

Miles Ombersley, driving the old "Silver Ghost," with its squat copper radiator, which he had bought in the easier days before the war (it was the only motor-car he had ever possessed), was appalled, as he breasted the top of Wychbury Hill, to see how, within a few years, the hated city had grown. Its western fringe had now reached the lip of the Tilton escarpment, and was spreading along it like an angry red rash: the raised edge of a brick erysipelas. There was no stopping the growth of a city like this, Miles thought; already the hamlet of Tilton had gone; it would be Halesby's turn next; after Halesby, Stourford and Wychbury; after Wychbury . . . Chaddesbourne. "But not while I live," Miles Ombersley thought. "Unless they break me, they'll never build villas in Chaddesbourne!"

He found the offices of Wilburn and Wilburn in

Sackville Row without much difficulty. For a firm of their reputation they struck him as unimpressive, though the room in which he was left to wait was ornamented with deed-boxes painted with names that had weight in North Bromwich: *Sir Joseph Astill, Bart., Sedgebury Main Colleries., Ltd., The Great Mawne Iron and Steel Co., The Rt. Hon. Lord Wolverbury,* it seemed to him that none of these had lately been opened, or even dusted; and the room with a door of opaline glass marked "Private," which he took to be Wilburn's, seemed as dead as the rest, until suddenly a freckled young man in a very high collar flung it open with a flourish and invited him to step in.

"Mr. Flower will see you immediately," he announced.

"But I want to see Mr. Wilburn."

"Mr. Wilburn no longer comes to the office, sir, on account of his health. Mr. Flower is Mr. Wilburn's partner. Kindly step this way, sir."

Mr. Flower received him. He was not Miles Ombersley's idea of a family lawyer, being an exceedingly smart young man with a military moustache, which seemed somehow incongruous, a pronounced Midland accent, a signet ring, with a crest, which he fingered as he spoke, and a familiar manner, designed to put clients at their ease, which made Miles uneasy.

"If there is any probability of my finding Wilburn here in the course of the next few days . . ." Miles hesitated.

L

"None whatever," Mr. Flower assured him cheerfully. "To be candid, I don't mind telling you I'm afraid poor old Wilburn's in rather a bad way. I think I may say I know quite as much about your affairs as my partner did. If you'll tell me your business. . . ."

"There are a number of things. First of all, my income-tax return."

"That's quite simple. I handed the papers you sent me to our own accountants, and I think their figures are ready."

"I had practically no income last year."

"That, unfortunately, doesn't make much difference. Assessments are calculated on a three-year average. The Inspector of Taxes will probably accept our figures: in which case the sum payable will, roughly, amount to this."

He handed Miles Ombersley a slip of paper with a flourish that seemed to say: "You see how efficient we are in this office—everything at our finger-tips!" Miles stared at the figures in alarm.

"This can hardly be right. It looks enormous," he said.

Mr. Flower wagged his head knowingly. "My dear sir, haven't you noticed it always does? These figures invariably look larger than we expect, just as bank-balances—you've probably noticed that too?—invariably look smaller. In any case they don't apply till next January. Sufficient unto the day is the evil thereof. There's the second instalment of this year's

income-tax due on July the first. Which reminds me:
there's also that little annuity payable under your late
father's will to a lady named Clarke. If you wish us
to pay it as usual, would you kindly send us your
cheque to cover the amount? Seven hundred a year, I
think? Yes, that's a hundred and seventy-five pounds.
I don't like to worry an old client over a small matter
like this, Colonel Ombersley, but, to tell you the truth,
Wilburn's illness has made our banking arrangements
a little complicated. You'll quite understand? The
same thing applies to the interest due on the various
mortgages which my partner arranged to handle.
That, also, will be due on the twenty-fifth. Would
you be so kind?"

Miles hesitated. He would have found it extremely
difficult to unbosom himself even to Wilburn, whom
he trusted, and the little he had seen of Mr. Flower
did not inspire confidence. With an effort, he forced
himself to speak: "As a matter of fact, I came here in-
tending to discuss that matter with Wilburn."

"Mrs. Clarke? I'm afraid we're too late for that.
I urged Wilburn at the time to contest the old gentleman's will. Now that probate's been granted nothing
but an act of grace on her part. . . . Of course, if
you wish it, I could approach the lady. . . ."

Miles flushed. "No, no. . . . That's a debt of
honour." (Mr. Flower nodded and smirked.) "I
was thinking of the mortgages. What with one thing
and another—death duties, the expense of taking over

the estate, and the sudden drop from full pay to my ridiculous pension—I am finding myself, at the moment, somewhat short of ready money. I've a troublesome tenant who owes me twelve hundred pounds. . . ."

Mr. Fowler nodded: "Ah! . . . you want us to see to that?"

"If you did, I doubt if anything would be gained; it would be throwing good money after bad; the fellow would simply go bankrupt. No. . . . What I had intended to discuss with Wilburn to-day was the possibility of increasing the existing mortgages."

Mr. Flower pursed his lips. "I should have to look into that. As far as I remember, they relate to a property called Moat Farm. They were contracted, unless my memory deceives me, about the beginning of the war, at a time when agricultural land had an artificial value. Your father, if you'll excuse my saying so, was somewhat secretive. He did not arrange the matter through his bank or through us, his usual legal representatives. The business was handled by a firm of solicitors in Stourton, and we knew nothing about it until the question of probate arose. To be candid, Colonel Ombersley, I think our colleagues in Stourton did very well for him. Now that land-values have declined I should say that the sum they borrowed on the property cannot be much less than its actual value to-day, and I'm afraid you must relinquish the idea of raising more—in that quarter at any rate.

There's one consolation: even if you should default, I don't think the mortgagee would feel inclined to foreclose. The court might insist on a sale, and at the moment people are cautious of acquiring land—land like yours, that is, away from main roads or railways or modern conveniences, such as electrical power, and not likely to be developed. Of course, there are always other possibilities. If I remember rightly, you have a property called Uffley Mill, about which we had an enquiry some time ago."

"From whom?" Miles asked quickly.

"From another firm of North Bromwich solicitors."

"I'm not going to sell Uffley Mill, Mr. Flower."

"So Wilburn told me. Of course, that's for you to decide. All I venture to do is to suggest that you can, if you want to. And why sell, after all? Mind you, I'm not at all sure that our colleagues are still interested in the property; but if they *are*—who knows? —they might not be averse to arranging a small loan which would free you from this—er—temporary embarrassment. There's nothing at all unusual in a transaction of that kind. People in your position are doing that sort of thing every day."

Miles was silent. "I dislike the idea," he said at last. "First of all, I have given my word to the tenant at Uffley, an old friend of mine, that he won't be disturbed Then again . . . I dislike this air of mystery. Who is it that wants to buy Uffley? Who's your colleagues' principal?"

"I have no idea. The procedure is perfectly normal."

"You've no other suggestion?"

"There's nothing more promising. Do you want us to see what we can do with your tenant at The Moat? We might try tactful persuasion?"

"Perhaps you had better. I must confess I'm not very hopeful; but every little will help. I'll post you particulars."

"Very good. And you won't forget Mrs. Clarke's cheque, will you? It'll be due on the twenty-fourth."

"I'll do what I can."

"And about Uffley Mill. . . . If you should change your mind, remember, we're at your service."

Miles laughed grimly. "I shall not change my mind," he said. "I wish you good day, Mr. Flower."

He was thankful at last to get the tang of North Bromwich out of his mouth—that and the taste of Mr. Flower's company, which had, somehow, offended him. If poor Wilburn, whom he had trusted though never liked, was retiring, Miles felt like making a change: this fellow Flower was altogether too smart for a family lawyer; he had an unpleasant air of knowing more than he admitted. Wasn't his persistence in speaking of Uffley a trifle sinister?

"I was unwise to consult a local man about money matters," Miles thought. "I should have gone to London, instead, and seen my bankers. I suppose I could raise enough money on the security of my pension to carry me through this emergency. . . ."

By this time, and at this distance from the heart of the city, the last shreds of moisture had left the sky; the kempt pavements of the Halesby road, with its detached mid-Victorian houses, protected by screens of laburnum and lilac, displayed a number of women, dressed with more expense than refinement, of smart nursemaids pushing perambulators, and dogs that appeared to be better bred than their owners. The bright afternoon had brought out coloured fleets of motor-cars of the newest and most luxurious design. Skimming over the road's surface like newly-hatched butterflies, they made the old "Silver Ghost" look sadly old-fashioned: as old-fashioned as himself, Miles reflected, sitting there bolt-upright in front of the open tonneau.

"This damned place is bloated with money like a fat tick," he thought: "blood-money, made out of munitions, most of it. All the money has changed hands; and the people who have it now don't know how to use it: a new class, without taste or tradition or sense of duty—with no vision beyond the fences at the bottom of their gardens, with no stake in the country except their suburban freeholds—yet half of them could buy me up to-morrow, and would, if they had the guts to face my responsibilities. A mean age," he thought; "a cowardly, decadent age!"

The impatient squawk of a klaxon horn made him swerve to the left. A long streak of red flashed by—

Mr. Hackett's Pearce-Tregaron. Mr. Hackett himself, who had recognized Miles, turned round and smiled at him and waved his hand gaily. Miles gave back his salute and returned to his meditations. "That fellow," he thought, "is an example of the way things are going." Yet somehow Mr. Hackett refused to fit into his preconceived picture. Mr. Hackett, he felt forced to admit, was neither mean nor cowardly nor decadent. On the contrary, he was generous, courageous (heaven knew!), and, according to his own lights, progressive. If Miles Ombersley disliked the man and all he stood for, he couldn't, exactly, despise him: if he was an enemy, he was at least an enemy worthy of his steel; and the prospect of the inevitable duel between them was, therefore, heartening, and put him in a less disconsolate—if sterner—mood. As he crossed the bridge and drove into Chaddesbourne Miles Ombersley smiled grimly.

"When he gets my letter to-morrow morning," he thought, "the fun will begin."

XIII

PROMETHEUS BOUND

SENSE of fun, unfortunately, was by no means Mr. Hackett's long suit; and Colonel Ombersley's reply to his lead took his breath away. Mr. Hackett was not so much offended as puzzled, not so much puzzled as hurt. He regarded himself—not unreasonably— as a man of patent goodwill. The two factories of Amalgamated Gunsmiths, Ltd., in North Bromwich and Dulston, were models of what such establishments might be, equipped with the most costly precautions against accident or industrial disease, with canteens, recreation-grounds, dispensaries, reading-rooms, baths and swimming-pools. Having no children of his own, he liked to think of his workpeople as a happy family. Every man employed took a share, apart from his liberal wage, in the profits of the undertaking; a large number of them lived in all-electric dwellings maintained, without thought of expense, by a landlord who regarded their condition as a matter of personal pride, and incidentally, a valuable method of advertisement. During the term of their employment their wives and children enjoyed the benefits of a paternal solicitude in matters of health and of education; at the end of

it they themselves could look forward to the security
of a generous pension-fund, the creation of which had
been Mr. Hackett's proudest achievement.

Retiring from business in the prime of life, he
had left this considerable monument of benevolence
behind him; but the fact that he had retired did
not imply that his restless and conscientious zeal
for the reform and improvement of social conditions
had cooled. His first contact with Chaddesbourne had
inspired an uncritical infatuation. He had fallen in
love with its quietude, its simplicity, its unworldly
picturesqueness, and that passion had soon (and sur-
prisingly) been reinforced by his discovery of a
romantic—an almost mystical—explanation for this
instinctive devotion.

For a time he had been content to indulge the sentimental pleasure of brooding over the village's superficial beauty: those humble roofs of velvety thatch
which clustered about the church-tower and straggled
away towards the Hall; the green paddocks and
cottage gardens and blossomed orchards; the great
elms, keeping guard over all, like benevolent sen-
tinels. Sometimes he would stand in the porch of his
house and look down on Chaddesbourne; he would
watch the grey spirals stealing up from a score of
chimneys, and hear the cries of children playing in the
street; sometimes, on a Sunday evening, he would
listen to the bells, whose voices, tremulous with age,
suspended on the still air like smoke, seemed to en-

hance the old quietude of the scene rather than disturb it; and his mind would go back to the men of his own blood who had assuredly heard that same music, yet now, though the sound poured down on them, could hear it no longer.

Yet these mild debauches of sentiment—though he enjoyed them at times as he enjoyed an occasional glass of whisky and soda—were the embroidery rather than the tissue of Mr. Hackett's thoughts about Chaddesbourne. He was a Liberal Nonconformist with a social conscience whose activities did not stop at theory. He had bought land and settled in Chaddesbourne parish, and by doing so had acquired responsibilities which he had no intention of evading. He had wealth, he had interest, he had knowledge of the mechanism of local government among enlightened communities which had set an example to the world; and all these, thanks to his leisure, were at the service of the home of his fathers, the village in which he had chosen to end his days. Was there any reason, he asked himself, why the people of Chaddesbourne should get less out of life, in a material sense, than his factory-workers at Dulston? There was no reason that he could see, apart from the fact that nobody had ever gone to the trouble of making the community conscious of itself as a social unit, or attempted to pull the people together, to open their eyes to the Progress of the outside world (Mr. Hackett believed in Progress), to instil them with ideals of self-respect

and ambition, to awaken in them that acquisitive sense
which would not only make their private lives fuller
and richer, but also, in its virtuous circle, contribute
towards Lubricating the Wheels of Trade. (Mr.
Hackett believed in Lubricating the Wheels of
Trade.)   He refused to accept what his friends in
North Bromwich told him: that rural England, as
represented by places like Chaddesbourne, was dead.
The only thing wrong with it was that it didn't know
it was alive: all it needed was galvanizing into consciousness.

Almost literally . . . for in the process of revival,
electricity would play a large part. Cheap power and
improved communications. If he had been asked to
confess his industrial creed, Mr. Hackett's first article
of faith would certainly have been: "I believe in Electricity." He believed in its future so firmly that
(apart from the interest he still maintained in the
manufacture of lethal weapons) he had sunk a large
part of his fortune in the electrical industry. Indeed,
one of his minor satisfactions in bringing current to
Chaddesbourne was the fact that his seat on the board
of the Power Company would enable him to obtain
for the job preferential treatment, not merely in time
but in cost, and convince Chaddesbourne people (particularly Miles Ombersley, who, hitherto, had not
shown himself so deeply impressed as he should be)
how influential (as well as benevolent) their new
neighbour was.

During the last six months Mr. Hackett had been elaborating this plan in secret; for the time being it had overshadowed his sister scheme—that of the arterial road which, piercing the hills, would "put Chaddesbourne on the map" by bringing it within nine miles of the City Centre and which would follow as a matter of course, for his two factories, in North Bromwich and Dulston, gave him equal influence in the North Bromwich Town Hall and on the County Council. His own engineers had worked out every detail of cost and construction—to the last fuse-box— except the wayleaves. Mr. Hackett had left these till the last because, in his innocent enthusiasm, he imagined that Miles would concede them as a matter of course; he had taken it for granted that his presentation of the all-but-accomplished fact would be regarded as a pleasant surprise. Miles might possibly, Mr. Hackett supposed, dislike being beholden to a comparative stranger for such expensive benefits and offer to take a share in the cost—in which case Mr. Hackett was prepared, under protest, to allow him to save his self-respect by some nominal payment. That Miles should turn down the scheme and knock the bottom out of it was a possibility that had never occurred to him, particularly after the charming talk he had had with Mrs. Ombersley.

He felt, frankly, bewildered. Such behaviour was completely outside his business experience. What, he asked himself, did Miles want? Was this letter of his a mere prelude to bargaining? Was he hoping, in spite of the advantages he was going to receive, to extract a handsome additional rent from the way-leave? Couldn't he see what he stood to gain—not merely the benefit of a modern instalment planted on his doorstep, which, if he had undertaken it him-self would have cost several thousand pounds, but a substantial, incalculable increment to the value of every building on his property, every square foot of his land? No reasonable man could look such a re-markable gift-horse in the mouth!

Perhaps Miles was not reasonable? Perhaps he was merely stupid? Mr. Hackett, still staring at the letter, shook his head. He had seen quite enough of Miles Ombersley to be sure that he wasn't as stupid as all that! Then what could be the explanation of this astonishing conduct? The whole thing was beyond him. Perhaps somebody better acquainted with the species to which Miles belonged could throw light on it. He jumped into his car and drove down to con-fide his troubles to Mr. Winter.

"I should like to know what you make of *that?*" he asked.

Mr. Winter was equally tactful and sympathetic, but disinclined to take sides. He saw, he admitted, his visitor's point of view.

"Was there any other?" Mr. Hackett demanded.

Perhaps, Mr. Winter suggested, Colonel Ombersley might have been better pleased if he had been consulted at an earlier stage in the proceedings.

"He ought to be thankful I've done all the work for him," Mr. Hackett maintained.

That was true, in a way, Mr. Winter agreed. Yet didn't the way in which Mr. Hackett had presented the matter rather imply that he had gone over Colonel Ombersley's head?

"If a fellow presented me with two or three thousand pounds—and that's putting it mildly"—Mr. Hackett hotly replied, "I shouldn't care whether he'd gone over my head or under my feet: I should keep my mouth shut and be thankful!"

Still, men were not all made alike, Mr. Winter said mildly. While he could see Mr. Hackett's position, one had to remember that people of Colonel Ombersley's class—a class whose preponderance, for a variety of reasons, was on the wane—were apt to be sticklers for——Mr. Winter was going to say "manners," but changed the word to "formalities". . . .

"You mean," Mr. Hackett burst in, "that Ombersley's cutting off his nose to spite his face? That 'ld be all very well if it was only his own nose that was concerned. But it isn't: it's your nose, Mr. Winter, and mine, and Hadley's and Selby's—it's the noses of the whole blessed village? Now is that *right* . . . I ask you?"

This aspect of the matter, Mr. Winter admitted, was . . . unfortunate. There was, of course, another.

(He had carefully kept this till the last.) The æsthetic aspect.

"The *what?*" Mr. Hackett asked.

"The æsthetic." Mr. Winter smiled apologetically. "What I mean is this: it's just possible that Colonel Ombersley may have been frightened by the prospect of seeing a diagonal procession of—er—masts, iron masts. . . ."

"Steel masts," Mr. Hackett corrected.

"Steel masts crossing the park in front of his house. He may fear they will spoil the view from the windows of the Hall. Some people are sensitive about things like that, you know . . ." he added timidly.

Mr. Hackett stared down his nose and wrinkled his brow. Then he sighed and shook his head obstinately.

"I can't follow you there, Mr. Winter," he said. "I confess that's beyond me. What's more, I'm prepared to say that in these days no reasonable man has a right to separate the appearance of things from their meaning. What do these masts of mine mean? They mean light, they mean power, they mean progress, they mean prosperity. And if you want these things, I tell you, they've got to come. And I assure you they're not unsightly. The young fellow who built my house on Green Hill—what I call Chaddesbourne Manor—and that's what it's going to be called!—he approves of them. People talked rot like that when railways came in, and canals, and telegraph poles.

Who notices things like that now? I bet Ombersley doesn't. And I don't mind betting you too that within six months the old boy wouldn't know they were there. It's like having a tooth out," Mr. Hackett added, obscurely.

"Don't you think you might put the—er—wires underground?" Mr. Winter suggested.

"Yes. . . . I might put the cables underground. If I did so it would cost me another two thousand pounds. I'm not a poor man, Mr. Winter; but I like to see value for my money. And that wouldn't meet the case either. Look at Ombersley's letter: *I have made it a rule not to grant any wayleaves for the passage of electric cables over the Chaddesbourne estate.* That's flat enough, isn't it."

Mr. Winter admitted it was flat. Would it be possible, he wondered, to complete the scheme without passing over Ombersley land?

"Possible, yes; but prohibitive; quite out of the question," Mr. Hackett replied. "Do you know what this means? I'll tell you in one word. The man's jealous: a dog in the manger. He's jealous of my money—though God knows I've worked for it. He's jealous of my name: he knows that we Hacketts were here before any Ombersley set foot in Chaddesbourne. He's jealous of his privilege; he and his have been cocks of the walk for so long that he thinks nobody has a right to set foot on it. And he's so blind, so wrapped up in his name and the rest of it, that he

can't see the signs of the times. What's happened to
Stoke Priory, the D'Abitots' place, where his wife
came from? Sold! Broken up! What's happened to
Mawne Hall, the Pomfrets' old house? Sold!
Walter Willis had it, and now it's for sale again.
What's happened to Stourford? Sold, and rebuilt by
Joe Hingston! What'll happen to Chaddesbourne?
I'll tell you one thing that'll happen as sure as my
name's John Hackett: and that one thing is—I shall
wash my hands of the place and leave it to fall to
pieces the way it's doing! And if anyone asks you
why . . . you just tell 'em to ask Miles Ombersley:
he's the fellow who knows!"

Mr. Hackett paused for breath. He was red in the
face; his usually kindly features had a look of
pugnacity, his fists were clenched, and his eyes, Mr.
Winter observed, were actually brimming with tears.
He presented, at that moment, the picture of a
contrary child: an overgrown child with a red face
and a bristling moustache. Mr. Winter was shocked
by the spectacle. He said:

"I do hope you will not be hasty, Mr. Hackett.
Just because of this unfortunate—this most unfortunate—er—contretemps. I should be really shocked
if I thought for a moment that you imagined your
interest in Chaddesbourne was not appreciated. On
the contrary, I assure you it is. As a matter of fact,
at the moment when you arrived, I was about to
trespass on your kindness by writing you a letter on

a subject with which I hoped to enlist your sympathy. In point of fact we are trying to raise funds for our little War Memorial. Colonel Ombersley has kindly given us the land. . . ."

Mr. Hackett laughed. "That won't cost him much!" he said. "What do you propose to spend on it?"

"Selby and I have agreed that it ought to be simple: the simpler the better. We thought that fifty pounds should cover it."

"Fifty pounds?" Mr. Hackett pulled out his cheque-book. "Will you lend me a pen, vicar? No . . . it's all right: I've got one. The name's Arthur, isn't it?" He bent over the table and wrote: *The Rev. Arthur Winter. One hundred pounds*—"No use spoiling the ship for a ha'po'rth of tar," he said. "This'll allow you to spread yourselves. I didn't do so badly out of the war myself," he admitted. "Put my name at the top of the list, and see what the others will do." He laughed, but the laugh was not ill-humoured. "And I'll tell you another thing, vicar: if you want this job properly done in the latest style, you might do a lot worse than get on to that young man of mine—the one that I spoke of just now who built my house—to make you a drawing and super-intend the erection. You can tell him to put his ex-penses down on my bill."

Mr. Winter, holding the cheque in his hand, found himself at a loss for words. "I'm afraid," he began, "so large a gift. . . ."

"Oh, that's nothing," Mr. Hackett broke in. "As I say, you can spread yourselves. Do yourselves proud."

". . . such a handsome sum," Mr. Winter went on, "will rather—what shall I say?—overshadow those of our less wealthy contributors. I should like you to understand . . ."

"Oh, I quite understand: I'm not shy."

". . . that—well, Mr. Hackett, in point of fact, Dr. Selby and I had more or less made up our minds that—the Memorial being rather in the nature of a votive offering from the parish as a whole rather than from—er—individuals, and seeing that many of the subscriptions would necessarily be quite small—we practically decided not to make public the names of the donors or the amounts they subscribe."

"But you've told me already that Ombersley has given the land?" Mr. Hackett said quickly. "He'll get credit for that as an individual all right!"

Mr. Winter smiled. "Well, we couldn't exactly conceal *that*, could we? He owns the whole village. And I think you must admit his position is rather exceptional."

"Exceptional? How? Why should it be?"

"He's the senior officer in the parish, the President of the British Legion and the Old Comrades Association. Quite apart from that, he has rather a special interest in our Chaddesbourne Memorial: he lost his two elder sons in the war."

Mr. Hackett was silent. Though he told himself that the attitude was illogical, that, by making munitions at all hours of the day and night, he had "done his bit" as effectually and with as great a sacrifice (to say nothing of the Excess Profits Duty) as many men of his age who had achieved decoration in khaki, he always felt slightly uncomfortable when people spoke, in lowered voices, of men who had actually lost their lives in the war. The subject was so thickly sown with pitfalls that he decided not to pursue it.

"Well, do what you like with the money," he said. "If there's any left over I reckon you'll be able to find some good way of using it, and if you want any more, you've only to let me know. I had a plan for a new Village Hall in the back of my mind; but when a man who wants to improve things meets the kind of obstruction I've had over this electrical business, he begins to sit up and wonder if the game's worth the candle. Good day, sir!"

Mr. Hackett retired. This visit to Winter had not been exactly a success. He was a hundred pounds out of pocket in cash, with nothing to show for it (not that he really minded *that*) and not much richer in sympathy. Mr. Winter had not shown the fine indignation which Hackett had expected of him; he had appeared, on the whole, to lean to Miles Ombersley's side. "But that's Church of England all over," Mr. Hackett told himself, "neither here nor there. A compromise—that's what it is and always has been. Vested Interests and Christian Charity: England and Rome. Thank God, I was brought up an honest Wesleyan with a mind of my own!"

Dr. Selby might be more sympathetic, he thought; but at that time of the morning Selby would hardly be back from his round. At that moment the church clock chimed twelve. Mrs. Hadley unbolted the door of the "Ombersley Arms" and waved her hand to him. "That's not such a bad idea," Mr. Hackett thought. "This man Hadley's a sensible fellow. I'll drop in and have a glass of beer and a chat and see what he thinks of it."

Mr. Hadley was naturally delighted to join him in half a pint. He stood leaning against the bar while John Hackett rehearsed his grievances. Mrs. Hadley sat knitting and nodding her head with clucks of surprise or approval.

Of course, speaking for himself, Ted Hadley said, there was nothing that would please him better than having electric light. It was a grand idea. He'd maintained all along that was the one thing Chaddesbourne needed. "But, mind you," he said, "it isn't as simple as all that, sir. You bring juice to the village. So far, so good. But that's not enough. I've got to get my house wired; I've got to put in meters and switches and fittings and bulbs and so on; and, to tell you the honest, as times are, I could no more afford it than I could afford to go in for a slap-up motor-car."

"But you wouldn't have to afford it," Mr. Hackett told him. "That's the landlord's job."

"It's certainly the landlord's job, Ted," Mrs. Hadley echoed.

Ted Hadley laughed. "I can see Colonel Ombersley taking that on! Why, Mr. Hackett, I daren't even ask him for outside repairs that ought to have been done years ago in the old gentleman's time. This here house, between you and me, is falling to pieces. We go on like we are because we know he does all he can, and it's no use hurrying a gentleman who's doing his best. And supposing he *did* put the light in, what happens? Up goes the rent! As an ex-sergeant-major, with all respect, I know a gentleman when I see one. And the Colonel's the goods, sir, you may take it from me, he's the goods: and when I say that, I'm speaking for the whole blooming village!" Ted Hadley brought down his hand with a slap on the counter.

"Then you know, sir," he went on, "it's all very well to talk, but Chaddesbourne *is* Chaddesbourne. I doubt if you'll find a more ignorant lot of people in the whole of Worcestershire—let alone Hereford. If you told them you were going to put electric light in their houses, would they thank you? Not them! They'ld be scared to death of the wires; that's the solemn truth of it. And what's more, in some of them thatched cottages you couldn't do it. If you hammered a nail into the wall of a house like Aaron Bunt's, it

would just about fall to pieces, and a good job too!
I suppose you've heard all the story of Aaron's
latest?"

Mr. Hackett did not even know who Aaron Bunt
was.

"What . . . you don't mean to tell me you've
never heard of our Aaron?" Ted Hadley cried.

He proceeded to enlarge on the shady Bunt family
history: Mrs. Bunt's notorious potations, the morals
of the two girls, Aaron's talent for poaching. It
seemed to Mr. Hackett what it was—rather sordid
and not particularly interesting—until it reached the
description of Aaron's last escapade, which Ted
Hadley obviously regarded as the cream of the
jest:

"So the constable, he says to me: 'Ted, I reckon
I've got that sly beggar this time, but I'm taking no
risks. Before I do anything more, I go down to the
Hall and get the Colonel to give me a warrant'. . . ."

Mr. Hackett sat up. "One moment! Didn't you
say the fowl was stolen from Ombersley's property?"

"From his keeper's. You must know Jim Roberts.
He's been there for years. So, as I was saying, P.C.
Page goes down to the Hall and gives sworn information in writing, according to law, and comes away with
his warrant safe in his pocket. *Feloniously entering
by night.* It's the word 'night' that does it. Well, no
sooner has he got to Bunt's cottage than out runs
Bunt's missus: like a spitting wild-cat, Page says, her

hair flying all over her face. 'What are you doing here?' she says. 'Get out of this quick!' Well, Page, he just smiles at her—he's a decent chap, ex-Grenadier—he says: 'Now Mrs. Bunt, you just calm yourself. I want none of your lip. What I want is a quiet word or two with your husband. You don't come into this. Shall I find him inside?' At that she went mad; started screaming at the top of her voice—that was to give Aaron the tip, don't you see?—and such language as you never heard! 'Yo' bain't going to poke your nose in this house, warrant or no warrant,' she says. 'There's a babby lying dead in this house, and no bloody copper's going to set foot in it!' Well, Page being a family man, like, that made it awkward, though duty *is* duty—and he knew, as well as I do, that the old besom didn't care a damn about Nellie's kid and was only playing for time, as the saying is. So he says: 'Mrs. Bunt, I'm afraid that makes no difference. I must do my duty,' he says, and at last, out comes the other one—not Nellie, you know, but the elder—what's her name, Glad?"

"Polly."

"That's right, Polly . . . I never know one of those two beauties from the other. Out she runs, and I'm blest if the two of them didn't set on him! 'Ted,' he says, 'it was like the blooming monkey-house at the Zoo!' And I don't mind telling you the man had a couple of scratches on his neck that long."

Mr. Hadley held two index fingers apart and

demonstrated. "Oh, go on, Ted," said Mrs. Hadley. "That's exaggerating."

"Well, have it your own way. . . . And then, in the middle of this scrap," Mr. Hadley went on, "out comes Aaron himself, with a yawn on his mug. 'What's all this about?' he says, as innocent as a lamb; and he copped the old girl a good and hearty one over the ear. 'That'll learn yo' to raise the place like this for a go-off!' he says, 'and here's another!' he says. But the second one missed her by inches, the old cat being used to his tricks. 'Why didn't you come out before, Bunt?' says Page. 'You knew I was here.' Aaron yawns. 'I'd just dropped off to sleep, sir,' he says. 'Oh, *that* was it, was it?' says Page. 'Perhaps you were out late last night, Bunt. Didn't happen to pass anywhere near Jim Roberts's, did you?' 'No, I can't say I did,' Bunt says, scratching his head. Then Page lugs out his pocket-book. 'I must make a note of that answer,' he says, 'and any statement you make may be used in evidence . . . Why—if I haven't broken my pencil! Will you lend us a knife, Bunt?' Aaron felt in his pocket and found his knife was missing. Page was watching him all along; he says he could see the beggar go pale underneath the dirt. 'So you've lost it, have you?' he says, 'I suppose it isn't anything like this?' And he shows him the one he picked up off the ground by Roberts's fowlhouse: horn handle, worn blade with blood on it. Aaron shook his head; but from that moment Page knew that he'd got him. 'You don't happen to have seen a Rhode Island Red hen about the premises either?' No . . . the only fowl Bunt had seen was a white Leghorn he'd picked up in the road, run down by a motor-car. 'Well, let's have a look inside, then, in case you're mistaken,' says Page. Then Aaron perks up. 'Not you! Not without a warrant!' So Page, he brings out his warrant, and with that he cautions him. 'And keep your women in order,' he says, 'or else there'll be trouble. . . .'"

"That was asking something," said Mrs. Hadley, severely.

Ted Hadley took a swig of beer to moisten his throat.

"So Bunt goes in first," he went on, "and Page, he follows; and he tells me the stink of that place nearly knocked him backwards. 'Ted, my boy,' he says, 'a fox or a badger weren't in it.' The old woman and Polly, that had set on him outside, had gone upstairs. Only the other one, Nellie, was there. She was sat in the corner of the room alongside the box they'd put her kid in. When Page come inside he took off his helmet, out of respect for the dead like, and apologized for intruding. Did she answer him? Not her! She set there like a waxwork, he says, with her hair hanging over her bosom, and those big black eyes of hers staring. 'Ted,' he says, 'I give you my word I never seen anything like it. I've seen some asylum cases in my time, and none too pretty, but that girl's

eyes, I tell you straight, they give me the creeps. No
expression. Nothing. Just eyes. Following you about,
and not seeing. You could feel them right through
your back. . . .' That's his very words.

"Well, he had a good look all round. There was
a pot on the fire with what was left of a fowl in it.
White Leghorn, Bunt stuck to it, picked up in the
horse-road the day before yesterday. Burnt feathers
in the ess-hole, charred black. At that Bunt began
to get cheeky. 'Have a look in the privy,' he says;
'don't mind me!' 'This room's bad enough without
that,' Page told him. 'If I was a human being I'ld be
ashamed to live in a pigsty like this. What's the good
of having three women in a house if they can't keep it
clean?'—and, to tell you the truth, it very near turned
his stomach. He'd looked everywhere except the
corner where Nellie was sitting, and he thought:
'Well, shall I, or shan't I?' Being a family man, as
I say, he felt . . . well, what shall I call it?"

"Ashamed of himself," said Mrs. Hadley indignantly. "At least that's what he ought to."

"Now be reasonable, Glad, and don't fly off like
that!" Mr. Hadley protested mildly. "The man did
no more than his duty, however unpleasant: you can't
deny *that*. He goes up to Nellie. 'I shall have to have
a look in this corner, Miss Bunt,' he says. Did she
answer him? Not a word. Just eyes! Page went
closer. It was downright pathetic, he says: the kid
lying there with its little eyes closed, just as if it was

asleep—and Nellie never moving a muscle, though he felt all the time she was like a cat ready to spring and scratch his eyes out. And there, if you please, right under the chair they'd put the coffin on, he saw what he wanted: a heap of red feathers Bunt hadn't had time to burn! He picked up a handful. It was like putting your hand in a wasp's-nest, he says; but Nellie never moved. Then he held them out and showed them to Bunt: 'White Leghorn!' he says. 'Aaron Bunt,' he says, 'you and me are going for a stroll just as far as Wychbury. Come along, my son. Get a move on! I've been waiting for the chance of taking a walk with you the best part of a year!' As I said to Page: 'They may talk about village policemen, but I call that a smart bit of work!'" Hadley ended triumphantly.

"And where is this wretched man now?" Mr. Hackett asked.

"In the lock-up at Wychbury, I reckon. Aaron won't mind that. He's at home there. The case comes up next Friday, and he'll go for a trip 'up the line.'"

"Has nobody offered to bail him out?" Mr. Hackett demanded.

Mr. Hadley laughed. "Aaron Bunt? I doubt he'd thank anyone if they did. The food's not too bad; and the lock-up at Wychbury's a palace compared with the house he lives in."

"One of Ombersley's houses?" Mr. Hackett said bitterly.

Ted Hadley stared at him. He had a feeling

that his rich bit of gossip had not gone down too well; that Mr. Hackett's attitude towards it was somehow inconsistent with his position as a man of property, that his views on the subject of larceny were dangerously unorthodox. He felt even more uncomfortable when Mr. Hackett abruptly rose and, without finishing his glass of beer, walked out of the house.

"What the hell's the matter with *him?*" Ted Hadley asked himself. "That chap's got a maggot in his head."

As, indeed, Mr. Hackett had. He had come down to Chaddesbourne that morning smouldering with resentment. Mr. Winter's lukewarm sympathies had not improved matters; Ted Hadley had not even pretended to share his indignation. By the time he had drunk half his glass of beer he was fully convinced that Levite and Publican were equally leagued against him, supporters alike of the obstructive feudalism, incarnate in Ombersley, which cumbered the path of himself, the Paladin of Progress. And then, at a point when frustration had fanned his resentment to anger, Ted Hadley's amused account of the Bunt case had thrown fuel on the flame.

This was the crowning example of the manner in which obsolete feudalism dealt with its weaker opponents: the case of a poor working man degraded by Ombersley's neglect of his houses, starved by Ombersley's callousness; arrested on Ombersley's warrant by Ombersley's myrmidon, torn away from his mourning family and locked up on disputable evidence, for the theft of a few wretched shillingsworth of Ombersley's property.

"And when he comes up for trial," Mr. Hackett thought, "Miles Ombersley will sit on the bench and preach him a sermon and send him to quod! But I'll see that the poor devil has a run for his money!" he told himself. "It's time I came out into the open and put a stop to this nonsense. Before the day's over, I'll see that he's out on bail, and when the case comes to court on Friday he'll be properly defended."

Mr. Hackett climbed into the Pearce-Tregaron and drove furiously to Wychbury. Any stick, at that moment, seemed good enough to him for beating Miles Ombersley—even that broken reed Aaron Bunt.

XIV

STILL LIFE AT UFFLEY

THE inmates of Uffley Mill remained ignorant of
these events. If life moves at all at Uffley, it flows as
quietly as that part of the brook which is turned aside
and imprisoned to feed the sluices, acquiring in that
suspension a new nature, passive and somnolent; becoming a right mirror for things that move not: such
as the bleached brick and silvery cross-timbers of the
mill-house itself and the dark verge of Foxall Wood
—or for things that move slowly: such as idle clouds
and old men with stiff sinews and no fret in their
blood, like Joe Warley or Eli Lydgate. When it
settles in the millpool, indeed, the once-lively water
appears to sleep; it is content to ponder the dream-
like images that fall on its surface, so deeply lulled
by the brook's constant music (like memories of childhood wandering through an old man's mind), so
drugged by the stagnant odours in which it is steeped
(of sallows and weedy snags and marsh-gas and mint),
that when movement stirs it—lash of rain or flurry
of wind; dipping swallows that skim and dimple its
surface; blue kingfisher's blur of flame; plop of
water-rat diving or splash of rising trout—it seems

no more perturbed than a dreamer who stirs in his sleep. Only on rare occasions, when black bellies of cloud are ripped by the hills and flood-water roars over its straining sluices, does the mill-pool at Uffley awake and find voice.

Such a freshet in the life of the Mill was the coming of Steve Lydgate. The odd thing about it was that his grandfather, who had pretended to grumble at the prospect of his visit ever since he heard of it, immediately took to him. This was hard to explain; for the old man's nature was deliberately withdrawn and solitary, and as loth to accept new acquaintances as new ideas. In his prime he had quarrelled fiercely with both his sons, and particularly with Steve's father. Perhaps it was in regret and atonement for this wilful alienation that he now accepted the son: perhaps (and this is more likely, for the man had the courage of his defects) he accepted Steve because now, being frustrated by age, yet not resigned to it, his mind craved for some expression of the strength he could no longer command, and found, to his delight, a fit vehicle for that vague purpose in this stalwart young man who was not only the sole bearer of his name, but also, in his outward appearance and abounding vitality, a reincarnation of his own lost youth.

From the moment when they met and clasped hands, Eli had been aware of this resemblance and flattered by it. Unlike his father, in whom the alien

M

blood had shown a predominance, Steve had bred physically true to the Lydgate type: he had Eli's breadth of shoulder and length of limb; Eli's hair, though Steve's was golden rather than bright copper; Eli's dark, smouldering eyes, and something of Eli's severity of feature—though here, indeed, the foreign strain had softened the Lydgate cragginess, as, again, in the form of the mouth, which was as bold and sensuous as Eli's without any hint of sternness, and in his nature, forthright and generous to the degree of rashness, impatient of silence, good-humoured, and given to laughter. Perhaps it was these very differences that touched the old man most deeply, showing him an image of his own youth as it might have been, of a happier self, care-free and unhampered by instinctive glooms and repressions, from contact with which, it seemed, he was able vicariously to renew in a richer form his ebbing vitality.

"This lad's a chip of the old block," he told Joe Warley. "A proper Lydgate! Don't you see how he favours me?"

"Ah, he favours you some roads—and others he dain't," Joe answered, without enthusiasm. For he saw in Steve Lydgate a quality which Eli did not perceive, but to which he, being writhen and crippled, was strangely sensitive; he was aware of the slender line that separated Steve's ruthlessness from cruelty, his good-humour from mockery; and because he was helpless and wary as a wild creature, he dreaded these things. Not only for himself, but for others who failed to see them.

His pet, Mary Lydgate, for instance. Mary had no misgivings. Long before Steve arrived, when his letter came from abroad with its exotic stamps of sphinx and pyramid, she had fashioned for herself, in her small lonely mind, a romantic image of what her cousin must be. He was to her not merely a young man (cousin, brother . . . what did it matter?), a human being of her own age and nature, miraculously sent to share for a while this life in which all things and creatures but herself were old and dry, somebody to whom, because he was young, she could open her heart, with whom she could talk as she longed to talk, and laugh, or—if she wanted to—cry. Her brooding imagination had made him far more than that. He had become for her a very incarnation of romance: of far lands, about which she had heard; of the sea, which she had never beheld; of stories, of adventure, and stories of love, by which she was thrilled and transported, although she knew nothing of either; until the image she had made for herself, like a precious seed planted in secret and nurtured with passionate hope, had taken such root in her fancy and flourished so bravely that, before she was aware what was happening, it had filled and coloured to the exclusion of all else a life that was empty of anything but trivial preoccupations and vaguer dreams. So that, soon, when she went about her work in the dairy or kitchen, she had caught herself wondering where the ship that was carrying him to England tossed at that moment, and whether he was fair or dark, and how his voice sounded, and if he was thinking of Uffley as eagerly as she thought of him, and whether, when the moment came, she would lose her courage and be shy of him. As the time of his arrival drew nearer this fear had increased; yet she had assured herself that surely cousins should understand one another; perhaps—and this made her smile—he would be shyer than she.

"But the time will pass quicker," she thought, "if I busy myself in making things ready for him."

So, when she had settled the room in which he should sleep—the best room, facing east, looking over the brook and the larchwoods towards the shoulder of Uffdown—and re-arranged the furniture and tied up the curtains with ribbons and smoothed the lavendered linen and put it to air, she would stand at the window, calculating what Steve would see when he opened his eyes in the morning, reflecting how, when he came, the larches, which now were feathery, would have come to full greenness and the gorse on Uffdown reached its glory.

"He must have flowers on his dressing-table," she thought, "and on the chest of drawers, too; for there are no flowers to see or to smell on board a ship."

So every day she picked flowers, such as she could

find, and filled the vases with water, and brushed away
fallen petals or pollen carefully, because sailors, she
knew, had a passion for tidiness. Her mind was so full
of Steve's coming, though he never came, that she had
felt almost inclined to evade Dr. Selby's invitation to
the dance in Chaddesbourne for fear lest, after all this
trouble, he might come when she was away and find
nobody (except Eli and Joe Warley) waiting to greet
him. She had been thinking of him all the time while
Jim Cookson was driving her home and talking so
solemnly about his "well-sorted" cattle and insisting
on their stopping to listen to the nightingale. Yet that
halt, as it happened, had been nothing short of a
miracle of Providence; for if the car had been moving
they might have missed Steve on the road—in which
case she would not have been able to guide him along
the dark passage into the kitchen; nor would they have
stood alone and gazed at each other in candlelight;
nor would he have kissed her.

Since that night he had never kissed her again—
at least, not in that way. When she thought of it now,
as she often did when she was lying in bed and straining her ears to catch the sound of his movements in
the room at the end of the passage, she found it difficult to recapture the precise ecstasy of that moment.
There were regrets in the memory as well. For if she
had known what was going to happen, if she had not
been stupidly fluttered and confused, she would
certainly have kissed him, too. But her lips had been

paralysed with surprise, and she had not kissed him.
And now, for all she knew, he might never kiss her
again.

Even so, his presence made life at Uffley far richer
than it had ever been before. He had brought summer
with him, along with his other trophies from the
south: he had shown her in his bedroom the curled
ostrich-feathers from Port Said in a long tin tube, the
Colombo moonstones milkily sparkling in his strong
palm, the picture of himself, done by hand on silk,
by a Japanese in Kobe, and the mantilla and tortoise-
shell comb which came from Malaga.

"You're a bit like a little Spanish girl yourself,"
he had told her. "This gear would suit you fine"—
and Mary had blushed with pleasure, for a moment
she thought he was going to give them to her; but
then he had started talking about a stunning girl he
had seen at a bull-fight in Cadiz, folding the mantilla
as he spoke and putting it back in the drawer and forgetting all about her.

Yes, summer had come with him. On the very first
morning when she had brought him his tea and tapped
at his bedroom door, and he had called to her not to
be shy, but to bring it in to him, she had been aware
of the dazzle of sun pouring in from that eastern
window. It had shone on the crisp golden hair of his
arms and his sun-browned skin, and lit flecks of fire in
his tawny, smouldering eyes. He lay there, sprawled
like some lazy luxurious animal (as he yawned, she

could see his teeth, which were white and strong, but irregular in front with two long pointed canines), and when once she had wakened him—for he slept like a log—he seemed disinclined to let her go, asking foolish questions, to which she knew that he knew the answers, as a pretext for keeping her standing by the bedside.

"But Steve, I can't possibly stay here like this," she would say. "I've all my rooms to do, and the butter to put up for market."

"Oh, leave the old rooms alone for once. Nobody'll notice the difference. I shan't, anyway. And don't go running away as if you were scared of me. I like you to stay and talk to me, and I like to look at you. No, honest, I mean it. I'm fed up with these foreign women who get up in the middle of the day and go slouching about in wrappers. Here you are, first thing in the morning, as bright as a daisy and as pretty as paint. You're cool and you're sweet and you don't use scent, Mary: that's what I like about you. And I like your hands, too. Yes, that one. Let's have a look at it! All right. . . . If you won't you'd better run away quick. I'm going to get up."

He always got up rather late, long after Eli had finished his breakfast. It was worth while planning little surprises for him; he enjoyed his fresh, country food so much after the stale ship-board fare, and teased her, saying that everything tasted better because she prepared it

"My word, what a wife you'll make for some lucky devil!" he said.

When breakfast was over he filled his pipe with an elaborate ritual, slicing "plug" with a thin-bladed knife and rubbing it up in his strong brown hands; and when he lit it, with the spill that she gave him, the aroma of the blue smoke ravished her—partly because it was proper to that ritual, but even more because it was so different from the familiar odours of Uffley, because it belonged to Steve, because it was male. When she had cleared the table he would stand by while she washed up the breakfast-things, and wander with her wherever she went, into bedrooms and kitchen and dairy, lazily talking and chaffing her and asking his childish questions; so that Mary, who for weeks on end had hardly spoken to a living soul save herself, grew gay and talkative, and her workaday life, which had been drab and mechanical, became tinged with colour and enlivened by the mild, adventurous excitement which Steve's company had power to radiate.

He was, he insisted, on a holiday: the first holiday he had spent ashore since the end of the war. He was frankly determined to relax and enjoy himself, and that enjoyment was infectious. Nature herself conspired to maintain this atmosphere of relaxation. May had been wet and squally, but the change of moon brought in a period of peerless June weather in which (or so it seemed to Mary) the sun always shone. The

hue of the sky was as hazy as that of a butterfly's
wings—a blue butterfly flitting through an air that
seemed windless until, of a sudden, wafts of perfume
floated over the fields where tassels of grass-flowers
scattered their pollen and mingled with heavier scents
distilled by the dying may. It was a period of sappy
growth, a season of suspension, in which the mere
process of living and breathing seemed sufficient to
human happiness, resembling, in its placidity, nothing
so much as the glassy surface of the mill-pool itself,
perpetually, insensibly moving, yet always appearing
to be still: serene vacancy that reflected nothing but
incalculable depths of luminous air.

It was a season of drowsy inaction; for the grasses
which shed their pollen had not yet ripened for haymaking. When their morning chorus was over even
the birds went to sleep. The silence of summer fell
on the garden like a firm hand laid softly on closed
eyes, inviting sleep. After middle-day dinner old Eli
slept in his chair—there was no hour of the day at
which he was not ready for sleep, but Steve was greedy
for the sun, which tried the old man's eyes. He had
found an old rod and tackle in the barn, and must
fish, or pretend to fish, in the mill-pool; and there,
when the washing-up was finished, Mary would join
him. She had washed and ironed the tropical "whites"
he had brought from China. The scanty gear gave his
body freedom and enhanced its strength. His canvas
shirt, open at the neck, displayed his strong throat;

the rolled sleeves showed his sinewy forearms that were like living, ruddy bronze. The glitter reflected from the mill-pool danced in his eyes as he sat watching the float, like sunshine broken by ripples and shining on gravel. Mary thought he never looked handsomer than when his mouth grew solemn with this childish intentness. She sat gazing at him as he lay there, his rod thrust between the ribbed blades of the yellow flags, whose still falls were like beaten metal, and the spears of grey-green reeds, in a silence that seemed so sweet and satisfying that she wished it might go on for ever, until, suddenly, the float dipped and bobbed up again—once, twice—and he struck, and the rod-top bent to the strain of a perch darting hither and thither in an invisible panic until, the fight being over, its barred shape lay flapping on the grass between them, the spined dorsal fin erect and the scarlet gills opening and shutting to pump in suffocating air.

"But do be careful of the spikes; they're so sharp," she would beg him.

He laughed. "Silly child! Do you think I don't know how to handle a fish? Look!"

Then one cunning brown hand passed over the humped back of the perch; the fingers closed on the erectile spined fin and pressed it flat. One finger of the hand slid into the gaping mouth: it pressed the perch's head backwards, backwards, until there was a little snap and a weak, clucking sound.

"That's done it," he said. "Broke its neck:" and proceeded, reflectively, to detach the barbed hook from the bloody tissue in which it was embedded.

Mary Lydgate watched the process, her face wrinkled with disgust. "It's cruel," she thought; "it's horrid!" But, because he was Steve, she watched his movements, fascinated. Some actions that would have revolted her in herself or in other people seemed natural in him. And she didn't want him to change—not in anything.

Once, at the end of a long, dreamy silence, in which she had almost nodded asleep, he whispered to her: "Come quickly, Mary, there's a whopper right under the bank, cruising round, deep down. I think it's one of those big trout Joe Warley talks about. Must be two pounds, if it's an ounce. Quiet now! Don't disturb him."

She turned over and edged herself forward by inches, lying on her face, till she reached his level. It was delicious, she thought, to stretch one's cramped limbs like that, to mould one's body to the cool earth, to feel the pressure of soft grass supporting one's breasts.

"Now look . . ." he said, whispering. He slipped his arm over her back to steady himself as he pointed; she felt its weight and the heat of the sun-warmed flesh. "Down there. Do you see him?"

She gazed into the cool depth of sunlit water in which every minute floating particle hung gilded, like motes in air, and made all the water mistily golden. In the midst of the water she could see a shoal of small perch striped like tigers, hanging motionless but for a perpetual quiver of translucent fins. On the tawny bottom an eel writhed in and out of the stones; its head, lifted inquisitively, questing from side to side.

"Can't you see him, you silly?" Steve asked impatiently. "There . . . *there!*"

As he stretched out his hand there was a swirl in the water, and a long shape, ploughing through them, scattered the shoal of small perch.

"Now he's gone. I've scared him," Steve said. "Do you know what he reminds me of? Last time we put into Beira I was on the bridge, looking down, with the sun astern. The water is about the colour of this: it's the River Zambezi that clouds it. And all around us, swirling and diving, there were dozens of sharks— great torpedo-shaped brutes, fifteen-footers, some of them. Nasty colour, too: greyish on the top, and a sort of pale, beastly purple below. Strong? I tell you, they made rings round us! And I thought what a lark it'ld be if one of our Chinks fell overboard from the fo'c'sle." He laughed. "My God, Mary, they'ld have gone for him, all the lot, like minnows worrying a bit of bread-crumb!"

She listened to the rumble of his voice, but hardly heard what he said. She was more conscious of the weight and warmth of his arm, which he had not removed, and of a strange transformation which had taken place in the water when the big trout disappeared. For now she was aware of the golden depths no longer, but only of the surface, on which, dusky against the bright sky, she saw two faces, her own and Steve's close together. And she thought: "How strange that Steve and I should be lying here side by side, our faces so close together and his arm round my shoulders, when only a week ago I had never seen him! His face looks darker than mine in the water," she thought, "though his colouring is lighter and my hair is almost black. I can look at him now," she thought, "without his knowing or my being shy. I should like to go on looking at him like this for hours. . . ."

But whenever she felt lazy and happy like this there always seemed to be things waiting to be done in the house about which her conscience pricked her; and when these were finished there remained the endless task of putting Steve's wardrobe in order. There was hardly a shirt or a vest that hadn't been torn by Chinese laundries or a sock that didn't need darning—though this work was a joy and a privilege rather than a labour, because Steve's clothes, oddly enough, seemed part of him, and she felt curiously contented when they lay in her lap. He never thanked her for these secret and intimate services, though surely he must have noticed how the shirts and underwear were ironed without a single wrinkle, how the socks were all darned and sorted into pairs and laid in rows. But why should a man, and a man on a holiday, remember small things like that?

Though sun suited him best, the evenings had their own sweetness. At that time of the year (except in the house) light lasted till bedtime. When the sun went down there was a short space in which the black-birds, that had spent the day hidden in thickets or pillaging the bitter-cherry tree, perched themselves on high branches up in the cooler air and sang. She liked their song better than that of the nightingale, though perhaps that was only because Steve, not Jim Cookson, heard it with her.

In the evenings, too, Eli was at his best, for the heat fatigued him. After supper, when she had drawn a quart jug of cider from the cellar—sometimes Steve went with her—he became almost talkative, recounting old stories of family history which she had never heard, and questioning Steve about his voyages to the East and to Africa. Eli was greedily interested in all Steve's adventures, almost as though he regarded them as a kind of compensation or proxy for his own narrow life. They would bring out a tattered atlas and pore over the maps, the strong brown and the frail white hands together, and Mary was astonished to find how much more the old man knew about the world than she did.

Most of Steve's stories seemed to be connected sooner or later with some woman in the background. He was extraordinarily frank about this side of his seafaring life, and made no attempt to hide it; and old Eli, whom Mary had always imagined to be severe in such matters, did not appear to be shocked by him. Nor yet, strangely enough, was she: Steve's frankness had a charm in itself, and the fact that women, all over the world, had run after him did not seem in the least surprising. Sometimes his stories of amorous adventure hurt her; he spoke so callously of his women; yet she didn't mind being hurt in that way. What really hurt her was that, apparently, he didn't think of her as a woman: she was merely a cousin, the nearest thing to a sister, a creature set in a category apart, not conceivably the partner of any romantic association. "But that isn't fair," she told herself. "Cousins often marry. Perhaps they shouldn't, but they do. . . ."

One evening she suffered a moment of agonised anxiety. Steve had been talking of his ship, the *Chusan*, which he had left at Barry, and Eli asked him how long it was likely to be before he would have to rejoin her. Mary held her breath. It had never occurred to her that, once having come, he would ever have to leave Uffley. Supposing he said "next week" or even "next month"?

"I doubt if I'll ever set foot in that packet again," Steve said. "When I left, they were going to tow her round Land's End and lay her up in the Fal. They may end by breaking her up and selling her for scrap-iron. There are dozens of ships laid up and chaps like myself out of a job. When trade looks up we shall

all get a look-in again. I've been lucky. When I was in Cardiff I ran into a chap I know with an extra master's certificate who'ld have given his eyes to sign on as third mate in a collier. It was his own fault: the fool was married and had a family. Sailors oughtn't to marry, I say. No . . . I reckon you or somebody else 'll have to put up with me ashore till the wind comes round and export trade looks up again."

"Well, you can keep your feet under the table at Uffley as long as I'm here," said Eli.

"I don't ask for a better table, Granpa," said Steve; "but when you've been on the beach a bit, you know, you begin to get restless, especially when the summer's over and the rain begins. A chap that's been used to the sun comes to miss it somehow. That's why I was never much struck on the Western Ocean. Give me something east of Suez, or the Pacific. Ay, the Pacific. . . . Now Samoa's a place! Did I ever tell you . . ."

"They begin to get restless," Mary thought. "But the summer has only just begun; he won't get restless yet. And soon there'll be lots of things to amuse him. The haymaking . . ."

They had already begun cutting their hay at The Moat. "A good week too early," Eli declared. "That chap Cookson's always in a hurry; and the weather can't go on like this, it's bound to break." The meadows at Uffley, poor feed at the best, lay higher and ripened later. In the stillness of evening they could hear the crake of Tim Cookson's mowing-machine in the fields that marched with Uffley. The noise went on steadily as long as light lasted and after. When it ceased, a landrail in their own meadows took up the creaking tune.

"That's the first sound of human life outside Uffley I've heard since I came here," Steve said. "Whose farm is that?"

"The man Grandpa spoke of: George Cookson. He's the father of the boy you met driving me home that night." (Was he getting restless?)

"Oh, that lout?" Steve answered contemptuously. "Are there any more like him?"

"There's a daughter. But she isn't like him."

As soon as she had spoken she wished she had hidden the fact of Elsie's existence. Steve was interested: "What is she like, then?"

"Rather smart and towny. She's been in North Bromwich."

"How old?"

"Oh. . . . About your age. We don't like the Cooksons much, Steve. Grandpa has never fancied them."

For the moment her discouraging answer satisfied him; but the sound of Jim's mowing-machine had detached his mind from Uffley; he was tired of fishing and lounging; he was beginning to be bored. Mary realised that one evening a few days later when she found him standing moodily on the bridge that spanned the brook. He was breaking a straw in pieces and tossing them on to the stream. Some pieces became caught immediately in tangles of brook-lime, but others, tilted and released, went floating away. Steve watched them moodily, so engrossed that Mary had stepped on the bridge before he noticed her. He let the last fragment of straw fall. "Do you know where that goes to?" he said.

"Down to Chaddesbourne, I suppose. What do you mean?"

"Down to Chaddesbourne!" He laughed. "Down to Chaddesbourne, indeed! Can't you see any further than that, Mary? It goes first to the Stour, and then to the Severn, and then to the Bristol Channel, and then to the sea. Blue water, my girl . . . the South Atlantic . . . until the trades catch it. There's the doldrums between, where you see the nautilus—little ships with rainbow sails—and the flying-fish. And then —I suppose it's a toss-up whether it'll go to the Plate or get washed ashore in the middle of the Bight of Benin. But, wherever it goes, I wish to God I was going with it! I loathe the sea when I'm on it, but when I'm not . . ." He laughed. "I don't know. I can't stick in one place too long. I reckon I'm like a dog: I like a change of smells. I like to have a sniff at China, or Burma, or Zanzibar where the cloves grow. Do you realize that since I've been here I've not even seen Chaddesbourne?"

There was not much to see in Chaddesbourne, she told him; she never went there, except, sometimes, to church.

"Well, let's go to church, then," he said, "and have a look at the girls."

The morning of Sunday was hotter than ever. The sun had a glazed look, and the horizon was ringed with motionless anvil-shaped clouds.

"There'll be tempest afore Cookson carries that there hay of his," Eli said. "You two mind you don't get caught on your way to church."

Joe Warley harnessed Rose, the old white pony, and put to, not in the trap, but in the governess-cart, which was sometimes used for taking produce to market. Mary was late at the start, for Sundays made no difference to the house-work, and she had stayed longer than usual at her mirror because she wanted to do Steve credit. She wore a demure muslin frock, a crinkly straw-hat and white cotton gloves. Round her neck hung a thin gold chain with a little cross on it which had belonged to her grandmother, and she carried a prayer-book and hymn-book in a case of red Russia leather which smelt, as Steve said, of Sunday.

"Why, how grand and proper you look, Mary," he said. "Shall I drive?" And he took the reins. But he jagged so much at the pony's grey lips that after a field or two the poor brute gave up trying to understand what he wanted and stood stock-still. "Why the devil didn't Warley give us a whip?" he complained.

"Rose doesn't need a whip," Mary told him. "Let me take the reins."

And as soon as she felt the familiar hands the pony

jogged forward under a sky that was turning paler, as though bleached by the sun which had already silvered the thin swathes of George Cookson's hay, the dog-roses in the hedge and the lilac cuckoo-flowers amid which Jim's cattle were grazing.

"Can't you make the beast get a move on?" Steve grumbled. "We shall never get there at this rate."

"Rose never goes faster than this," Mary said. "She's old and she feels the heat, and there's really no hurry." Why should one hurry? she thought; for she wanted to make the most of this memorable journey: the two of them, all alone, slowly ambling through an air that was drowsy with quiet thoughts and meadowsweet and new-mown hay. "Listen!" she said. "You see, we have plenty of time: the bells are only just beginning."

That morning they could hear not only the five bells of Chaddesbourne, but also the Wychbury peal, whose conflicting notes, welling and fading on currents that moved invisibly in the upper air, broke the pattern of sound into a confusion of overtones, vaguely quivering above the Chaddesbourne tenor-bell's bourdon like a swarm of metallic bees. As the pony-cart turned at the bridge a motor-horn hooted behind them, and Mary pulled in to let a car pass. It was the Cooksons' Ford, with George Cookson, recovered from his sciatica, in the driver's seat. Beside him sat Mrs. Cookson, a severe black hat balanced on the top of her head, and behind them, Elsie and Jim, who turned

and blushed and raised his hat as they passed. Elsie
also turned and stared out of curiosity.

"My God . . . that's a pretty girl," said Steve.
"Who is she?"

"Elsie Cookson; Jim's sister."

"The one you told me about? You never let on she
was like that. Are they going to church, too?"

"I expect so. You see, Mr. Cookson's the people's
churchwarden. I don't really know them, except Jim."

By the time they reached the "Ombersley Arms"
and tied up the pony, one bell was tolling. Miss Loach,
whose cough had improved with the warmer weather,
sat installed in her window, her prayer-book and
hymn-book in her lap. Even though she herself could
not go to church, she liked to see who did and who
didn't. With the window a little open, she could hear
the growl of the organ and the feeble bleat of the
Psalms, and, more or less, follow the service. The
appearance of Steve excited her. "Who is that young
man?" she enquired.

Jane Trost thought it must be Eli Lydgate's grandson from Uffley.

"This is the first *I've* heard of anyone being at
Uffley," said Miss Loach indignantly. "Are you guess-
ing, or do you *know?*"

Jane Trost thought she had "heard something."

"Then why didn't you tell me?" said Miss Loach.
"I dislike people being secretive. The vicar is late this
morning."

On a morning like that Mr. Winter preferred to put off going to the vestry as long as possible. He had risen for the Early Celebration, which was what really mattered, and so, being at peace with God and his own soul, he had walked to and fro in the garden in his black cassock, thinking how sweet the pinks smelt and how gracious the Creator had been in the contrivance of such rich variation of colour and scent for the delight of men's eyes and nostrils. That was how he preferred to think of it, though Dr. Selby had explained, in his roguish way, that the colours and scents of flowers were sexual characteristics designed by Nature (he never said "God") to entice fertilizing insects to visit them. But if that were all, he reflected, how would Selby explain the fact that during his own manhood, all the musk in the world had suddenly lost its perfume? Did this imply a sudden and vindictive decision on the part of God to rob the poor musk of its sexual attractions, which it had doubtless abused? Hardly that. For, now that he came to think of it, the odour of musk (the memory of which, so it seemed, must die with his own generation) had associations of transparent innocence; since, when he was a boy, he remembered, a pot of musk with its pale hispid leaves had been part of the furniture of every well-ordered nursery, and its scent the very perfume of well-to-do childhood. For a moment, indeed, Mr. Winter was transformed in the spirit into a little boy in a sailor suit with a lanyard and a whistle which must not be blown in company—until, suddenly, the bell stopped tolling, and he became once more a middle-aged priest of the Anglican Church with a vagrant mind which he recalled from these old vagaries, closing his eyes and dedicating the words of his mouth and the meditations of his heart to the duties of his office. As the clock in the tower struck eleven, Miss Burton hurriedly brought her voluntary to a close, and Mr. Winter, in the white surplice and Cambridge hood which made his long face look so sallow, entered the chancel, his head bowed, his hands folded on his breast. . . .

XV

THUNDER WEATHER

As the congregation rose on Mr. Winter's entry, Morgan Jones slipped into his place in the rear of the school-children. Though he was impressed, against his will, by its sonorous liturgy, his heart despised the rites of the Church of England. If he had been forced, at the stake, to confess any formal religion (and Shelley and Swinburne were religion enough for him), he would have chosen the variety in which he had been nurtured, for he loved to hear the reading of the Bible and the saying of the Psalms in Welsh and the sweet Welsh hymns, and, though he disclaimed any capacity for sentiment, tears always came into his eyes when he heard the tune "Aberystwyth"—even when it was droned and whined by feeble Saxon voices. He attended the Church services at Chaddesbourne partly because it was evidently supposed to be one of his duties, but even more because it gave his eyes the chance of devouring Elsie Cookson.

Since the night of the dance, Mr. Jones's condition had steadily become more desperate. He had reached a degree of despair in which he could not even write poetry. Only one person in Chaddesbourne shared his

secret: Miss Burton, who, piously tidying Mr. Jones's
desk in the schoolroom, had found the fragments of
rhapsodical verse which he had failed to complete and
the impressions of other and happier attempts on blot-
ting-paper, which she had deciphered by means of a
looking-glass—not out of mere curiosity, but because
she had Mr. Jones's true interests at heart. And those
verses had hurt her: not because they were obviously
not addressed to herself—indeed, she would have been
far more hurt if they had been—but because, in a
moral, not a prosodical sense, they were extremely
free. They were scattered throughout with anatomical
details about which Christian young men never thought
before marriage. They were verses, in short, which
no modest woman could possibly have inspired without shame or perused without a blush. And Miss
Burton knew who his inspiration was. That had been
clear enough at the dance; it was just as clear now,
when she saw the direction of Mr. Jones's glances reflected in the mirror, set at an angle, by means of
which, from her organ-seat, she was supposed to time
her music to Mr. Winter's movements. Mr. Jones's
eyes were fixed greedily on Elsie Cookson, and his
thoughts no more occupied that morning by religious
emotions than—alas!—were Miss Burton's own. . . .

Or than the minds, for that matter, of many others
who now knelt, as did Miles and Helen Ombersley,
repeating the phrases of the General Confession after
Mr. Winter. Not many years since the spectacle of the

Ombersleys' devotions had been hidden from their inferiors' eyes by the walls of a high box-pew closed with lock and key. During the vicariate of Miss Loach's father, when the church was "renovated" by the substitution of pitch-pine for worm-eaten oak, the high walls of the box had disappeared, and discovered the Ombersleys and their guests grouped, rather like museum specimens, against an explanatory background of family tombs and monuments.

Miles Ombersley never missed going to church for the Sunday morning service, not because of any depth of religious conviction, but because he regarded it as being in the nature of a parade. It was important, he felt, that the village should know that the national church had his support. He loved the church service; its very familiarity made it soothing. It imposed no strain on his intellect, and allowed most of his mind to stray idly through those by-ways of family history, so comforting to his pride, which the monuments suggested. He even liked reading the lessons—which was odd in a man so reserved—partly perhaps because walking to the lectern renewed the sensation he had known as a commanding officer inspecting his regiment, and even more because he remembered his father reading them when he was a boy.

On this thundery morning, however, his mind was a prey to many anxieties which took the opportunity of invading it in this hour of relative vacuity. First of all financial. The last weeks, in a way, had been critical

His visit to his lawyer's in North Bromwich had produced discouraging sequels. Flower's attempt to "ginger up" George Cookson had brought nothing but regrets and excuses: times were bad; Cookson hoped they would soon be better; he was expecting, when markets improved, to sell his surplus stock and perhaps to dispose of some of his hay; to clear the arrears of rent was, for the moment, out of the question, but he was hoping to make some payment on account in a few weeks' time.

"In a few weeks' time" was all very well, Miles Ombersley thought. In a few weeks' time his own income-tax would have to be paid, to say nothing of the quarterly interest due on his mortgages and Mrs. Clarke's pension. Still, as Flower said, one couldn't draw blood from a stone. There was always the chance (a thin one) that Cookson might be compelled by judicious pressure to pay some of his arrears, while if payment were forced he would almost certainly go bankrupt—in which case his creditors would descend like a pack of wolves, and all Miles would get would be an incalculable share in a meagre dividend.

As for the possibility of increasing the mortgages on The Moat, Mr. Flower wrote, he had explored every possibility and had not been encouraged. As things were, the mortgagees felt by no means pleased with their bargain, which had been made at a time when money was cheap, and by present standards, offered a poor return for their capital on a security whose value had decreased and was still decreasing. No hope there: on the contrary, the shadow of a threat. For in the case of a default in the payment of interest, the mortgagees, Mr. Flower gathered, would be only too glad to foreclose and reinvest their capital to greater advantage.

"For they know quite well," Mr. Flower wrote, "that a man in your position could not possibly consent to the indignity of a sale by their order and, if it came to a point, could raise money on other properties to meet their claim. That is why," he went on, "I once again take the liberty of reminding you that the obvious way of meeting your present embarrassments is to dispose, as so many of my clients have found it necessary to do on succession, of some of your outlying property. As the result of confidential enquiries made from my colleagues since your visit, I am in a position to say that the party lately interested in Uffley Mill is still in the market and sufficiently keen on acquiring the property to make an unexceptionable offer probable. I should like to add," Mr. Flower concluded, "that I mentioned it to Mr. Wilburn, who is still indisposed, and that he entirely agrees with me."

Miles Ombersley knew that letter by heart; he hated its clumsy jargon. It was a sign of weakness in himself, as he knew, that the mere mention of Uffley was sufficient to put his back up. Why? Because he was convinced that the "party" concealed by Mr. Flower's "colleagues" was none other than Hackett; and because Mr. Hackett's name as a symbol of antagonism and frustration was beginning to obsess and dominate his thoughts precisely as his own name obsessed and dominated Mr. Hackett's. Wherever he turned, he suspected that Mr. Hackett's hand (or, more subtly, Mr. Hackett's money) impeded him. It was Mr. Hackett, he guessed, who had upset the balance of decency by his huge anonymous subscription to the War Memorial Fund. Mr. Hackett was behind the bill, affixed to the stable wall of the "Ombersley Arms" beside the preliminary notice of Bromsberrow Fair, announcing a three-hourly motor-bus service between Chaddesbourne and Wychbury, and significant enquiries from the County Council (of which Hackett was a member) as to the strength of the bridge over the brook, which was his. Mr. Hackett, at the annual meeting of the cricket-club, an Ombersley preserve, had unanimously been elected vice-president: a position which Jack should have filled. Mr. Hackett's influence was actually, within the law, beginning to tamper with the administration of justice.

The Bunt case showed that. When Aaron Bunt, quite properly, had been taken to the lock-up, Mr. Hackett had driven to Wychbury and bailed him out. There was nothing in that to which Miles could take exception. In the ordinary way he would have regarded it as an innocent example of misguided humanitarianism. But was it so innocent? Would Hackett have bailed Bunt out if the theft had not been committed on Miles's property, and if Miles had not granted the warrant? That was only the beginning. When the case came up at Wychbury, with himself in the chair, Miles had found Bunt represented by the leading criminal lawyer from the North Bromwich Stipendiary's court. The presence of this notability had evidently been widely advertised. The press-bench was full, the court crowded with faces, among which Miles recognized a large number that came from Chaddesbourne.

From the moment the case began, the North Bromwich lawyer made it quite clear that the person actually on trial was not Aaron Bunt, but the chairman of the bench. Bunt elected to be judged summarily: which meant that Miles personally must bear the responsibility for the sentence inflicted. It was to assure this, no doubt, that the gentleman from North Bromwich did not stress (though he took care to mention it) the doubtful propriety of the presence on the bench of a magistrate on whose property the alleged larceny had been committed.

This suggestion got Miles on the raw. His first impulse—though there was no reason in usage or law why he should follow it—was to retire from the bench. "But if I do that," he reflected, "they can say I turned tail, and I'll be damned if I'll let them do that!" No doubt "they" had banked on this particular reaction of his stubbornness compelling him to hold his ground, knowing that even if he stayed (as they wished him to stay) the suggestion of unfairness, once made, would

stick in ignorant minds; that, in short, they could
"have" him both ways.

The whole conduct of that defence, as Miles remembered it now (the choir, dominated by Joe Atkins's
bass, breaking into the *Venite* with Miss Burton lagging a quarter of a bar behind), had been built on suggestions of this kind—suggestions which no judge in a
court of assize would have tolerated, but which, precisely because they were directed against himself, Miles
found it beneath his dignity to repress. Again and
again the Justices' Clerk attempted to keep Bunt's
solicitor's questions to the point; but before he could
stop him speaking, the mischief had been done and
the answers scribbled down in the reporters' note-
books.

By the time Constable Page, all injured honesty,
and Bunt had given their versions of the affair, he had
firmly established the implication that poor Bunt had
been the victim of a particularly unsavoury piece of
feudal spite; that the privacy of a working-man's house
(and, thanks to Miles, what a house!) had been
violated on the slenderest of evidence and with a dis-
regard of all decency that stopped short at nothing; a
brutality which had even failed to respect the sanctities
and solemnities of death. The word he would apply
to this case was not prosecution, but persecution. He
sincerely hoped that the Chief Constable would take
cognisance of the policeman's behaviour, and that the
bench—even if they did not dismiss the charge, as he

urged that they should do—would consider how deeply this British workman's feelings had been lacerated already by the police's gross intrusion on a private sorrow.

Of course, the case was a clear one, and the evidence good enough even without the confirmation of Bunt's finger-prints on the bone-handled knife. He was a man with a shocking record—as witness the inspector's catalogue of previous convictions—caught, so to speak, red-handed.

When the justices retired, Mr. Pomfret of Wychbury had unbottled his indignation. The mere fact of Bunt's being defended shocked him. It was a symptom of class warfare.

"What is the lawyer fellow from North Bromwich doing here, Ombersley? Who's paying him? I don't like it. . . . I say I don't like it! A bad case. What's the most we can give him? Three months with hard labour? He'ld have got more if he'd gone to a jury."

Miles Ombersley had found himself curbing Mr. Pomfret's corrective zeal—not that he had any doubt as to Bunt's guilt or as to the propriety of poor Constable Page's behaviour, but because, as he looked at Bunt in the dock, he couldn't help feeling that petty theft of one sort or another was as natural to him as any other bodily function, and that three months in jail would no more cure it than it would cure the cast in his foxy eyes: it was no good "larning" Bunt not

to be what heredity and environment (environment?)
or both had made him. He had said:

"Let's give him a month. At any rate, they'll cut
his hair and give him a bath and bake his clothes."

Mr. Pomfret was horrified at this leniency. If
poaching blackguards once got it into their heads that
they could come to this court and "get away with it"
like that, then good-bye to any chance of preserving
game in the district! Was Ombersley intimidated?
Presumably he knew his own business. Chaddesbourne was *his* village, anyway. . . .

"You will go to prison for a month with hard
labour," Miles Ombersley had said. "The bench consider that the criticisms which have been made of the
conduct of the police in this case are entirely un-
justified."

But the evening papers were full of it, and the local
weekly, which went to every cottage in the village, had
a verbatim report of the case, including Bunt's lawyer's
reflections on housing conditions in Chaddesbourne,
which had a headline to themselves.

Was it this unfortunate publicity, Miles wondered,
rather than Selby's report, which had set the machinery
of Local Government in motion against him? (By this
time the choir had begun to stumble through the
Psalms, in which, since their words were less familiar,
Miss Burton had not merely made up her quarter-
bar's lag, but spurted and taken the lead.) Did that
headline account for the sanitary inspector's visit?

N

The man had been respectful, speaking as one in authority to another, but fully aware of the advantages attached to his position. Under the powers conferred by the Housing and Town-planning Act of 1919, he had made an official inspection of five houses in Chaddesbourne on which adverse notices had been received, and compiled a report covering such details as the condition of walls, ceiling-plaster, windows, damp-courses, roofs, water-supply, ventilation, food-storage, facilities for cooking, lavatory accommodation, sleeping arrangements, and rent. He had also, in accordance with the Act, compiled a priced specification of the necessary repairs, and an estimate, in each case, of the house's value.

"You see, sir," he had explained, "the legal position is this: When the Local Authority are satisfied that any house is unfit for human habitation and not capable of being repaired at a reasonable cost—that's the wording of the Act—it is their duty to serve notice on all persons interested to attend a meeting. And that's why I've come to see you. I want to know first if any other person than yourself has a financial interest in these properties. . . ."

"A financial interest?"

"It's a matter of form, sir: Mortgagees or Lease-holders or Trusts."

Miles had laughed. "No, they're mine, worse luck. What about this meeting?"

"The owner is asked what he is prepared to do. It's

all in this notice. You are legally bound to appear with a prepared specification. From what we've worked out, considering everything, including the rent. . . ."

"Which is not always paid."

"Exactly . . . it seems quite clear that you couldn't repair these old properties to our satisfaction, at current rates, for less than five hundred apiece—which makes two thousand five hundred in all. That, of course, is ridiculous."

"I agree. Not only ridiculous, but impossible. What's the alternative?"

"An order for demolition, sir."

"That's all very well. Where are the people to go?"

"That is always the difficulty. As a general rule, the Council erects new houses."

"Where?"

"As near to the site of the old one as possible."

"But if there's no land available?"

"We can make it available, sir. We have powers of Compulsory Purchase."

"The deuce you have! People have been living comfortably in these houses for three hundred years."

The inspector smiled: "Well . . . comfortably?"

"Nobody's complained . . . until now. Can I resist a Demolition Order?"

"If you repair them to the Council's satisfaction, none will be made. Otherwise you can lodge an appeal to the County Court within twenty-one days of the

Demolition Notice. You'll find the exact information on the back of Form 5."

"H'm. . . . It sounds very complicated. Do you realize, inspector, that demolishing these five houses would spoil the whole village?"

"Well, there's spoiling *and* spoiling, isn't there, sir? Of course, being what I am, if you'll excuse me saying so, I look at it from the sanitary point of view."

"Are there any local members—I mean Chaddesbourne people—on the Council's Sanitary Committee?"

"Let me see, sir. Yes, two. Mr. Cookson and Mr. Hackett."

Mr. Hackett. . . . There was something positively devilish in the way this man's name cropped up wherever he turned. Hackett's finger was in this pie as well, or soon would be. A policy of encirclement! That was what the Germans complained of in Europe in nineteen-fourteen. It had forced them to fight. But what about the sinews of war? Two thousand five hundred pounds! Once more, in the familiar doxology, the choir left Miss Burton floundering behind. Miles Ombersley, recalled to the exigencies of the moment, rose, put on his reading-spectacles, and walked to the lectern.

"Here beginneth the Twelfth Chapter of the Second Book of Samuel. *And the Lord sent Nathan unto David. And he came unto him, and said unto him. There were two men in one city: the one rich, and the other poor. . . ."*

"He looks tired and grey this morning," Helen Ombersley thought. "Something's worrying him; I'm afraid he's not sleeping."

During the night she had heard the boards in the next room creaking under Miles's weight; they creaked louder than ever when you tried to move quietly, treading on tiptoe. That was the worst, she thought, of married people having separate rooms. No doubt it was far more hygienic, and one slept with less risk of disturbance, yet one lost something by it. Something quite definite in the way of complete understanding which couldn't be supplied by any other kind of intimacy. And when anyone happened to be sleeping badly or restless or worried, the loss was incalculable. There was something extraordinarily soothing and steadying in the touch of the hand of somebody who loved you, even if they were asleep. Often, lying awake at night, she would have given the world to have Miles by her side—not necessarily to hold her (to have and to hold), though that, of course, would be lovely, but just to be near, physically near, and to turn when she turned. It was a pity, she thought, that he snored so dreadfully, though she supposed that most men *did* snore, after fifty, anyway, and Miles snored so terrifically, poor darling, that she often heard him in the next room. What was troubling him now? she wondered. Could it possibly (and her heart went cold) be anything to do with Jack?, There had been no news írom Oxford now for more than a fortnight. No news was good news, they said; yet that wasn't always true. Supposing there *was* something, after all, in Lady Clun's letter? Supposing Ledwyche had written more definitely to Miles, and Miles had not told her? She felt herself going hot and red in the neck. The morning was really exceedingly oppressive. Sooner or later it must end in thunder, or, as Follows said, "tempest." "And then—oh, my poor roses!" she thought, though her roses, indeed, would suffer far less from thunder-rain than her pæonies with their heavy heads and their sappy stalks. She composed herself to listen to Miles.

"*. . . as the Lord liveth,*" he read, "*the man that hath done this thing shall surely die. And he shall restore the lamb fourfold, because he did this thing and because he had no pity. . . .*"

Mrs. Cookson trembled in her heart. How stern Colonel Ombersley's voice was! *Because he had no pity.* Looking down on her over the top of his glasses, his eyes appeared pitiless. A hard man, she thought. He had sent that wretched creature Bunt to prison. She hadn't had time to read through the whole of the report in the paper, but from what the North Bromwich lawyer suggested, Colonel Ombersley didn't appear to have come out of the case any too well. What kind of mercy, of consideration, could a tenant expect from a man like that? Twelve hundred and forty-two pounds three shillings and sixpence. Then the seedsman's account: one hundred and ninety-seven. Dips and fertilizers: seventy-three pounds. Dr. Selby: sixteen (one should always pay doctors first: you never know when you mayn't need them). Fifteen pounds at the blacksmith's. Ninety-two to James the grocer. (And a good bit of that was port wine and whisky.) That was one of the things a woman could never keep track of; George dropped in when he was passing: "I'll just slip this in my pocket, Mr. James. Put it down in the missus's bill. I've no change." *She* knew. But how many pounds of butter did it take—butter separated and churned and made up with a woman's own hands—to pay for one bottle of whisky? (What did he owe—he'd never told her— at the "Ombersley Arms"?) And then what was the end of whisky but debts, debts, debts, and pushing your wife in the fire? On a Sunday afternoon, too!

"And yet nobody," Mrs. Cookson thought, "would dream it to look at him. George always looked well in his black clothes in church. Who, looking at him now, would credit the fact that within a few days—if the seedsmen persisted in their demands—he was going to be forced to petition for a receiving-order in bankruptcy? That was what it had come to now. Yet he didn't look like a man who was going bankrupt. When he walked down the aisle distributing the velvet collection-bags to the sidesmen, you had to confess he was every bit as fine a figure of a man as Colonel Ombersley: much stouter, of course, and a good deal redder in the face, but always well turned-out and solid and prosperous-looking. That was part of his trouble. He always looked prosperous, and spoke like it, too, so that it took people in. When they saw George's good-humoured face they couldn't hardly help giving him credit- -at least, up till now they couldn't. But lately they'd begun to wear a different look on their faces. When they said: "Good morning, Mrs. Cookson," the shopkeepers no longer smiled. For the last month or so she hadn't hardly liked to show her face in Bromsberrow High Street, they spoke so short to her. They knew, as she knew, that the crash must come soon. Nearer every day. (Twelve hundred and forty-two pounds three shillings and sixpence. One hundred and ninety-seven. Seventy-three. Fifteen pounds ten. The figures began their dance again.) And to think of Elsie there, pretty as a picture and innocent as a lamb. Brought up with ideas too big for her; she'd always said so, though George wouldn't have it. "Nothing in the world's too good for my chicken!" That was what he said. Well, well, perhaps it was fortunate for Elsie that she knew nothing of what was coming. Jim did, though. Poor Jim! The anxiety was beginning to tell on him, though she wouldn't encourage him to speak of it, out of respect for his father.

As her thoughts embraced him (Colonel Ombersley, by this time, was nearing the end of the lesson) Mrs. Cookson turned her tired eyes, suddenly transfigured with tenderness, in the direction of her son. As a rule,

Jim knew when she was looking at him; he, too, would turn and smile back at her; but this morning his eyes were set in another direction, following which, instinctively, Mrs. Cookson's glance arrived at the transept-pews, diagonally opposite, where Mary Lydgate sat at her cousin's side.

When she realized who was the object of Jim's gaze, Mrs. Cookson was stabbed with jealousy. Jim was all she had in the world. That demure child, all black and white, had stolen his glances—which meant (if Jim had any of his father's impetuousness) that she would soon steal him, too. But the Lydgate girl, she noticed, was cunning. Her eyes were downcast. It was the young man by her side, the sanguine young man with the tanned face and coppery hair, who returned Jim's attention, unless—ah, now she had got it!—he was staring at Elsie. Yes, that was it. Elsie. "And you're not the first, my boy, nor you won't be the last," Mrs. Cookson thought. And she smiled wanly to herself; for Elsie, it seemed, was unaware, or pretended to be unaware, of Steve Lydgate. "Well, the sooner she makes up her mind and settles down with some steady young man and gets out of this cruel muddle," Mrs. Cookson thought, "the better for her." And she sighed so heavily that Jim heard her, and suddenly looked up. She patted his hand. It was going dark; and, through Jim, her thoughts went back with anxiety to the lying hay. . . .

Steve Lydgate continued to stare at Elsie Cookson.

N*

His first glimpse of her in the passing car had in-
flamed him. When they reached the church he had
been careful to ask Mary where the Cooksons sat.
Even if she had not told him, Jim's bulk would have
betrayed them. Thus examined, though still at a
distance, Elsie's frail blondeness—her combination
of brittle porcelain fragility with radiant health—
entranced him. It was of a type which he had
encountered (and had found satisfactory) in Cali-
fornia and occasionally in New South Wales. The prospect of an adventure made him feel more like himself,
and forget the boredom with which he had been
afflicted that morning. The Cooksons, it seemed, were
near neighbours, which made Chaddesbourne seem not
such a bad place after all. "Yes, my beauty," he
thought, "you know that I'm staring at you all right!
This maiden meditation business doesn't wash with
me! You won't turn your head because you know
you've a pretty profile and want me to see it. Well,
you have, and I do."

A ricochet of the looks that Steve wasted on Elsie
passed by her and found a second target in Nellie
Bunt, who, sitting four pews behind her, appropriated
them to herself. Nellie Bunt had conformed to the
established Chaddesbourne convention of going to
church on the Sunday after a funeral. She liked going
to church in any case, particularly in the evening, when
it was easy for a lonely girl to pick up an old friend
or a new acquaintance. This morning, in view of the

formal occasion, she had paid a great deal of attention to her appearance, putting on the black afternoon dress that she wore in service and a shady black straw hat retrieved from her last mistress's waste-paper-basket.

She was so conscious of looking her best that she was hardly surprised when the ardent glance which she imagined this handsome stranger to be aiming at her reached her. It showed that in spite of the dreadful events of last week, her life was not finished and hope need not be abandoned. She was still attractive to young men! But what was this? Colonel Ombersley, nearing the end of the lesson, to which she had listened vaguely, lowered his voice and spoke more impressively:

"*And it came to pass on the seventh day that the child died.*"

"The child died . . ." Nellie thought. "The child died . . ."

All the wild desolation of her tragedy rolled back on her. The sly smirk of invitation which had come to her lips in answer to Steve Lydgate's scrutiny quickly faded. Her lax mouth trembled; tears swamped her eyes. For she saw that the story which Miles had been reading was hers. God had killed Bathsheba's baby to punish David for his sin. God had killed her baby to punish her for hers. And she hated God for it. It was a mean, dirty trick to go killing innocent babies. If God was like that she would never go to church again . . . no, never set foot in the beastly place full of sanctimonious people, all dolled-up, who, if the truth were told, were no better than herself—not one of them! George Cookson, for instance. If she told what she knew about *him!*

At that moment the storm broke overhead in a crack of thunder. It shook every window in the church. Nellie Bunt had always been terrified of thunder, though not of lightning. When she heard it at home she would crawl under the kitchen table and throw her apron over her head. But this particular storm, she knew, had a personal significance. God had roared at her out of the sky because she had said she hated Him. Perhaps He would kill her, like He had killed her baby. She wouldn't much mind. All the same, she crouched down in her pew and took cover beneath the book-ledge. Another crash made her tremble. She knew it was no good pretending that she hadn't meant what she said, because God knew everything and would only laugh at her. Then rain drummed on the leaden roof and slashed the stained-glass windows. It continued to rain, and God continued to growl at her like a savage dog until the morning service was over.

By that time, though the air still smelt of wet dust, the sun had burst out again. It shone, dazzling, through the humid air as through a burning-glass; the flags of the churchyard path and the mossy gravestones steamed. Morgan Jones was the first of the congregation to move. He had determined, during the service, to catch Elsie Cookson on her way out and invite himself to The Moat to tea. "For if I keep on seeing her at a distance like this," he told himself, "I think I shall go mad." He hurried down the path and waited by the lych-gate, while the congregation streamed past him, idly chattering about Mr. Winter's sermon and the noise the thunder had made. (They were thinking all the time of their Sunday dinners which, for the sake of economy, had been carried in roasting-tins to the bakery.) But though Morgan Jones waited for what seemed to him an eternity, Elsie Cookson did not appear.

Could they have left by the Vicarage gate? he wondered. So he hurried back, only to see his idol talking, with hateful vivacity, to the handsome stranger whom he had noticed sitting by Mary Lydgate. That was Jim Cookson's fault. Though his mind was vexed by fear lest the thunder-rain had drenched his hay, Jim had made a bee-line from the porch towards Mary Lydgate.

"You promised you'ld bring your cousin to see us at The Moat," he reproached her, "and you've never come. What about tea this afternoon?"

Steve accepted the invitation before Mary could answer.

"That's a grand idea, Cookson. By the way, I've never properly thanked you for that lift."

Elsie hovered towards them, a bored look on her lovely face. Jim had kept her waiting. He introduced her to Lydgate.

"I was wondering in church who you were," she said.

"Then I'd the advantage. I knew who you were," Steve told her. "I saw you in your car at the bridge."

"And remembered my face? How clever of you!"

Steve laughed. "No, you don't, my lady!" he thought. He said: "Yes, wasn't it?" And Elsie laughed, too; she knew how to play at that game.

(Morgan Jones thought: "I can't butt in while they're talking like that; but I shall go to The Moat about tea-time just the same. Why shouldn't I? She practically asked me.")

"Between four and half-past then?" Jim said triumphantly. "If you like I'll drive down and fetch you."

"No, no," Mary protested eagerly. "We can come with the pony."

In the back of her mind she was worried, wondering how old Eli would take this visit. She told Steve so on the homeward drive: "You don't know how queer he is." But what worried her even more was the certainty that Steve was taken with Elsie. That was why he had jumped at Jim's invitation so quickly.

"I think you're ridiculous, Mary," he said, "allowing yourself to be tyrannized by Grandpa like that. What right has *he* to say where you shall go or not go? I'm damned if I'ld stand it."

"Well, he doesn't fancy the Cooksons, and he's old, and I don't like to vex him. You can do as you will. You'd much better go alone. I shall be quite happy at home."

But she knew she would not be happy at home. If Steve were going to start a flirtation—an "affair," as he called it—with Elsie, she knew that she would be wretched unless she went with him and watched; for the suffering of seeing what actually happened would be nothing compared with that of imagining it. All morning she had been miserable; she was even more hurt when he said:

"Well, it's all the same to me. I'll go alone if you like. It's not worth making a fuss about, anyway, is it? For God's sake don't look so solemn."

He himself looked angry, and spoke roughly. "I'm nothing to him," she thought.

As the church clock chimed half-past three, Morgan Jones left his lodgings and turned his face towards The Moat. Ever since "church" that morning he had been so excited that he could hardly contain himself. Mrs. Webb had scolded him for only "pecking" at his dinner, which was a beautiful juicy roast shoulder of young mutton, fit for a king. "Won't you help yourself to the onion sauce, my dear?" she had said. (She had fallen into the way of calling him "my dear," for her own sons had been ravished away by marriage and lived in London, and her maternal heart yearned to embrace even such an odd substitute as Morgan Jones.)

But Mr. Jones had declined onion sauce; and this particular mortification of the flesh was pathognomonic. It signified, beyond doubt, that Mr. Jones was going courting. "It's Miss Burton," Mrs. Webb thought. After all, what could be more suitable? Though she would be sorry to lose Mr. Jones—for no house seemed like home unless there was a man in it—she felt strongly that a young man of Mr. Jones's age should be thinking of "settling down." After dinner Mr. Jones confirmed her suspicions by retiring to his bedroom, where he plastered his hair down with water and put on a new red tie. He also put the last poem he had finished (the one which began with *Child, by what chance* . . .) in his breast-pocket. He had other poems, addressed to Elsie, in Welsh. It was easier to write love-poems in Welsh, which was a more expressive and more poetical language than English; but Elsie, unfortunately, being imperfectly educated, would not understand them, so he left these behind.

It was hotter than ever. The morning's storm, furious as it was, had failed to lay the dust. A dry wind blew from the south-east and whirled it in eddies, not merely dimming the lustre of the new boots which constricted his swollen feet, but fogging his spectacles and making his eyes smart behind them, and mingling in a caked compost with the sweat that trickled from under his plastered hair. But Mr. Jones, being momentarily a hero as well as a poet, plodded on magnificently. To-day he must do or die.

It took him the best part of an hour to reach The Moat. As he approached it he saw a governess-cart turning into the yard, and in it the abominable shape of the prepotent, bronzed young man who had been talking to Elsie that morning. He saw him, with Mary Lydgate, tie the pony up in the yard and proceed to the front door with an enviable air of cool confidence; so, in order that his own arrival should not be confused and overshadowed by theirs, he waited, panting, behind a barn and dusting his boots with his clean pocket handkerchief and wiping his spectacles. Then, with heart wildly beating, he, too, approached the steps and rang.

He heard the bell tinkle distantly (as he heard his own heart), but nobody answered it. From inside the house he could also hear a careless babble of loud English voices. "I will *make* them answer me," he thought; so he rang again, loudly; and at this the babble of voices suddenly ceased. He heard a door open, and steps on the flags of the hall. George Cookson came and opened to him; his red eyes blinked with sleep (for after the beef and beer of Sunday dinner he always dozed), and he stared at Morgan Jones as if he were an apparition.

"Mr. Jones?" he said. "What on earth . . . ?"

Morgan Jones explained that he had been passing and had just dropped in. Miss Cookson, he said, had kindly invited him to do so. "But I see you have company," he said.

"Not at all, not at all," George Cookson said heartily. "Come in, Mr. Jones. This is open house on a Sunday. We never know who may turn up. Step this way. . . . Hi, Elsie!" he called, "here's another young man for you!"

His gross bulk towering above Morgan Jones, he thrust him forward into a drawing-room crowded with hostile eyes that seemed to stare critically at his small, dusty figure and to take a savage delight in his nervousness. Elsie came forward to greet him. She looked deliciously cool in a billowy muslin frock; her cheeks were bright with excitement; she smiled, but the eyes with which she surveyed him from his dank brow to the dusty turn of his trousers were hard and contemptuous. When she shook hands, politely, Morgan Jones was aware of the moistness of his hot palm against her cool fingers.

"Miss Cookson," he said humbly, "I hope you won't be thinking this an intrusion. You were saying at the dance, you remember, that you'ld have no objection to my dropping in; but if you're finding it at all inconvenient . . ."

"Not at all, Mr. Jones," she said. "I'm so glad you've come." (But though her voice was enchanting—like light bells, he thought—he knew she was not glad, but embarrassed.) "You wanted to see the house, didn't you? I must tell Mother. Mother, darling, this is Mr. Jones. You know him by sight."

"Yes, yes. Indeed, this is a very great pleasure,"

Morgan Jones said eagerly. But before he had shaken hands with Mrs. Cookson, Elsie had left them. Her mother was talking to him now ("Won't you sit over here, Mr. Jones, away from these noisy young people?"), but he couldn't listen to what she was telling him about the house having been built in the reign of Henry VIII ("1509–1547," his scholastic mind thought automatically), and restored in the reign of Queen Anne ("1702–1714"), and, again, sixty years ago; because, though she took such pains to inform him intelligently and correctly, Mrs. Cookson's mind, he knew well, was no more interested in him than he was in her.

While the sweet mouth spoke, the tired eyes were watching every movement of her husband, who, restlessly prowling, seemed suddenly to make up his mind and slunk out of the room. (Mrs. Cookson knew where and why: he was going to the dining-room to whip himself up with a swig of whisky.) And Mr. Jones's eyes, though he listened and smiled and nodded, were glancing at the "noisy young people" who, no longer noisy, had broken apart into two couples—Mary Lydgate and Jim in one corner, Steve and Elsie in another.

Jim and Mary seemed ill at ease, the young man was showing her photographs taken on the farm, which she examined listlessly: but Elsie and Steve were getting on like a house on fire—Elsie glowing in the light of Steve's bold eyes and of the teasing compliments he paid her, more radiantly alive than he had ever seen her before. Once she caught Mr. Jones's jealous eyes and became self-conscious. Her own eyes, still soft with the smile which Steve had left in them, suddenly hardened. Mr. Jones saw her lay her hand on his arm and whisper. Then Lydgate, too, glanced at him savagely, and they rose together. Elsie's billowing muslin passed through the French window into the garden in front of him. Mr. Jones could hear them laughing outside, and the laughter was cruel. He believed they were laughing at him.

"But the inscription is in the next room," Mrs. Cookson was saying. (If they hurried, she thought, she would be able to catch George before he found the key of the cellarette, which she had hidden in a vase on the mantelpiece.) "Won't you come this way, Mr. Jones?" Jim Cookson looked up thankfully: he and Mary were to be left alone.

The cruel laughter had been succeeded by a silence even more cruel. Where had they gone? Morgan Jones thought. What were they doing in the garden? Would she allow him to kiss her? Would a man like that wait to be allowed?

"I believe the motto is very uncommon," Mrs. Cookson said. "Ah, here you are, George!"

George Cookson, the key of the cellarette in his hand, edged away from the sideboard and scowled at them, then started humming a tune and slunk out again.

"You see," Mrs. Cookson said, "it goes all round the cornice: *Plenty and grace be in this place*. . . . But the spelling's old-fashioned."

Mr. Jones burst into a compliment: "It's nice to be thinking that though they put it up such a long time ago, the motto's still true to your home and your family, Mrs. Cookson. Yes, yes, indeed!"

Mrs. Cookson smiled pallidly. "Yes . . . It *is* nice, isn't it?"

"She doesn't look any too well, whatever," Morgan Jones thought. "An ill woman. I wonder if there's any disease in the family? Consumption. . . ." And he shuddered; for in the valleys from which he came, consumption was the scourge to be dreaded above all others, and he remembered the flush on Elsie's cheeks, which, in his innocence, he supposed to be natural. In the silence a clock on the mantelpiece, one of George's prizes, decorated with a silver name-plate, struck five.

"Why, it's tea-time," Mrs. Cookson said. "We must call the others."

She hurried to the open window and called: "Elsie . . . Elsie. . . ." There was no answer. "How like her! She's taken Mr. Lydgate down to the arbour by the moat! Having a pretty daughter is a great responsibility, Mr. Jones. Here's another conquest, I'm afraid—though one gets quite used to them. Shall we go into the garden and fetch them?"

Morgan Jones had gone pale. Every word she

had spoken fell like ice on his heart. His pride, his
hot hopes, had been sufficiently humiliated already,
and the possible sight of Elsie (who knew?) in
Lydgate's arms was more than he could bear. He took
out his watch—which was ridiculous, since the clock
had just struck—and said brusquely:

"I ought to be going."

Mrs. Cookson stared at him: "But surely you'll
stay to tea?"

"It will take me an hour to walk home and tidy myself," Morgan Jones replied grimly, "and the evening service is beginning at half-past six."

"Well, you've time for a bite and a sup," Mrs.
Cookson pleaded. "I'll send Jim to fetch them. It
won't take a moment to get you a cup of tea. It's
dreadful to think of your coming all this distance and
then running away. You see: they've laid a place for
you."

"Indeed, it's very kind of you, very kind," Mr.
Jones said firmly, "but I shall be being late. I'm
afraid I must go whatever."

He could have kicked himself for using that word,
which with infinite pains he had expurgated from his
vocabulary; but Mrs. Cookson had not even heard it.

"Why, here they are coming," she said. "So you
can say good-bye to Elsie."

Panic seized Mr. Jones. He grasped Mrs. Cookson's hand. "Good-bye, thank you," he said, then
moved hurriedly to the door. "I can find my way

out: please don't trouble to show me," he said, disappearing.

Mrs. Cookson could only imagine that he had been taken with colic but was too shy to admit it. What a very extraordinary young man!

Elsie, arriving a few moments later, was astonished and apparently delighted to find he had gone.

"Didn't you ask him to stay to tea, Mum?" she asked.

"Of course I asked him. His behaviour was most queer."

Elsie smiled contemptuously. "Well, I never said he could come here, and I can't imagine why he came. Do you know, Mr. Lydgate, he dances quite beautifully, but I think he's a little mad. I've heard he writes poetry, so he must be."

Mr. Jones himself believed he was mad. His mind was full of broken madness and hatred. When he left The Moat he found himself running, in spite of the heat. He did not know where he was running or why, until, suddenly, he found himself not in Chaddesbourne as he had expected but on the crown of Uffdown Hill. He lay there prostrate, crushed and panting. He wished he could cry; but he was too utterly miserable to cry, and, perhaps, too proud. He lay there a long time, his brain swept by gusts of wild words like a burning wind. When it cooled at last, the Chaddesbourne peal had stopped ringing; the tenor bell tolled its single funereal note. He sat up and rubbed his dusty eyes. They saw, beneath them, the green Severn plain, and beyond, smoky mountains of Wales.

"*Unto the hills,*" he thought, "*from whence cometh my help.*. . . If I could go there I could find healing. This is a strange, hateful land, and a strange people. I hate them, as my fathers hated them. They're soft and treacherous. They smile, and they steal your soul. . . ."

Then he thought of the verses folded in his breast-pocket; and the hot words, coming back to him, carried him away on their rhythm; and with them, the frustrated passion that inspired them flamed up anew.

"I shall love her and suffer as long as I live," he told himself. "That is my fate. There is no escaping from it. I shall always love her."

It was dark when he returned to Chaddesbourne: not a soul in the street but a woman hurrying in the distance whom he recognized as the girl called Nellie Bunt. Mrs. Webb had gone to bed, but had left him his supper. The sight of food nauseated him in spite of his hunger. He went to bed. The night was as quiet as death until, just after midnight, its silence was ripped by the roar of a racing motor-car. Though Morgan Jones did not know this, it meant that Jack Ombersley had come home.

XVI

DECLARATION OF INDEPENDENCE

JACK OMBERSLEY was unfeignedly thankful when the last roar brought him to the level of Aaron Bunt's cottage. These six-cylinder *Grand Prix* Pearce-Tregarons were the devil to drive. When they chose to go, they went like the wind and passed everything else on the road; but when they conked out on you —as this brute which Trevor Tregaron had lent him had done no less than three times between Oxford and Chaddesbourne—the strength which had previously propelled them like flying projectiles appeared to be concentrated in resisting all human efforts to restart them. Jack liked "messing about" with cars, he liked nothing better: he was passionately interested in their intricacies of carburettor-settings, ignition and timing; but to have been held up thrice for an hour at a time in less than a hundred miles by this monster's sullen inertia was more than a joke.

This last time the self-starter, instead of turning the fly-wheel, revolved by itself with the faint whirr of a vacuum-cleaner. "The damned Bendix-engagement's gone west," Jack thought, "and if the brute thinks I'm going to crank her over now she's mistaken. I've had just about enough of her." So he got out and pushed the two tons of dead metal to the side of the road.

"Not much fun coming home like this, anyway," he thought, "even without troubles of this kind. Everybody will have gone to bed, and all the doors will be locked."

He entered the drive and stole round the front of the house, keeping carefully to the grass verge, which would muffle the sound of his footsteps. "What an ugly great barrack!" he thought, "what a rotten white elephant! Why does Dad want to go and bury us in a dull hole like this, miles away from anywhere, when, for half the money he wastes on it, he might take a service-flat in Belgravia or Mayfair, where he could keep touch with his army friends—if he wants to— and Mum and Catherine and I could have a good time? Why can't he understand that Chaddesbourne means nothing to us? After all, why should it? We never set eyes on the place before six months ago!"

On the southern face of the house two windows showed light. They were those, Jack was almost certain, of his mother's bedroom, and the thought of her lying there still awake softened his harshness and filled his mind with a boyish tenderness. Catherine and he were "good pals," she was miles superior to any girl he had ever met; but in the case of Helen

Ombersley such comparisons did not arise: she was his "little mother," the object of an unquestioning devotion which took count neither of age nor sex nor appearance nor any other attribute; the one human being in the world whom he blindly loved, from whom he was assured of an equally blind understanding and sympathy.

"If she's awake," he thought, "I shall go and tell her. Much better to get it over."

At the back of the house he found a pantry-window which Langley had neglected to see fastened. Jack climbed through it and groped, by the side of the door, for an electric switch. There was none. "What a house!" he thought. "Not even electric light." So he struck a match. A mouse scuttled along the wainscot. He saw on a shelf a plateful of sausage-rolls, and becoming aware that he had eaten nothing since tea-time, crammed one greedily into his mouth. "If I could find a bottle of beer . . ." he thought. But the unhasped window was Langley's only lapse.

Jack made his way to the hall and lit a candle. Half a dozen dead Ombersleys stared at him from the walls in sleepy surprise. "Solemn old blighters," he thought. On the stairs he was stopped by a sudden vision of the huge Snyders picture of a heron driven down by falcons, which he had never noticed before. He stared at it now because the sight of it illuminated in the depths of his mind a suppressed desire. "Before the end of this year," he thought, "I must learn to fly." At the top of the stairs he halted. There were so many doors on the landing, all alike, that for the moment he couldn't be quite sure which belonged to his mother's room; but when he examined them more closely he saw a faint glimmer of light beneath the bottom of one of them. He opened it softly and entered.

Helen Ombersley was lying half propped-up on the pillows with a candle-lamp at her elbow. She had been reading; but the book had fallen of its own weight on the coverlet. She lay there, in a little pink bed-jacket trimmed with swansdown scarcely paler than her silvery hair, which made her look curiously child-like—more like a girl who from some caprice had powdered her hair, than a woman who might easily have been a grandmother. When Jack opened the door, she started (for she had been lost in a dream); but as soon as she saw him her face became radiant with love.

"Jack . . . My darling!" she whispered; then put a finger to her lips; for surprised as she was, she did not forget that Miles was sleeping next door.

"Mother, dearest. . . ."

In a moment he was beside her; she was in his arms: strong young arms which held her and instantly banished her loneliness. His face, cooled by the rushing night-air, lay against her cheek. And he, too, for the first time in the last wretched forty-eight hours, was happy in holding her, in feeling the warmth and softness of her face, in smelling her faint perfume of lilac.

"But, my darling, what does this mean?" she whispered. "You've not written for ages."

"I couldn't, Mum. Things have been much too hectic. I'm in an awful mess."

"An awful mess?" Helen Ombersley's heart went cold. She remembered Lady Clun's letter. So it was true after all. Why hadn't she acted on it at once, hurried off to Oxford to see him? "This is partly my fault," she told herself. But panic would never do. She said, quietly:

"What do you mean, darling? Is it something to do with . . . some girl?"

Jack laughed suddenly—and so loudly that she was frightened lest Miles should hear him. But that laugh lifted the ice from her heart. She thanked God for it. After that nothing really mattered. If it was only money. . . .

"Some girl!" he repeated scornfully. "You ought to know me better than that, Mum. I've come rather a mucker, that's all. I've been sent down."

"Sent down? What does that mean exactly, darling?"

"I can't go back to the House, Mum. Not this term, anyway. The Dean was most awfully decent about it, I must say. But there it is. Discipline and all that. Trevor's in it as well."

"That Tregaron boy? You know, darling, I never liked him."

"Oh, old Trevor's all right. He's one of the very best. We got caught out, that's all."

"Is it anything to do with a place called 'The Blue Fox'?"

"Mum, how did you know? Did the Dean write to you?"

"No."

"Then I know who it was," Jack said indignantly. "It was that rotter Ledwyche!"

"Never mind about that, darling. Tell me what happened."

"Well. . . . It's all very simple. Trevor and I have been trying to beat the speed-record from Oxford to Hyde Park Corner. He has one of his father's new 'sixes,' and we did it all right. It was such fun hareing up to town over the Chilterns in the middle of the night when the roads were all clear that we sort of got into the habit of it. We kept on beating our own time—they're marvellous cars, Mum; perfectly astonishing performance—and when we got up to town we used to feel a bit dizzy. So we used to go along to this place that Trevor belongs to, put in an hour or so dancing and stoking up with kippers and beer, and then back to Oxford before daylight. The last time we did it we jolly near averaged sixty, and that's moving, you know! But just short of Oxford Trevor got into a skid and we crashed. He's a topping driver, Mum. I don't believe anyone else, except Segrave or Campbell, could have corrected it as well as he did. We slewed round into a lamp-post and ripped off one wing and buckled a wheel. I thought the back-axle must have gone: no other car could have stood it; but you know what marvellous material old Tregaron uses."

"And you weren't hurt, darling?"

"Not a scratch on either of us. The only trouble was the wire-wheel was so twisted that we couldn't get the blessed thing off to change it. We had such a job over it that we clean forgot about time, and before we could get it clear it was nearly daylight. I told Trevor we'd much better leave the bus where she was and make a bolt for it; but he's an obstinate fellow and hates being beaten, so there you are! And he *did* get it right, you know, Mum. But just as we started to push off, along comes a bicycle with a fat don on it, trying to get his weight down by a ride before breakfast. I didn't know who he was; but old Trevor did. He'd met him before. When he saw us he hopped off his bicycle and came over to us with a nasty gloating look in his eyes. 'Are you gentlemen members of this University?' All the usual stuff. Name and college and the rest of it. He was one of the proctors. Sheer bad luck! Any decent proctor would have been in bed, but this blighter suffers from in-somnia: overfeeding, like most of them. And there we were! *Ça y est*, as the French say. Next morning—

that's yesterday—an invitation to visit him. He belongs to Pembroke—a little place just round the
corner. Next thing, the Dean sent for us. Awkward
questions. What were we doing? Where had we
been?"

"And you told him?"

"Of course, Mum," Jack answered indignantly.
"The old Dean's a fine fellow. We'd been fairly
caught out. He was extraordinarily nice, as I've told
you: so decent, in fact, that he made me feel rather
an ass. As for sending us down—well, we'd both
of us one or two minor bad marks against us,
and I honestly don't see what else he could have
done."

"How did you get here to-night?"

"I ought to have been here hours ago. Trevor had
another bus—one of their old *Grand Prix* models—
in Morris's garage, and he lent it me. We were going
to try it out against the new six, make a race for it as
far as his home in Warwickshire and spend the night
there; but as soon as we started he shot off out of sight
—my word, those new sixes can move!—and after
that I had three packets of trouble on the road. Then
I saw a fingerpost pointing to Worcester, and I
thought, 'Well, this game's not good enough. I'll
push on to Chaddesbourne to-night and 'phone Trevor
in the morning.' But we're not on the telephone, are
we? Lord, Mum, what a place!"

"You can telephone from the post-office, darling.

You look tired. There's no bed made up for you."

"Oh, don't worry about that, Mum. I can roll myself up in some blankets. And don't move. Shall I put your light out?"

He bent over and kissed her in the dark.

When he had gone, Helen Ombersley felt an access of relief that approached exultation. It seemed odd that a mother should be enraptured by the news that her son had been sent down from Oxford. That only showed how deeply she had been distressed—more deeply than she knew—by the implications of Evelyn Clun's letter. Why was it, she asked herself, that the mere hint of Jack's being indefinitely associated, even innocently associated, with an unknown woman should appear to her so much more serious than the actual breakdown of his Oxford career, than what amounted to a false start in life? Why was it that the first, reacting through her emotions, devastated her, while the second, reacting through reason, left her almost unmoved? Was it, she wondered, because of the tradition, bred in her bones, that had for centuries made the D'Abitots dread misalliance more than disgrace: an instinct, in effect, for the protection and accumulation of property? (A fallacious instinct, after all: for if the D'Abitots had been less correct in these matters and had admitted less attenuated strains to their family blood, the title which had died with her father might not now be extinct!) Or was it an instinct more primitive still: the tigerish jealousy which

o

some mothers feel for the women who attract their sons?

Helen Ombersley would have been ashamed to admit it was either of these. Indeed, now that the danger had passed, it appeared unprofitable (as well as humiliating) to examine the secret springs of her past emotion too closely. What concerned her now was the present—or rather the immediate future: not what she had felt, but what Miles was going to feel. How would he take Jack's catastrophe? she wondered.

First of all there was the question of discipline: that strict adherence to the rules of the game—in war as in cricket—which was the beginning and end of his ethical creed. Jack was going to be tried by court-martial, and courts-martial were merciless. In her quality as Jack's defender she began to search for extenuating circumstances. There could be none. Her son was an Ombersley, and because of that, rather than in spite of it, must be judged more strictly. Or for precedents? It occurred to her that a number of distinguished men had been sent down from Oxford; but the only one she could remember at the moment was Shelley—a most unfortunate example, she reflected, smiling to herself, for even now the quiet sense of humour with which she regarded her husband's rigidity did not quite forsake her. There must surely be other distinguished names, she thought; but, even if there were, it seemed doubtful if they would help Jack's case. No Ombersley had ever yet been distinguished or ever would be; and what Miles demanded was that Jack should behave like an Ombersley. He would probably blame her for having sent him to Eton. . . .

It was all very difficult; but something had to be done. In the morning, when, by following the orderly succession of sounds, she knew that Miles had finished his exercises, she put on her most attractive wrapper and entered his dressing-room.

"Jack came home late last night, Miles," she said.

"Why? Is anything wrong?"

She told him, as gently as she could, what had happened. He listened in silence.

"I think the Tregaron boy is to blame," she said.

"That fellow Jack picked up at Eton!"

(She could almost have smiled. How calculable his reactions were!)

"There was no harm in it really, Miles darling," she said. "Nothing . . . nothing to be *ashamed* of. . . ."

Miles grunted. "It's the lack of discipline in this generation. Particularly at Oxford. Jack should have gone to Sandhurst."

"Don't things like that happen at Sandhurst, too, darling?" she innocently asked. But she felt sorry she had said that: it seemed hardly fair. Rather like shooting a sitting hen. Miles evaded the question.

"I'll see him after breakfast," he said.

That, again, was one of his cast-iron rules. Under

no conceivable circumstances would Miles permit any personal problem, pleasant or unpleasant, to enter his mind until he had breakfasted. Not even a letter must be opened. (She had often wondered how he had managed to preserve this integrity sacred through the war.)

And his behaviour that morning, although she had broken that rule, allowed no exception. Miles sat down at the table, having nodded good morning to Jack, without giving the least sign that anything unusual had happened. He moved slowly, methodically through his accustomed programme—first porridge (which he always ate standing), then bacon and eggs, then a shaving of the admirable Chaddesbourne ham from the sideboard, then toast and marmalade—with a regularity which suggested that even if Langley had announced that the house was on fire he would have gone on eating.

Catherine came in, as usual a little late and as usual apologizing. At the sight of Jack her face lit up with pleasure.

"Why, Jack . . . how lovely! When did you come?"

"Last night."

"And how long are you staying?"

"Not quite sure."

"But the term isn't over?"

"No. This is a surprise."

Miles went on with his breakfast. When he had

swallowed the last mouthful of coffee he folded his *Morning Post*.

"Come along to the smoking-room, Jack, when you've finished," he said.

"I've finished now, Dad. I'll come with you."

They went. Catherine stared at her mother. "What's it all about, Mum?"

"They want to talk something over, darling," Helen Ombersley said. "I must fly at once. I ought to catch Follows before he goes to the kitchen-garden."

"Well, I think you might tell me," Catherine said. But her mother was gone.

Miles Ombersley closed the door of the smoking-room behind them and sat down at his desk. On the other side of it, Jack stood, like an orderly-room defaulter, in front of the six-inch map of the Chaddesbourne estate. Miles sat back and folded his arms and looked at his son. He surveyed him judici-ally, dispassionately, and knew that he loved him; but his eyes betrayed none of this tenderness. A good-looking boy, he thought, well-made and clean-cut. Though he's neither D'Abitot nor Ombersley, he has the stamp of a thoroughbred. Nobody seeing him as he stands there could doubt for a moment he was English. But he's soft, he reflected: he hasn't the look of a stayer as yet; he needs pretty strict training; and, from what I can see, he's not likely to get that at Oxford. Of course Sandhurst would have done it, but now it's too late for that. If I take him in hand and put him over some stiffish fences he should be able to make up what he's lost. On the whole I'm glad he's finished with Oxford—or Oxford with him. He said: "Well, Jack. . . ?"

"Mum's told you, Dad. I've nothing to say . . . except that I'm terribly sorry."

Miles thought: "When I was his age I called my father 'sir.' It's better. More manly. Less sentimental."

He said, looking the boy in the eyes:

"Rather a poor show, don't you think?"

"A rotten show, sir."

That was better: more like man to man. The boy stood up to it well.

"Well, we'll say no more about it," Miles said.

Jack flushed quickly. This was generous. He felt grateful to Miles and proud of him. A smaller man would have sermonized. But Miles hadn't finished. He went on:

"What d'you propose doing now?"

"I don't want to go up again."

"They don't seem very anxious to have you."

"I mean later. I've loved being at the House; but I think I'm through with it."

"Through with it . . . through with it," Miles thought. "That's an Americanism. . . . Why can't he speak English?"

"You see," Jack went on, "I'm not really *doing* anything there. If I went up again and read hard I might get a 'third' with luck. But what's the use of it, anyway? I'm not going to be a parson or a school-master."

"I'm inclined to agree with you," Miles said. "To tell you the truth, I'm not altogether sorry you've come home—although, of course, I should have pre-ferred your coming home less—dramatically." He smiled, and Jack, too, smiled uneasily. "You see," Miles continued, "we have rather a long furrow to plough and a hard one at that. You know I've got rid of Healey?"

"Mother told me."

"I had to do so for a number of reasons which I won't go into; but the best of them all was simply that I couldn't afford to keep him. Your grandfather left this estate much neglected, I'm sorry to say—that wasn't entirely his fault—and considerably encum-bered. When I succeeded, I found myself faced with a great many expenses besides death-duties, and nothing to meet them with except my very small savings. There were mortgages too, and . . ." Miles hesitated . . . "and other charges." (Even though he wished to be candid, his code of piety prevented him from mentioning Mrs. Clarke.) "I've met them as well as I can. It hasn't been easy, and we're by no means out of the wood yet. I'm not, as you know, Jack, exactly a young man. We must face that, and think for the future. When you succeed me, as you will before you're middle-aged, I don't want you to have to face the wretched conditions I found when I came here. I want to leave everything in order and so arranged that if I died to-morrow . . ."

"I wish you wouldn't say that, Dad."

". . . that if I died to-morrow," Miles went on firmly, "you would be able to take over the reins. I've been waiting to talk to you about this for some time, Jack, and this is a good moment. Of course, Chaddesbourne doesn't quite mean to you what it means to me. Not yet. I don't see why it should. You weren't born here; you didn't grow up in it. But now that you've come home, I'm quite sure the place will take hold of you. You'll get to know every path, every field, every hedge—pretty nearly every tree of it. . . ."

(Miles spoke quietly, unemotionally; there was no feeling to be heard in his voice; yet his son was conscious of the passion that underlay the flat words, as one is aware of the power beneath the gentle hum of a dynamo. He was aware, and rather afraid of it. It was strong, and it threatened his liberty.)

"This is a full-time job," Miles went on. "It fills your mind all the time. You wake up in the night and find yourself thinking: 'That hedge on the far side of Tump Piece ought to be laid and pleached this year,' or: 'Where did I see that wire in the hedge? On the Uffley side of the wood. I must remember to speak about that before they start cub-hunting.' Things like that. Then there's forestry . . ."

("What do *I* care about forestry?" Jack thought. "How should I ever care about forestry?")

"Foxhall Wood's past redemption. It was badly used forty years ago and hasn't recovered. It will never be much use to anyone except as a covert. But there are spinneys and copses all over our land that need systematic thinning, and others that ought to be cut and replanted. I had an expert down from the Ministry a few weeks ago, and he advised me to get out a regular planting-plan for the whole estate. A nice fellow, and extraordinarily clear-headed. Of course, trees we plant now won't come to maturity in my time; but they may in yours, with any luck, and even more in your children's. You see what I'm driving at? Things like this give you something to work for. . . ."

Jack Ombersley was puzzled and surprised. He had never before heard his father deliver himself of his thoughts at such length. He had generally regarded him as an impersonal, taciturn figure, who, appearing on rare occasions, made life uncomfortable by suggestions of discipline, and stole his mother from him. But his surprise was far less disturbing than the embarrassment he felt when, suddenly rising from his desk, Miles approached him and slipped his arm round his shoulder. It was the first gesture of intimacy or affection Jack had ever known in him, and Miles, too, seemed a little shy of the caress, for he quickly removed his arm, and when he next spoke his tone was almost peremptory.

"You ought to know this map by heart," he said. "There's not a lot to learn. Our boundaries, as you see, are washed in with red. They've not changed in my time, though if you look at those shaded patches you'll see that your great-grandfather sold a couple of farms on the Wychbury side sixty years ago. I've always hoped to get them back again. If you'll ride up to Uffdown some day and keep this map in your mind, you'll be able to plot out the whole estate quite easily; you see, it's roughly a triangle. . . . Now all this land here"—he pointed with his pencil—"is shockingly badly drained, which means, of course, that it's sour and unproductive. Sooner or later we ought to deal with this—for our own sakes as well as our tenants'—though for some years to come we certainly shan't have enough money to tackle it. But that doesn't mean we oughtn't to keep the matter in mind and work it all out and lay our plans carefully. As I say, there's no end to the interest and excitement of a job like this. . . ."

("Does he really find it exciting?" Jack thought. "That's an odd word to use!")

"I suppose part of it's pride: one doesn't forget— and I don't think one ought to forget—that our people have been handling it, some of them well and some middling badly, for a few hundred years. But there's more to it than that—at least, so I feel—more than pride or even than sentiment. . . ." Miles hesitated;

he smiled nervously, almost apologetically. "More than that," he went on. "This place is a bit of England."

("Oh, Lord!" Jack thought wearily, "I'm in for a bout of flag-wagging. He might cut that out.")

But Miles, having broken the ice of his own shyness, plunged boldly.

"Don't imagine," he said, "that I'm going to give you a lecture on patriotism. We had plenty of highfalutin stuff of that kind during the war. I shouldn't say what I'm saying now to anyone but yourself—not because I'm ashamed of it—I'm not—but because one doesn't talk about the things one feels most deeply. But the fact remains: in our own time we've had to fight for our country. Several millions of us, including Dick and Roger, have died for her. I had the luck to come through, and you, thank God, were too young. And the country's not what she was, Jack. She's bled white; she's desperately tired, and desperately poor. But in spite of all that, she's still the most important thing in the world—in *my* world, at any rate, and yours. That's where *we* come in, you and I—and remember, there are thousands of others thinking just like us, although they don't talk about it, and thousands of Chaddesbournes, too. It's our job to build up what the war destroyed. It's a devilish hard job, and we can't see much farther than the end of our noses, either. Well, I don't think that matters. The only thing we're concerned with is to do our duty

as well as we can by our own bit of land and our people.
If everyone else does the same—as most of 'em will,
for we're an amazingly stout-hearted race, although
I say it—there's nothing to fear except a longish spell
of collar-work and short-commons, which won't hurt
anybody who has the guts of a louse. You and I can
stand it, anyway. That's our job, as I see it. Are
you ready to weigh in?"

Miles asked the question point-blank. He still
smiled, as though anxious to qualify by a hint of
raillery, which could be accepted or discounted at
pleasure, this long dissertation which—although he
meant every word of it—had been so awkward to
deliver, even in confidence. He looked at Jack almost
pathetically, as if waiting for an assurance that he
needn't really have felt shy about it, and that everything was all right.

But the boy did not answer. His black brows were
obstinate, his lips petulant. He stood with his back to
the wall and the map of the Chaddesbourne estate,
his mind full of surging antagonism and resentment
which he couldn't, or dared not, express.

All this threadbare, canting talk about England
and the war! Hadn't he been fed to the teeth with
it for the greater part of his life? It was all very
well to smile apologetically; but didn't Miles realize
that all those clichés were out of date? When one
heard them from elderly strangers one laughed and
felt slightly ashamed: one felt, naturally, much more

ashamed when they fell from the lips of one's father. Duty. . . . That was another of those high-sounding words that meant nothing. Duty, discipline, drilling—interchangeable, and equally unpleasant. Duty to one's forbears (Why, in God's name?)—to one's country (What was wrong with it, anyway? Look at the new roads!)—to the land. (All his friends were agreed that the land was a bore.) What about one's duty to oneself? Life was short enough in all conscience—it had been too short for Dick and Roger, poor devils!—and while it lasted, a man "with the guts of a louse," as his father put it, ought to make the best of it. Could he be said to be making the best of it if he buried himself in Chaddesbourne, away from his friends, away from his interests, away from everything that gave it colour and vivacity? The young men of his generation, for the first time in history, knew their own minds. They could see where fine words like "duty" had driven their blindfold elders. They were all individualists—self-expression was the magic word—and if solemn, old-fashioned people preferred to label it 'selfishness,' what the hell did it matter? Let them call it just what they liked and leave him alone!

They wouldn't leave him alone. That, unluckily, wasn't the worst of it. They wouldn't play fair. His father would be shocked to the roots if he suggested such a thing; but there it was. Was it "cricket," he asked himself, to sugar hard reason with sentiment?

To drag in one's ancestors, one's dead brothers; to throw in (most unfair to all!) that gesture of paternal affection; to make it appear—if one had the courage of one's convictions and refused to be bluffed—that one was behaving, to say the least of it, with shocking bad taste? Miles was waiting for his answer. "If I don't stand firm now," Jack thought, "I might just as well throw up the sponge." He said awkwardly:

"I know what you mean, Dad. And I know how you feel about it; but I'm afraid I don't feel the same."

"You don't feel the same? About what?"

"About most things, I'm afraid. Particularly about Chaddesbourne. I'm not saying this on the spur of the moment; I've been thinking an awful lot about it during the last year, and I've talked it over with a lot of fellows of my own age who are in the same boat, so to speak, as I am. And we've nearly all of us agreed that we don't want to drift."

"To drift? My dear boy, I don't want you to drift. I want you to settle down to your oars and pull your weight. There's a strong tide against us."

"Always 'us'," Jack thought. "I'm afraid I shall have to be brutal." He said:

"I know, Dad. That's just what I mean. Isn't it rather a waste of strength? You pull like the dickens and think you're no end of a swell, but when you look at the bank you find you're just where you were when you started. That's why we ask ourselves; 'Is it good enough?' "

"Is *what* good enough?"

"This business of sweating your heart out over being a landowner. It's all right for a fellow who has mineral-royalties and that to fall back on; but everyone I've ever heard of loses money over farming— tenants expect more and more every year, from what I can see—and so ... well, I mean what *is* the use of throwing good money after bad? You wear yourself out, and at the end of it all, if you're lucky, you may make two ends meet. Or you don't—and the wretched fellow who comes after you starts with a bigger handicap. Just as you did. And then it begins all over again. Whereas a chap like Sir Robert Tregaron ..."

"Ah, I see. ... But go on, Jack."

"Well, there is a case in point. Trevor Tregaron has an uncle, a man called Sir Esmond Delahaye, who lives down in Radnorshire."

"I know whom you mean. His father knew your grandfather."

"Well, these Delahayes are more or less in the same position as ourselves. Trevor's uncle came into this place, Glan Escob, or whatever it's called, and he thought it was his duty to hang on by the skin of his teeth, as he has done, and by all accounts it's jolly uncomfortable. While Trevor's grandfather sold all his land for a waterworks for a pot of money ..."

"And lost every penny of it afterwards. I know that story."

"Yes, Dad, but my point is this: Trevor's father,

who was his son, pushed off on his own and went into the motor-car business, and now he's a millionaire. Whereas, if he'd stuck on at home like Sir Esmond, he'd have been just where we are. It was a good bit of luck for him that his father sold out. Otherwise he might have been tied to this place down in Wales."

"Sir Robert Tregaron, by all accounts, is a mechanical genius. Besides which the war helped him," Miles added grimly. "It didn't help us." ("The war," Jack thought, "always the war! Can't they ever forget it?") "Am I to gather from this," Miles went on, in a tone of irony, "that you'ld advise me to sell Chaddesbourne?"

"I wish to goodness you would, Dad!"

How passionately he spoke! Miles gazed at him, almost too much puzzled and hurt to be angry. "There's something wrong with him," he thought. "Neither D'Abitot nor Ombersley. Something missing. Neither Dick nor Roger could have thought or spoken those words. But Dick was killed and buried in Flanders, and Roger missing. Four years missing. . . . If Roger could come back!"

He said dryly: "I'm afraid your wishes will not be realized. Not while I'm alive, anyway. You don't want to stay at Chaddesbourne and help me?"

"It sounds rotten of me, Dad; but I really can't help it. I should hate it. You see, really I'm not cut out for it, and that's that."

"What are you cut out for? Or what do you *think*

you're cut out for? What can you *do?*"

"I can drive a car . . ."

"A chauffeur may possibly get three pounds a week. If I may say so, you're not very ambitious."

"Well, of course, Dad, I don't mean *that*. You see, Trevor's a friend of mine. I think I could get into Pearce-Tregaron's with his influence."

"But you're not an engineer. Rather late in the day to talk about that, don't you think?"

"Oh, I don't mean actual designing. There are plenty of other jobs: superintending, advertising, testing. Then there's racing as well; I'ld like that best of all. Then they're building enormous new London showrooms near Berkeley Square. I might get in there, you know."

"I see," Miles said. "What you want to be is a shopwalker: one of those young men with Old Etonian ties who condescend to sell expensive motorcars to the new rich?"

"Well, lots of fellows I know have done that, Dad, and done rather well out of it, besides having a good time. If you get hold of somebody on your own and sell him a Pearce-Tregaron, there's a good bit of commission at once." (Miles grunted.) "I don't think you quite realize, Dad: selling motor-cars is different from selling anything else. It's nothing to be ashamed of nowadays—and one *must* start somewhere."

"Indeed, yes," Miles said grimly. "It merely struck me that you were aiming rather high."

Jack looked up at him doubtfully. He was not, that morning, in a mood to appreciate irony. Miles Ombersley was smiling, as he habitually smiled when things were going against him (when he lost a set-point at tennis; when, leading his dismounted regiment, he went over the top at Loos), and Jack, who did not know him well enough to appreciate the dangerous significance of this facial gesture, was stung, when he saw it, by pangs of pity and remorse. He had dreaded this interview, expecting what he called a "bust-up," and the composure with which Miles had received first the news of his rustication and later his declaration of independence completely disarmed him.

Miles wasn't after all, it seemed, an old-fashioned "heavy" father, but an enlightened parent of the most modern school, appreciative of the new generation's superior wisdom and its right to live its own life and express itself. Such decency and sensibility, in a man of his father's advanced age, were so remarkable that he felt it imperative—no, that word would never do! —say, rather, polite, to apply a salve to the wound which he had been compelled to inflict—just as one might give half a sovereign to an old man who had been stupid enough to get knocked down by one's motor-car. After all, having won this bloodless victory, he could afford to be generous. He said:

"You know, Dad, I feel rather badly about this; I loathe disappointing you, but, honestly, I haven't made up my mind in a hurry. I've discussed this business again and again with Trevor and several other fellows, and they've all agreed it's the only thing to do. I've got to have a shot at it, anyway. If it comes off, as I'm sure it will, you'll have nothing to grumble about. If it doesn't, well, it won't be your fault, will it? There's nothing lost, anyway. If things come to the worst, I can always fall back on Chaddesbourne . . . provided you don't sell it, as I honestly think you ought to. Perhaps, later on . . ."

Miles gave a short laugh. These childish excuses, this childish importance wearied him. It was time to end them.

"Very well, Jack," he said. "I'm not going to force you to bury yourself, as you call it, at Chaddesbourne. What are your plans?"

"If I can get the bus Trevor lent me going, I shall drive over to the works at Coventry and ask for that job. I'll see Trevor's father myself."

"Is the car insured?"

"I expect so."

"Let's hope it is. There's just one more matter: have you left any debts at Oxford?"

Jack flushed quickly. "I didn't intend to mention that. Oxford tradesmen are awfully decent, generally speaking."

"Yes, until you go down. I dislike owing money. They must be paid. Will you make out a list? A full list. Don't keep anything back, as people usually do."

"I'm afraid there'll be rather a lot. You see, I

hadn't been expecting this. I'd been hoping to go easy during my last year and pick up a bit."

Miles nodded. "One always does, but it never works. A full list, mind!"

He took up a paper-knife and began to open his letters. It was a signal of dismissal. Jack moved towards the door, then turned suddenly:

"Dad . . . I'm terribly sorry."

No reply save the sound of the thin knife-blade slitting envelopes, methodically, one by one. Then the click of an ancient latch. Miles Ombersley put down the paper-knife. He was alone.

Most bitterly alone. . . . And that at a moment when he had found himself looking forward with an eagerness which he now saw to have been pathetic to the long, uphill task of rehabilitating Chaddesbourne, not alone, as heretofore, but with the collaboration of Jack's lively youth and enthusiasm. He had imagined the two of them, working together in that same room; riding over the fields side by side, planting, draining, scheming, laying plans for the future, countering present emergencies. Jack was going to have all the experience of which his own service and his father's odd ways had deprived himself. Little by little, as things grew easier under prudent management, he was going to leave more and more of the guidance of the estate in Jack's hands, until finally, when Jack married, he would probably hand over the whole of it to him, so that before he died he would be able to say a *Nunc*

Dimittis, with the consciousness that, in spite of the war's catastrophe and the shocks of quaking society, an Ombersley still held Chaddesbourne, and held it more firmly than the hands from which he had received it.

His confidence in this event had never been coloured by the faintest shadow of doubt, and was so deeply rooted that even now, when the last hour's convulsion had shattered its foundations, it still seemed valid—his condition reminding him (it was odd how these images returned!) of a subaltern in his regiment whom he had seen at the battle of the Somme staring at his own leg, torn away by a shell, with an incredulous smile on his face. No more than that wretched fellow—they had picked him up dead when the line fell back—could Miles Ombersley believe what had happened to him. He was not even angry with Jack—it was no use being angry—he was merely stunned. With the trained instinct of a man in whom action must always take precedence over emotion, his mind was already adapting itself to the changed conditions. The line had given way, at a point where he least expected it. This was no time for apportioning blame or giving way to recriminations: the gap must be closed, the line re-formed, reserves hurried up; for in war (and at that moment he was in the thick of action) disaster was certain unless the man in command kept his head.

Only once did Miles Ombersley permit himself to reflect on what had passed, when, gazing out of the window, he saw Catherine pass down the drive, tall and slim in her spotted muslin, moving swiftly, delicately. The sight of her stirred him then, not because he felt tenderly towards her (and in his rigid, inarticulate way he adored her), but because, even at a distance, he was suddenly struck by her physical resemblance to Roger, the younger of his two sons who had been posted as "missing" at Gheluvelt.

"My God," he heard his heart crying, "how I wish she was a boy!"

"But I have no boys left," he told himself bitterly, "and I've no time to spare. I must get on with my business."

He returned to the morning's letters. There was one from the Dean of Christ Church. He laid it aside, unread. That matter no longer interested him. Another, from Miss Loach, he did not even trouble to open. There were two circulars, one relating to Bromsberrow Fair, and another a time-table of Mr. Hackett's new motor-bus service, over which his eyes hardened: the enemy was showing persistent activity. Bills . . . bills . . . He found he had opened one by mistake It was addressed to Jack by a tailor in Oxford. Ninety-three pounds eight shillings and sixpence. A stiffish beginning: he hoped they were not all on that scale. He replaced the bill in its envelope; he scribbled on the back: *Opened in error. M.O.*, and tossed it aside. Smaller bills of his own. ("But they mount up," he thought. "The first lot of the Midsummer Quarter. I'll pay them later.") A long envelope. Wilburn's, perhaps? Or was it his banker's? Yes. No good news to be expected there: one had always spent more than one thought. That could wait. And this? A copy of a letter:

S.R.D.C. Stourton Rural District Council. *Housing and Town Planning Act, 1919. Section 19. I have to report that in my opinion each of the under-mentioned houses is unfit for human habitation, and is incapable of being rendered fit at a reasonable expense. I ask permission to serve the appropriate notices under this section.*

"At a reasonable expense ..." Miles thought. "Two thousand five hundred pounds. If I don't do it, they'll pull them down and stick up their own abortions. I can't do it, can't possibly do it, unless I sell Uffley. And, after all," he asked himself bitterly, "why shouldn't I sell Uffley? What's the use of clinging to it? Nobody cares for it but myself: as soon as I'm gone it'll be sold."

It seemed to him as if the Chaddesbourne he knew and loved were already disintegrating, beyond recovery, beneath his eyes.

XVII

HAMMERCLAVIER

CATHERINE OMBERSLEY, left alone in the breakfast-room, wrinkled her brows. This delicious midsummer morning which had begun so sweetly with a luxurious awakening to the whisper of scythes mowing the "adlands" of a meadow (which the machine could not reach) and had continued with the glad surprise of Jack's unexpected appearance, had all gone wrong. The family pretended that there was nothing the matter; and this annoyed her, because she was normally inquisitive, and disliked being "shielded" or "put off" like a child. Even her mother had evaded her questions with a hollow excuse; she hadn't in the least wanted to "catch Follows before he went to the kitchen-garden"; she was walking to and fro beside the long border, which was visible from the breakfast-room window, alone, and evidently preferring to be alone. And this hurt Catherine, too.

It was a shame, she thought, to allow such a peerless morning—full summer at its best, though the note of the cuckoo was cracking—to be spoiled by their wilful mysteries. She had felt so nice and fresh and serene in her clean white muslin spotted with black, and now life was a muddle. There was only one cure for such a nonsensical mood, she told herself: to go to the drawing-room and play the piano and forget all about it.

Yet this morning she couldn't play; couldn't even begin. She sat moodily turning over the pages of a volume of Chopin. With the turn of each page, a condensed version of its contents flickered through her mind. She heard it with the inward ear and dismissed it impatiently. Nothing answered to her mood or subdued it: not even the little mazurkas could tempt her fingers to dance. She closed the volume of Chopin and put it aside, and suddenly, arbitrarily, a string of words ran through her empty mind: *I should cut out Chopin and Schumann and Tschaikovski and Scriabin*. . . . She seemed to be hearing not merely those words, but the voice that had spoken them: a deep, pleasant voice, she thought, without any affectation—less affected even than Jack's with his lazy Oxford inflection: a firm voice, a confident, sensible voice. Could a voice be confident, sensible? Such adjectives surely belonged more properly to the voice's owner. "He has nice hands and nice eyes," she thought—which was rather straying from the point—"and he's perfectly right about Chopin; that's very wise of him. How did he know?"

Since the night of the dance she had often asked herself questions about Dr. Selby. His voice (or himself) kept invading her mind with a persistence she found hard to explain, unless it were an example of that haphazard telepathy which can exist, without any particular emotional sympathy, between strangers, and means no more than that a stray thought launched into space happens to reach a brain which by chance is tuned to receive it. She had dreamt of him several times, too, which was only remarkable because her sleep was usually dreamless. Yet the fact that, asleep or waking, she continued to be reminded of him, excited her curiosity.

"I suppose," she thought, "it's because he's so different from everybody else."

Even socially different. His position was equivocal. Nobody knew "where he came from" or what his "connections" were. It was quite certain that if he had been married the "county" would not have called on his wife: "Which would be lucky for *her*," Catherine thought, remembering the boredom she had suffered from her mother's callers. "But even though he'ld find them boring," she reflected, "it's quite ridiculous that they should look down on him just because he lives in a little house and isn't cut to the pattern of bridge-playing colonels and glossy subalterns and hunting-men who can talk about nothing but hot baths and horses. He's much more alive and refreshing, for instance, than Mr. Winter, whom the Abberleys and Pomfrets and all their kind adore. And Heaven knows," she thought, "Worcestershire isn't so crowded with interesting people that they can afford to despise him."

"Despise" wasn't exactly the word. The attitude of the "ingrowing county" (as she and Jack privately called them) was less active than that—"ignore" was more accurate, suggesting the right noun: "ignorance"—and, in a way, more irritating. Even her father, though he confessed, with an air of surprise and apology, that he "liked that fellow Selby," always spoke of him as of a member of a different species from himself who had succeeded by some sort of miracle in becoming almost presentable. Of late, indeed, Miles had rarely mentioned his name. One day when they had met him, riding down the street together, and Selby had saluted them, Miles had barely troubled to raise his crop in return. What could poor Dr. Selby have done, she wondered, to upset him? Probably nothing of any importance: he was so easily upset. Yet, whatever it might be, she believed it accounted for the way in which her mother had hedged whenever she happened to remind her of Selby's invitation to herself to use his piano.

"If I never go there, it will look so ungrateful," Catherine had said.

"Oh, I don't suppose he's given it another thought, darling. He may not have meant it seriously."

"Of course he meant it seriously, Mum," Catherine answered indignantly. "I can see you don't want me to go there. Why don't you?"

Helen Ombersley evaded the question. She had

heard about all the fuss over Aaron Bunt's cottage. She saw Selby's side of the question, but was not going to give Miles away.

"Well, next time he comes here," she said, "we'll find out if he really did."

But Selby had not been asked to the Hall since the night of the dance, nor had he come of his own accord; and that, too, puzzled Catherine, for she flattered herself that after their long talk that evening he would surely want to come. This morning, being hurt and bored and moody, and left out in the cold, and having had Selby's "prescription" (as he called it) so oddly and vividly brought to her mind, she felt suddenly rebellious.

"They're jealous of his understanding my music," she thought. "They're being stuffy and proper and 'county,' and I'm not going to stand it, because, if I do, the poor man will imagine I'm like them, which I'm not. Nobody wants me here. So I shall go and use his piano this very morning."

The mere fact of having made up her mind raised her spirits. This was precisely the right hour. Selby's "morning surgery" would be finished and himself away on his round. Often, passing the door with the brass plate on it, she had wondered what that poky little house would look like inside and what sort of life a lonely bachelor could live in it; for the insides of people's houses (as witness Miss Loach's where she had once been received in state) were generally a fair index of the insides of their minds; and having glanced, as it were, through the front window of Selby's and liked the look of it, she was not only anxious to see more, but also a little excited by the prospect of exploration. There was an element of adventure (as well as of rebelliousness) in the whole affair. She even looked forward to meeting the devoted housekeeper with the odd name. What was it? Hussingtree . . . Yes, Mrs. Hussingtree.

Hurrying past the window where her father stood gazing at her, Catherine Ombersley was equally unaware of his scrutiny and of his suffering. By the time she had reached the drive gate the last of her sombre preoccupations had been dissolved in the joy of action and movement. Once more she was aware of the morning's drowsy, comforting sounds: the creak of drought-shrunken cart-axles; the clatter of a distant mowing-machine; that high note, thrummed by innumerable quivering wings, of gilded flies and brown chafers and predatory wasps, which is the true music of summer, suddenly broken by the drone of a bumble-bee booming close to her ear, swinging heavily past in his mead-drunken flight from one side of the road to the other—for, at this end of the village, its trodden verges were white (and the soft air saturated) with honeyed clover-blossoms amid whose ivory claws the pollen-dusted drunkards crawled and stumbled.

"How quickly the season passes," Catherine

thought. When last she had ridden down the length of the village with Miles the apple-blow had been bleaching amid the pale leaves. Now the petals had fallen, the pale leaves had darkened. Even the elms in whose golden tops, a few weeks ago, young rooks had fluttered and scolded about their nests, were now burdened with such opulent hanging festoons of leaf that she felt the trees ache with their weight; the rooks had flown, and their nests were hidden by leaves. All Chaddesbourne, indeed, seemed sunk in July's heavy greenness; a hidden village, its existence only betrayed by ridges of brown thatch emerging from the heaped green like the backs of furry monsters patiently browsing.

"There's no peace, no security in the world like this," Catherine thought, "and no beauty so healing. Peace that passeth all understanding. No poet can put this into words. Poets need mountains and lakes and spectacular beauties to fit their fine phrases. This land is too quiet; the weight of a word would snap its silence, which, of course, isn't really silence because, when you listen, it tingles. This needs music to express it—but such simple music! Or rather such complicated music! Tristan's shepherd's piping? No, no, that's Kareol, not England—nor even Kareol: I really believe it's Bayreuth. It belongs to footlights and painted scenery. (He was quite right about Wagner . . .) A folk-tune, perhaps? But folk-tunes become so sophisticated. Ah, yes—it has been done once in music, by Elgar: in the little interlude of *Falstaff* in Shallow's orchard. I wonder if I shall ever hear an orchestra again? Does *he* go to concerts in North Bromwich?" (She meant Dr. Selby.)

"But how strangely insensitive it was of me," she reflected, her thoughts running on as she walked, "not to have realized all this when first I came to Chaddesbourne! Of course, at that time, I didn't much mind what was done with me: I'd been dead, and I hadn't really come to life again, and one place was the same as another. Yet now I believe I should hate to live anywhere else. I feel rather as Dad does about it. Why? Because the old Ombersleys lived here for hundreds of years? I don't believe that's the reason. Jack doesn't feel it. He says he hates Chaddesbourne, though, of course, he may change, as I've done. No, that isn't it. It's simply that I've fallen in love with it, just as Dr. Selby fell in love with it; and the best thing about falling in love is that it doesn't need explanations. Half the trouble of life is explaining things. And how jolly it is," she thought, "when two people who like each other (for I *do* like him) fall in love independently with the same thing!"

By this time the slow drift of thought had carried her, without her perceiving it, to the centre of the village. That morning it appeared to have awakened to an unusual activity. Beside the wide doors of the inn-yard a small knot of people had collected to stare intently into an excavation made to contain an underground petrol-tank, the first stage in the construction of Ted Hadley's new filling-station. Inside the smithy a red pump stood propped against the wall. Attached to the windows of the "Ombersley Arms" strips of printed paper announced: *Teas, Lunches, and Light Refreshments.* As Catherine drew near, Ted Hadley himself turned and raised his hat.

"Good morning, Miss Ombersley. Lovely morning, isn't it? You see, Chaddesbourne's going ahead. We've been needing a pump here this long time, and now we've got it. What with that and the bus-service starting next week, we shan't know where we are. Glad to see Mr. Jack's home: he'll liven things up a bit, too."

Catherine smiled. Though she had heard that he drank—most publicans did—there was something one couldn't help liking about Ted Hadley; he seemed so pleased with life in spite of his limping leg, so friendly for all his vulgarity. As she crossed the road, the church clock chiming a quarter to eleven, a shadow appeared to dart aside from behind the curtains of Miss Loach's bedroom window, like a trout moving under water. It was Jane Trost, who, stationed there to report on the erection of the petrol-pump, had just recognized Catherine.

"Are you sure it's Miss Ombersley, Jane?" Miss Loach enquired weakly. "You make such wild statements all of a sudden, and you know your sight's not what it was."

Jane Trost screwed up her ferret eyes. "I'm quite positive it's her, miss."

"And she's going to the doctor's? Now what could she be going there for?"

"Well, I really can't say, miss."

"Of course you can't say," Miss Loach answered irritably. "What time is it?"

"The clock's just this moment gone a quarter to eleven, miss."

"Then she's too late to see him. He always leaves on his round at half-past ten. Besides which I heard his motor-car starting. Though I really can't think that a girl of her age and position would visit the surgery alone. People of that class expect their medical attendant to wait on them. And rightly. No doubt she is leaving a note or a message—though what it could be about I can't imagine: perhaps one of the servants is ill. Has she rung the bell yet?"

"Yes, she's just rung it now. Mrs. Hussingtree's come to the door, and Miss Ombersley's gone in."

"Gone *in*, Jane? You must be dreaming. Why should she go in?"

"I really can't say, miss."

"How I wish you wouldn't repeat yourself. You said that before. You've made a mistake. You're always making mistakes. I shall have to have your eyes seen to, or get a new maid with good eyesight," Miss Loach added malignantly. "Now don't start crying like that and lose your head, but watch carefully

P

and see who comes out. This is most mysterious. How's that man Hadley's hole getting on? Have they reached the bottom yet?"

Mrs. Hussingtree had opened the door as soon as the bell rang, almost as if she were a jack-in-the-box, Catherine thought, released by the spring of the bell-push. A motherly body, tied in at the waist like a boiled pudding in a bag.

"Good morning, ma'am. It's Miss Ombersley, isn't it? Please step in, my lady."

"Dr. Selby has told you . . ." Catherine began.

"We've been looking for you every day, miss."

Catherine smiled. That "we" sounded at once welcoming and proprietary. The servants at the Hall—even Langley, who was "dug in" for life—were a community apart, vaguely curious, no doubt, about the family's odd humours and ways as a source of entertainment, but always aloof from them. Servants came and went, but their private lives were mysteries. In a small house like this, Catherine thought, the relation was much more intimate. If the Hussingtrees humbly venerated Dr. Selby as a benevolent deity, the fountain of all favours, it was evident that they also, proudly, regarded him as a personal possession.

"Every morning for I don't know how long," the housekeeper said, almost reproachfully, "that there room's been set for you, madam. The last thing the doctor says before he goes out on his round is: 'Now, Mrs. Hussingtree, don't be surprised if the young lady turns up this morning, and mind you look after her properly and make her feel thoroughly at home. And if she looks a bit tired, as she may when she's finished,' he says, 'just you give her a glass of hot milk and a biscuit or a piece of your cake like. But for God's sake,' he says—if you'll excuse the expression, my lady, for he means no harm, bless his heart!—'don't you go near the room while she's playing. You wait till you're quite sure she's finished,' he says, 'but have the milk ready in a saucepan on the side and a tray with a nice clean cloth on it, like she's used to; and don't you forget,' he says, 'to open the window wide and let out the smell of tobacco.' Which I've done, half an hour ago. So please step this way, miss."

Catherine followed her. After the spaciousness to which she was accustomed, the dimensions of the house seemed tiny. "But how clean it all is," she thought, "and how austere!" The passage was dark to her sun-dazzled eyes, yet wherever light entered it shone on waxed tiles and brass door-knobs that were pale as silver. A faint smell of some antiseptic permeating the air instantly carried back her mind to the hospital at Wyshford. Before she came to Chaddesbourne some instinct of self-protection had invariably made her fly in panic from such poignant reminders; at one time the mere sight of a chemist's shop had compelled her to cross the road for fear of encountering them. To-day, though she momentarily jibbed at it, out of sheer habit, the hospital-smell seemed to have lost its power to wound her; if she still associated it with her tragic romance, it was also an attribute of Selby, and, of the two associations, his was the stronger. She perceived this fact with a tremulous emotion in which surprise mingled with thankfulness, resembling that of a fever patient who wakes, wondering, when delirium has passed, to a consciousness of coolness and sanity.

"Here you are, miss." Mrs. Hussingtree opened a door and bustled into the room in front of her. "Now, if there's anything you require, you've only to ring."

"I'm sure I shan't want anything, thank you."

Mrs. Hussingtree left her. Though the last words Catherine had spoken were no more than a conventional phrase, she knew, in an instant, that they were unconsciously but profoundly true. From the moment she set foot in it she found this small room, so unlike any other she had known, so different, particularly, from those at the Hall, with their faded graces and splendours, completely satisfying and also strangely familiar—not in the manner of those rooms which one recognizes and accepts, having known them in dreams, but because, in some equally mysterious way, it answered to her desires and her expectations. That, of course, she told herself was ridiculous. She had not consciously expected anything: Dr. Selby had told her nothing, but that there was an empty room with a Blüthner piano in it. Why, then, should it seem so familiar and she so completely at home in it?

"I suppose," she thought, "it's because this room is an expression of himself, because everything in it is part of him, and the most intense part. But that theory won't do either," she told herself, arguing against it; "for I can't really know a man whom I've only met half a dozen times in my life—except that there are some people one seems to know without having to think about it. Is this room really like him?" she wondered. "Perhaps it makes me feel happy because it's like *me*. And that brings us no further," she thought, smiling at herself; "for heaven only knows what *I'm* like!"

Taking off her hat, she began to examine her surroundings in detail. The church clock had not yet chimed eleven: there was plenty of time. The room was long and low, with walls and ceilings distempered the colour of Jersey cream or mild sunlight, a floor covered to the skirting with a soft patternless beige-coloured carpet. No pictures hung on the walls: their creamy expanse was unbroken by anything but a mirror in the form of a triptych over the mantelpiece and the brooding bay-crowned death-mask of Beethoven above the piano. From the floor to a height of three feet or so, save only in the space where an open French window gave on to a walled garden completely occupied by a lawn, the circumference of the room was lined with books and bound volumes of music on shelves of pale pine so unobtrusive that they themselves seemed part of the walls.

Catherine glanced at them swiftly. The music claimed her first. She had never before seen a library so complete and so orderly; it made her ashamed for having doubted the depth of his interest and knowledge, for the scores covered the whole gamut of classical music from the Elizabethan lutanists and Purcell to Delius, from Bach to Schönberg and Prokofieff.

The books tempted her next, though among these she moved with less confidence. There were no medical books—these evidently belonged to a part of his life which had no connection with this room. The volumes she saw were nearly all English, and most of them novels—sets of Scott and Hardy and Meredith—or poetry. Unlike those on the ornamental shelves of the Adam library at the Hall, they appeared to have been read. She had a feeling, too, that they had been loved, that when she examined them, as now, taking out the first volume that came to her hand, she was intruding on something more personal than mere printed paper. The book at which she gazed was a "collected" Wordsworth, a school-prize heavily bound in calf with a gilt coat-of-arms; on the fly-leaf she read his name, Anthony Selby, written in a serious schoolboy hand.

"A firm, sensible hand for a boy," she thought. "In essentials he must have changed very little. I suppose people don't. He must have been rather a charming boy. Quick, generous. . . ." She smiled at herself.

"Good heavens, what nonsense I'm talking!"

Was it nonsense altogether? she asked herself, putting back the book, taking guilty care to straighten the line she had disturbed. Couldn't one deduce from this well-ordered room a tidy mind—and a rich mind, surely? Couldn't one go even further than that? Was it fantastic to suppose that something of personality (and of good more than evil) might cling to material things which a man had used—and particularly things he had loved; that, in this room, the atmosphere of light, of serenity (of austerity, too) which answered to her present mood was a product of the spirit of the man who had made it and dwelt in it, still pervading it—faintly, perhaps, like that whiff of antiseptic in the hall or the odour of his tobacco which, for all Mrs. Hussingtree's careful attempts at "airing," persisted, contributing through another sense to its masculine flavour?

"To its bachelor flavour, too," Catherine thought—for the timid ministrations of Mrs. Hussingtree had left very little trace on it. It was, above all, a man's room. No woman, she knew, could possibly have created it; for no woman's mind could have resisted the temptation of small, added graces. Even now, gazing through the window, she caught herself thinking how she would like to pick a handful of irises out of the garden, to arrange them in a tall glass vase with their green stems gleaming through water between the stiff, sword-like leaves—not, of course, on the sacred piano, but on this table of polished mahogany from which they would seem to rise as from a dark pool.

"I would put them," she thought, "where that mirror could catch their colour: it looks so empty."

But now, glancing towards it, she perceived that the empty mirror was inhabited by a reflection of herself: a pleasing reflection, for the spotted muslin became her, the warm light softened her features, and her lips, though she had not been aware of it, smiled. She examined this image with curiosity, because, for a long time, she had hated looking at herself, seeing nothing in her glass but a hollow mask of serenity, unrelated to herself, which a protective instinct had fashioned to hide her emptiness. Yet the face she saw now in Selby's mirror was no longer a mask, but an expression of what she felt, what she supposed she was; the serenity it showed was not feigned, the smile no conventional gesture; and beholding it gave her the effect of having surprised herself in the process of some secret physical transformation not ordinarily seen—like the opening of a flower that frees its clenched petals in darkness. She put up her hand to press back her hair, and the rapt vision was broken.

She became conscious of the urgent passage of time. How long had she stood there in contemplation? If the church bells had chimed, her ears had not heard them, and there was no clock to tell her the hour. That seemed as it should be: this room should be timeless, like a contented mind, given over to quiet thought and silence—or else to music, to sound more beautiful than silence. She laughed at her own bemusement.

"If I go on dreaming like this," she thought, "he'll be back from his round before I've touched his piano, and I don't think I want him to catch me here . . . not to-day. But what shall I play?" she thought. "What would he *like* me to play?" The answer, as clear to her mind as if it had been spoken, was "Beethoven." She went down on her knees before the deep shelves and found the volume of sonatas. The *Appassionata?* No . . . The *Waldstein?* Perhaps . . . but not quite. She turned over the pages till she came to the last great four. Opus 106: the *Hammerclavier*. "Can I remember it?" she wondered. "I believe I could play anything in this room; and that covers all my feelings: the challenge of the first movement; the brave *scherzo*, and then the *adagio* that goes on and on, so mysteriously, like thoughts in the dark . . ."

She approached the piano's stark form of lucent ebony. How could people say that a grand-piano was ugly? It seemed to her one of the most lovely shapes in the world. . . . "If only people would leave them," she thought, "to speak for themselves. . . ." How delicious it was to sit there, in that long empty room with no exciting colour or form to distract one, with the sweet air wandering in from the walled garden— that cloistered garden—over the smooth lawn, and swaying the curtain silently!

She put her music on the stand. "Shall I lift the

P*

top?" she wondered. "Yes, I think I will: this is strong, tempestuous music; it should have freedom. And nobody will hear me, so I needn't be shy." She sat down on the stool and raised the lid of the keyboard. There was something inside it: a card lying on the black notes of the middle register, and, written on the card, the words: *This is yours,* initialled *A. S.*

Catherine smiled. "How sweet of him!" she thought. "How many days has he left that there, expecting me to come, and been disappointed? And Mum wondered if he meant what he said—or pretended to wonder!"

She began to play. The superb affirmation of the sonata's first phrase flung forth its challenge, its everlasting "yea." . . . How brave a world, enlivened with what splendour of hope and strength and high endeavour! "And what a piano!" she thought, as the confident hammers spoke. "How different from my poor little Broadwood, with its sweet, quavering strings! This is a man's piano: it's used to the touch of firm fingers, to the expression of sounds clear-cut and masterful and courageous; one couldn't play woolly music on a piano like this; it would resent it. And how richly it responds—giving back to me more than I give to it, as though it were alive and had a soul of its own—not its own soul, perhaps, but a memory he's left in it, added to it. The notes that I'm playing now don't all come from me; I've never before played like this," she told herself. "Is it the piano, the room, or what? Not merely myself, at any rate. Something strange has happened to me. *Something rich and strange. . . ."*

So she thought, while her fingers played. Enraptured with sound, inspired, she had forgotten to turn the pages; the music appeared to flow from some source unconnected with memory. The first movement ended, and now the *scherzo* began; its gay, tripping phrases fluttered out like newly-hatched butterflies in sunlight . . . but suddenly the sun went in; a mutter of far thunder was heard; there was dread in the air; and now the light, tripping notes were less gay than pitiful, like butterflies dancing under a threatening sky, over the brink of an obscure abyss, until there came a sudden angry stutter of impatience: Enough! Away with this levity! And the poor thing gave three feeble flutters. Then came silence. . . .

And now the *adagio*. . . . That dark and dreamy communing; those sombre, unanswered questions, dim speculations, blank misgivings. . . .

Catherine Ombersley thought no longer. This strange, brooding music transcended thought and quelled it. In these profundities of human consciousness, without form and void, darkness was on the face of the deep, a darkness through which she seemed to grope without guidance, not knowing whither she went nor when, if ever, it would end. Her eyes dimmed; the visible world, of which she was now barely conscious, grew blurred and faded. She was lost in a maze of dark sound, insentient, discarnate. . . .

And God said: *Let there be light . . . He divided the light from the darkness.* Like the light of creation, one wave welling after another, the mounting major triads declared themselves; a long trill rippled like light over the sea at dawn. She shivered and woke; and no sooner was she awake and alive than the flood of the great fugue caught her and rolled her along with it, irresistibly, so that she no longer cared where or who she was or whither it carried her. "This," she thought, "is pure joy; this is living at its best; this is ecstasy! Grasp it now, while you may. It may never return to you."

Her hands fell to her knees. It was over. "So soon," she thought. "After that I can play nothing more." When she raised her eyes to the ivory-coloured death-mask, it seemed that Beethoven's face was benevolent.

Strangely shaken and a little tremulous, she left the piano and moved to the mirror to put on her hat. Once more her own image faced her; she saw that she was pale (and why not?), but her face reflected the happiness of her heart.

"I must close the piano-top," she reflected, "and put back his music"; but, on second thoughts, it seemed to her better to leave the music on the stand, so that Selby could see what she had been playing. "Although we seem to have shared it already," she thought, "and it's hardly necessary."

When she came to close the cover of the keyboard,

she became aware of Selby's card which she had put aside. She found herself picking it up and examining it again. Then, obeying an impulse which made her smile, she opened her bag and found a pencil, with which she crossed out one letter of Selby's message and his signature, adding her own; so that now it read: *This is ours . . . C.O.* So, astonished at her own boldness, she put the card where she had found it and closed the piano.

Jane Trost, glued to the window, reported the moment of her departure. Miss Ombersley—for it was certainly she—had remained in the doctor's house exactly one hour and a half by the Chaddesbourne church clock, which now chimed a quarter-past twelve.

"A quarter-past twelve," Helen Ombersley thought anxiously. "Surely they can't go on talking much longer? I do hope Miles won't be too hard on him."

She slowly returned from the garden—where she had been listening, or pretending to listen, to old Follows' recital of infinitesimal troubles—the frost that had nipped the dahlias in storage, the slugs which had gnawed the delphinium-shoots, the bullfinches that already played havoc with the ripening white-hearts—and stealthily re-entered the house through the drawing-room window. This was Catherine's usual time for practising, but the piano was closed and Catherine nowhere to be seen.

"Where can she have gone?" Helen Ombersley thought. All her thoughts were anxious that morning.

She moved quietly into the hall and listened at the smoking-room door. If Jack was still there with his father, they had evidently finished their discussion; no sound reached her standing outside but a faint rustle of paper. She listened to this till she could bear it no longer, and then tapped gently.

"Come in!" That was Miles's voice; but the tone, she thanked heaven, was not irritable.

He was sitting at his table, an unruly sheet of the six-inch ordnance-survey spread out before him, in his hand a pair of dividers. As she entered, he looked up and smiled; but the smile was so pathetic and his face looked so grey and old that her heart ached for him. He lowered his eyes and went on with his work.

"Where's Jack?" she asked quickly.

"He's gone over to the Tregarons'."

"To the Tregarons'? What for?"

"To ask for a job as a shopwalker."

"Miles . . . what do you mean? You've not sent him away?"

"Indeed, no. That's his ambition. Rather an odd one."

"I don't understand, darling."

"Neither do I, my dear. We've talked the whole matter over. He doesn't like Chaddesbourne."

"But that's nonsense, Miles."

"I agree. But the fact remains. I've no intention of forcing him: it never pays. So I must manage without him."

"He's not gone altogether? You've not quarrelled?" she asked, in alarm.

"Dear me, no. He's assured me he'll come back when it suits him," Miles answered bitterly.

"He's so young, Miles. He'll soon change his mind."

"Perhaps. I hope so. Will you pass me that india-rubber? Thanks."

The subject was closed. "What are you doing, darling?" she asked.

"Trying to plan out a new plantation beyond Foxhall Wood."

She bent over him. "What trees are you going to plant?" she asked.

"Larch and oak."

"But won't they take a terribly long time to mature?"

"The larch will come out for pit-props in fifteen years or so."

"And the oak?"

"Perhaps eighty. Perhaps more . . ."

She was silent, deeply moved by this act of faith; she had rarely admired Miles more than she did at that moment. She bent over and kissed his forehead. She sighed.

"I wish I could help you, darling."

He took the frail hand that lay on the table and pressed it.

"You do, Helen," he said. "I must finish this before luncheon."

XVIII

TROUBLE AT THE MOAT

GEORGE COOKSON'S luck was out. It seemed as if the elements themselves were leagued against him; for the Sunday tempest which broke the June drought brought in, with July, ten days of steady downpour with the brook in flood overflowing his lower fields, and his cut hay soaked, steaming, rotting where it lay.

This season of stifling greenness, in which all virtue seemed to have been sucked out of the sodden air, while the very walls and window-panes streamed with moisture, was no treat for a man of plethoric habit, who sweated easily, suddenly forced to deal with a financial muddle which had reached the point at which facts must be faced.

Even now, if he could have had his own way, George Cookson would have shirked facing them, his optimism sustained by a succession of "nips," which tricked his mind into an unreasonable sensation of well-being; but, much to his disgust, he could not have his own way. During his attack of sciatica, fate had delivered him into the hands of his wife, who stood over him as he lay there helpless, until the sheer weight of incontestable figures compelled him to admit that, however hopeful he might feel, he was actually bankrupt.

The wretched woman allowed him no peace. "It's no use pretending anything different," she said. "Even if people are soft enough to give us credit, I refuse to take advantage of them. From this day, George, nothing's going to come into The Moat that hasn't been paid for in cash: if you can't find the money to pay for things—well, then, we must go without them. And it's no good your going on writing letters, George, putting people off with excuses that you know aren't true and that nobody believes. If you've any decency left in you, you must go and face them. You know how we stand to a penny, and it's only honest to tell them so. Take the rent, for instance . . ."

Take the rent, indeed! That just showed how hopelessly unreasonable she was.

"You make me sick, Annie," he said. "Can't you get it into your thick head that the rent's the one thing you've no call to fret about?"

"There's that letter from the lawyers."

George laughed. "That'll cost Ombersley six and eightpence, but it won't cost *me* anything. Old Ombersley can't afford to have The Moat empty, and you don't catch many fools nowadays taking on farms as big as this. What can he *do*, I should like to know? Sell me up? All right. Let him try it! There'll be plenty of others besides him scrambling for what they can get, and *he* won't come off any too well. Do you think his lawyers don't know that? Lawyers' letters!

You can't scare me with lawyers' letters."

Mrs. Cookson shook her head desperately. "I don't know what's come over you. Have you no conscience left? Nobody could have been kinder or more considerate to us than the Colonel and the old gentleman before him: and now you've the face to laugh at him and take advantage of him to cheat him."

"Now it's no use talking like that, Annie," George Cookson declared. "Is it *my* fault the luck's been against me? You know it isn't. Well, my luck's against Ombersley, too, and if he don't like it, I say he must damned well lump it, the same as me. It's the war that's upset things. They're bound to come right in the end, as I've told you a hundred times. As for pitying Ombersley . . . *He* hasn't got much to complain of: living a gentleman's life at the Hall with a fine house like that and coming into an estate of three or four thousand acres! If he doesn't like the risk of owning land, he can sell it to-morrow. What's our little bit of rent to him? He can afford to wait for it! If he won't, that's his funeral. As I've told you, he'll lose the lot, and have a vacant farm going to waste on his hands as well. I've answered the lawyer's letter and had no reply. Well, that's that. Can't you leave well alone?"

Other creditors wouldn't. The bills that rolled in with every post were no longer polite, but accompanied by peremptory letters threatening legal action unless they were paid by a specified date. It looked as if all the creditors had taken alarm simultaneously. Some of them called in person. Mrs. Cookson, working in the house, went pale when she heard the squeak of motor-car brakes in the yard; her heart stood still when the front-door bell rang. Then she took off her apron and tidied her hair and went to meet them. She always "answered the door" herself, being frightened lest the visitors should let the girl guess what they had come for. When they saw her they were usually polite; she looked such a superior woman.

"Good morning, madam. Is Mr. Cookson at home?"

"No, I'm afraid he's gone out." (George took good care to go out.)

"That's bad luck. When d'you expect him back again?"

"I really can't say. I'm sorry. Can I take any message?"

"Well, as a matter of fact, I've come from North Bromwich—from Stevens's, Limited, on a matter of business."

"Won't you step in for a moment? You can leave the message with me."

(She always received these callers in the dining-room: the furniture was so solid and George's cups made such a good show; it gave an impression of prosperous solidity which ought to be reassuring; and it pleased her to see the visitors taking this in.)

"Please sit down," she said. "I know all my husband's business."

(She had found that this forced serenity of hers had a good effect. Sometimes it appeared to take the wind out of their sails, as though they felt a little ashamed to find themselves dunning a woman, and a woman so obviously honest and respectable at that.)

"Well, to tell you the truth, it's this bill for seeds, Mrs. Cookson. A hundred and ninety-seven pounds. That's a tidy figure. My people don't like making trouble with old customers; your husband's name and his father's before him have been on our books many years. Please understand that we don't want to be unpleasant; but we're feeling the pinch of bad times the same as everyone else, and this bill, as you probably know, has been rendered a number of times. . . ."

"Yes, I know."

". . . so that—well, taking everything all round, Mr. Stevens thought it would be better, as I happened to be passing this way, that I should call in and enquire about it. No offence intended, you know."

"I'm sure there isn't. I quite understand."

"If Mr. Cookson could pay us something on account. . . ."

"I'll speak to him about it and ask him to send you a cheque. I'm afraid, at the moment, he won't be able to manage a big one. We've had terrible luck this year. I don't want to deceive you."

"I'm sure you don't, Mrs. Cookson. That's much

better for both parties. I'll tell Mr. Stevens what you
say. I'm glad I caught you in."

"Won't you take something before you go?"

"Very kind of you, Mrs. Cookson. I don't mind if
I do."

There was nothing like a gill of whisky for sending
them off in a charitable state of mind.

But not all of them were so easy. Indeed, some of
them arrived with faces hardened by suspicion. When
she ushered them in, their eyes cannily quartered the
house, as though they were making rapid estimates of
the value of its contents. Sometimes as they went they
dropped hints:

"That's a nice grandfather clock over there, ma'am.
Eight-day, I suppose? Does it chime? I should guess
that's worth something!"

"Yes, indeed, and we're proud of it. A gentleman
who came from North Bromwich valued it at a
hundred pounds."

"My word! You don't say so?"

"I believe it's worth much more than that. The
whole house is full of old pieces that came to us from
my grandfather. It seems almost a pity to use some of
them. As the gentleman I was speaking of said, they
ought rightly to be in a museum, not in a private
house."

"I can well believe it."

"And the price of antiques is going up all the time,
I'm told. They say it's the Americans having more

money than they know what to do with."

"I wish we could say the same!"

Things like that were almost as encouraging as a gill of whisky.

But sometimes the callers were truculent. They stalked into the house (she never turned them away) as though they already owned it. They refused her drink, swept aside her polite conversation. Occasionally, disappointed at not finding George, they turned nasty and declared they would wait until he came home. These were usually small creditors, themselves on the rocks, who came for their money in person and made Mrs. Cookson's task more difficult because she felt sorry for them and guessed they were in the same plight as herself; for most of them were dressed shabbily and, indeed, looked less prosperous than George, and the sight of their obvious need humiliated her even more than the fact that George had kept them waiting for the money they had earned.

To these she made promises which, when George came home, she forced him to fulfil. George was much more submissive to her now than of old, as well he might be, seeing that it was she who stood between him and his creditors and shielded him and bore the whole brunt of this losing battle, yielding ground inch by inch, yet always retreating towards the inevitable end. For at last, having realized that the end was inevitable and that it was no use blustering or trying to bluff her, he had thrown in his hand and abandoned the whole desperate business, going his own way and leaving her to fight for him. This submission on his part was her revenge for the slights and violences and infidelities he had inflicted upon her. It was a barren and bitter victory which she would willingly have forgone.

One day in the cool of the morning, when she was "making up" the butter, the front-door bell rang. It was so early that she thought it unlikely that any creditor had called, so she sent the girl to answer it. There were two gentlemen at the door, she told Mrs. Cookson, wanting to see the master. That sounded like the old story. Mrs. Cookson sighed.

"Did you show them in, Ethel?"

"They didn't wait to be showed, ma'am. They've gone into the drawing-room."

"The drawing-room? What impertinence!"

Mrs. Cookson took off her apron and hurried to the front. She had great natural dignity, and was prepared to put these mannerless intruders in their place and even to show them the door, but as soon as she saw them she decided that this was not worth her trouble. They made a comical couple, like a pair of music-hall comedians, one short and one tall. The tall man looked pale and anxious and carried an umbrella. The shorter, a regular little beer-barrel, with puffed cheeks and a nose that looked as if it had been reddened with paint, was apparently the leader. He was wearing a bowler hat on the back of his head, but when he saw Mrs. Cookson he took it off, revealing a white bald scalp, that resembled a bladder of lard, bedewed with sweat which he mopped with a red cotton handkerchief. When he spoke he screwed up one eye, as though announcing that what he was going to say must be treated as a joke.

"Mrs. Cookson?" he said. "Good morning, madam. Good morning. Very close for the time of day." He winked. "Mr. Cookson about?"

"Mr. Cookson's gone out, I'm afraid."

"That's a shame, now. When do you expect him?"

It was the same old dialogue: "I really can't say. I don't think he'll be back till this evening."

"Oh, well, well. If that's how it is, I reckon we'll have to wait."

"I said he won't be back till this evening."

"So I understood, ma'am. We can't go till we've seen him, though."

"I know all my husband's business. Perhaps, if you'll tell me what you want. . . ."

"Oh, I can tell you what we want all right, ma'am: that's not so difficult. Have you got that writ, Alfred?" The tall man produced a long, folded paper. "Let me see. . . . Twenty-three pounds seven and fourpence. That includes the judgment and the costs and the execution."

"If you'll leave the bill, I'll ask my husband to deal with it."

The red-faced man winked and shook his head.

"Can't be done, lady. We've come here to put in an execution. If your husband pays up, well and good. If he don't it's our duty to stay here."

Mrs. Cookson went pale. "Then you're bailiffs?"

"Sheriff's officers, madam. Don't you trouble about *us*, now," he went on, reassuringly. "We can make ourselves comfortable. Me and my mate are quite used to it. It's our job, so to speak. If you'ld prefer us to stay somewhere else, you've only to say the word: we like to perform our duty in a friendly manner without any unpleasantness."

Mrs. Cookson scarcely heard what he said. It had come, at last: the dread moment which had haunted her imagination for thirty years since that evening in Stourton, when her father had come in from the shop and told them that the bum-bailiffs were "in" at Rogers's! This was the end, she thought. It was almost a relief to know it was the end; to relax that eternal effort of "keeping her head up," of pretending that "everything was all right" when she knew it wasn't, of concealing the truth from Elsie and Jim and the "girl," who had probably already guessed what was happening. The man with the red face yawned and put on his hat again. "How dare he put on his hat in my drawing-room?" Mrs. Cookson thought; and the anger that filled her made her mind work again. She said quickly:

"How much did you say?"

"How much was it, Alfred?"

"Twenty-three pounds seven and fourpence," the tall man repeated gloomily.

"And if I pay you that now, you won't have to stay here?"

"Of course not. The sooner it's paid the better for all parties."

"Will you please come this way?" She led them into the dining-room. "If you'll wait here a moment, I'll see if I can manage it. Do you mind locking the door?"

The little man put his head on one side and looked doubtful.

"Look here, ma'am, you know you're not allowed to take anything out of the house?"

Mrs. Cookson blushed. "I promise you I won't. It isn't that. I was only afraid my daughter might come in, and I didn't want her to see you."

"All right, ma'am. I'll see that nobody comes in. There's no need to lock it."

Mrs. Cookson closed the door softly and hurried upstairs. In the spare room next to Elsie's stood a chest of drawers in which lately she had hidden and locked her dairy-money. In the old days she had always kept it downstairs in a bureau in the drawing-room; but George had discovered her little hoard and raided it, only laughing when she protested, so that now, to foil cunning by cunning, she changed the hiding-place every week. She stole along the passage on tiptoe; for Elsie, who liked to waste hours over her toilet, was not yet up. Mrs. Cookson could hear her singing to herself as she did her hair; and, of course, the door creaked in spite of her care, so that Elsie stopped singing and called: "Hello? Is that you, Mum?"

Mrs. Cookson stood still as stone and did not answer. She crept into the room and unlocked the drawer and opened it, feverishly counting her hoard. It was much less than she thought: for a moment she imagined George must have discovered her hiding-place. She picked up the notes and coins together and carried them to her bedroom to count. Twenty pounds, two grubby ten-shilling notes and a collection of odd silver and copper. Twenty-one pounds seven shillings and threepence halfpenny: and, as far as she knew, not another penny in the house! Two pounds and a halfpenny short! What could she do about it? She remembered that the girl had been paid her wages at the end of last week. That was two pounds; but as soon as the money was paid, Ethel sent home a postal order; besides which, Mrs. Cookson disliked the idea of borrowing from a servant, and the creature would put two and two together and guess what it was all about.

"But I must get them out of the house," she told herself, "before Elsie comes down."

She wondered if they would be kind enough to take her gold watch in part payment. That ought to be worth three pounds, though jewellery was always less valuable than one imagined. If she could get hold of

Jim and tell him some plausible story? But Jim was
away in Keck Furlong, carting the ruined hay. Perhaps Jim kept a little money loose in his bedroom?
This, at least, was worth trying. She picked up her
hoard and hurried to his room. With a sensation of
guilt she proceeded to burgle it. Three drawers
she drew blank. In the fourth, where he kept his
collars, she found a small wooden box. It was locked,
but when she shook it, it gave forth a metallic
sound.

"If I force it," she thought, "he'll know it's been
tampered with, and then everything will come out;
but, sooner or later, in any case, that must happen,
and now that it's come to this, nothing really matters.
Besides, I've no time to spare."

On the dressing-table she found a pair of scissors
with which, though they bent in the process, she forced
the lock. The box revealed an odd assortment of
treasures: imitation gold cuff-links which had once
belonged to her father, studs of metal and mother-of-
pearl, several newspaper cuttings relating to cattle-
shows, and the real gold tie-pin representing the horse
Bend Or. And here—what could this be?—was an
envelope containing a muslin handkerchief. What on
earth could her Jim be doing with a woman's handkerchief? What woman's? A swift pang of alarm and
jealousy swept everything else from her brain. She
examined the corners rapidly in search for a mark,
and found initials in faded ink: *M.L.*

"Mary Lydgate!" she thought fiercely. "That sly little cat! Why hasn't he told me? It's the first time in all his life he's kept anything from me. Is he going to turn out like his father? Now he'll know that I know."

Another envelope . . . and, this time, thank heaven, a crinkle of paper inside it. Quite a lot of money: six five-pound notes and seven more of a pound! Mrs. Cookson extracted two of these eagerly. She closed the box. The lock was broken beyond all concealment; but that didn't matter now. All that mattered was to get those two dreadful men out of the house before Elsie came down, and Elsie, providentially, still sang to herself at her toilet.

Mrs. Cookson ran down to the dining-room and tapped at the door. It had not been locked. The taller of the two men opened it; the other was sitting in front of the empty grate, still wearing his hat and slowly sucking at a pipe of shag. She spoke breathlessly:

"Here's your money," she said. "I'm afraid it's a halfpenny short, but it's all I have. Does that make much difference?"

The red-faced man winked at his friend: "What about it, Alfred?"

The question was intended for a joke; but Mrs. Cookson could not see jokes; she waited in agony for the tall man's reply.

"Toss you double or quits, Bert," he said.

The little man counted the money. How clumsy

his fingers were! He looked puzzled and began to count it all over again. Mrs. Cookson grew tense with anxiety. Had she made a mistake? Finally, he folded the notes and put them in his breast-pocket.

"That's all right, ma'am," he said. "We won't bother about the odd halfpenny. You'll excuse the 'at, won't you, madam? It's a question of habit. When you're bald on the top, like I am, you feel every draught, particularly in summer, when the scalp gets moist, so to speak." He sucked his teeth wearily. "Well, Alfred, I reckon that's all our business this morning; we'd better be getting a move on. You've some nice things about, Mrs. Cookson. It's a pity those cups and trophies, or whatever they call 'em, aren't as valuable as they look. I've seen stuff like that go for nothing at sales again and again; but you know what sales are. You don't happen to have a pen handy to sign the receipt, ma'am?"

Mrs. Cookson hurriedly brought him one from her husband's desk. He wrote slowly, laboriously. Would they never go? She heard a door slam upstairs and feared Elsie was coming. He finished and handed her the paper.

"Now that's all in order," he said. "All's well that ends well, as they say. Don't trouble—we can find our way out." He hesitated again. "You don't happen to have a time-table?"

"No, I'm afraid I haven't."

"Well, that's of no consequence. If there's a train

there's a train, and if there isn't, there isn't. That's right, Alfred, isn't it?"

The tall man nodded his head lugubriously. They went.

Mrs. Cookson's first impulse was to lock the front door behind them as soon as she heard it close; but it seemed as if all the strength had gone out of her body. She sank down on a chair by the dining-room table and put her hands to her head. In the silence she became aware that she was crying. Silent tears ran down her cold, lined cheeks and lay in a pool on the polished mahogany. It suddenly struck her that it must be years since she had cried.

"It will never do for our Elsie to see me like this," Mrs. Cookson told herself, dabbing her eyes and hurrying back to finish making up the butter before the day began to swelter. She need not have worried herself, for Elsie was well content to take time over her toilet, and rarely appeared before the middle of the morning. When she came downstairs she noticed the reek of shag which the pipe of the red-faced man had left in the dining-room, and the smear on the table where her mother had dried her pool of tears; but neither of these demanded an explanation: her mind was far too deeply engrossed in her own affairs—or rather in the progress of one affair, with Steve Lydgate.

Since that Sunday afternoon when he had come to tea at The Moat, Steve had given her no peace. She had plunged into this flirtation, hoping to find in it a diversion from the boredom of life at home, somewhat flattered by having made a new conquest, and confident in her own ability to handle "men." But Steve Lydgate was different from those she had learnt to handle in North Bromwich, the well-groomed, suburban boys who had taken her for "rides" in their side-cars, paid her shy, clumsy compliments, and bought their timid kisses with boxes of chocolates, which seemed the right kind of payment for her chocolate-box prettiness. The young men she had known were always extremely well-bred; they treated her like a lady and behaved like gentlemen. Steve Lydgate did nothing of the sort. Perhaps he wasn't one. And he paid her no compliments. His manner was, by turns, careless, brutal, and extraordinarily tender. He teased her more often than he made love to her. He made no pretence of observing the conventions of gallantry; there were no rules in the game as he played it. But when he *did* make love . . . "Well, thank heaven," she thought, "I've a fairly hard head!"

On that very first afternoon, before they had known each other two hours, he had kissed her—not with the chivalrous hesitations to which she was accustomed, but without preliminaries, boldly, possessively. When she took refuge in the little display of offended prudishness which, in such cases, was usually effective, he had merely laughed at her. And his laugh, oddly enough, moved and troubled her almost as much as his kisses.

It was so easy, so confident: as confident as the veiled glance of his tawny eyes which, even across the tea-table or in church, made her cheeks blush and her heart beat tumultuously, for they seemed to strip and possess her against her will.

Was it against her will? She couldn't be sure: that was the disquieting part of it. If Steve had pursued her ardently she might have felt better pleased with herself. But he didn't pursue her; he waited for her, with that lazy smile on his mouth, his strong, ruthless mouth, which at times seemed so curiously sweet and at others so cruel, with its air of mingled mockery and possessiveness. Every day when they parted she was becoming more and more conscious, through some special sense of which, before, she had not been aware, of Steve's physical preponderance. Her mind could not escape from it, and did not want to escape. The more roughly he treated her the more she was drawn to him and the more she was thrilled by the sensation of what she had been taught to think of as "playing with fire."

"Though why shouldn't I play with fire?" she asked herself. "I'm not so innocent as all that. I know how to look after myself. I can play this game quite as well as he. After all, it *is* only a game. If it weren't for him I believe I should die of boredom in this deadly hole."

All through the hot afternoon she lived in waiting for the moment when they would meet, her mind lost in a kind of listless suspension, vaguely conscious of the life of the farm that moved about her. Her mother seemed more than usually harassed to-day, but that did not trouble her. Mrs. Cookson was never happy unless she had something to worry about. Jim stayed out in the fields for his dinner; her father had gone to North Bromwich; when once he got there with his farming friends he rarely came home before dark. All the time she was waiting, waiting for the cool of the evening. After their first few meetings she had begged Steve not to come to The Moat, because, though she was ready to boast of her independence, she was actually still a little intimidated by her mother. Mrs. Cookson was always ready to imagine "the worst," she was so old-fashioned; and Jim, too, had taken a sudden dislike to Steve, being jealous, she supposed, of him and his shy little mouse of a cousin. (If only Jim knew what small reason he had to be jealous!) It was not only more prudent but also, because it was secret, much more exciting for her and her lover to meet on the edge of the wind-break of larch and pine which ran down from the hills to the brook midway between Uffley and The Moat. Nobody ever passed that way when the day's work was over; not even Roberts, the keeper.

These midsummer nights had been quick with a strange enchantment; full of melting raptures and panics and hairbreadth escapes. She lived for them, feeling her heart go softer as dusk approached. So now, when supper was finished, she slipped upstairs and tidied her hair and anxiously examined her face in the glass to see that all was well with it. Then, cautiously, secretly, she fluttered forth round the garden hedge, like a pale ghost-moth flitting silently over the drowsy fields, till the shadow of the dark wood and Steve's arms enfolded her, and, at last, she was happy.

Not entirely happy. Even to-night, when she had thought it was going to be more perfect than ever before, she felt something dividing her from unmixed happiness. "To-night," she had determined, "I'm not going to think of anything but loving and being loved. I'm going to forget who I am and who he is . . . everything." But now that the hour had come, there flashed through her mind, as before, vague monitions of peril, icy fears, more potent than conscience (unless conscience were fear?) which stiffened her lax body to alertness and quelled her deliberate rapture, making her suddenly aware of material things with which, momentarily, her reeling senses had lost touch: the smell of pine-needles, the crack of a broken twig under Steve's straining foot, the whinney of an owl—until, incredibly, she saw herself, Elsie Cookson, on the point of yielding to a swarthy young man in a white duck suit, a stranger of whom she knew next to nothing. "This is happening to *me*," she told herself: "This is happening to *me!* What am I doing? What have I done?"

In a panic, pulling together her scattered defences, she managed to free herself.

"I do wish you wouldn't do that," she said, "I don't like it. You *know* I don't like it. I've told you already. You make me hate you."

Steve laughed. He had heard words like that before.

"If you hate me as much as all that," he said angrily, "why the devil do you come here? You set out to be such a woman of the world, and then act like a silly schoolgirl. You don't hate me at all. You know perfectly well you're in love with me. And why shouldn't you be? Can't you trust me? I know what I'm doing. And what's wrong with it? You're a woman and I'm a man."

By this time she was steadier and able to produce the correct reply:

"I'm not that kind of woman, anyway. That's where you make a mistake."

"All women are that kind of woman," he told her, "when they're in love. I know a damn sight more about women than you do, my dear. When it comes to the point there's not twopence to choose between you. But of all sorts of women the one I hate most is a prude like you who leads a man on and then sells him a pup. You feed me up, Elsie."

"Well, you needn't insult me, anyway," she said. "Let's go for a walk. I loathe this wood: there's no air in it."

She felt safer in the open; but beneath her sulky

silence and her prim affectation of shocked modesty, as they walked side by side, an unspoken doubt troubled her.

"After all," she reflected, "he's quite right: I am desperately in love with him; nobody else has ever made me feel like this. And I *do* lead him on: I can't help it. Why should I be silly and prudish? Why shouldn't I trust him? Why should I be different from all the other women he talks about?"

For, when she had eluded him like this, Steve always persisted in talking about other women: the various women with whom he had made love on his travels abroad. He had found the recital of these amorous escapades an effective weapon in his armoury as a practised seducer. With a slightly different intention—for in her case it was partly boasting and partly sheer cruelty—he would harrow poor Mary Lydgate's feelings with his adventures with Elsie. She hated to hear them, yet could not bear to stop him; for it was better to know the truth (if he told her the truth) than to suffer in imagination. So Mary would listen to him, as Elsie, although she protested, listened now.

"I wish you'ld stop talking about your women," she told him. "If you think you can make me jealous in that way you're completely mistaken. It's hateful and disgusting. Please talk about something else, or I shall go home."

But she didn't go home; and he knew quite well that in spite of what she said she was more excited than

disgusted. More than once when a girl had been difficult he'd got her by making her angry.

This evening, however, his trusted prescription
failed. The girl was not even angry; she was merely
sulky and frightened. He could make nothing of her;
her behaviour conformed to no type in his roll of experiences. He had wasted no less than three weeks
of skilful planning on this gamble, and ended by back-
ing a loser. Why waste any more? Though the frustration wounded his pride, he had never been above
cutting his losses. Elsie Cookson was a pretty little
piece; but there were other pebbles on the beach, and
better fish in the sea than ever came out of it. He had
noticed another girl in church at Chaddesbourne: a girl
dressed in black, quite attractive at a distance, who had
certainly smiled at him. He would find out who she
was (Ted Hadley would probably know); he would
stroll down to Chaddesbourne one evening and have
a look round.

That was, if he stayed on at Uffley. In his present
mood, to tell the truth, he was getting pretty sick of
the place. At the beginning, newly come from the sea,
he had found it attractive; he had liked the fresh
country fare, the green fields, the flowers; it had
amused him to lounge in the sun and fish in the
mill-pool; to listen to Eli's tales and flirt with
his little cousin; but even before he had met
Elsie, he had been getting restless, as he always did
after a bit of kicking his heels on the beach. He re-

membered an evening when he had stood on the bridge
with Mary, idly tossing fragments of straw into the
Chaddesbourne brook, and how his imagination had
followed them—to Severn, to the Bristol Channel, to
the South Atlantic. Now, walking the fields with Elsie
in the pale July night, he was suddenly smitten with
a vision of Capetown, of mist spilling over the flat top
of Table Mountain to lose itself in the silver-tree
kloofs of Kirstenbosch; he could see the flower-stalls
in Adderley Street, the rime-white sands of Muizen-
burg fringing False Bay; above the breath of an
English hayfield he could smell the reek of Boer
tobacco. In a moment his soul was five thousand miles
away under the Southern Cross, and his heart was crying: "My God, what am I doing here? That's where I
ought to be!"

Elsie suddenly stopped and recalled him. They
were almost in sight of The Moat. She had determined before they parted to make her peace.

"I'm sorry I was so stupid to-night, Steve," she
said. "What about to-morrow?"

To-morrow. . . . Within the last half-hour she
had ceased to be an attraction; she had become a
hindrance.

"It's all very well to talk like that," he said roughly.
"What's the use of going on like we are?"

"I've told you, I'm sorry, Steve darling. The same
place?"

He rebelled against this new softness. He had had

enough of her. It was no use her clinging to him like this. He said:

"I'm afraid I can't manage it." He saw the pale face of the girl in black. "I'm going to Chaddesbourne. I'm booked for supper with Ted Hadley."

"What a shame! And the day after that will be Bromberrow Fair. You said you'ld go with us. Mary was coming as well."

"All right. If I promised, I'll go."

"Only because you promised?"

"Don't be a touchy little fool! How do we get there?"

"Dad or Jim will drive us. We always go. It's such fun when it's lit up at night."

"Righto, then. What time?"

"About eight at our house?"

"All right. Make it eight. I'll bring Mary along."

"Aren't you going to kiss me?"

He laughed: "I thought you didn't like my way of kissing you."

"Oh, Steve. . . ."

Lamplight streamed from the dining-room window over the mossed path; in the beds it illumined the bells of Madonna lilies. Elsie, passing, peered through the window. George Cookson had come home. He, her mother, and Jim were sitting at the table. It was covered with papers. George Cookson's face looked flushed and obstinate; Jim's puzzled; her mother's drawn, grim.

"My word, I'm not going to poke my head into a den of lions like that!" Elsie thought. Avoiding the light, though nobody inside the room would have troubled to look at her, she slipped round the back of the house and ran upstairs to her bedroom.

It was fortunate for Mrs. Cookson that George had come home that night in a state of comparative sobriety: if he had been market-peart he might have been more difficult to handle. Drunk or sober, she had determined to bring their affairs to a head. When, at half-past nine, Jim yawned and showed signs of going to bed, she had detained him.

"I want you to wait till your dad comes home, Jim," she said. "And I want to tell you something." Her mouth quivered. "I've taken some money."

"Taken some money, Mother?"

"I broke open the box in your drawer. I had to, Jim."

Jim blushed. He remembered Mary Lydgate's handkerchief. But his mother went on:

"I took two pounds. You may never get it back. I had the bailiffs in the house this morning and I had to pay them or else they'd have stayed here. We're in a terrible mess, Jim. It's not your fault nor mine; it's your father's. We can't go on. I've been fighting against it for the last two years, but now I can't do any more. I've got to make him face it, and you've got to help me."

"He won't hearken to me, Mother."

Q*

"He'll have to hearken this time. I want you to be with me and help me. You're all I've got."

Mrs. Cookson's face worked; a tear dropped on the tablecloth.

"Oh, Mother, don't cry!"

"I'm not crying," Mrs. Cookson said firmly. "I think I hear him. Please get all those papers from the desk over there and put them on the table by me."

A moment later George Cookson came in, blinking at the light. When he saw his wife sitting at the table with the papers beside her, his face fell. Then he smiled good-humouredly:

"Hello, Jim boy," he said. "Not turned in yet? You're a late bird to-night. Have you carted Keck Furlong?"

Mrs. Cookson said: "Come and sit down, George. Please look at this."

It was the writ which had been served that morning. George Cookson screwed up his face and held it at arm's-length.

"What is it? Can't see the damned thing without my glasses."

"Give your dad his glasses, Jim. They're on the mantelpiece," Mrs. Cookson said casually. "He'll want them. This is a county-court warrant, George; it was brought here this morning by the bailiffs. I had to pay them to get them out of the house. I did it with my own money and what I took from Jim's box.

George, why didn't you tell me you'd had a judgment against you?"

George Cookson was still staring at the writ. He cleared his throat and glanced furtively at the sideboard, looking for whisky.

"My throat's as dry as a bone. It's the dust," he said. "I could do with a wet."

"Give your dad a glass of water, Jim," Mrs. Cookson said icily.

George glowered at her. "Where have you hidden the key of that cellarette?" he demanded.

"I've put it where it'll be safe," Mrs. Cookson said.

George blustered. "I should like to know one thing: Is this my house or isn't it?"

"That is what we want to find out, George. I wish you'ld sit down."

George savagely gulped the water Jim had handed him. He was no longer defiant. With a stiff tot of whisky he might have plucked up some courage; without it he was disarmed. He sat down and glared at his wife with red, sullen eyes. How he hated her! How he feared her! Mrs. Cookson, instead of addressing him, spoke to Jim.

"I've been working all evening," she said, "at your father's debts. I've made out a list of the ones I can get hold of. Of course, there's no knowing what others he may have kept back from me, like the one that turned up this morning; but even without counting those, it mounts up terribly. I've checked all the items carefully and put a tick by them." She handed the paper to Jim. "Just run your eye over it."

"Look here, Annie," George Cookson protested. "You've no call to drag Jim into this. Here, give me that paper, Jim!"

Mrs. Cookson interposed her hand: "If you shout like that, George, you'll rouse the whole house," she said. "I want Jim to know everything. He isn't a child. It's his business as much as ours. At any rate, he stands to suffer by it more than we do."

Jim stared at the list incredulously. "But Mother," he said. "You must have made some mistake. It can't be as much as this. We can't owe all this rent!"

"We do, Jim. It's probably worse."

"It 'ld take us a lifetime to pay up all this!"

"We can't possibly pay. What's more, they won't wait for us. We've been bankrupt the last three years, from what I can make out. After dinner I walked over to Green Hill and saw Mr. Healey in his office. He was always a friend of your father's, and I thought he might help us."

"What business have you," George broke in, "to go jabbering about my affairs to Healey? I like your damned impudence!"

"He said there were only two things to be done," Mrs. Cookson continued calmly: "either to petition for a receiving-order—I think that's what he called it—or to wait until one of your father's creditors did the same thing. In any case, he said, we ought to find out what our assets are: that is, make a list of everything we can turn into cash to satisfy them. Well, I don't want to wait for the creditors to start it; I can't wait any longer, Jim. I've come to the end of my strength and my patience; I can't do any more. So to-morrow your father will have to write to the Court at Worcester, and in the meantime we must try and find out exactly what we've got."

George laughed. "Well, you seem to have it all cut and dried," he said. "Since you're so damned clever about it, I reckon I'll get off to bed."

"You're not going to bed, George. You're going to listen to me. Please sit down." She waited for George to obey her. "First of all, there's the furniture. Some of that may be valuable, thank heaven. There's that clock in the hall, which must be worth quite a lot. I've made a full list of everything like that. Then we come to the farm machinery."

"And how am I going to make my living without that, I should like to know?" George protested.

"I don't know. When it's sold we shall have to start over again. Some of it isn't paid for yet: I don't know what will happen to that. Then there's the hay you've just made, Jim, and the standing crops. You must make out a list of them."

"That won't take me long, Mother."

"And then, of course, there's the stock."

"I can give you those figures right away: I've got them down here in my note-book. Here they are.

That's the lot, apart from those grade Herefords of mine in Far Leasowes."

"You must put them in, too, Jim."

"What? Put in my Herefords, Mother? You can't mean that! I bought them with my own money: every penny I'd saved!"

"Their feed wasn't yours, Jim. Their feed was Colonel Ombersley's, and your father's not paid for it. Put them down on the list with the others."

Jim went red. "That isn't fair, Mother. Father, what do *you* say?"

"I say nothing. I keep my mouth shut. Your mother's gone cracked: that's all I say."

"Put them down, Jim, please," Mrs. Cookson persisted. "It wouldn't be fair to keep them. If you kept them you couldn't look the world in the face. Don't forget, Jim, the best of the furniture's mine, not your dad's."

"That's right: rub it in, rub it in!" George Cookson said savagely.

"But, Mother . . ."

"How many are there, Jim?"

"There's nine of them. They're beauties. They cost me a hundred and thirty pounds . . ."

"Please God they'll fetch more than that when they're sold," Mrs. Cookson said. "Every little will help." She sighed. "If it wasn't for the rent . . ."

"But that's what I've told you a dozen times," George Cookson cried angrily. "And I've told you, too, Ombersley won't turn us out. He knows which side his bread's buttered on! If he thought it worth while he'ld have done so long ago. What does it matter to him—just come into the old man's money?"

Mrs. Cookson gazed at him coldly. "Remember the eighth commandment, George: *Thou shalt not steal*."

"Oh, my God, if you're going to talk religion, woman, I'm finished!" He rose and pushed back his chair, which fell over with a crash. Jim picked it up.

"And the third as well," Mrs. Cookson said: "*Thou shalt not take the name of the Lord thy God in vain.* Jim, bring your dad the pen and the paper. He's going to write that letter. You can go to bed now. Come here and kiss me good night."

She put up her face to him. It was cold and expressionless.

CARNIVAL

Miss Loach lay in bed with an attack of acute bronchitis. Though she was resigned to coughing all through the winter, she found such an infliction, in the height of summer, unreasonable and hard to be borne. She attributed it to the numerous excitements which had compelled her to leave her bed and sit at the window: the arrival of the first motor-bus from Wychbury and her anxiety to see what Chaddesbourne people wasted their money by using it (one of the first was Nellie Bunt), and what strangers it brought to the village; the initiation of Ted Hadley's petrol-pump, which, although she disliked it, she found extremely ingenious; the clearing of the site, between the church and the "Ombersley Arms," for the War Memorial, which Mr. Winter hoped to have ready for unveiling on Gheluvelt Day; and, above all, Catherine Ombersley's frequent visits to Dr. Selby's house.

These last she considered a glaring breach of propriety. It was discreditable enough that any young lady should visit a bachelor's house unchaperoned even when it was empty; but that she should have dared to enter it when his car stood outside the door for all the world (consisting of Miss Loach, Jane Trost, Mrs. Hadley and Mrs. Webb—to say nothing of the innocent school-children) to see, transcended daring; it verged upon immorality. Such goings-on had never been witnessed in her father's time. They showed the Decay of Religion not only among the Upper Classes (who were already suspect), but also among the Great Middle Class, to which she and Dr. Selby belonged. A man who could stay in his house after an unmarried lady had entered it was guilty of Infamous Conduct in a Professional Respect, and should be struck off the register. In the first shock of indignation she had instantly resolved to write to Miles Ombersley about it; but she had written to him so many times calling his attention to abuses which concerned him as Squire, such as the noise the motor-bus made, without receiving any reply, that she hesitated to lay herself open to another rebuff. And now, what with distress and anxiety and draughts, she found herself in bed and entirely dependent on Jane Trost for her knowledge of how other people were misbehaving themselves!

A less conscientious woman than herself might have relaxed the vigil she kept over the village's behaviour; but Miss Loach could not treat her responsibility to her Maker so lightly. Even now, late at night, as she lay there wheezing, her grim face jutting out of a cashmere shawl in the direction of a plume of steam spouting from a bronchitis-kettle, Miss Loach's ears, though plugged with cotton-wool, became aware of an unusual

sound in the street—a sound innocent enough in itself,
yet as sinister in its implications as the tramp of armed
men. The Army of Sin was on the march; Sàtan himself was hurrying up his heavy artillery: what Miss
Loach's ears heard in the street was the rumble of
caravan-wheels and the puffing of traction-engines
hauling dismantled booths and coconut-shies and
stacked roundabouts and swing-boats cross-country
from a village in Shropshire to Bromsberrow Fair.

Even in her father's time, when Sin was less
rampant than now, Bromsberrow Fair—and even more
than the Fair itself, the walk home through the dark—
had been a pitfall for the youth of Chaddesbourne, an
occasion for Licence if not for Immorality. Mr. Loach,
stalwart, black-cassocked Puritan that he was, had got
up in the pulpit and, stroking his prophet's beard, had
denounced the fair in language quite properly derived
from the Old Testament. But Mr. Winter was no
bearded prophet; and since now there was nobody but
herself left to set an example (and it was extremely
difficult to set an example in bed), Miss Loach could
do nothing but lie still and shudder and fear the worst.

Bromsberrow Fair, in fact, meant even more to the
people of Chaddesbourne than Miss Loach imagined.
It was a fixed festival, and therefore more useful for
reference than the movable feasts of Church and
State: it was easier to say "Last Bromsberrow Fair"
than "Last Whitsun." Indeed, a festival so ancient
may possibly in the remote past have had a religious—

though not a Christian—significance. It lay midway between the two harvests, of hay and of corn, being, in this sense, a sort of *mi-carême* in the Lent of labour. More than midsummer day, which no longer stood for anything but the end of a quarter in commerce, it marked the height of the season: at Bromsberrow Fair, so children were told, the cuckoo bought the horse on which he would ride away. It was more even than a horse-fair or hiring-mop. It was the one day in the year on which the Merry England of legend was actually reborn in an abandonment (a "licence," Miss Loach would have called it) rarely seen in our slow Saxon natures, yet none the less native. It was an occasion on which country folk of both sexes and all ages from the remotest of farms flocked into the market town and "let themselves go" in a manner that made the prim streets of Bromsberrow resemble a Flemish picture (a Breughel, perhaps) of a summer *kermesse*. No man, woman or child in Chaddesbourne could bear to miss Bromsberrow Fair.

All the school-children were already agog with anticipation. Morgan Jones found it impossible to hold their attention. They had seen or heard, like Miss Loach, the long strings of show-caravans rolling past with their florid baroque ornamentation; they had spelt the enticing inscriptions: *White's World-renowned Galloping Horses, Joe Collins's Fire-dragons, The Hall of Mirrors, Petter's Joy-wheel, Hancock's Racing Motor-cars.* Already, in imagination, their heads were flushed and spinning, their palms sticky with brandy-snaps. As they gaped at Mr. Jones's irritated questions, small boys' hands, in their trouser-pockets, anxiously turned over the threepenny-bits and pennies they had saved for this magical moment ever since Christmas.

When afternoon school was over, Miss Burton approached Mr. Jones.

"Are you going to Bromsberrow this evening?" she asked.

Mr. Jones glared back at her. Did the wretched woman imagine he was going to take *her*?

"I have better use for my time than that, Miss Burton," he answered severely. "It seems to me all the village have lost their head . . . has lost its head," he corrected quickly—for, particularly before Miss Burton, he was anxious to be grammatical.

"Oh, I quite understand how you feel," Miss Burton replied.

She was thankful, in a way, to hear what he said; for her fancy, too, had been straying towards Bromsberrow, seeing Mr. Jones there in the company of Elsie Cookson—not indulging, indeed, in anything so vulgar as swing-boats or roundabouts, but walking about in a detached and dignified way with Miss Cookson on his arm. And, of course, if he *had* suggested taking her, she would have consented gladly; for the fever in the air had infected her. Even staid, old-fashioned people like Mrs. Webb were going to the fair; and life in Chaddesbourne, in spite of the ardours of unrequited love, was not exciting. It was at this point that the devil tempted her to blurt out what was in her mind.

"I expect your friends from The Moat will be there, Mr. Jones," she said.

Mr. Jones blushed hotly.

"The Cooksons are no friends of mine, Miss Burton," he said. "They are merely acquaintances. I doubt if respectable people of that kind will go to Bromsberrow."

But from that moment his mind knew no peace. The idea which Miss Burton's malice had implanted in it haunted him. Was this, perhaps, he asked himself, the opportunity for which, since that disastrous visit to The Moat, his soul had been hungering? She would be there with that bounder Lydgate, he told himself, and who knew what might happen? A dozen possible emergencies presented themselves: Lydgate might even get drunk—he had seen him himself coming out of the "Ombersley Arms" late at night; in an ill-mannered English crowd Elsie's beauty might attract unwelcome attentions; she might fall from a swing-boat, or slip from a roundabout and sprain her ankle. In each of these emergencies Morgan Jones saw himself as a potential knight-errant, stepping in, superbly, at the crucial moment, to rescue a damsel in distress, as a dark guardian-angel watching over her unsuspected, but ready to swoop down from the sky whenever his aid might be needed.

"And perhaps, by this time," he told himself, "she may have tired of that brute and be glad of my company. In any case, it's far better to know the worst than to stay here eating my heart out imagining everything. Besides which, it is almost my duty to keep an eye on my boys and see that they don't get into mischief. I shall hate the whole business," he told himself, "but I suppose I ought to be there."

Mrs. Cookson was shocked at the very idea of anyone from The Moat going to Bromsberrow. From the moment when she had forced George to sign his letter to the Bankruptcy Court, she regarded the house as being in the same condition as if somebody were lying dead in it; it seemed even wrong, in a way, not to pull down the blinds. George himself had washed his hands of the farm and everything belonging to it. On the day following the debacle he had rushed off to North Bromwich—where on earth he found the money, she couldn't imagine; but George always found money in some mysterious way. He had come home after midnight, presumably the worse for liquor, and slept on the drawing-room sofa. At breakfast next morning he had not spoken to her: he sat drinking cup after cup of tea and glaring at her with the eyes of an offended animal. When breakfast was over, without saying good-bye, he had gone off again.

"What on earth's up with Dad?" Elsie asked her innocently.

"Your father's worried," she told her.

"Well, he never even kissed me good morning!" Elsie pouted. "I hope he'll be back to go with us to the fair this evening."

"*Who's* going to the fair?" Mrs. Cookson demanded.

"Why, all of us. The Lydgates are coming. We settled that weeks ago."

"We promised to drive them, Mother," Jim put in anxiously. "We can't very well go back on it."

"Go back on it?" Elsie cried, in alarm. "I should jolly well think not! What on earth do you mean, Jim?"

"I know what he means," Mrs. Cookson thought. "It's that Lydgate girl. That's why he's blushing. He knows I found her handkerchief locked in his box. And he still has money to waste on her. I ought to have taken the lot. He's no right to spend that money —not another penny of it. If once he starts that game he'll have no time to think of anything else—least of all of me." She said: "If your father's gone off in the car, you can't take the Lydgates to Bromsberrow—unless you walk, and I don't see Elsie walking that far."

"He hasn't taken the car, Mother," Jim told her. "I looked in the shed."

"And who's going to pay for the petrol, I'ld like to know?"

"Mother, how cross you are! What's the matter with you?" Elsie reproached her.

"The tank's full; I measured it this morning," Jim replied. "I'd thought of that."

"Oh, you think of everything when your pleasure's concerned," Mrs. Cookson said tartly. "I can't stop you going, Jim, but you *know* . . ."

She did not finish the sentence. If she did, it meant telling Elsie the truth, and she hadn't the heart to do that.

"I wonder if the Ombersleys will be there?" Elsie mused.

Dr. Selby was wondering, too. He had asked Catherine the same question when he had caught her for one entrancing moment that morning. In these days Selby's morning "surgery" tended to drag on— not because more patients came to consult him, indeed work, at this season, was slack, but because, at that time of the day, he found it increasingly difficult to concentrate. All the time that he sat listening to long stories of trivial ailments, his ears were strained to catch the tinkle of the front-door bell, the sound of a light step (so incredibly light!) in the hall, the first, hesitant notes of the piano. It was only when he heard these that he began to live, briskly bustling the last patient out of the waiting-room and dashing round to his music-room for one moment. For proprieties apart —and nobody worried about such nonsense nowadays (he forgot Miss Loach)—it was ridiculous to miss the last chance of seeing Catherine. Only to see her was enough.

"I only looked in," he would say, "to make sure that everything was in order. I'm late as it is."

("You are more utterly lovely," he thought, "every time I see you.")

"Yes, everything is perfect," she would tell him, "including your dear Mrs. Hussingtree."

("When you smile," he thought, "I can scarcely bear it: life is too sweet for me.")

"Then I won't disturb you," he said. "Do you know, my piano's quite different now that you play on it? You leave part of yourself behind."

"I've thought that of you, too."

And she glanced at the card at the side of the keys. He had never moved it. After that there was silence between them; for the words that came to his lips were not to be spoken. Not yet. And, this last time, he had said:

"Is there any chance of your going to Bromsberrow Fair? If you've never been, you ought to. It's rather jolly. All the country people enjoying themselves."

"When is it?"

"To-day. The fun doesn't start until it's dark. Then it's really worth seeing: the lights and the movement . . ."

"It sounds too enchanting. Perhaps Jack will drive me over."

"Then he's still at home?"

"Yes . . . and rather bored by it, I'm afraid." Her face clouded momentarily. "Sir Robert Tregaron's still in America. Jack's determined to work for them. He still has that monstrous car Trevor lent him."

"I've seen the brute. Don't let him drive you too wildly, Miss Ombersley."

"If we crash, you could patch me up again."

"That cuts both ways: I should love patching you up, but hate having to do it. Such a delicate business: like mending the Portland Vase."

("Of course," Selby thought, "that's precisely what has been bothering me. She's Greek, pure Greek, in her peerless classic symmetry: *Forever wilt thou love and she be fair . . .*")

Catherine laughed deliciously:

"Really, really, doctor, I'm not as fragile as that. I'm a healthy young woman, thank you, and putting on weight every moment."

"I shall look for you at Bromsberrow, anyway."

"Perhaps."

"There's no 'perhaps' about my looking. Do come: you'll enjoy it. And now I must really go. Good-bye, and bless you."

"Good-bye, and thank you."

"If I go and see Miss Loach now," Dr. Selby thought cunningly, "and don't hurry over the visit, I may see Catherine come out."

He left his car standing in front of the surgery door and approached Miss Loach's. Somebody whistled a tune down the street. Selby turned to see Roberts, the keeper, passing the steps of the "Ombersley Arms," where Ted Hadley stood yawning and sniffing the early air. Their voices reached Selby:

"Good morning, Mr. Hadley."

"Morning, Joe."

"Going to the fair to-night?"

"I never miss Bromsberrow Fair. What about you?"

"Oh, I reckon I shall have a look round some time. I shall get back early, though."

"There's a special bus running both ways to-night. A shilling return."

"Is there now? Well, I've always walked to the fair, and I reckon I'll go on walking. I don't fancy them things. D'you mind what happened last time I took a night off? That beggar Bunt come mouching round and broke into my hen-house."

"Well, that's all serene: Bunt's in quod."

"Ah, but he comes out to-day. His month's up."

"You don't say so? My word, how time goes!"

"I bet Nellie Bunt'll be there all right," Roberts said, with a leer, "with all them chaps knocking about."

"Well, there's no accounting for tastes, Joe," Ted Hadley yawned.

Jane Trost opened Miss Loach's front door. She looked redder in the eyes and more like a ferret than ever.

"Oh, doctor, we've had such a terrible night," she sighed. "The caravans kept her awake. She was all rambling like. She made me close the window."

Selby went upstairs. The air of Miss Loach's bed-room was suffocating. Her black eyes peering out of the shawl shone like beads through the steam of the bronchitis-kettle.

"Well, Miss Loach," he said cheerfully. "Sorry you've knocked up again."

She was breathing in quick little gasps; her beady eyes fixed him, but did not appear to see him.

"It ought to be stopped," she gasped. "It ought to be stopped. I shall write to the Bishop, Dr. Weir."

Selby nodded sympathetically. "We'll see to that later on." He took hold of her thin wrist, discovering a small, thread-like pulse that beat like a kitten's and missed occasionally. "May I have a look at your chest?" he said. "I'll try not to disturb you."

The thin hands wavered upwards feebly, disclosing a minute triangle of yellowish skin, like a chicken's breast.

"I'm afraid I shall want more than that," Selby said, with a smile. Miss Loach showed alarm and horror: no male eyes in seventy years had beheld more than that.

"I consider that quite . . . unnecessary," she said.

"Well, turn over on your side. Gently now!" He lifted her over as if she were a child. In the process the shawl slipped from her head, carrying away with it her black wig with the net attached to it and reveal-

ing a small, insect-like head, bald except for a few thin
white hairs. Jane Trost quickly dashed in to replace
it, as if to conceal an indecency—which, indeed, this
was; but Miss Loach was too dazed to resent her
nakedness. Selby lifted the flannel night-dress and
listened to her chest. Through the tubes of the
stethoscope there came to his ears from both lungs
sounds of rasping and bubbling.

"Broncho-pneumonia on both sides," he thought.
"The poor little monkey!" (For that, at the moment,
was exactly what Miss Loach resembled: a little, sick
marmoset bundled up in the vast four-poster.) "That
will do," he said, and Jane Trost darted in once more
to restore the night-dress. Miss Loach, gasping for
breath, subsided on her back. "You know," Selby said,
"it's quite warm outside: you ought to have this
window open." Miss Loach stared at him blankly.

"I blame the vicar," she said. "It's his duty to put
his foot down. And I blame Dr. Selby, too. It should
not be allowed. When *I* was her age . . ."

Her voice faded away. Selby beckoned Jane Trost
to the door.

"I'll send Mrs. Hussingtree round with some
medicine at once."

"Is it serious, doctor?"

"Of course it's serious. I'll look in again this
evening. But for heaven's sake, open those windows
. . . all of them! The room's like a furnace. She
needs all the air she can get."

He went back to the surgery and put up an expectorant mixture. Catherine was playing the *Italian Concerto* of Bach. He resisted the temptation to listen or linger.

"I shall see her to-night at Bromsberrow," he thought. . . .

Wherever he went people talked of the fair; but all through the day, what occupied his thoughts was not this general excitement nor even the entrancing prospect of seeing Catherine, but an obstinate vision of that odd little bald-headed monkey-shape in the four-poster bed. It was one of those cases, he told himself, in which medical skill was impotent: its issue depending on the amount of vital force that remained in that nexus of muscular fibres which drove the thread-like stream of blood through Miss Loach's arteries. What reserves of energy were left there he could not guess. Miss Loach had never yet confessed to her age. She was very old. From what he had seen that morning she must surely be older, far older than he had imagined. She was obstinate, too. Would the unconscious organism, clinging to life, exhibit the same obstinacy as that with which her conscious mind, even in delirium, clung to its principles? Creaking gates, people said, hung long. There might be something in it. There was nobody in Chaddesbourne whom he disliked so much as Miss Loach. To-day, for the first time, that dislike dissolved in pity.

After dinner that evening he found himself con-

sidering Miss Loach's life in perspective. It was difficult to imagine that Miss Loach had ever been young.
Yet once—heaven knew how many decades ago—she
must actually have been a young girl, a girl of the
age of Catherine Ombersley. Had she ever been
beautiful? Hardly that; by no stretch of imagination
could he read beauty into her shrivelled features. Yet,
in youth, those black eyes of hers might easily have
had charm and a certain dark sprightliness which some
man—incredible though it seemed—might have found
alluring: and he saw Miss Loach as a slender figure
moving through one of du Maurier's summery draw-
ings—the vicar's daughter, in a looped skirt and, perhaps, a bustle, swimming over a croquet-lawn decorated
with willowy, whiskered young men in cricket-caps.
Then he saw that first sprightliness fading, slowly
fading; the willowy young men in cricket-caps faded
away with it; gay parties no longer came to flirt and
play croquet on the lawn; and the one who had walked
with her alone between the box-borders had vanished
completely, having probably been presented with a
living and married a widow with money. Or perhaps
(for by now Selby rode his fancy on the snaffle) he
had not been a parson at all, but a soldier, who had
sailed away and lost his life in some frontier war,
leaving Miss Loach's black eyes to lose the softness
his whispers had given them; so that now, resigning
herself to Fate, she had sought consolation in the
service of God and the ecstasies of religion.

"Such an arid, repressive religion!" Selby thought to himself, remembering the portrait of Miss Loach's father that hung in the looking-glass drawing-room: the portrait of a man with a beard who resembled, indeed, a Semitic Jehovah. He saw Miss Loach's soft lips going slightly hardened, with the bloom of a black moustache on them now, as she walked down the street of Chaddesbourne, from the vicarage to the church, from the church to the Sunday school, from the Sunday school back to the vicarage. The Vicar's Daughter must always set an example; she must walk erect and sit with her feet together; she must rise in the vicarage pew whenever her father enters the chancel, and keep a strict eye on the school-children; she must watch all the girls whom she taught to say the Catechism grow up like young trees and blossom and fruit, she must dandle their babies and go to their christenings as godmother; but she herself must never think of marrying now, because the race of willowy young men in cricket-caps has become extinct, because her duty is to her father, who is growing old and spills egg on his beard at breakfast and soup on his waistcoat and catches cold easily; it is her duty to stay at home, because, being the Vicar's Daughter, she must never permit familiarity—or even admiration—from superior young farmers or school-teachers who are inclined to be friendly; she must nip such friendliness in the bud; she must become an old maid. . . .

And when her father dies at the age of eighty of a stroke, she must not go to live with her sister in Bournemouth, where the climate is milder, but must stick to her post in Chaddesbourne, because now, more than ever, the decency of the village depends on her example as the only remaining witness of things as they were; she must continue going to church whenever the bell rings, no matter how cold and damp affect her weak chest, because, if she neglects to do so, the new incumbent—there have been two since her father died—will almost certainly insert into the services the thin end of the wedge called Rome, and, even if she cannot dictate, at least she can show disapproval; and when service is over and people come out of church, she can impart a few words of timely encouragement and advice to her god-daughters' children—her god-grandchildren, so to speak. ("Now don't be contrary," their mothers say crossly, "there's nothing to be frightened of. Look up, and shake hands with the lady at once, or I'll give you a smacking!") And, later on, when her legs are too weak to carry her over the road to church, and every winter seems longer and blacker than the last—for the climate has certainly changed since her father's time—she can still insist on the Vicar's coming to see her and tell him how things used to be done and *should* be done, world without end, and be wheeled down the street to the gates of the Hall in a chair, though the ill-mannered children do laugh at her, and crawl back to bed again—to the mahogany four-poster in which her father died; until, suddenly, a stray microbe, blown up from the dust in the road, settles into her lungs and gives the Vicar's Daughter broncho-pneumonia, and the bedroom goes hot and is filled with oddly familiar phantoms, such as old Dr. Weir, who has surely been dead a long time, but with whom she feels strangely at home after so many years of tired loneliness . . . so many years . . .

"This will never do," Dr. Selby told himself firmly. "No doctor who allows his imagination to play tricks like this should be allowed to practise!" He looked at his watch. By this time they should have finished dinner at the Hall. "I'll drive over to Bromsberrow now," he thought, "and have a last look at the poor old girl before I turn in."

By this time all the roads that led to Bromsberrow were empty; the whole country-side had been sucked dry of its population. No stars or moon shone that night, but the hedgerows were luminous with high plumes of elder-flower and ivory panicles of cow-parsley, which gave an impression of moonlight. At a distance of more than a mile from the town, the lights of the fair could be seen as a glow in the sky, and a babel of broken music reached his ears. As Selby drew near the confused noise of steam-organs grew louder, rising in snatches above a steadier high-pitched hum of human voices, resembling the note of an enormous dynamo which his fancy conceived as giving light to the tawny sky. Bromsberrow itself seemed deserted;

not a single shop was open; but on the farther side of the town, where the fair-field lay, the side streets were so thickly lined with charabancs, traps and motor-cars abandoned by their occupants that Selby had difficulty in finding a place for his car. Among them he thought he recognized Jack Ombersley's *Grand Prix* Pearce-Tregaron, and his heart-beats quickened.

"She is here," he thought, "she is here! I should have come earlier."

Now the themes of the great steam-organs grew distinct. Like monsters trying to drown one another's voices in a barbarous triangular contest they screamed out the war-time tunes: *"Tipperary"* competing with *"Everybody's Doing It"* and *"Pack Up Your Troubles"*; and suddenly barbarity of colour was added to that of sound, when, entering the ground through the gap between two caravans, Selby saw the three huge revolving pavilions—White's Galloping Horses, Joe Collins's Fire-dragons and Hancock's Racing Motor-cars—spinning round in their garish splendour of scarlet and gold. Above their striped canopies, steam from the engines' exhausts rose in spurts and plumes which the glare reflected from below illumined; and in the same mysterious region, from time to time, swing-boats decked with white human faces leapt into light like sparks flung up from a bonfire of straw. Below, the fair bubbled and simmered like a cauldron, the packed crowd moving restlessly to and fro, jostling, pullulating, interpenetrating: a

kaleidoscope of fragmentary colour, shifting perpetually under the yellow flare of hissing naphtha-
lamps and white arc-lights that fizzed like cicalas. It
moved wrapped in its own subdued clatter of excited
speech issuing from a multitude of faces flushed and
dazed with happiness, amid the shouts of the showmen,
the thuds of wooden balls hitting canvas or smacking
coconuts, the sharp cracks of rifles aimed at celluloid
bubbles that danced on a jet of water.

It was a jolly crowd, Selby thought as he edged his
way through it; an English working-class crowd with
its good-humoured spirit of "give-and-take," its instinct for order; a sober crowd. Here and there it in-
dulged in mild horse-play, when the temptation to use
feather "ticklers" and lead water-squirts overcame it;
but it did him good to see the red-faced farm-boys with
their girls on their arms, so proud of their Sunday
clothes and their bits of ribbon; the old men in
corduroys with quiet blue eyes, the timid old cottage-
women in black with their wrinkled cheeks; the prosperous young farmers in cord-breeches and leggings.
Though he knew very few of those he saw, Selby felt
curiously at home with them; he was conscious, above
all, of their inherent stability, honesty, decency.

"These are my own people," he thought. "I am part
of them; I belong to them; I am proud of them. There
is no decadence here, whatever folk say!" And there
flashed into his mind a passage he had read, a few
evenings before, in one of Milton's letters: *The cheer-*

fulnesse of the people is so sprightly up, it betok'ns us not drooping to a fatal decay.

But where was Catherine Ombersley?

In this swarming, buzzing hive (that was how he thought of it, for like bees on a sill they clustered round the steps of the side-show booths), how should any figure as delicate as Catherine's be seen? He wandered to and fro persistently, searching everywhere; but in this heaving sea of faces he had not as yet seen one from Chaddesbourne, till, of a sudden, two dark eyes smiled at him familiarly, and he found himself smiling back at Nellie Bunt.

"Hello. . . . Enjoying yourself?" he said.

"Yes, Doctor. Isn't it lovely?"

Nellie Bunt was in heaven. She had walked over from Chaddesbourne early in the evening, and though her feet already burned and ached something chronic, she didn't mind that. This was her last day of real freedom before her father came home from Worcester jail, and she was determined to make the most of every minute. She hadn't yet managed to pick up a young man, and she had only a shilling to spend; but one never knew, and, for the moment, the mere fact of being on the fair-ground entranced her. She moved to and fro from stall to stall like a child picking prim-roses, darting hither and thither whenever a new sound or sight caught her fancy, always clutching the little purse with her shilling in it, which, together with the black straw-hat and patent-leather shoes she was wearing, she had retrieved from the waste-paper-basket at her last place but one.

What a treat it must be, she thought, to be attached to a show, to move over the country from place to place in an air of perpetual holiday! How she envied that swarthy wench, with her own gipsy colouring, who handed out the wooden balls at the coconut-shy, or the red-haired girl at the rifle-range who loaded the young men's air-guns and laughed when they missed the leaping balls, and chaffed and encouraged them. What a life! she thought. Or the young ladies in pink tights, with legs no better than hers, if as good, who did step-dances on the platform in front of the set-up theatre! To travel the roads and cook and sleep in a caravan, all yellow paint and bright brass, with a fellow like that tigerish young man with the broken nose who stood stripped to the waist in front of the boxing-booth and showed off his biceps, or the other one, who sparred at the back with a negro! She wouldn't even mind "taking up" with the negro, if she could only travel with a fair.

If she had had any money she would certainly have paid to go into the boxing-booth, for the man with the broken nose fascinated her. Perhaps, if she went round to the back of it, she could peer through a slit in the canvas. She stole round behind it. There was a yellow-and-red caravan standing there with the shafts turned up. A woman sat on the steps, a dark, sulky woman with lank hair in two plaits.

"Hello, kid! What do *you* want?" she said in a lazy voice.

She had a baby in her arms, and as she spoke she opened her bodice to give it the breast. This sight hurt Nellie Bunt; it gave her a sudden pain in her heart; for she thought of the weeks during which she had fed her own baby before they snatched her away from it and sent her into service. She gazed at the black-headed baby greedily (it was so like hers) and envied its mother.

"How old is your baby?" she asked.

"Two months and three days," the woman replied. "What d'you want here? We don't like people mooching round the back."

"Can't a girl take off her shoe when it hurts her?" Nellie Bunt asked indignantly.

"Well, take it off then," said the woman.

"Can I look at the baby?"

"I can't *stop* you looking," the woman said sullenly. The child was butting at her breast like a hungry lamb. Nellie shivered.

"It's lovely to feed them, isn't it?"

"Oh, *that* part's all right," said the woman. "What do *you* know about it?"

"I had one. It died of the whooping-cough." Nellie Bunt's mouth quivered.

"Lots of 'em do," said the woman callously.

"I only nursed mine ten days," Nellie said pathetically. "Then they sent me away." She was aching to touch the baby, which was so like hers. She put down her hand, and the baby's fingers fastened on it; its knuckles were pink and swollen and shiny. What a fat little pig! Nellie shuddered to feel the tiny palm close to her finger.

"One's all right," said the woman bitterly. "You wait until you've had seven. Then you'll know all about it!" She plucked the leech-like creature from her breast and re-fastened her bodice. The baby's fat face puckered; it began to cry.

"Oh, hold your bloody noise, you," said the woman violently. She glared at Nellie. "Look here, I've told you before, the boss don't like strangers mooching about the back of the booth. You clear off, afore he catches you."

She clutched the baby and climbed up the steps into the caravan.

Nellie Bunt retreated. This interlude had upset her. She wished she could do something violent and desperate: go whirling round on one of the Galloping Horses that rose and fell so superbly on their brass rods, or fly up in a swing-boat, soaring into the sky to the sound of music. The crowd surged past her, uncaring; all its faces were strange, inhuman. Sometimes a man looked for an instant and caught her quick smile, then straightened his face severely and hurried on.

There, there was one face she knew! The face of the young man who had stared at her more than once in Chaddesbourne church. And here was another: George Cookson's son from The Moat. But each had a girl on his arm, and neither saw her. The mere fact of knowing them slightly assuaged Nellie's loneliness. She proceeded to follow them, lagging a few paces behind.

The members of the party did not appear to be enjoying themselves. They had left The Moat less than an hour ago under the gloom of Mrs. Cookson's mute disapproval, and had had a puncture on the way. The task of repairing it had smothered Jim's clothes with dust, and made his hands so greasy that he dared not even touch Mary Lydgate's waist, which was the one thing in life he desired to do most, and had hoped to achieve.

Steve Lydgate and Elsie looked equally miserable. Elsie had tried to "make it up" with Steve, to repair the breach on which they had parted, with a submissiveness which implied that she regretted her prudishness; but Steve was not having any more nonsense of that kind: he had wasted three weeks over Elsie and had had enough of her—or, rather, so little of her that his interest had cooled. When she slipped her hand into his in the car, he had not responded to her. That vision of Capetown had finished him; his mind was no longer at Chaddesbourne; all he thought of now was getting away from it as quickly as possible.

He had told Mary Lydgate so that morning; and the casual way in which he broke the news had shattered her world. She had gone pale when he told her he was going, but had managed to keep back her tears until she reached her room, where she had thrown herself on the bed and sobbed tragically till she had no tears left. She would rather have allowed him to make love to Elsie (as if she could stop it!) and endured the agony of seeing them together than lose him completely like this.

"It's time I went back to sea," he had said. "I'm dead sick of loafing on the beach."

"But when the voyage is over, you'll come back to Uffley?" she pleaded.

"Come back here? I don't know about that. I may roll up some day."

"Elsie Cookson will miss you," she said, almost eagerly: she was ready to grasp at anything that might bring him back to her.

"Elsie Cookson can whistle for me; I'm through with that little bitch. She's no more to me than you are," he added brutally.

After that it was no wonder that Jim found her remote and distracted. As if his troubles at home—and, above all, the loss of his cattle—weren't enough without *her* turning queer!

"Mother was right," he thought sadly; "we never ought to have come here. I don't know what's wrong. It's as if there's a curse on all of us. How can I tell her I love her, like I want to, when I know we're going to be sold up and leave The Moat?" he asked himself, as they walked on in silence and Nellie Bunt followed them.

"How unhappy Jim looks!" Mary thought. "I'm afraid that's my fault. He must find me poor company. It's a shame, for he's nice; he grows nicer and nicer the more you see of him. But that's different from falling in love, entirely different."

Elsie clung to Steve's arm. "I wish you'ld say something, Steve darling. I can't think what's the matter with you."

"There's nothing the matter. Men don't want to be jabbering all the time."

"And a crowd's horrid, isn't it? To-morrow we'll have to make up for it."

"What d'you mean?"

"To-morrow night in the wood." She pressed his arm to her. "Steve, I'll promise faithfully never to be so silly again. Steve, I love you so dreadfully."

"I'm going to Cardiff to-morrow to look for a job. You've missed the bus this time, my girl."

"Oh, Steve, don't tease me! You will come?"

"Can't you hear what I say? Let's get on to this roundabout." He turned round. "Hi, Jim, come for a ride. I'll treat the party."

The revolving platform was just slowing down. Steve jumped on to it; Elsie scrambled up after him; Jim and Mary followed. The roundabout had teams of three galloping horses abreast, moving up and down with contrary motion as the circular platform swung

them round. In the centre of the circle the steam organ
blared out its tune; four grotesque caryatids at the
corners clashed brazen cymbals and regarded the
swinging riders with fixed, archaic smiles.

When Nellie Bunt saw the Cookson party mounting
the step, her heart burned with envy. A single ride
would cost twopence, she told herself, and they didn't
last long: two minutes, perhaps. Then she thought of
her shilling. "Why shouldn't I?" Her purse clutched
in her hand, she made a wild jump as the roundabout
started moving, and giddily clutched the third horse
beside Steve's and Elsie's.

The great platform gathered momentum; the horses
began to plunge; the gilt figures clashed cymbals more
rapidly and always smiled; the steam organ blared
forth its old-fashioned rag-time tune:

Everybody's doing it, doing it, doing it!
Everybody's doing it, doing it, doing it!
Everybody's doing it now. . . .

What a superb combination of movement, up and
down, round and round! The pace quickened; the hot
air rushed past Nellie Bunt; it blew up her skirts—she
didn't mind showing the hole in the knee of her stock-
ing—it nearly blew off her straw-hat. She forgot the
baby; she forgot her aching feet; forgot everything
but this sublime motion, this intoxicating sound. When
her horse plunged downward, Steve Lydgate's horse,

next to her, rose. She was breathless with ecstasy, yet she sang at the top of her voice:

"Everybody's doing it, doing it, doing it!"

Steve Lydgate heard her and looked round. The girl who had smiled at him in church! Had she chosen the horse next to his on purpose? As they crossed in mid-air, plunging up and down, he took stock of her. Not so bad! He liked a girl who could let herself go. He smiled, and Nellie smiled back at him. Her teeth were all right. He said:

"My word, aren't you just enjoying yourself!"

"Isn't it lovely?" Nellie Bunt gasped ecstatically. "I could go on like this for ever."

Elsie hit him on the sleeve. "Steve! Did you speak to that girl?"

"Of course I spoke to her. Why shouldn't I?"

"I know her, Steve. She's from Chaddesbourne. She's a bad girl."

"Well, thank God for that!"

"If you dare speak to her again . . ." (The horses' wild plunging separated them.) "If you speak to her again I shall get off."

"Well, get off if you want to! Who are you to say who I shall speak to?"

"I mean what I say. I think it's disgusting of you."

Steve laughed. The roundabout slowed down. He turned his face towards Nellie Bunt provocatively.

Elsie, flaming with anger, slipped down from her horse. Steve appeared not to notice her. How she hated him now! She stepped down from the platform into the crowd. Steve took Nellie Bunt's arm.

"My girl's left me," he said. "Do you want to have another round?"

"As many as you like. I know who you are," Nellie Bunt said softly.

"And I know who you are, too. Why did you smile at me in church?"

"Oh, I don't know," said Nellie Bunt. "I reckon I liked the look of you."

Elsie Cookson, with a burning face, pushed her way through the crowd.

"He insulted me," she thought. "Deliberately. He insulted me! And *that* girl, of all people! I shall go back to the car and sit in it. Oh, why did I come here?"

Morgan Jones, perspiring in the midst of the crowd and hating it, found himself suddenly faced by her. Surprise and joy overwhelmed him: she was actually alone. He took off his hat.

"Good evening, Miss Cookson. Well, this *is* a fortunate coincidence."

Elsie gasped good evening and brushed past him. The mere fact of anybody speaking to her nearly made her burst into tears. Morgan Jones, undaunted, pursued her. She was in distress! His dream had been justified.

"Can I be doing anything for you, Miss Cookson?"

She continued to flee. "No, nothing, thank you. I'm all right."

"But you aren't all right. Something has happened, Miss Cookson. You must allow me to help you."

"Why shouldn't I tell him?" she thought. "It will do me good to tell somebody. He wants to help me, and at least he'll behave like a gentleman."

"A man has insulted me," she said.

Morgan Jones's face reddened.

"Insulted you? Who? Where is he?"

"Oh, you can't do anything, Mr. Jones." He looked positively ferocious. "If you'll come with me to our car I shall be much obliged."

"Anything in the world, Miss Cookson," Morgan Jones said superbly. He was longing to tell her that it was only because he had feared an emergency of this kind that he had come to Bromsberrow.

"If you'll oblige me by taking my arm," he said, "we can find our way through this horrible crowd more easily."

It was nice of him, Elsie thought. She took his arm, and made Mr. Jones feel prouder than if he had been chaired for a prize poem at the National Eisteddfod; his head swam with glory; his stature became gigantic; he was a hero of the Mabinogion, Macsen, Emperor of Rome, escorting the British Helen through the vales of Cær Seint. Yet the glory was an inward glory: it would not come out in speech.

"I expect you find the air oppressive this evening, Miss Cookson?" he said.

Elsie admitted it was hot.

"Yes, yes, indeed—but no more than one might reasonably expect," Mr. Jones said judicially, "in the height of summer. The day I came up to The Moat I, myself, was feeling the heat extremely. I owe you an apology, Miss Cookson, for that unfortunate. . . ."

"Why, there's Dad!" Elsie cried, "and he's talking to Dr. Selby. Thank you so much for escorting me, Mr. Jones. I shall be all right now."

Abandoning Mr. Jones's arm, Elsie hurried towards them. "Is this to be the end, then?" he asked himself gloomily. She seemed to have forgotten him. Not even so much as good-bye! "It is beneath my dignity to thrust myself forward whatever," he thought.

"Dad! I never expected to see you here," Elsie said. "What luck!"

George Cookson caught her in his arms and kissed her. The sustained debauchery of the last two days had played the deuce with him. He was unshaven; his eyes were bloodshot, his movements uncertain, his speech blurred. "This is my chicken, doctor," he said, "my little chicken; my one and only daughter!" He slipped his arm round Elsie and kissed her again. "You know her, doctor?"

Of course Selby knew her. He had not enjoyed himself, standing there in the crowd and listening to

George Cookson's maunderings. In his fuddled condition George might easily get into trouble, so he had
not liked leaving him; he liked leaving him less than
ever now that Elsie was with him. The right thing,
he supposed, was to drive them both home before anything desperate happened, and miss seeing Catherine.
This was the devil's own luck!

"How did you get here, Dad, darling?" Elsie asked
eagerly. "I thought you were in North Bromwich."

"I *was* in North Bromwich," George Cookson
answered solemnly. "I *was* in North Bromwich,
passing the day with a few friends. And now I am
here," he explained, "at Bromsberrow Fair. And
when it comes," he added, "it brings good cheer. Like
Christmas . . ." He chuckled feebly. "Just listen to
that darned music!"

"I shall have to do something," Selby thought.
"If I could only keep him quiet until I've seen
her!"

Somebody slapped him on the back: "So here you
are, doctor, at last! I've been looking for you everywhere." Selby turned to see Jack Ombersley.
"Catherine told me you'ld be here. Not much of a
show."

"Where is she? I've been looking for you, too."

"Mother and she are dining at Uffdown with the
Steven Hingstons. When Cath told you she might be
here she'd forgotten about it; so I promised that I'ld
find you and make her apologies or whatever you call

them. Phew! I've had about enough of this mob! Now I've given you the message, I think I shall push off home. Want a lift?"

"In your monster? I managed to get through the Somme, my dear fellow, and I'm running no risks. Besides, I've got my own car here." A new idea suddenly struck him. "Look here, Ombersley, there's something I wish you'ld do for me. . . ."

"Anything you like, as long as you don't ask me to stay here."

"There's a tenant of yours here, George Cookson of The Moat."

"I know. Pretty daughter."

"Don't speak so loudly. She's just behind me. She'll hear you."

Jack laughed. "Well, she'ld like to hear that!"

Selby whispered: "George Cookson's been drinking. He's all right: only mildly oiled. I don't like leaving him with that girl, and I can't very well spare the time to drive them home: there's an old girl in the village —you know her, Miss Loach—whom I ought to have seen before. Will you be a Christian and take charge of them and dump them at The Moat? The sooner he's safe at home the better for everybody."

"Of course I'll take 'em. Delighted. You'd better introduce me."

Selby tapped George Cookson on the arm and recalled his enraptured attention from the revolving roundabouts.

"Here, Cookson," he said. "I've managed to get you a lift home."

"A lift home? I don't want to go home," said George Cookson rebelliously. "I've only just come. Spent the day with some friends in North Bromwich. Now me and my chicken are going to have a turn on the roundabouts."

"You'd better take the chance while you can. Mr. Ombersley says he'll drive you. Here he is."

Cookson shook hands heartily. "Pleased to meet you, I'm sure, Mr. Ombersley. I know your dad and I knew your grandpa, *and* they know me!" He laughed knowingly. "Yes, they know *me* all right."

"And this is Miss Cookson," Selby said.

Elsie smiled. "I know Mr. Ombersley quite well— by sight."

"And I know you, too," Jack said. He had never seen her at such close quarters before. He found her extraordinarily pretty in her shop-girl way. It would be fun driving her home through the night. He felt sorry for her, too. Selby was right. It was beastly to think of her dragging about on the arm of her fuddled father. "Would you like me to drive you home?"

Elsie glowed. "I should love it, Mr. Ombersley. In that wonderful car!"

"She's not such a bad old bus. She can move, I I promise you."

Elsie tugged at her father's arm. "Come along, Dad," she said.

"What? You don't want to go on the round-abouts?"

"No, I've had enough of it. I'm rather tired. Do come, Dad!"

"Well, have your own way." George Cookson smiled weakly. "You see how it is, Mr. Ombersley; she does what she likes with me. She's my chicken, she is. . . ."

"Oh, Dad, come along. Don't be silly." Elsie grasped his arm firmly. "We'll follow you, Mr. Ombersley. There's only one thing: I must leave a note in my brother's car, or he'll wonder what's happened to me."

"That's perfectly simple. Good night, Selby. This way, Miss Cookson."

Selby waved his hand. So that was all right: one thing off his conscience. Poor old Cookson: a good man run to seed. That was an ugly tragedy. Now that the hope of seeing Catherine must be abandoned, his mind returned to Miss Loach. "I must get back and have another look at her," he thought, and became aware, during the process, of the white face of Morgan Jones hungrily staring after the Cooksons. Mr. Jones looked so haggard and tired that Selby was touched. He was impelled to speak to him.

"Hello, Jones," he said. "What are you doing here? I shouldn't have thought this was your line of country."

Morgan Jones, with a start, recovered himself.

"No, indeed it is not, Dr. Selby. I've never been here before, and I shan't come again."

"Do you want a lift back to Chaddesbourne? I'll give you one if you like."

"I should be most grateful."

Three miles away, at that moment, under the lee of a newly-made haystack, Aaron Bunt awoke and sat up and rubbed his eyes. He had taken his discharge from Worcester jail at midday. The warder had given him back his familiar clothes, including the skirted tweed coat with the hare-pockets; they had been baked in a sterilizer and felt dry and brittle, but, for all that, after a month in convict's uniform, he was happily at home in them. The warder had also given him money, the reward of his labour, in addition to the few odd coppers which had been in his pocket when he was arrested. When he stepped out into the streets of Worcester the pubs were open. He had stayed in a bar at the back of Foregate Street till they turned him out into a world that was not only free but also, seen through a mist of beer, of a unique and novel splendour.

On the road he had fallen in with a tramp who had reminded him that this was the first day of Bromsberrow Fair. After his month of seclusion the idea of mingling freely in a crowd enchanted him; but, approaching Bromsberrow, he had remembered that by this time the pubs would be opening again, and as

he felt somewhat depressed by the reaction from his
previous potations, he had turned into a wayside inn
and put down another two quarts of cider; after which,
forgetting the fair, he had staggered on vaguely in the
direction of Chaddesbourne, leaving Bromsberrow to
the east, until, tired and feeble (for he had tasted no
food since the prison-breakfast), he had decided to
look for a convenient haystack and sleep it off. When
he woke, it was dark. His head was still throbbing
and dazed with the effects of alcohol, to which he had
become unaccustomed. He swayed out into the road
and zigzagged on towards home.

"If you'll sit in the back, Mr. Cookson," Jack
Ombersley said, "your daughter can ride in front with
me."

George Cookson lurched into his seat. Elsie stepped
in delicately. Jack Ombersley slammed the door and
started the engine.

Elsie Cookson was thrilled. This was a marvellous
end to that devastating adventure. Steve Lydgate and
the humiliation he had inflicted on her were almost
forgotten. It was an ugly experience; she only
thanked heaven that by the skin of her teeth she had
escaped the additional humiliation of losing her head
and letting him have his way with her. She found it
impossible to believe that she had ever been fascinated
by a man with so little sensibility, a man who could
stoop to "pick up" a revolting creature like Nellie

Bunt. The thought of it made her feel sick; it sickened her, too, to remember, unwillingly, that she had actually kissed him. She shuddered at the memory.

Yet Virtue, however fortuitous, had its rewards. Here she was, in the ecstatic present, sitting by the side of a genuine gentleman, the grandson of a Viscount, the son of an Honourable, at the front of a car which had cost at least two thousand pounds! And he was awfully nice to her. Not a suspicion of "side." He laughed and spoke so naturally. It was evident that he admired her—this young man who could take his pick, at hunt-balls and so on, of the whole British Aristocracy! Her only regret was the fact that the drive would so soon be over, and that her father had not exactly shown himself to advantage. "But now that we know each other," she thought, "we may meet again."

She said, speaking carefully with accents of deliberate refinement:

"Do you know, Mr. Ombersley, it has been the ambition of my life to ride in a Pearce-Tregaron. This *is* a Pearce-Tregaron, isn't it?"

Jack laughed. "Well, now your ambition's realized. This is a Pearce-Tregaron all right. It's the *Grand Prix* model."

"It goes terribly fast."

"Do you call this fast? Why, we're only crawling. Would you like to go really fast?"

"It's the thing I love best in the world."

"So do I. There's nothing like it. This old bus is a bit of a crock, but she'll do eighty-five."

"I've never been more than fifty."

"Well, you shall to-night. Just you wait till we come to a good length of road where I can whip up the 'revs', and I'll let her out."

"Oh, that would be marvellous. I *am* enjoying this so."

Jack smiled, and stole a side glance at her. In the light reflected from the luminous banks of cow-parsley and elder-flower the girl was quite ravishingly pretty: a little bit like Trevor Tregaron's friend at the "Blue Fox." But more innocent: those young women in night clubs frightened him. It was a shame, he thought, that she had such an unfortunate father. She spoke like a lady . . . almost. She was simple and well behaved; quite different from what you'ld expect in a farmer's daughter. He liked her voice; he liked the confiding way in which, when she spoke to him, her arm pressed against his. And she looked the least bit unhappy beneath her naïve enjoyment. Poor child! What wonder?

"Now here is a good stretch of road," he said. "Are you ready? Hold on!"

He pressed down the accelerator and opened the cut-out. The great car roared through the night. He said: "Watch the speedometer!" Elsie saw the needle creep up, from fifty to sixty—sixty-five—seventy—

seventy-five—seventy-seven. She was as far lost in happiness at that moment as Nellie Bunt, walking through the long alleys of light, five miles away, with Steve Lydgate's arm round her waist. Seventy-eight. The needle quivered on eighty. Far in front the huge headlights illumined a tunnel of oak. In the middle of the road it picked out the figure of a man standing still, a mean, scraggy figure in a sagging tweed coat with hare-pockets. Jack's klaxon shrieked at him. He appeared not to hear. He stood in the middle of the road staring, like an animal fascinated by the glare of the headlights. Then he waved his arms, wildly gesticulating, and began to run, zigzagging like a frightened rabbit from one side of the road to the other, but never leaving it.

Jack slammed on both brakes. As he did so, George Cookson, behind, suddenly awoke to the danger. He reached over and tugged at Jack's shoulder; pulled Jack's arm away from the wheel.

"Let me go, you damned fool!" Jack shouted.

But he shouted too late. The car swerved; the wheels locked; there was a screech of dry rubber tearing, a smell of rubber burning. A tyre burst with the sound of a gun-shot, but that sound was drowned in the crash of the great car hurtling into a telegraph-pole, the splinter of glass. Then the wreckage turned, like a stick in an eddy; it crashed into the opposite hedge and burst into flame.

Jack crawled from the débris unhurt. He saw Elsie

Cookson lying on the verge of grass by the broken telegraph-pole. He staggered towards her and picked her up.

"My God . . . are you hurt?"

"I think I'm all right. My head's cut. It was the glass." He saw her pale face streaming with blood. "Is Father all right?" she asked feebly.

Jack had completely forgotten George Cookson. Horror seized him. A drunken man in a burning car! No, thank heaven! The blaze revealed another figure lying flat in the middle of the road. He knelt down and shook him. "Mr. Cookson," he shouted, "Mr. Cookson!"

But George Cookson heard nothing. George Cookson's neck was broken. With incredible effort Jack pulled his dead weight to the side of the road. He put up his hands to his reeling head. He fainted.

Over the fields towards Chaddesbourne, Aaron Bunt was running as though the devil was after him. Looking back from time to time, he saw the flames of the wrecked car licking the tops of the oak trees. A terror greater than this pursued him: the fat face of Constable Page. If anyone was hurt, they were not going to drag him into it. Not if he knew it! He ran on like a hare.

XX

CROWNER'S QUEST

A MOTH-EATEN bison's head hung on the wall above
the table at which the deputy-coroner sat. This totem
of the Royal and Ancient Order of Buffaloes, in which
Ted Hadley himself held high office, gave the impro-
vised court in the "club-room" of the "Ombersley
Arms" the air of some summary tribunal in which
prairie law was savagely administered. So Selby
thought, looking up at the heavy-browed emblem and
waiting for the scratching of the coroner's pen to cease.
He was an elderly man, methodical, punctilious, exact-
ing, and being ill-paid in this capacity and unpros-
perous in others, inclined to insist on the powers which
his brief authority gave him.

"Please proceed, Dr. Selby," he said. "At ten
minutes past eleven. . . ?"

"At ten minutes past eleven I saw a light in the sky
ahead of me. I imagined a barn or haystack was on
fire, and hurried on to find out where it was so that I
could report it. By the time I reached the site of the
accident, within a few yards of the milestone which
says 'Stourton 7—Bromsberrow 5,' the flames had died
down. The car lay on the north side of the road in

the ditch; the body of the deceased on the opposite verge, about thirty yards behind."

"Thirty yards? How did you measure the distance?

"I stepped it."

"You stepped it. I see. And then?"

"I examined the deceased where he lay, as best I could. It was extremely dark. I found he was dead. Then I hurried on to the others."

"They do not concern us. Later, under my orders, you performed a post-mortem. What did you find?"

"The deceased met his death through a fracture— dislocation of the cervical vertebræ."

"One moment." The deputy-coroner turned to the jury. "That means a broken neck. Go on, doctor."

"I formed the opinion that death was instantaneous. This injury might have been caused by a jerk of unusual suddenness, or by direct violence. There were others: compound fractures of the left frontal bone, the right arm and the left thigh. The impact that caused these must have been terrific. The deceased was a heavy man."

"And if he was hurled out of the car that would make matters worse?"

"I agree."

"Did you find anything else in your routine examination? Anything germane to the case?" (Joe Atkins, the foreman of the jury, wrinkled his brows. What had the Germans to do with it?)

"Yes. I found fatty infiltration of the heart, some local thickening and adhesions in the membranes of the brain, and hepatic cirrhosis—what is commonly called a hob-nailed liver."

The deputy-coroner instructed the jury: "That's what some people call a gin-drinker's liver," he said. "That is generally the result of a prolonged indulgence in spirits?"

"That is so."

"Anything else, doctor?"

"Nothing else *post-mortem*. If I may offer evidence on another point. . . ."

"You are called as an expert."

"I think this can be called expert evidence."

"Very well."

"Half an hour before his death I saw the deceased at Bromsberrow. I formed the opinion that he had been drinking heavily that day. It was for this reason that I asked Mr. Ombersley to drive him home."

"We are enquiring into the cause of his death, doctor."

"This circumstance may help you to ascertain it. If the deceased, at the time of the accident, was not in full possession of his senses or control of his muscles, he would have been much less capable of saving himself at the moment of the impact. I regard this as an important contributory cause of his death. Perhaps the most important of all."

"I see your point, doctor. The jury will appreciate that. I don't want to keep you here; I know you're a busy man. If you'll be good enough to read through the record of your evidence and sign it, you may go."

The police-superintendent from Bromsberrow called "John Ombersley."

Jack rose hurriedly from his seat at his father's side and stepped forward. He looked gaunt and chastened and grey—as pale as his flannel suit or the faded stripe in his tie. The coroner administered the oath. Jack repeated it without a tremor:

"I swear by Almighty God that the evidence I shall give to this court shall be the truth, the whole truth, and nothing but the truth."

The coroner spoke slowly: "Mr. Ombersley, before you testify, I have to warn you that anything you say will be taken down in writing and may be used in evidence. You need not answer any question or say anything that may incriminate you as a party concerned in the death of the deceased."

"I quite understand. I wish to give evidence."

"Your name?"

"John D'Abitot Ombersley."

"Age?"

"Nineteen."

"Occupation?"

"None."

"Will you tell us, in your own words, what happened?"

Jack began his story. Once or twice the coroner interrupted him. "Not so fast, please. Say that over again. I could hardly catch what you said, and I'm sure the jury couldn't. You consider the deceased was under the influence of liquor?"

"He was certainly a bit muzzy."

"A bit muzzy, did you say?"

"Well, pretty well oiled."

The coroner considered the word critically, but let it pass.

"You say you got into a 'dry skid.' The phrase is new to me. What do you mean exactly?"

"The road wasn't wet. The wheels locked when I put on the brakes, and the car . . . well, it skidded. I could have got out of the skid all right if Mr. Cookson hadn't stood up when he saw that fellow in the road and wrenched the wheel away from me. It gave me no chance."

"About this man in the road. Do you know who he was?"

"I haven't the least idea."

"Are you certain there was a man in the road?"

"I'm on my oath, sir."

The superintendent of police leaned over: "That is corroborated by the evidence of Elsie Cookson, taken in hospital."

"You're of the opinion that the deceased had been drinking. Had you been drinking yourself?"

"I had a couple of glasses of beer at dinner and one

glass of port. That was at eight o'clock: three hours previously."

"Nothing else?"

"Nothing else. If I had had anything else I should have said so."

"You need only answer my questions, Mr. Ombersley. The next one is important to you. How fast do you think you were going at the time of the accident?"

"I know that exactly. When I put on the brakes the car slowed down. I was doing seventy."

"Seventeen miles an hour? Come, come, Mr. Ombersley!"

"I said seventy, sir."

"*Seventy* miles an hour! That's greater than the speed of an express! You say you 'slowed down' to seventy?"

"The car I was driving is one of the fastest on the road. It's capable of eighty-five. I've touched that myself."

"I need hardly ask you if you are aware that the legal speed-limit for motor vehicles on the road is twenty miles an hour?"

"It's a limit that nobody observes, sir."

"If you had observed the legal speed-limit, would this man have lost his life?"

"No. I don't think he would."

"I entirely agree with you. I don't know if Mr. Flower wants to ask any questions?"

The lawyer rose: "None, sir. My client has given evidence with complete frankness—I think you will appreciate that—and I have nothing to add."

The coroner summed up ponderously. He reminded the jury of their function. "You are here," he said, "to enquire into the death of George Cookson and find how he came by it. The medical evidence is clear. He died of what is commonly called a broken neck. Dr. Selby has suggested, and I think quite rightly, that the fact that the deceased was under the influence of alcohol contributed to his death. Remember, this is not a Court of Justice but a Coroner's Inquest; no person is on trial. You can return a verdict of Accidental Death. On the other hand, if you are satisfied that this man met his death directly through the negligence of the driver of the motor-car, it is your duty to say so. The driver, John D'Abitot Ombersley, has admitted that, at the time of the accident, he was driving his car at the enormous—I think I am just in saying the monstrous and dangerous speed of seventy miles an hour, considerably more, that is, than a mile a minute. He has told you that the road was clear up till a moment before the accident, and that a man suddenly appeared in it. It is extremely unfortunate that this man has not come forward voluntarily to give evidence; his testimony would have been valuable, though I doubt if it would have added much to what we know already. Whoever he was, he had as much right to use the road as the driver of the car. If, during your retirement you decide that the death of George Cookson was caused by Ombersley's negligence, it will be my duty to direct you to bring in a verdict of culpable homicide, that is to say manslaughter, against him. This is a painful case, an extremely painful case; and I know that you will wish to express your sympathy with the victim's bereaved ... er ... family. You may retire. I should have said that your verdict must be unanimous."

Miles Ombersley turned towards Flower: "What will it be?"

"It can only be one thing, I'm afraid."

"And what happens next?"

"He will be arrested and committed to prison for trial on the coroner's warrant."

"To prison?"

"The coroner is empowered in his discretion to accept bail. No doubt he'll do so."

"Will my bail be sufficient?"

"You can leave all that to me."

"And the next stage?"

"Bromsberrow police court. The accident was inside their boundary."

"They may dismiss the charge?"

"They may; but I don't think they will. The public is beginning to get nervous about motor-cars."

"The man was certainly drunk."

"Oh, we've got a good case."

"When do the assizes come on?"

"After the vacation."

"That's a long time to wait."

The jury returned. In the silence Miles heard their hob-nails clumping over the club-room floor. The coroner looked up from his notes.

"Have you considered your verdict?"

Joe Atkins cleared his throat noisily. "Yes, sir. Unanimous." He read slowly from a paper that trembled in his hand, in a monotonous voice, without pauses: "We find unanimous that the late deceased met his death by death by accident caused by a broken neck as the result of being thrown out of a motor-car under the influence and being negilently driven by . . ." he gasped for breath . . . "Mr. Jack Ombersley through skidding, and the jury likewise unanimous recommend him to mercy expressing sympathy with the late deceased's family."

The coroner knitted his brows. "I shall have to word this rather differently. Your verdict is one of culpable homicide against John D'Abitot Ombersley."

"That's right, sir. Recommended to mercy. While under the influence."

"The question of a recommendation to mercy does not arise. You are not trying Mr. Ombersley. He has not even been charged."

"Very good, sir. But we thought if we put that down, like . . ."

"I shall record your verdict. The sympathy you have properly expressed will take the form of a rider."

"I beg your pardon, sir?"

(The word, though indirectly connected with Joe Atkins's calling, was unfamiliar to him.)

"A rider: a supplement to your verdict. Superintendent Withers! I shall issue my warrant for the arrest of John D'Abitot Ombersley on a charge of manslaughter."

Mr. Flower jumped up: "In the matter of bail, sir. . . ."

"All in good time, Mr. Flower."

"I must go and see my wife, Flower," Miles Ombersley said. "She'll be anxious."

"Of course. I'll stay here with your son and arrange things. I'll come down later."

Helen Ombersley awaited the news of the verdict in the garden at the Hall. She would gladly have gone with Miles and Jack to the inquest. Her place, as she thought, was by their side, but Miles wouldn't let her. She supposed he was right: he was always right in those things. It seemed such a long time since they had left her. Surely an inquest was not so complicated as all that? She hoped the coroner wouldn't keep Jack standing too long; for, although he said he was none the worse for the smash, she knew better: his nerves were really in a dreadful state; the least noise made him jump; his face twitched; his hands shook; he had lost his colour; he looked miserable.

After all, it was a dreadful thing to have happened to him; he was only a child. And it wasn't his fault.

If that wretched man hadn't clutched him from behind and torn the wheel out of his hands, he wouldn't
have hit the telegraph-pole. As for George Cookson,
everyone agreed it was almost a blessing for his
family, if not for himself; but she was sorry for the
girl—she remembered seeing her at the dance in rose-
coloured taffeta and remarking how pretty she was,
in the way such girls could be. Since the war, of course,
surgeons were terribly clever with facial scars; they
lifted people's faces and even gave them entirely new
noses. Dr. Selby assured her the Cookson girl's face
wouldn't be too dreadfully disfigured: just a thin line
across the forehead. And with a girl of that class looks
were not so crucially important. If a thing like that
had happened to Catherine . . . Mrs. Ombersley
shuddered.

Would they never come back from the inquest?
It was a horrid day. She had always thought that
August, except in Scotland, was the ugliest month of
the year. She remembered torrid Augusts as a child at
Stoke Priory: people always declared that the Severn
basin was relaxing.

"In August," she thought, "though it's hot, the
summer is really over. There's a hint of autumn in
the air; the elms become touched with gold; the leaves
of Virginia creeper begin to redden; red's the colour
of autumn: these dark velvety dahlias mark its beginning; they will go on blooming till the first frost; in
six weeks or so I shall wake up one morning to see

the lawns white and every one of them dead. I suppose the year really grows old when the wall-fruit ripens, and you see wasps drowning in bottles of beer, and Red Admirals and Peacocks sunning themselves on fallen plums. Yes, the year's really turned," she thought, "when the birds stop singing. In the spring they were almost a nuisance—the thrushes and blackbirds shouted so loudly, the rooks made such a clamour, and even the cuckoos ended by getting on one's nerves—but now that their love-affairs are over they seem to have gone dumb, just like human beings; though, of course, they're still there," she thought, watching a speckled young thrush hopping hither and thither clumsily as if he couldn't fly.

"How still everything is!" she thought. "The whole garden seems listening. On a day like this you could hear a peach drop from the wall. I wonder if Follows has sent in more peaches? Jack does so enjoy them, and they won't last much longer. Of course nothing will last much longer. That's why people of my age and Miles's find autumn a little sad. When I was a girl like Catherine I couldn't see an end to anything. I knew people had to die, but I didn't believe in it. It was one of the things that happened to other people, like one's house catching fire. And how delicious it was to get up early for cub-hunting! It's a pity that Catherine and Jack don't hunt, though I suppose, when you come to think of it, it *is* rather cruel. Are they never coming? Would Miles mind my going to meet them? I think I'll go back to the house; that will be nearer at any rate."

As she turned at the end of the long walk she saw Miles approaching. He was alone. "Why isn't Jack with him?" she thought. A vague fear chilled her heart. He looked very thin and old and sere as he walked towards her, as though the first frost of autumn had nipped him already. Yet he smiled when they met.

"Miles darling," she said, "I thought you were never coming. Where's Jack?"

"I left him behind with the lawyer fellow. He'll come along later."

"What happened?"

"This is going to hurt you, Helen. They brought it in manslaughter."

"Oh, Miles!" For an instant her heart stopped beating. "But how could they? It wasn't his fault, Miles."

"On the evidence they had to. I should have done so myself. The coroner's issuing a warrant. It's all right. I've arranged for bail. It will probably go to the assizes."

"But that doesn't mean. . . ."

"I don't think so. But there's always the possibility. It'll have to be faced."

"How terrible for him, poor darling. I wish I'd been there."

"I'm thankful you weren't. He must have suffered

horribly. But he came through it remarkably well, Helen. His evidence, I mean."

"What else did you expect?"

"You're quite right to say that. But this horrible business has—what shall I call it?—it's stiffened him. Jack needed something like this."

"Oh, Miles. . . ."

"Yes. He did. To tell you the truth, I felt proud of him. There was another odd thing, Helen. You know people say that stress brings out family likenesses? Well, when he stood in the box there to-day, he looked like your father. Quite ridiculously." He paused. "You realize we're in for a pretty bad time, my darling? The waiting will be the worst part of it: I gather the case can't come on till October at the very earliest."

"We've had pretty bad times before, Miles; but we've got through them somehow."

"You're a brave woman. I think you've been told that before. We shall get through this, too, never fear."

"As long as you tell me everything," she pleaded.

"Yes, I'll tell you everything."

"And you won't be too rough with him, darling? It hurts me more than him."

He smiled at her fears. "No, we're in this together, all three of us. It's the only way. We must make the best of it."

He kissed her. For an instant she clung to him, as

a girl to her lover. At that moment Helen Ombersley felt that a cloud had been lifted from her spirit, the one cloud which had shadowed the joy of her return to Chaddesbourne with its threat of a thunderous clash between the conflicting natures of Jack and her husband. For she loved them both, understood them both, and she knew that either might wound her tender heart (and Catherine's, too) through the other. As they walked back to the house arm-in-arm, very slowly—for the ardour of youth had left them both— and in silence, Helen Ombersley's calm face smiled, the faint lines left by suffering softened. Indeed, though the immediate future looked stormier than ever since the war, her heart was full of thankfulness, of new courage, and strangely happy.

"We must behave with him just as if nothing had happened," she said.

"Yes, that's much the best way," Miles agreed.

In the smoking-room Flower awaited him. Jack had gone straight upstairs, he said: he was tired, and what wonder? Since his first discouraging visit to North Bromwich Miles had modified his dislike of Wilburn's partner. Flower wasn't, to put it crudely, exactly a gentleman; but then members of the professional classes needn't be, and he was, without doubt, an extremely shrewd fellow in matters of law. Miles had only stuck to the firm because he dreaded changing horses in the middle of a stream. He was now convinced that he had acted more wisely than he knew. Flower handled this situation with a matter-of-factness, a lack of emotion that was almost brutal. That was just what Miles wanted. Affecting an equal nonchalance, he said:

"What about this bail?"

"That's all arranged. Five hundred pounds. That sounds a lot, but it's merely a matter of form."

"When will the case come on at Bromsberrow police-court?"

"Within a couple of days."

"We should be represented by counsel?"

"Good lord, no. They're bound to commit him. It would only be waste of money. I shall reserve the defence."

"At the assizes, then?"

"We must have the best we can get. I suggest Sir Edward Cronshaw."

"That theatrical bounder?" Miles exclaimed. "I admit that I've never met him; but I've seen his photographs in the papers, and I know the kind of case he's associated with."

Flower smiled. "Your description is perfectly just. Cronshaw *is* a bounder; he *is* theatrical. Great criminal advocates are often both. But we have to deal with a jury, and no jury—particularly no provincial jury—can resist him. I'm thankful to say your son makes an excellent witness. I liked the frank way he came out with his 'seventy.'"

Miles was flattered. "I thought, myself, that he didn't shape badly. What will Cronshaw cost?"

"I can't say off-hand. You'll have to pay for his name. I imagine his brief will be marked something like five hundred, with refreshers on the same scale. The case won't last long."

Miles looked grave: "I shall have to raise money, Flower."

"I realized that. There's another aspect of the case. If the verdict should go against us, Cookson's family will be in a position to get heavy damages in a civil court. Of course, Jack's a minor."

"I couldn't shelter myself behind that."

"You could, but you won't. That's why you must be prepared. You'll have to sell Uffley."

Miles Ombersley was silent.

"Yes," he said at last. "I suppose I shall have to sell Uffley. But please understand, I can only do it on one condition. I've given my word to my tenant, Eli Lydgate, that he shall not be disturbed. I can only give the buyer possession after his death. He's an old man."

"H'm. . . . That may complicate matters. However. . . . I'll see what can be done. I'll write to my colleagues this evening. By the way, I'm afraid you'll have to write off the arrears of rent for The Moat as a bad debt."

"That debt's been discharged."

"Well, yes . . . if you look at it in that way."

Flower rose to go. "Of course," he said, "I shall keep in touch with you. As soon as I hear any news of Uffley I'll let you know. You had better leave the question of price to me. If they know that you're forced to sell and you insist on conditions, you'll naturally get less."

"Beggars can't be choosers, Flower."

When the lawyer had gone, Miles Ombersley sat on at his desk gloomily staring in front of him. On the opposite wall he could see the six-inch map of the Chaddesbourne estate, its irregular equilateral triangle outlined with a wash of red water-colour. That shape, which he had always considered as permanent and immutable as the triangular outline of England itself, no longer represented the geographical truth. The equilateral triangle had become an isosceles. The Moat, though still nominally his, now remained irrevocably in the hands of the mortgagees; within a few weeks, if his hopes were realized, Uffley would be sold. The losing battle was over; he had been forced to capitulate.

The one thing he found intolerable at that moment was inactivity. This drab little room and the map were getting on his nerves. He left it abruptly, went round to the stable and ordered a horse to be saddled, then rode out, carrying his mood with him, over the hot, silent fields. The air of late afternoon hung more sultry and lifeless than ever. His horse sweated as he walked, switching his tail and tossing his head to shake off the flies. Miles Ombersley himself sat erect and still as a figure in an equestrian statue, vaguely aware of the panorama of blue-green woods that unrolled itself under the drooping sky, doggedly moving towards the performance of two duties that could not be avoided.

The first was a visit to Uffley. Nearing the mill along the dense verge of Foxhall Wood, he remembered the day, soon after his succession, on which he had renewed Eli Lydgate's acquaintance. That day, too, had been gloomy, with a yellowish blight in the air; yet he could not forget the high spirit, the hopes, the determination with which he had approached it. Of these emotions none but determination remained to console him. If he were no longer master of Chaddesbourne, he was still, he reflected grimly, master of himself.

He tied up his horse and crossed the bridge over the brook. In the storm-light that shone from under the tattered fringes of thunder-cloud, Uffley Mill appeared unsubstantial; its pale brick and bleached timbers gave it the aspect of a mirage that might vanish before his eyes. Miles knocked at the door. Mary Lydgate opened it. She, too, looked pallid and ghostly, her great black eyes widened with surprise in her matt-white face. "What has happened to her?" he wondered, as she led him into the kitchen where Eli was sitting.

Eli Lydgate rose and shook hands with him. "Glad

to see you, Mr. Miles. Sit you down. I had an idea you'ld be coming."

"That was more than I had, Eli."

"It's a fact, none the less. I've heard of the inquest. News of that kind travels like thistle-down. A bad business. I'm sorry for you. Not that Cookson isn't a good riddance," he added, grimly.

"A bad business, as you say. Are you all alone here?"

"Ay, we're all alone. My grandson's gone off to sea again. Some folk are born rovers. Some aren't. I'm one of them. Eighty years and more I've stayed in one place."

Miles spoke with an effort:

"Eli, I've got to sell Uffley."

The old man smiled. "That doesn't surprise me, Mr. Miles. I've seen it coming."

"But I want you to realize one thing before you hear of it, as you probably will do in the course of a day or two. Bad news, as you say, travels fast. I am making it a condition of the sale that you stay here. I promised you that, and I hold to my promise."

"Well, that's handsome: it's like you, too, Mr. Miles. But suppose the buyer don't like that?"

"Then Uffley will not be sold."

Eli gazed at him without answering.

"Well," he said at last, "I reckon my time's about up. I shan't stand in your way for long. But look here, Mr. Miles, if you find yourself stuck——"

Miles Ombersley shook his head:

"I shall look for some other way out. Good-bye, my friend."

Mary waited for him at the door. "I'm afraid you'll miss your cousin," he said.

Mary blushed. "Yes, it's lonely without him."

Miles rode on to The Moat. This visit was even more difficult than the last. The Moat looked less ghostly than Uffley, but even more dead. Mrs. Cookson received him in the room with the plaster frieze. She was dressed all in black, but wore a clean white apron. Though her eyes were haunted, her face showed no signs of unusual suffering. She displayed, in her grief, extraordinary dignity. The manners of a duchess . . . an old-fashioned duchess, Miles thought.

"Mrs. Cookson," he said, "it's difficult to find words for what I want to say. . . ."

She smiled faintly; the smile struck him as strangely sweet.

"Colonel Ombersley, there is nothing to be said. We each know what the other feels. My husband was not all he should have been, but I loved him. The Lord's will be done." Her lips quivered, then hardened again. "I'm afraid," she said steadily, "that his affairs are in a bad way. My son and I will do what we can about them; but the money we owe you. . . ."

"I wanted to speak about that too. I understand

the position. Your son is a good farmer by all
accounts. . . ."

"And a good boy, too—though I say it."

"So everyone tells me. I don't want you to leave
The Moat if it's possible for you to stay. We don't
like changing our tenants at Chaddesbourne, and your
husband's family has been here for three generations.
If you can straighten out your affairs, I should like
your boy to stay on."

Mrs. Cookson shook her head sadly.

"George's debts must be paid. I'm afraid there'll
be nothing left. We shall have to make a new start in
a smaller place."

"Your daughter is better?"

"Yes, thanks be to God. She'll come home from
hospital next week."

"I'm thankful for that. Ask your son to come down
and see me, Mrs. Cookson. If I can help you in any
way, you may trust me to do so. As for the rent, you
had better forget about it."

"You are more than kind, Colonel Ombersley."

"And you're a brave woman, Mrs. Cookson."

She sighed, and Miles rode away.

Three days later Flower drove over to Chaddesbourne. He carried his brief-case into the smoking-
room. The brusque, business-like air which had
troubled Miles Ombersley when first they met was
now reassuring.

"My agents in London have got into touch with Sir

Edward Cronshaw," he said. "They've sounded his office, and they gather that he will be disposed to undertake the defence. What makes it a little difficult for him is the fact that the case will be tried out of London. The Old Bailey is his favourite—what shall we say?—stage. He's been briefed already for the defence in the Pimlico murder, and the dates may be awkward. However, I think we may count on him. At a figure. . . ."

"What figure?" Miles asked.

"I'm afraid a rather substantial one. We gather that he won't look at the brief for less than six hundred."

"Six hundred?"

"It does sound a lot; but he knows your name and your position as Deputy-Lieutenant and all the rest of it."

"He doesn't know 'all the rest!'" Miles said sardonically.

"In any case I doubt if you'ld get a man of equal eminence to come to Worcester for less."

"So it appears we have no alternative. What about Uffley?"

"I was coming to that. I'm now in a position to tell you the name of the prospective buyer."

"I know it already. John Hackett."

"He's not a friend of yours?"

"On the contrary."

"So I supposed. Mr. Hackett is difficult."

"You mean he is haggling about money?"

"Not in the least. He's objecting to your conditions. He insists on immediate possession."

"He can't have it. I'm bound by a promise."

"A promise in writing?"

"My dear Flower, a promise is a promise."

Flower smiled: "Not in law, Colonel Ombersley."

"I know nothing about that."

"What is more, he insists on conditions of his own. Very odd conditions. First of all, a wayleave over your land for an electric cable to Green Hill. He's willing to allow you to tap it and take current for yourself and for the village, which strikes me, I must confess, as rather handsome: he's offering, in short, to improve the value of your property. Then he wants you to sell him a site for a Village Hall. That, too, seems to me unobjectionable. And lastly, he wants you to grant him a lease for The Moat. He's by way of being an amateur farmer, I gather; and from what my colleagues have hinted it rather looks as if he knows of the existing mortgages: if you refuse, he may possibly acquire them. The curious thing is that, on the face of it, every condition Hackett suggests appears to be in your favour. To be candid, I can't make it out. Of course none of these questions will arise if you refuse him possession of Uffley."

"I should refuse his conditions as well. Every one of them. This is nothing short of blackmail!"

"Not in law, Colonel Ombersley," Flower repeated.

"I'm not a lawyer. But I'm not going to be what *I* call blackmailed. This damned fellow apparently thinks he's got the whip hand of me. Can't you find another buyer?"

"I very much doubt it. They don't grow on trees in these days."

"I must think about this."

"Are we going to brief Cronshaw? There's no time to waste."

"We must brief Cronshaw."

"And the money? Can't you arrange matters with your tenant at Uffley?"

"That's quite out of the question. I must find out some other way."

"Don't take too long over it, I beg you. Cronshaw's much in request."

"I'll promise to let you know in three days."

"Very well. By the way, here's a letter, addressed to you 'care of' my office. Three days: that means Friday?"

"Yes, Friday."

That night, after dinner, Miles retired alone to the smoking-room to take stock of his position again. The air was still tepid and soft as new milk; a continuous flicker of summer-lightning washed the sky; through the open window there buzzed and fluttered a succession of night-flying insects, floury chafers, grass-moths with filmy fans and impetuous yellow underwings. The bronze bodies of these smote his lamp-shade one after another. The glass rang like a bell and startled him; then they fell stunned, upside-down on his papers, spinning round, their weak legs aquiver. Outside the bats dizzied, taking toll of the insects which flew to the constant light. Miles worked on or dreamed hour after hour, sitting upright there in his starched collar and shirt, adding sums of figures or staring at them.

There were the last quarter's bills for the estate, which had not all been paid; there were Jack's Oxford debts, and these were debts of honour; there was a separate estimate for the repair or rebuilding of the five cottages which he had now been ordered to demolish; there were the various documents relating to the mortgages on The Moat, on which a new payment of interest would fall due before the trial. He looked through them and turned them over again and again, and could see no glimmer of light through the forest of his embarrassments. For Sir Edward Cronshaw's six hundred pounds was only the beginning of that story.

It was long after midnight when he put out his lamp and closed the smoking-room window. Choosing his candle from among the thicket of candlesticks at the foot of the stairs, he was reminded of the night when he had come home to Chaddesbourne immediately after his father's death. He remembered going slowly upstairs to the room where the old man lay dead. He remembered re-winding and starting a clock that had stopped, a small bracket-clock by Tompion, with a charming chime. As he reached the landing he glanced at it to see if it was keeping time. For some reason, he had no idea why, it had stopped at five minutes past ten. Such an incident, at any other time, would not have troubled him. It did not trouble him seriously now, but he found it a little sinister; it was in keeping with the darkness of his mind, and continued to haunt the depths of it with a stirring of vague disquietude.

And he could not sleep. With him sleeplessness was most unusual, but, when it came, quite incurable. He re-lit his candle and tried to read a novel by Thackeray; but though his attention wandered, his brain would not rest. He got out of bed and drank water and looked at the night. Chaddesbourne church-clock chimed and struck three. In another hour or so the dawn would be showing. He heard a soft rustle behind him and started. His nerves were or dge. The door opened. It was his wife.

"My darling, why aren't you sleeping?" she said. "You came up so late, and I've heard you moving all night. Come into my room. I don't like you to be waking alone."

He kissed her. "Yes, Helen. I think I'll come into your room."

He followed her submissively and lay by her side.

She said: "What is it, Miles darling?"

"Well, we've plenty to worry about, haven't we?"

"Of course; but you don't tell me everything. The weight would be lighter for you if you'ld let me share it."

"You've quite enough to bear, Helen, without being troubled by details."

"I should be far happier if you told me, Miles, and so would you." She paused. "You're not frightened of things going wrong at the trial?"

"I'm not frightened. No. We have a good case, Flower says. Though one never knows with a jury. But I'm not worrying about that."

She was silent, and, thus encouraged, he began to talk about money. The relief to his soul was enormous. Not even with Flower had he shown an equal frankness. He told her of the mortgage on The Moat, of Mrs. Clarke's pension, of the demolition order, of Jack's debts, of his fight against selling Uffley and his final capitulation, made fruitless by John Hackett's rejection of his conditions.

Helen Ombersley listened gravely. "You poor darling," she said. "Oh, why didn't you tell me all this before, Miles?"

"What could you have done, Helen?"

"It isn't always 'doing' that matters. The real trouble is Mr. Hackett. I'm afraid you got on the wrong side of him, Miles. Men like that are so sensitive."

"John Hackett, sensitive? In any case I've never set eyes on him since the day he came here."

"Yes. That's a pity."

"Of course I turned down his proposals about electricity. I suppose that annoyed him."

"There are so many ways of doing things like that. If I'd seen your letter. . . ."

"What good would it have done?"

"I think I understand Mr. Hackett better than you do. I had a long talk with him at that dance, and I rather liked him."

"*Liked* him? My dear Helen!"

"Yes, I did. I found him pathetic. I believe he means awfully well."

"I'm not concerned with his meaning. It's his actions that trouble me."

"He's misunderstood you. . . ."

"I made my position quite plain."

She smiled in the dark. "I know, darling. You always do. And I think you've misunderstood *him*."

"I'm afraid you're wrong there. The present situation proves that I summed him up rightly from the first."

"Well, we won't talk any more about it. Turn over and try to sleep, darling."

She embraced him tenderly, gathering him in her arms as if he were a restless child. She was happy to have him in bed with her, to end this long separation. Her hand lay in his, and this contact seemed to calm him. After two or three turns Miles slipped over on his back and began to snore. For once she was thankful to hear him.

Next morning he woke to feel the urgent necessity of seeing Flower again. He had little knowledge of financial procedure—this vital subject had not been included in the staff-college syllabus—but money-lenders' circulars had often reached him by post. He had always presumed that the senders were necessarily rogues; but surely, in a calling regulated by law (they had to be registered), there must be some reputable firm with whom Flower could put him in touch? At first he had thought of telephoning to Flower about it; but a vision of Mrs. Webb, with ear-phones clipped to her head and goggling eyes, listening-in on his private affairs, deterred him. Immediately after luncheon he took out the old Silver Ghost and drove in to North Bromwich.

(Helen Ombersley saw the car turn the corner of the drive. He had not told her he was going; his habit of secretiveness was declaring itself again; and this hurt her, although, for another reason, she was glad of it. She, too, had made secret plans.)

At the office of Wilburn and Wilburn, Miles drew a blank. The managing clerk was reproachful. Why hadn't he made an appointment? Mr. Flower had gone to London by the breakfast train. Without any breach of professional confidence, he thought he might say that he had actually gone there on Colonel

Ombersley's business. Would Miles like to leave any message?

Miles would not. In the local paper that morning he had read the advertisement of a North Bromwich moneylender, and scribbled the address on the back of an envelope. Even if the firm were not reputable, he could do no harm by calling and making enquiries. On the steps of Wilburn's office he pulled out the collection of papers from his breast-pocket to find his note. He looked for it in vain. The last thing he found was a sealed envelope addressed to himself. It must be the one which Flower had handed him the evening before. He opened it idly and read:

Mrs. Clarke will take it as a great favour if Colonel Ombersley will excuse this most unusual request and be kind enough, at his convenience, to call at the above address. She is always at home in the afternoon, and begs him to give her the opportunity of talking over a matter of importance which cannot properly be discussed on paper.

Miles read the message through twice. His instinctive response to it was indignation. How could this woman, the authoress of so many of his troubles, dare to approach him? She herself admitted that the request was unusual. *A matter which cannot properly be discussed on paper. . . .* If the creature wanted more money she had backed the wrong horse! Yet something in the oddly-formed wording of the note and, above all, in its delicate, pointed Victorian calligraphy, made him hesitate. The writing, as well as the phrasing, was that of a lady. Though he shrank from having anything to do with the woman, he could not help feeling curious about her. *A matter of importance*. . . . He had time on his hands. He decided to go there.

The house in which Mrs. Clarke lived was a small detached "villa" in the smug, mid-Victorian suburb of Winsworth. It lay retired from the road behind a screen of overgrown laurels, and was approached by a semi-circular gravelled drive too narrow to admit his car. Miles opened the gate and tugged at the front-door bell-pull. He was conscious of an odd distaste; felt as though he were secretly visiting a house of ill-fame. A wrinkled housemaid in black uniform buttoned up to the neck and a cap with old-fashioned starched streamers admitted him. He handed her his card; but she did not even look at it. He had the impression that the family likeness had been recognized.

She showed him in to a small room at the back of the house giving on to a carefully-tended patch of lawn with set borders of lobelia, calceolaria and geranium. The furniture of the room belonged to the same period as the housemaid's cap. In spite of the sultry day, a fire burned in a cast-iron grate with an aperture shaped like a Norman arch. Before the fire stood an arm-chair heavily upholstered in red rep, before which lay a footstool covered with bead embroidery. The hearth was guarded by a painted glass firescreen mounted in mahogany; on either side of the fireplace hung a series of silhouettes of early-Victorian ladies and military gentlemen. In the middle of the mantelpiece itself, a gilt Empire clock ticked discreetly in front of a large gilt mirror. There was one photograph on the mantelpiece: a faded portrait of his father, erect, smiling and confident in his High Sheriff's uniform, at the age of sixty. Comparing this with his own reflection in the mirror, Miles found it not extraordinary that the maid had recognized him.

The Empire clock suddenly burst into a tinkling chime and struck three. Out of a habit of precision Miles looked at his watch. The clock was correct to a few seconds. This was an orderly house. It was, he admitted, a comfortable house, restrained, and in no way vulgar.

The door opened quietly with a metallic shiver of portière-rings. Miles found himself bowing stiffly to a little, bent, wrinkled old woman who advanced towards him slowly, hobbling with the aid of an ebony stick. She smiled, and the smile on that shrunken face had a remote and chilly beauty. She held out her hand to him. It was a delicate hand, though the knuckles were distorted with rheumatism. On the other, which grasped the stick, he noticed two wedding-rings. He gave her his arm to the chair that stood against the light. She thanked him.

"I am obliged to you," she said, "for coming so promptly. I almost feared. . . ." She stopped. "You are very like your father. No wonder Constance recognized you! She was devoted to him. Won't you sit down? That is your father's chair."

Miles bowed once more. He felt oddly out of water: the woman, no less than her house, was so different from what he had imagined. Her voice was refined; she had a strange dignity; she was obviously a lady. He found it impossible to treat her in the way he had thought of her. She gazed at him long and fixedly, with eyes that had certainly been beautiful. Then she shook her head and sighed.

"I do not suppose," she said, "your father ever spoke of me?"

"I knew you existed; that was all," Miles told her.

"I loved your father," she said. "He was a very great gentleman. A courtly man. We were friends for a great many years. Forty years: more than half a lifetime. We met by accident at a railway-station. I was thirty-five, and he in the prime of life. I was married —unhappily married, alas!—and he was a widower. My first husband—my husband, I should say—was a professional man in this city. It is a very tragic story: he went out of his mind and was put away. He was a healthy man otherwise: he died only two years ago. And then, of course, it was too late."

Miles nodded sympathetically. "I see." Mrs. Clarke continued:

"Before that, of course, marriage was impossible, though I know he would have liked to marry me. Our relationship was much more worthy of respect than a great many marriages. We regarded it as a marriage. I wore the ring that he gave me. I'm wearing it still. Your father bought me this house and frequently came to see me. We were both of us lonely, and it gave us both a feeling of settled happiness. He used to come here and sit in the chair you're sitting in now. We were both quiet, simple people. He told me all his troubles. He regarded this as a second home. I am sure, indeed, he found it more homely than Chaddesbourne." She smiled: "But I mustn't detain you by talking about myself. I didn't ask you to come here for that. I'm afraid you're in trouble. I read about that terrible accident in the paper. It distressed me greatly."

"It is a great anxiety for all of us. The uncertainty is wearing."

"Your son has been committed for trial?"

"Yes, at Worcester assizes."

"Will you forgive me if what I am going to say offends you?"

"I shall not be offended by anything you say, Mrs. Clarke."

(How could one be offended by anyone so gentle, so pitiful, as this crippled, quiet-voiced woman?)

"It is kind of you to say that. I hesitated. I said to myself: 'He has been accustomed to thinking hardly of me. Dare I write to him?' But I'm glad I did. I suppose a case of this kind must entail a considerable expense?"

"Unfortunately."

"And I know that your father left you in difficulties. It was a great worry to him, I assure you: you mustn't judge him too harshly. In his will he left me an annuity. I want to explain how that happened. Some thirty years ago—yes, it must have been thirty—your father had a fright: he was thrown from his horse in the hunting-field, and might easily have been killed. After that he insisted on giving me a regular allowance—nearly twice as much as I needed, but he was always generous. And . . . this is what I hesitated to tell you . . . I don't need it now, Colonel Ombersley; it is entirely superfluous. I have never lived up to it, and the balance has accumulated year by year, so that now, quite apart from that, I have a considerable income—larger, indeed, than the annuity your father so generously left me. I don't need this money. Is there any reason why I should take it?"

"It was left to you, Mrs. Clarke," Miles said. "As far as I am concerned it must be paid as long as you're living."

"But surely I can refuse to take what I don't really need? I am sure *he* would say so."

"I know nothing about the law. But whatever the lawyers may say, the obligation remains."

She smiled. "You looked so like your father when

you said that! Do you mind if I talk this over with Mr. Wilburn?"

"Mr. Wilburn is ill. I'm afraid he's retired from the business."

"I'm sorry to hear that. Your father was fond of him. In any case, if I refuse to take this annuity what can you do?"

"I really don't know," Miles said.

"And you see," she went on, as though coaxing an obstinate child, "it will come to the same in the end. When I go to join your dear father—you can see for yourself I am old and not very strong—all the money I have, apart from a small pension to my maid, will go to your son. I have no relatives left whom I care for. When your father and I became friends we thought it better to sever all other connections. There will be twenty-three thousand pounds, more or less. That is all of it Ombersley money. My husband left me penniless. All that money came out of Chaddesbourne. It must go back to Chaddesbourne. I made my will the week after your father died, leaving everything to your son."

"That was generous of you."

"It was just, Colonel Ombersley. It is what he would have wished. I knew him so well! I think, perhaps, if you don't mind my saying so, I knew him better than you did."

Miles sighed: "I daresay you are right. We were always strangers."

"I should be sorry to think that was my fault, even unconsciously."

"I don't think it was, Mrs. Clarke. I'm afraid it was mine. If we had met forty years ago, I might have understood the position better."

Mrs. Clarke shook her head: "Somehow I don't think you would. You are an obstinate race. I know you. Don't be too obstinate about this!"

She leaned forward and put out her knotted hand.

"I am only anxious to do the right thing," Miles said.

"You will do the right thing—towards me, at least —if you'll forget my annuity. You will make me more than happy if you'll allow me to help my heir. Of what use is money to me? You can see how I live. I've no wish to live differently. You can't stop me giving him money, can you now?"

She paused, gazing at him anxiously, her head on one side. In that attitude her face had the charm of appealing innocence. Then she picked up her ebony walking-stick. "Do you mind helping me?" she said. Miles gave her his arm and she rose, slightly wincing with pain. She took his hand in both of hers and pressed it. "It was good of you to come and see me," she said. "You realize that it would have been quite impossible for me to come and see you. I have always wondered what you were like, Colonel Ombersley. He was enormously proud of you. You see, we had no children. And now, I will say good-bye to you.

Would you mind. . . ." She hesitated. "Would you mind very much if I kissed you?"

Miles Ombersley bowed his head. On his cheek he felt the pressure of those soft, wrinkled lips.

"If you will ring the bell, Constance will show you to the door," she said.

At the moment when her husband left Mrs. Clarke's house at Winsworth, Helen Ombersley had embarked on an adventure hardly less strange. This adventure was not, like Miles's, the result of chance circumstances (such as looking for a moneylender's address on the back of one envelope and finding another) but of a deliberate purpose which had grown in her mind while she listened to Miles snoring in the small hours.

As soon as she saw the Silver Ghost steal round the corner of the drive she knew that the moment for the performance of this purpose had come. Carefully evading Jack and Catherine, she slipped up to her room, put on a hat and made herself tidy. Then, with equal cunning, she left the Hall grounds by way of the kitchen garden and, encouraged by the secrecy of her escape, walked more slowly down the length of the village without meeting another soul. As she reached the church, the clock in the tower chimed half-past two. She looked up at it.

"What sweet bells!" she thought. "What a lazy summery chime! *A land where it is always after-*

noon. . . . If only life were as unhurried and simple as that! Perhaps," she thought, "it *was*, in the days when those bells were cast. But am I too early?" she asked herself. "Does he take a nap after luncheon? He's the kind of man who very easily might."

She paused for a moment, waiting till the echoes of the chime died away, then passed on, deciding that it would take her at least twenty minutes at this pace to reach Mr. Hackett's doorstep.

"For I mustn't appear to be hurried," she told herself, "and I mustn't look hot: there's nothing so unprepossessing."

To keep cool on that August afternoon was no easy matter. Only at the point where the Chaddesbourne Brook rippled under the bridge out of beds of water-speedwell was there any movement in the air; and Mr. Hackett's new gravel-drive, climbing Green Hill obliquely, burned like lava under her feet. In this part of her pilgrimage she felt terribly unprotected: she knew that the drive was visible in its whole length from Mr. Hackett's front windows; she had the sensation of a soldier scaling a smooth glacis under fire, and the drive was so steep that when she quickened her pace to escape from its nakedness she soon lost her breath. "Which shows I am growing an old woman," she thought. "What a terrible shame that everyone notices one growing old but oneself!"

It seemed that the main entrance to Mr. Hackett's new house was at the back of it. There were two bell-pushes on it (just like a town-house!), one marked "Visitors" and the other "Tradesmen." This struck her as odd. When she had recovered her breath she pressed the one marked "Visitors," and a butler (presumably), who appeared to be finishing his dinner, showed her into a hall, hung with heads of big game which she found it difficult to believe Mr. Hackett had shot, and then into an empty drawing-room.

The view from the windows was superb, and the view in every other direction was awful. Yet the room, if all Mr. Hackett's furniture and pictures and everything that was his had been removed from it, would have been delightful. "The poor darling!" she thought. "If only some woman with a glimmering of taste could take him in hand! Such a pity, with all that money!"

At that moment Mr. Hackett entered. He looked puzzled; his waistcoat was unbuttoned, and his face showed the flush of a man who has slept heavily after eating.

She said: "How d'you do, Mr. Hackett? I've been admiring your view." For she thought it as well to begin by admiring something, and her tactics were justified, for Mr. Hackett was evidently pleased. He smiled:

"Yes, I'm very proud of it. But it's even better from the window over there, Mrs. Ombersley. On a clear day you see the Black Mountain."

"How delightful!" She flattered him. "You know

we've nothing like this at the Hall."

"Won't you sit down?" he said. "It's a bit of a pull up that drive." ("So I do look hot after all," she thought. "Oh dear!") "Is there anything I can do for you?"

"You were kind enough," she reminded him, "to ask me to see your new house. I've been meaning to come for a long time. And then . . ." She hesitated. "I've been wanting to talk to you, too, if you won't mind listening. We've been through a bad time, as you know. . . ."

"I was going to mention it," Mr. Hackett said quickly. "I was going to mention how sorry I felt for you—for you personally," he corrected himself. "You almost took the words out of my mouth."

"That is nice of you. All our friends have been marvellously loyal. What I wanted to talk about was my husband."

His eyes became shrewd. "Indeed?" ("What's she up to? Has he sent her to try and borrow money?" he asked himself.)

"I want you to treat what I'm going to say," she went on, "as between ourselves. I know I can trust you. My husband has not the least idea that I've come here. I'm worried about him."

"How 'worried,' exactly, Mrs. Ombersley?"

He was still on the defensive.

"About Uffley Mill, Mr. Hackett. You know he is being compelled, much against his will, to sell it?"

"I know nothing about his being compelled. I know it's for sale. And *you* know, I suppose, that I've made him an offer for it?"

"An offer he can't very well accept. That's why I am worried."

"It's a straight enough offer. Mrs. Ombersley, may I be candid?"

"Of course. I'm trying to be candid too, Mr. Hackett."

"Well, that being so, I don't mind telling you this matter of Uffley Mill has got my goat. Colonel Ombersley knows, and I expect you know, it's the home of my fathers. I fancied it when I came here. No reasonable person could blame me."

Helen Ombersley shook her head. "I certainly don't."

"Very well. I offered to buy it. Nothing doing! And I don't mind telling you he might have been more polite about it."

"Yes. His manner is difficult. He didn't mean not to be polite."

"All right. We'll admit he didn't, though that's how I took it. What comes next? I offer to build a village hall if he'll sell me the land. Nothing doing! What happens next? I offer to supply your house and the whole blessed village with cheap electricity. I'm ready to bring it to your door, free, gratis and for nothing. Nothing doing! And if the letter he sent me about that's a polite one, I'll eat my hat! Do you see where we are? Every blessed thing I suggest to him, no matter what it is, he turns down: throws it back in my face! You may tell me he's out of touch with the modern world. Well, you can't be that now-adays. And if *I* don't teach Colonel Ombersley that, well, someone else will. I love this place, Mrs. Ombersley. It's in my bones, as you might say, and I love it dearly."

"I know you do." Helen Ombersley shook her head sadly.

"I want to turn Chaddesbourne into a going con-cern." ("Going . . . going . . . gone!" Helen Ombersley thought. "Poor, poor little Chaddes-bourne!") "And whenever I put my hand to a thing, your husband just digs in his hind legs and says: 'None of this!' It's aggravating, you know. I'm not used to that kind of attitude in business circles. To be perfectly frank with you, I've had just about enough of it."

"I quite see how you feel."

"Very well. Now he comes along, just as if I were a dog on trust with a lump of sugar on my nose, and says 'Paid for! You can buy Uffley Mill if you like, but only on certain conditions. I'll condescend to sell it, because it suits me, but you can't have possession.' Well, two can play at that game, Mrs. Ombersley. What about *my* conditions?"

"I've heard what they are."

"Well, now, aren't they perfectly reasonable?"

"There's a question of sentiment involved."

"Oh well, there you have me! I've been talking business."

"May I tell you how I look at it?"

"I'm always ready to listen to reason, Mrs. Ombersley."

"All the time you've been talking I haven't been able to get out of my mind this thought: 'What a pity it is that two people who love the same thing—I mean Chaddesbourne, of course—can love it so differently!' You see, the tragedy is, you're both of you right, and both of you obstinate."

"Well, really, nobody can say. . . ."

"Oh yes, you *are* obstinate, Mr. Hackett. And what's more, you're both proud of it."

John Hackett laughed for the first time. "Well, I daresay you're right."

"About Uffley Mill to begin with. My husband is unable to feel he can give you possession because he's promised old Lydgate not to turn him out during his lifetime."

"I guessed there was something of that kind. Needless to say, I recognize the fact that a promise is a promise, and I respect him for it. As a matter of fact, I should look at it that way myself. I should no more think of turning the old fellow out than flying."

"Then why not accept the condition?"

"I don't like having conditions forced on me."

"Isn't that rather. . . ."

"Go on!"

"I'm afraid I was going to say 'childish.' "

"I don't like being compelled. If he'd told me his difficulty and trusted me to do the right thing. . . ."

"I'm quite sure he would trust you if you put it to him that way. But you didn't."

"Well, if that's understood between you and me, I'll buy Uffley. Provided your husband falls in with the other conditions I've laid down."

"Yes . . . 'laid down' is the word. I'm afraid he's as little in love with conditions as you are. Particularly when they're 'laid down.' "

"He can take it or leave it."

"Can't we, rather, make it a matter of 'giving' as well as 'taking'?"

"I don't get you, I'm afraid, Mrs. Ombersley."

"Let's look at the other conditions. You're holding such a lot of pistols to his head; it's a regular blunderbuss. Such an old-fashioned weapon, Mr. Hackett, and you so up-to-date! There's The Moat. . . ."

"It would be best off his hands. It's heavily mortgaged. If somebody doesn't buy it soon, the mortgagees will foreclose. I happen to know this."

"And because you know this, you want to force him to sell it? Isn't that rather abusing your strength?"

"Would you like to know my real reason?"

"I want to."

"To tell you the truth, I'm sorry for those Cooksons. She's a decent woman, and the boy is as nice a fellow as I know in Chaddesbourne. They're bankrupt, quite hopelessly, and your husband's the principal creditor. They're going to be sold up, and that means turned out. So it came into my head that I could do myself and them a good turn at the same time: kill two birds with one stone, so to speak. If your husband sold me The Moat, or gave me a long lease, I should take over their stuff, stock and so on, at a valuation, without any sale, and hand the place over to Jim Cookson to run it for me as a sort of bailiff. When old Lydgate dies, I should make one property of the two. That was all my idea."

"But what makes you think my husband will turn out the Cooksons?"

"I know that he's pressed for money. He can't afford to do otherwise."

"If I told you that he'd called on the Cooksons yesterday and told them he wanted them to stay on and not worry about the rent, you'ld be rather surprised?"

"I don't deny it."

"Well, he did, Mr. Hackett. You see, you don't *know* my husband. And he doesn't know you. Don't you realize you've both of you been trying to do the same thing, and fighting each other just out of sheer suspicion?"

"If I'd known Colonel Ombersley had that in his mind I shouldn't have mentioned The Moat. The rent's more than half their trouble."

T*

"Let's forget about The Moat then. If you two put your heads together you can make things quite easy for the Cooksons. Then there's the Parish Hall. . . ."

"Now there I consider your husband treated me badly."

"Because you distrust each other so stupidly, both of you, that you've never discussed it. My husband is tremendously keen on the beauty of Chaddesbourne."

"So am I, Mrs. Ombersley. And I'm keen on the village having public conveniences. I'm afraid I've expressed myself badly. You know what I mean. To say nothing of electric light."

"The problem's the same. My husband is frightened of your architect."

"Then he's wrong. That young man has built seven police-stations, all over the Black Country. He's the chap who remodelled this house."

"I know. To tell you the truth I'm afraid of him too. And I'm frightened to death of your pylons."

"They're not unsightly."

"In the right place, no. But I should hate them crossing our park. Tastes aren't things about which one can argue. I think, if you'd asked my husband, you'ld have found that that was his only objection."

"He didn't give me a chance, Mrs. Ombersley."

"I know. He was wrong. Couldn't you run your cables underground?"

"It would double the expense."

"It would save the landscape, Mr. Hackett. If I

told you he'd give you your wayleave without hesitation provided the cables were hidden—I only mean that part of them which runs across the park—what would you say to that?"

"I'ld damn the expense and do anything to oblige you, Mrs. Ombersley."

"It's sweet of you to put it like that, Mr. Hackett." She meant what she said. "Since the long talk we had at Whitsuntide I've always felt that we were capable of understanding one another. It seems to me that what you and my husband needs is an interpreter."

"I don't ask for a better than yourself," Mr. Hackett said gallantly.

"If you talk like that you will turn my head," she protested.

"Well, I promised to be candid."

"And there's no other misunderstanding? You know, that is all they were."

"There's none than I know of."

"I'm afraid I disturbed your sleep. What time is it? Not half-past four? I can hardly believe it. My children will be waiting tea for me. And I've not seen your house after all."

"Won't you bring your daughter up some day?"

"That would be delightful."

"If I telephone you. . . ."

"I'm afraid we're not on the telephone. Yes, you think it's my husband's fault, and you're right. But that's only one side of him. Good-bye, Mr. Hackett."

John Hackett showed her to the door.

And now the hot drive no longer burned her feet. They flew, winged with happiness and, perhaps, excusable triumph. Rain threatened; but that did not trouble Helen Ombersley. If it had soaked her she would not have cared.

John Hackett stood gazing after her till the tall, frail figure was lost at the last turn of the drive. His mind was divided between admiration and a suspicion that he, shrewd business-man that he was, had been "done in the eye." By a woman, too: a gentle, soft-spoken woman. In the end he found himself smiling.

"By gad, if she can get away with it like that," he told himself, "she damned well deserves it! That's a woman, that is! She's worth two dozen Ombersleys!"

He was pleased to reflect that, provided his new pedigree was genuine (and considering what he had paid for it, it certainly ought to be), he had a dash of D'Abitot blood in his veins himself.

XXI

ORDEAL

BEHIND the lace curtains of Miss Loach's bedroom
window there proceeded a struggle far more intense
than any that vexed the Ombersleys. For no less than
a fortnight Miss Loach had been fighting for her life.
Not the Miss Loach whom Chaddesbourne knew as
an intelligence always inquisitive and sometimes malignant, like that of a black spider, watchful in the middle
of her web: that conscious Miss Loach had long since
ceased to impose her censorship on her little world,
having given place to another and inner Miss Loach,
who revealed herself in snatches of delirium as a
tremulous and romantic young lady of the eighteen-
seventies; until at last she too faded away, disclosing an ultimate or (as Mr. Winter would have
maintained) a penultimate Miss Loach, bereft of all
personality malignant or romantic, a mere concatena-
tion of cells in the shape of a little old woman, desperately vitalized by a force, dumb, blind and obscure,
called the Will to Live. Dr. Selby, who, in spite of
his concentration on the material aspects of the case,
was an imaginative man, saw this last Miss Loach as
a little red ember still obstinately glowing amid a mass

of cinder that had already gone black.

Could he breathe on the glow and coax it into an incandescence that would catch the dull cinders and bring them to life? He did what he could, whipping up the tired heart with strychnine and the doses of brandy which a conscious Miss Loach would have rejected indignantly. He had replaced the amiable and incompetent Jane Trost by two trained nurses; for nursing, in such a case, was more important than medicine, and (since Miss Loach could not afford them) he and Winter had decided to defray the expense. Five or six times a day, and often in the middle of the night, he stole into the room (its windows were wide open now) and bent over the small, monkey-like figure, looking, listening with an attention which had little sentiment in it yet partook of tenderness. He had not to deal—as in a case of lobar pneumonia—with an organism gallantly resisting a massed assault which must end, at a moment of crisis, in spectacular victory or defeat. The struggle which he witnessed was a grinding war of attrition in which, up to a certain point, time fought on the side of the defence.

At the end of the second week, when the glow in the ember grew so faint as to be hardly perceptible, he took counsel with Mr. Winter and sent for Miss Loach's widowed sister. She came up from Bournemouth with her luggage distributed in a number of cardboard boxes, one of which she left in the train. Though she did not resemble Miss Loach—indeed, she was her physical antithesis, being as plump and pale as her sister was spare and swart—she emanated, Dr. Selby discovered with delight, from the same fantastic world: she was as like the White Queen as Miss Loach was like the Red. Selby had never encountered a human being more inanely talkative or more completely diffuse.

"I'm afraid you'll be shocked by your sister's appearance," he told her.

"Oh, Laura was never a beauty," Mrs. Aspinall said blandly.

He escorted her upstairs to Miss Loach's bedroom; but their progress was slow, for she found it difficult to finish telling him about the contents of the cardboard box she had lost at Didcot, or possibly at North Bromwich, or perhaps at Stourton Junction, unless it had been mislaid in the ladies' waiting-room at Bournemouth; until it suddenly struck her that she might have left it at home, or even have miscounted the number of packages when they had been stowed into his car at Wychbury.

"In which case, of course," Mrs. Aspinall said, "it's all right, isn't it? You see, Dr. Selvedge, I have no head. Not a vestige of head. My late husband constantly chaffed me about it. In the most sympathetic way. I only wish you had known him. The handsomest and kindest of men. You know," she went on confidentially, "I always trimmed his beard. He wouldn't let anyone else touch it. It was trimmed to a point. More than one lady in the congregation has confided to me that he resembled Our Lord. As he did, indeed, in his nature as well as his beard. And you know," Mrs. Aspinall continued, "of course, there is always the weeniest chance that my maid, who has even less head than myself, forgot to pack it—I mean the kimono Captain Rogers brought from Japan (or was it Jamaica?)—because we're both unaccustomed to travelling since my dear father's funeral, and she did forget the dog's breakfast, poor little mite! Belgian griffons are so intelligent: they notice everything."

"It's the door on the right," Selby said. "Those stairs lead up to the attic."

"Well, that only shows you, doesn't it?" Mrs. Aspinall said.

She stood at the foot of the four-poster bed, breathing heavily, for the stairs had tried her, and gazed at the remains of Miss Loach.

"Well, Laura!" she shouted cheerfully.

Miss Loach lay still.

"She doesn't hear me," Mrs. Aspinall said despondently. "Fancy that!"

But Miss Loach had heard her. Miss Loach's black eyes opened. They were as tiny as boot-buttons, but they seemed to occupy the greater part of Miss Loach's face. She moistened her lips and spoke thickly, for the first time in five days.

"Arabella," she said. "Where . . ." She panted.

"Where is your mourning. . . . A widow has . . . no right . . . to wear . . . pansies in her hat."

Mrs. Aspinall laughed heartily.

"There you are, now! You see. She knows me!"

From that moment, indeed, Miss Loach took a turn for the better. It was as though the irritation of Mrs. Aspinall's presence were a more powerful stimulant than strychnine or digitalin. That she should have pulled through at all was nothing short of a miracle. Dr. Selby felt the relief; the whole village was relieved; though it detested Miss Loach as a person, it was proud of her, in a way, as an institution, and had been deeply impressed when Mr. Winter prayed for her publicly in church.

Her recovery was a relief to Selby, yet, otherwise, he was not happy. Since the inquest he had never set eyes on Catherine Ombersley. She came no more to the surgery to play on his piano. Every day, coming back from his round, he eagerly asked Mrs. Hussingtree if she had been; but even if she had not told him he would have known. There was something lacking in the long room nowadays. An added sweetness had gone out of it. Even the music he made there had lost the savour he knew. Of course, he told himself, they were suffering at the Hall. They would go on suffering beneath the weight of suspense until the assizes opened. And then. . . . Heaven only knew.

They were suffering less than he imagined. The misery of the situation at the Hall had its own com-

pensations, of which nobody was more conscious than
Helen Ombersley herself. If they "kept to themselves," they were, more than ever before, a united
family, each member pathetically anxious to comfort
the others. Helen felt this new unity between herself
and Miles, and was thankful for it. Since the ice of
his reserve had been broken on the night when she had
taken him to her arms and held his hand while he
slept, he had admitted her to his confidence with an
openness that had been lacking during all but the
earliest days of their married life.

She felt even more deeply and gratefully the growing communion of feeling and interest between Miles
and Jack. Ghastly though the immediate cause of
their reconciliation had been, Helen's heart was thankful for it. It seemed almost as though each of them
had needed some violent catastrophe to reach this new
understanding. Miles was softer, more human than
she had ever known him before, and Jack, too, was
changed. Even physically changed. The predominance of the latent D'Abitot strain which Miles had
noticed when he stood in the witness-box declared
itself more emphatically every day. No doubt he was
feeling the stress of his own situation, regret for the
small part (as his conscience still told him) he had
played in George Cookson's death, remorse, even
more persistent, for the anxiety he had inflicted on
the rest of the family. If his pale face had lost its
gaiety and impulsiveness, that air of a laughing cornet

in Rupert's cavalry still preserved in the Janssen portrait which hung in the library, it had gained a new firmness of feature and gravity of expression which, though it aged him, had made him undeniably handsomer.

This physical change was reflected in his mind, which was no longer careless and flamboyant, but oddly sober not merely for himself, but for his years. From the moment when he returned from the inquest in Flower's company he had evidently determined within himself to adopt a new manner of life. He proved this resolve not by words—there was something in him now, Helen Ombersley noticed, of his father's reticence—but by the interest he began to show in the working of the Chaddesbourne estate.

Helen watched these overtures anxiously. She was afraid—and not without reason—that Miles would discourage him, not by rejecting Jack's help but by regarding his interest as superficial and spurious, as a self-imposed penance rather than as the change of heart which she believed it to be. But Jack, it appeared, possessed his own share of his father's obstinacy. He had made up his mind, and it mattered little to him whether Miles discouraged him or welcomed him. He had chosen his path and followed it with persistence; so that now, when Miles rode out over the fields inspecting his workmen and deliberating on the plans he had made for a future which he himself would not witness, his son rode with him; and the sight of them riding together warmed Helen's heart. When they returned from these rides Jack retired to the smoking-room. He spent hours there alone (for a whole month he had never left Chaddesbourne) poring over maps, files of accounts and old correspondence, making himself master of every detail in the management of the estate. When Miles spoke his thoughts, as he did more frequently, he was surprised to find that Jack knew what he was talking about, and astonished by an intelligence for which he had not given him credit.

He admitted as much to Helen. She found it hard to resist the temptation of telling him that this was what she had always begged him to believe.

"The D'Abitot men are always like that, Miles," she said, "and Jack is a D'Abitot. They develop late and suddenly. One day they seem to be children with childish interests, and the next they're men. I've heard my grandmother say that my father was just the same, though, by all accounts, in his youth he was much wilder than Jack's ever been. You, of course, are quite different: that's why you don't understand him. I think all you Ombersleys are born old with the weight of the universe on your shoulders. Thank heaven, it works out the other way round. You're younger than you were five years ago."

Miles laughed. "I don't feel any younger, my darling."

"Just now we can none of us feel anything." She sighed. "We're simply waiting. When this dreadful business is over, we'll all be young again."

Miles was grateful to her for her courage. At times he was haunted by a dread which must not be spoken, that the case might miscarry. The jury might find Jack guilty, the judge send him to prison. It was necessary for his peace of mind that he should behave as though this event were impossible. The fact that the sale of Uffley was going through had freed his hands. He had already accepted contracts for the repair of the five condemned cottages. Every day he walked down the village and watched the workmen stripping mouldy thatch from the rotten timbers that must be replaced and hammering at the walls to make room for a damp-course. He was pleased with the work. They were making an honest job of it: a job, he reflected, that badly needed doing. He had quite forgotten his first indignation against Selby. It was Selby's evidence, he told himself, that was going to save Jack.

It was now mid-September. The Michaelmas-daisies made a mist of diaphanous blue and amethyst resembling the vapours that rose from the ornamental water, on whose banks the spears of Japanese iris grew shabby. The grass of the lawns sprouted no more; at dawn it lay white with rime and gossamer. In a single night of frost the dahlias wilted and went brown; the blackened buds, which would never open, hung dismally down. Red Admirals, seeking the flowers they had left overnight, found only decay, and flew drowsily over to the orchards where windfalls rotted in wet grass, or to the garden-wall where green ivy-bloom held the year's latest honey. Yet this season was less silent than summer. Soon, though the thrushes and blackbirds were still chary of song, stray robins appeared to fling their bright challenge on the air, hopping hither and thither perkily amid the rusty rose-buds; and at eventide, when the hot September sun failed and the air hung still and chilly, there was a rushing of wings overhead as the packed starling hordes, in one black cloud after another, came whirring westward from upland stubbles to their communal roosting-beds by the banks of Severn.

"And now it is really autumn," Helen Ombersley thought.

The assizes opened at Worcester on October 8th. The same day the Grand Jury, two-thirds of whom were his father's friends, returned a true bill in the matter of John D'Abitot Ombersley. The case, which would probably be tried on the tenth, excited a good deal of interest in Worcester because of the name of the accused and, even more, his defender's. It was not often that criminal lawyers of Sir Edward Cronshaw's eminence pleaded on circuit. The inhabitants of the city and its neighbourhood, though mildly interested in Jack's fate, looked forward to Cronshaw's defence, for which Miles had begun by

paying six hundred pounds, as a kind of gratuitous
dramatic entertainment in a theatre provided at the
county's expense.

On the morning of the trial Selby scrambled
through his work as best he could. Apart from
Elsie Cookson, he was the only Chaddesbourne witness. Though he watched the road carefully, the
Ombersleys' car slipped past without his seeing it,
so he could not tell whether Catherine had driven
to Worcester with the father and mother. From the
opposite side of the road Ted Hadley watched his
departure.

"Nice day for the trial, Doctor," he shouted
cheerily. Selby smiled to himself. It was odd how
little the average man concerned himself with the
distresses of others. Would he be much concerned
himself, he wondered, if Catherine's feelings were
not involved?

"Jim Cookson and his mother and Elsie have just
drove off in front of you," Ted Hadley shouted.
"Glad saw them go by. It looks like you've made a
good job of that cut on her face, Doctor."

"Yes, poor child," Selby thought. "It hasn't come
out so badly." During her convalescence he had called
at The Moat fairly often, and had been struck, once
more, by the admirable qualities of Mrs. Cookson.
"She actually looks happier," he thought, "than when
her husband was living. The trouble with poor George
Cookson was that he bit off more than he could chew."

Whyle everi man is plesed in his degre there is both peas and uneti. Yes, that was the truth of it. It had looked, at one time, as if the Cooksons would have to leave Chaddesbourne. On the auctioneers' notice-board outside the "Ombersley Arms" he had seen a bill announcing a sale at The Moat. Then, one morning, the bill had been defaced with a red-lettered strip: *Sale Cancelled,* and the next thing he had heard was a rumour that John Hackett had taken over the Cooksons' affairs, lock, stock and barrel, and was putting in Jim as his bailiff. It was not a bad arrangement, he thought, and decent of Hackett. Mrs. Cookson would still be mistress of The Moat, and that nice fellow Jim would continue to farm the land he knew, though Elsie could hardly remain a young lady of leisure. Even in this, it seemed, a kind Providence had its eyes on the Cooksons; for only last week Miss Burton had resigned her post to take up another in the south of the county where her home was, and Elsie, who had qualified as a teacher in North Bromwich, would probably fill her place. Miss Burton complained, Mr. Winter told him, that Chaddesbourne had never suited her nervous headaches ("As a matter of fact," Selby thought, "I'm sure she has astigmatism"); but what Winter dreaded, unreasonably, was the loss of an organist.

"Do you think," he had said, "I dare ask Miss Ombersley to take over the choir and the organ?"

"If she does," Selby said, "the attendance at church

will improve." When Winter looked shocked, he added: "By one, at any rate."

"Oh, I see what you mean," Winter said.

Selby put up his car in a garage in Foregate Street and entered the Shire Hall by the door reserved for witnesses. A farm-labourer stood in the dock, on trial for arson. He had the head and face of a congenital defective, if Selby had ever seen one. He sat dumb and dazed in the box while the judge, an old man with a heavy red jowl and gold pince-nez perilously clipped on the end of his nose, summed up, addressing a stolid-faced jury.

"So these are the men who will try Jack Ombersley," Selby thought. "If I had my choice, I would choose that old man every time."

He searched the packed faces anxiously for Catherine Ombersley's. She was not there—in a way he was thankful that she wasn't, though he longed to see her—but he soon discovered Miles Ombersley and his wife sitting side by side. There was no missing them: their distinction dominated the whole of the court-room. Both were pale, and both looked years older than when he had seen them last. Beside Mrs. Ombersley he saw the too-obviously handsome head of Jack's counsel, Sir Edward Cronshaw. From time to time he appeared to engage her in whispered small-talk: he had a great reputation as a "charmer" of ladies as well as juries. Selby saw Helen Ombersley incline her head and listen to him. He saw her smile with her lips, but her eyes did not smile. "Why can't that fool leave her alone?" he asked himself indignantly.

Miles Ombersley made no attempt to listen to what Cronshaw was saying. He sat upright with his stiff cavalryman's port, with eyes front, like the officer commanding a crack regiment at a general inspection. Selby had never appreciated the shape of his fine head and profile before. "It is a piece of pure feudal architecture," he thought, "transitional, or early English. How well that type wears!"

The stolid jury returned a verdict of "Not guilty" in the case of arson. ("A good sign!" Selby thought.) The labourer, free, but still dazed and dumb, shuffled out of the box.

Jack's name was called again and again: "John D'Abitot Ombersley!"

Miles Ombersley did not wince.

Selby heard the case for the Crown begin. It seemed to him that the counsel conducting it was luke-warm: a languid and rather desiccated man, a mere windlestraw beside the enormous physical preponder-ance of Cronshaw. Within a time that seemed to Selby incredibly short, he found himself in the witness-box and repeating the evidence which he had given at the inquest With a superbly theatrical gesture Cronshaw rose to cross-examine him.

Much as he disliked the man, he soon knew that he was in the hands of a master who could draw tones from a witness (even an unwilling witness: and Selby was willing) with the virtuosity of a great violinist playing on his chosen instrument. Left to himself, with no mean intelligence and the best will in the world, Selby could not have made his evidence a quarter as effective as Cronshaw made it, extracting from him, by suggestion, it seemed, a picture of George Cookson's fuddled state (George Cookson's injuries did not interest him) more vivid than any which he himself could have presented. When he had finished with him, Cronshaw smiled triumphantly at the jury. "Yes, I'm worth coming many miles to hear," his smile assured them. He sat down, manipulating his silk as a duchess might manage her train.

"That is all, Dr. Selby."

Any questions? A few questions from the prosecution: telling questions, too. The picture was not what it had been. But the jury, still dazzled by the afterglow of Cronshaw's virtuosity, preferred the more highly-coloured original. Even when he was silent, Cronshaw remained the centre of their interest. The judge suddenly looked at the gold watch lying in front of him. He took off his pince-nez, rose, stretched his legs, and instantly became a plain man, hungry for luncheon. The Shire Hall emptied slowly. Miles and Helen Ombersley did not move.

Selby wandered out into the city. He was glad to feel the sting of the amber autumn air. He walked briskly down Foregate Street and High Street to a point where the pinkish sandstone of the cathedral rose before him, the great tower pallid against the pale October sky. He skirted the western end of the nave and looked down on the river. Severn ran swollen and turbid with rain from the slopes of Plynlimmon; a noble river, the greatest of all rivers to him. Between it and the cold blue line of the Malverns he saw the pale green of the County Cricket Ground, that paradise of his boyhood, where his eyes had seen the giants of old days: Harry Foster, blue-eyed and stubborn, and his brother Tip, that peerless paladin of the cricket-field; but to-day those bright memories hardly tempted his mind. It was in need of a mood more solemn and meditative. He turned his back on Severn and entered the cathedral.

The vast church of Our Lord and the Blessed Virgin seemed empty, and so quiet that his footsteps echoed on its paving. He had always loved it; it was *the* cathedral to him; a graceful, mediæval lady of a church compared with round-headed Norman warriors like Durham and York; it was the reliquary, too, of rich personal memories, such as the day, long since, when he had first perceived the emotional significance of Elgar's *Gerontius*, being moved not only by the complicated loveliness of its Gothic traceries (so comparable to the soaring shafts and fans of the vaulted nave), but also by the unique spiritual beauty of Gervase Elwes's voice. In its shadows, too, he had first learned and loved the heartening magnificence of

Bach: not the "little Bach" of Catherine's *Italian Concerto*, but the magnitudes of the great choruses in the *B Minor Mass*, which were themselves cathedrals in sound.

He remembered such moments of ecstasy, as rare as those of first love or of a mystical religion, while he walked in silence down the empty northern aisle where worn banners of the Worcesters, the old twenty-ninth, hung like cobwebs from the walls ("How pathetically eager," he thought, "men are to sanctify violence and bloodshed!") until he reached the stone screen which separates the aisle itself from the Jesus chapel.

Sitting there and meditating on the more sombre glories of the place—John, brother of Cœur-de-Lion, lying dead with the shrines of St. Wulstan and St. Oswald on either side of him—Selby became aware of a sound which seemed more appropriate to his present mood than any he could have chosen. In the far organ loft invisible human fingers began to play. They played the slow movement of Beethoven's *C Minor Symphony*, and that ambling melody, with its smooth yet hesitant gait, so richly serene, so wise in its consolation, had the power of lending the immediate human distresses with which he was preoccupied a new value, a more just perspective in his vision of life; so that, rapt in those strains which wandered hither and thither with the freedom of thought through the airy spaces of galleried choir and clerestory, his mind was liberated at last from all memory of the grim scene he had left: the judge sitting on the bench in his scarlet robes, the stolid-faced jury, the packed Shire Hall smelling of ghoulish humanity and repressive law.

By that enveloping beauty of vagrant sound, enclosed, as it were, within the beauty of a dream in stone, he was inspired to think of life as something more noble and spacious than he had lately imagined. When the echo of the last note died away, he knew that by beauty and solitude together his soul had been purged of its restlessness.

He waited for a moment, wondering if the unseen player would begin again. But the music had ceased as mysteriously as it had begun. It would be wise, he decided, to depart while his mind was still full of it, before any discordant sound or sight had the chance to invade or disturb. He rose quietly, and, making his way to the porch, became aware that he had not been, as he imagined, a solitary listener. Other steps moved parallel with his down the length of the nave. He turned, and saw that the second listener had been Catherine Ombersley. They met in the cathedral porch. Her face, too, it seemed to him, showed traces of the serene influence they had shared.

"I had no idea you were here," he said.

"Nor I that you were here."

"In Worcester, I mean."

"I drove in with the others. I've been in the cathedral all morning. I couldn't face the Shire Hall.

Besides, they didn't need me."

"I think you were wise." (How pale she looked, for all her serenity!) "Have you had any luncheon? That's a medical question."

"You're quite right to ask; but I couldn't dream of it. Has the case begun?"

"Yes. The court rose when I'd given my evidence."

"And . . . ?" Her eyes were pleading.

"There's really nothing to tell you. I believe it will be all right. It's important that we should believe it."

"You have faith, Dr. Selby: I envy you."

"Yes, I suppose I have faith. I think Jack has paid his penalty. You've all of you paid, worse luck! Redemption by suffering! Don't millions of people believe in it? That's the idea which built this cathedral."

"Can it last much longer?"

"I don't think so: the court won't open for another quarter of an hour."

"And then you'll go back?"

"I'ld much rather stay with you. If I may . . ."

"I wish you would."

"Let us go and look at the river."

They walked round the west end of the nave side by side. "This is heaven," Selby thought. "It's heaven for me, and yet this sweet child is suffering. How gentle and fine she is, in spite of all this!" They stood gazing at the river.

"I've seen nothing of you for such a long time," he said. "I've missed you."

"I've missed your room, too." (Why did she put it like that?) "For the last six weeks I've found music quite impossible. We've been huddled together at the Hall, all four of us, like sheep when a dog runs into a field. We had to be close together to keep up our courage. I was probably wrong. That slow movement of the Fifth made me cry for the first time. I expect it was good for me. I felt almost happy alone in there."

"Until I broke in on you?"

"No, that isn't true. I'm glad you were there. I should have hated anyone else, though."

(But what could he say? Not the words that were in his heart: this was no time for them.)

"That makes me more happy than I can tell you," he said. "There is nobody else in the world who would have said that to me. I have very few friends: the best part of my generation disappeared in the war. And I've no women friends."

"Yet your life is much richer than most lives, I think," she said gravely. "You live every moment of it, which is more than most of us do. You've your music—I can understand that—but you've your books as well. I envy you those."

"You've no need to envy. You've ten years' start of me."

She smiled. "What a melancholy old man! And

that isn't all. You've your work, and that's surely the most enviable thing in the world. Every day you help people who are suffering in body or in mind. Isn't that wonderful for you? And you're wise in your helping, too. You were wise when you helped me, when you 'prescribed' for me, as you called it. And of course, you know that you're helping me now."

"You make me more happy than ever, Miss Ombersley."

"Why, if I had your work and your tastes and your knowledge, I think I should be so pleased with myself as to be quite intolerable. You have every possible thing that a human being could wish for!"

Selby smiled and gazed at her ardent eyes, then spoke slowly:

"Not quite everything."

Her eyes fell. He reproached himself for having passed the bounds he had set. From the grey tower above them a slow chime floated on the air. A deep bell boomed twice. In the glove factory down the river a steam whistle shrieked. Two o'clock. The court would be opening. Solemnity fell on them. They watched the far hills and the full, turbid flood of Severn in silence. For five minutes—perhaps more—no word was spoken. Then Catherine said:

"Ought we to stay here much longer? I can't stand still like this. It's more than I can bear. I must do something."

"If we walk up slowly towards the Shire Hall . . ."

"Yes, I think we'd better. It can't last much longer, can it?"

"No. The only witnesses are the Cookson girl and Jack himself. Then the judge will sum up."

"Let us go."

They left the river-side parapet and walked up the narrow street. A stream of workmen and factory girls, coming late from their dinners, impeded them, hurrying towards their works down by the river. The men puffed at their pipes, the girls laughed and chattered like daws as they went. The whole crowded street was callously intent on its own bustling business. Selby placed himself between Catherine and the jostling multitude; she had never before seemed so fragile, so much in need of his protection. He took her arm to protect her. She smiled and seemed grateful.

The street suddenly widened, the crowd thinned; they crossed the road in the Foregate. He was aware of the black railway-bridge with its embossed coat-of-arms, the three black pears on a silver shield, and the Faithful City's motto. As they passed into Foregate Street, Selby looked at his watch. Twenty-seven minutes past two. How much could have happened in twenty-seven minutes! He imagined Sir Edward Cronshaw's rich flow of rhetoric; he saw the blank faces of the jury, the red-jowled judge with his pince-nez perched on his nose; he saw Miles and Helen Ombersley sitting side by side motionless; his heart bled for them.

The gates of the Shire Hall courtyard opened on the right. Two policemen kept guard over them with an air of bored nonchalance.

"We can wait outside in the courtyard," Selby said.

"Yes, if they don't move us."

"I should hate to think of you waiting here alone," he said. "I'm glad I came with you."

"So am I."

The doors opened, and a stream of people emerged. Could it be over so soon? Selby caught a man by the sleeve.

"The manslaughter case," he said; "is it finished?"

"They've just brought in the verdict. Young Ombersley's acquitted. Cronshaw hardly said anything."

"He's acquitted, Catherine!"

"I heard. I can hardly believe it. Oh dear!"

"Let me take your arm."

"I'm all right. It was almost too much for me. I must go in and find Mother." She held out her hand to him. "Thank you so much."

"One moment before you go." He would not release her. "Catherine. . . . Will you marry me?"

She laughed, though tears ran down her cheeks.

"Yes . . . I think so. Now let me go, and do lend me a handkerchief."

"Thank heaven, I've a clean one!"

She took it, laughing, and left him.

XXII

DEDICATION

On the morning of October 31st, which is Gheluvelt Day, Mr. Winter walked in his garden waiting for his friend the suffragan bishop, who was coming to Chaddesbourne to dedicate the War Memorial, appropriately, for Mr. Winter and he (before his translation) had been comrades in arms at Gheluvelt itself on the day when the Worcesters earned the glory of that name. Mr. Winter was pleased with his War Memorial. At one period he had been anxious lest it should not be ready for dedication by this date; there had even been disputes or differences of opinion as to the form of it. Mr. Hackett, the donor of the largest subscription, had wanted value for his money in respect of bulk; he wished Chaddesbourne to have a bigger War Memorial than Wychbury or any of the adjoining parishes; but later on, to Mr. Winter's relief, his desires had become more modest, having been influenced, Mr. Winter gathered, by Mrs. Ombersley, who had, strangely, become the æsthetic dictator of Mr. Hackett's life and had collaborated with him in choosing an architect for the new Village Hall. It was a pity, Mr. Winter thought, that Hackett had not succumbed to Mrs. Ombersley's persuasions before he built his house on Green Hill. That, of course, was past saving; but the War Memorial had turned out exactly as Mr. Winter desired. It was a plain cross of Cotswold stone, of gracious proportions, with a carved inscription and the Roll of the Fallen engraved on a plate of bronze. He had watched its erection with careful anxiety, and now it stood there, between the church and the "Ombersley Arms," draped with the Union Jack, which the bishop would remove at the ceremony of dedication.

There were moments that morning when Mr. Winter had felt anxious lest the flag which draped the memorial should be blown away. It was a brilliant day, midway between autumn and winter, with a steel-blue sky through which a north-easter blew, tossing the tops of the elms (several branches had crashed in the night) and stripping their boughs of leaves which flew helter-skelter and lay in golden drifts against the walls of the gardens opposite. The trees had been so thrashed in the night that now one could see the rooks' nests which had been invisible since their broods forsook them in late spring.

"How quickly this year has passed!" Mr. Winter thought, walking briskly up and down the garden path to keep his blood moving. "All the Michaelmas-daisies are over," he told himself. "I must cut the clumps to-morrow as I cut the phloxes last week. Not a single flower is left in the border now; I shall see no flowers there till the snowdrops open in February. And next spring I must get some weed-killer," he thought. "This path is disgraceful. Why, surely that must be musk!"

His mind returned to a thundery Sunday, the sixth after Trinity, which was the last time he had wondered about the musk and its scent's mysterious extinction. Thinking back on it now, and still wondering, he found himself forming a new theory to explain this miniature catastrophe. Had the musk lost its scent after all? he asked himself. Wasn't it possible that human beings, who blamed the poor musk, had themselves lost the faculty of smelling it? That was a pretty parable, he thought, well worth noting for use in a sermon. Since the war we could not smell musk, and blamed the Creator, though, perhaps, its scent was still there. Since the war a large number of disillusioned men could not smell the world's sweetness, refusing to admit the existence of goodness in human nature, though God's world was still sweet and human nature still capable of astonishing goodness. The parable struck him as so useful that he hitched up his cassock and found a pencil and scribbled the word "Musk" on his cuff; but, as he did so, standing in the wind, he heard the swish of tyres and a motor panting in the vicarage drive, which meant that the bishop had arrived. So he hurried to receive him.

On such a cold day, the first day of winter, Miss Loach decided, her bedroom windows, which Dr.

Selby insisted on her opening during the day, must surely be closed, more particularly as she had determined to sit at them and take part at a distance in the dedication. This would be the first time she had witnessed a public ceremony since old Mr. Ombersley's funeral. But for the grace of God, she reflected, she might not have lived to see it, though now, since her illness, she had taken on a new lease of life and felt stronger and better and more fit to shoulder her moral responsibilities towards her neighbours than for many years past.

Mr. Winter had sent her a programme of the procedure. It would begin with a short service inside the church which she could not follow, though if the day had not been so boisterous (How the leaves scurried!) she might possibly have judged by the sound of the organ what stages the services had reached. It was a long time, she reflected, since she had seen a real bishop, and, though Mr. Winter's friend was young and only a suffragan, she looked forward to the sight of lawn sleeves and a pectoral cross as a rich source of edification.

Now the church clock struck two. The service, no doubt, was beginning. Miss Loach opened her programme and followed it as well as she could: a psalm, an anthem, a lesson and various prayers. She sincerely hoped, that the bishop would not introduce idolatrous ritualistic movements into the service. Judging by the reports which Jane Trost brought her, she gathered that Mr. Winter had been behaving with moderation in this respect. No doubt he would explain to the bishop the customs of his church and dissuade him from any indecent extravagance, though bishops, of course, were a law unto themselves, and one never knew nowadays.

Surely the service must be over by now? This delay was fatiguing. The wind roared through the elms. There! Another great branch went crash. Miss Loach grew anxious. Supposing a bough should fall on the bishop? Or even on the War Memorial draped in its flag? She had not, unfortunately, seen the memorial since its erection; but Mr. Winter had shown her the drawing of it, and it had seemed to her unobjectionable, though it was true that a cross was less suitable than the figure of a soldier, being conducive to idolatrous adoration, which a soldier wasn't. On the whole, she did not regret the half-crown she had subscribed to it.

At last! They were coming. The procession wound out of the churchyard. First the ex-Service men. They were all of them wearing their medal-ribbons. She noticed particularly those on Ted Hadley's broad chest, a long rainbow stripe beginning with the Queen's medal from the Boer War and ending with the D.C.M. As he limped forward she saw that Ted Hadley was carrying a bugle slung over his shoulder with a green cord. What was he doing with that? It was astonishing what a number of ex-

Service men there were for a small village like Chaddesbourne. She counted them walking slowly in twos. Colonel Ombersley, at the rear, kept step with Roberts, the keeper. Miss Loach disapproved of that. In her father's days the Squire would have walked alone. It was a sign of the degenerate times. She pursed her lips firmly and shook her head. Ah, there was Dr. Selby, too. She was pleased to see him. People said he had saved her life, and his charges were certainly moderate. His bill for the whole of her illness was less than three pounds. She had thought there must be some mistake; but he had assured her, quite reasonably, that it worked out so small because he happened to live next door.

Next the choir. She could never quite forgive Mr. Winter for putting them into surplices; but their mothers liked it, and it certainly brought them to church. They were singing a hymn. What was it? Jane Trost was able to tell her. *For all the Saints who from their labours rest.* It was in her hymn-book, but, for all that, Miss Loach was not quite certain that she ought to approve of it. Didn't it savour, however remotely, of *Prayers for the Dead?* She wondered . . .

And now the people. There were more of them even than she had seen at the old squire's funeral. Old people, too. There was actually Eli Lydgate from Uffley Mill, whom she hadn't seen for five years at least. An old, old man. A handsome old man. Miss Loach remembered him at the time of his marriage to the papist woman he had picked up at Miss Abberley's. His granddaughter walked by his side: a nice, modest girl. Jim Cookson was looking at her. Miss Loach hoped that didn't mean he was taking after his father. She thought of George Cookson's end and shook her head.

Then the Ombersleys: Mrs. Ombersley, Catherine and Jack. Mr. Hackett was standing near them. That man *would* thrust himself forward! Mrs. Ombersley could always be trusted to look distinguished; but the boy had improved out of all recognition since last Miss Loach saw him. Perhaps that dreadful affair had pulled him together. A blessing in disguise. No doubt now he would make a fine man. And Catherine. . . . Well, really, Miss Loach had never seen such a change in a girl. She no longer needed a back-board; she was as erect as her mother, and her face looked positively radiant. Though Miss Loach had never forgiven her those clandestine visits (that was the word) to a bachelor's house, she had been relieved, in a way, to hear of her engagement to Selby. A girl who had compromised herself so deeply could have no alternative, "though such an engagement would never have been countenanced in my father's time," Miss Loach had affirmed.

Next the clergy. She hardly took the trouble to look at Mr. Winter. Her little black eyes were greedily fixed on the bishop. He was not her idea of a bishop, Miss Loach decided. He was lanky and tall;

his robes flapped about a spare figure, and he had no beard. It was almost as easy to imagine an apostle without a beard as a bishop.

Mr. Winter was holding a parchment that blew in the wind. He was reading the roll. Miss Loach had a copy of it.

"George Attwood."

"*May God bless him for evermore*," the people murmured.

"Henry William Bagley."

"*May God bless him for evermore.*"

"Herbert Cooks."

"*May God bless him for evermore.*"

"Thomas Hipkiss."

"*May God bless him for evermore.*"

The reading of the roll went on. Here and there a white handkerchief fluttered out, heads were lowered. So many names for such a small village.

"Henry Lydgate."

"That's the girl's father," Miss Loach thought. "I remember his christening."

"Richard D'Abitot Ombersley."

"Roger Ombersley."

Miss Loach saw Helen Ombersley's lips move:

"*May God bless him for evermore.*"

Not a tremor! Miss Loach glowed with pride. Here was true aristocracy! "But I *do* think," she thought, "they should separate the names of the officers from those of the rank and file."

"Frederick Sheppy."

The name of Frank Vincent Waldron was last on the roll. Mr. Winter folded his parchment. The bishop stepped forward. What was he saying? Miss Loach read:

"In the faith of Jesus Christ we dedicate this Memorial in thankful remembrance of those our Brethren who gave their lives on our behalf, in the name of the Father and of the Son and of the Holy Ghost."

As Miss Loach began to fidget for her handkerchief the flag fluttered down; the tall, pale cross stood naked. Ted Hadley caught the flag blowing away in the wind. The bishop raised his hand in the Benediction. The people knelt and he prayed. He rose and spoke to them. Miss Loach could not hear what he said: she could hardly have heard in any case, for, in spite of her efforts to check them, tears obstinately brimmed in her eyes. She could not tell why; she had lost no relatives in the war. Yet so it was. Instead of an arbiter of the proceedings, she became a little withered old woman crying to herself behind a lace curtain.

They sang hymns. There was one which Miss Loach had heard of and now read with approval. *"O valiant hearts,"* it began. But what was the next? This was not a hymn, but a poem! Mr. Winter must surely have been dreaming when he put it into the service.